KATHERINE BUCKNELL was born in Saigon and grew up in Washington, D.C. She is a literary scholar and the editor of *Juvenilia: Poems 1922–1928* by W.H. Auden and of *Diaries Volume One, 1939–1960* and *Lost Years: A Memoir 1945–1951* both by Christopher Isherwood. She lives in London with her husband and three children.

Visit her website at www.KatherineBucknell.com

'In *What You Will* the characters, like those of Henry James, are people on whom nothing is wasted. Their cleverness and sensitivity does not preserve them from any of life's disasters but at least they are fully conscious as they enter the maelstrom. This is social comedy at its most poignant' EDMUND WHITE

'Splendidly worked and full of surprising things'
FRANK KERMODE

'*What You Will* contains beautifully realised passages'
Observer

'A dense, layered portrait of three people's interlocking relations, the ways they sustain each other and the ways they let each other down. What gives Bucknell's geometrical story its rich complexity is the time and intelligence the author devotes to the professional ambitions of her characters' *TLS*

'Elegant, incisive prose' *Vogue*

'*What You Will* beautifully and sharply explores one of literature's greatest and most mysterious themes: the unnervingly close relationship between creation and destruction – and its darkest side, possession – which is at the core of art and love'
DAVID MICHAELIS, author of *Schulz and Peanuts: A Biography*

By the same author

Canarino
Leninsky Prospekt

WHAT YOU WILL

KATHERINE BUCKNELL

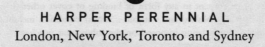

HARPER PERENNIAL
London, New York, Toronto and Sydney

Harper Perennial
An imprint of HarperCollins*Publishers*
77–85 Fulham Palace Road
Hammersmith
London W6 8JB

www.harperperennial.co.uk
Visit our author's blog at www.fifthestate.co.uk

This edition published by Harper Perennial 2008
1

First published in Great Britain by Fourth Estate in 2007

Copyright © Katherine Bucknell 2007

Katherine Bucknell asserts the moral right
to be identified as the author of this work

A catalogue record for this book is available from the British Library

ISBN 978-0-00-722511-8

Set in Bembo by
Palimpsest Book Production Limited,
Grangemouth, Stirlingshire

Printed and bound in Great Britain by Clays Ltd, St Ives plc

FSC

Mixed Sources
Product group from well-managed
forests and other controlled sources
www.fsc.org Cert no. SW-COC-1806
© 1996 Forest Stewardship Council

This novel is entirely a work of fiction. The names, characters and incidents portrayed in it are the work of the author's imagination. Any resemblance to actual persons, living or dead, events or localities is entirely coincidental.

For Bob

CHAPTER 1

'How on earth could she fuck things up so badly?' Lawrence asked.

'I know.' Gwen shrugged with her scant brown eyebrows. 'She commits in a big way. It's one of the great things about her. One of the things I love.'

He settled a pillow behind his head, slouching down into bed with his book, and put on his nearly invisible reading glasses; their delicate wings, spreading from the little gold clip on the bridge of his nose, made him look stern and scholarly yet somehow motherly, concerned. 'Her engagement, her job, her flat in New York all scuppered in – what – twenty-four hours? Over an imaginary love affair with her assistant while she was working here in London this summer? Something of a minor masterpiece, don't you think? She's not – dumb? Your American slang dumb?'

'No. She's not dumb.' Gwen studied the green paint underneath her fingernails, first with her grime-whorled palms upward, fingers curled towards her, then, flipping her hands over, with her fingers stretched out straight. 'Not dumb – except maybe the way beasts are. Silent and unprotesting. She just takes what comes. She's open-hearted, and she has the appetite for anything. She's not – suspicious, you know, so she doesn't try to protect herself from hurt.'

'Sort of a hero to you,' Lawrence observed, nonplussed, finding the page where he had left off. 'Because she's not afraid to suffer?'

'But she doesn't *want* to suffer.' Gwen was sharp with him. 'I mean – she says she has to fight it out for her job and finish what she was trying to do.'

'How old is she getting to be?' he asked vaguely, pulling his eyes up to his wife from the book. Behind his spectacles, the curves of flesh from lid to brow were broad and high, overlaying his grey-blue eyes with a permanent look of melancholy grandeur. His wax-white skin was ruddy around the nose, a little ruined by living. His once blond hair still grew thickly, to the verge of chaos.

'Thirty-four. Same as me. Exactly.'

'Funny, how she's always seemed younger,' Lawrence muttered. 'Like a little sister somehow. Though I guess you were both in my class that year. I remember she used to work terribly hard. And sit in the back row. Silent, just as you say. So – she needs to grow up; there'll surely be new vistas and new opportunities. She just doesn't know yet what they are. Neither do we. And we won't find out tonight.' He yawned.

'It's this *willingness* she has,' Gwen persisted. 'Doing things for the sake of what other people want. Picking up on everyone else's signals.'

'She doesn't appear to pick up on everyone else's signals very well,' Lawrence scoffed. 'One feels she ought to stay away from men for a while.'

Gwen was silent.

Lawrence caught her eye, sensing her concern.

At last Gwen said, 'She should be with someone, you know? It's just so tough – thinking of her alone. And I feel like – well, I never did that.'

'Weren't you alone when I met you? It seemed so to me. Anyway, you're not Hilary. Why do you want to put yourself in Hilary's shoes?'

'Would you like me in Hilary's shoes?' The tease was perverse.

Lawrence laughed. 'Your feet wouldn't fill them, would they? Your actual rather tiny feet. You'd have to grow yourself – quite a lot.' And then in a tone of admonishment, a little impatient, 'Why do you admire it, Gwen? Her blindness? Her inability to think clearly or to make sound judgements about other people?'

Gwen didn't like being admonished, and she answered hotly: 'I don't admire it; I feel moved by it. By the way she exposes herself to things – to life.'

'Yes, well, that you *have* done – taken your chances, huge ones. On me, for starters, and on living in England. You've shown plenty of nerve. It's just that you've shown a surer instinct, don't you think?'

'A surer instinct for Englishmen?' She was engaging him again, light-heartedly. They both laughed.

'There does seem to be generous play on that theme,' Lawrence said drily. 'So perhaps she wants what you have and just doesn't know how to get it? Perhaps it's only natural? A little rivalry between the pair of you, being so close?'

'An Englishman of her own? I don't know that she likes you all that much, darling.'

'I suppose not, or she might have made it up to see us at the cottage. She adores you, though. And we've been happy?' The question trailed away, a wisp of interrogative, then he punctuated it flatly: 'She's well aware of that.' His attention was wandering. He turned his eyes to his book.

Gwen nodded, pondering, tried to draw him back with a note of drama. 'It's major, Lawrence; she's way out there now. Precarious. How does anybody deal with that?'

She hardly got more than a stock reply. 'They turn to friends, my dear, just as she's done. Lucky for her, she has you. And evidently plenty of aeroplane tickets.'

'Maybe no more tickets, though; she has to be low on money, don't you think? Which is another reason she really ought to stay here for at least a while. She needs us to take care of her.' It was an explanation and also a plea.

'She needs *you* to take care of her, my love.' Lawrence gave a half-smile.

'All of us,' Gwen said emphatically.

'I don't see what I have to contribute apart from general fondness. I don't mind at all, Gwen, if you feel you can persuade her. It's nice for Will to spend time with his godmother. And nice for you. Especially when I'm in Oxford and staying at the cottage so much. I expect family life will wear thin with her quite quickly, and she'll be off back to the States again no matter what you do for her or say to her.' He paused; his eyes grew serious, his mouth settled in a forceful line. 'But will you be ready for your exhibition, my love? That's what you need to be sure of. She's going to be hanging about, needing sympathy, endless conversation. It might prove to be like having two children. You've only just managed to settle Will at school and get shot of childminders. How will you paint? How long have you got?'

'The show's not till after Christmas. I've been thinking about it ever since she got here – Hilary sleeping up in the studio right now. I'm close enough. It's about four months away, and there are plenty of canvases that are nearly ready. But the real point is that the work's going well and I don't want to stop. There are new things happening.' She tested the very tips of each thumb against their first two fingers, rubbing lightly, then pincering open and closed like a crab, as if her hands tingled with energy and with excitement. Her eyes gleamed, her strange opaque green eyes. They had the look of cabochon emeralds, milky, as if she were threatened by cataracts, and they were shaped like drops turned sideways, spreading from the narrow tips inside the bridge of her nose. The deep brown lids were slow to blink, like the lids of a bird of prey.

Lawrence smiled and gave a little snort of pleasure. 'There, you see – you grow all the time; nothing can stop you. Not even the safety of your happy marriage. You pull the sunlight to yourself, the nutrients, the H_2O. You don't need to cast yourself out of the garden into a wilderness of error. Just keep painting. Can you? With Hilary up there?'

'I can do – whatever I want. I've already told her I need to work. It's not as if anyone has died – or – well . . . But she can deal with how we are. And she's great with Will; she'll help. She doesn't have anything else to do.'

'I've got to get the early bus to Oxford.' Lawrence put down his book and reached for her, across her small back, around her smaller waist, a broad, familiar hand on her stomach, low down, the heel of his palm on her hip bone, his thumb edging into her belly button, pulling her towards him down into the depths of the mattress and the worn white sheets.

'I've still got paint on my hands.'

'I've been reading Petronius.'

Once again, they both laughed.

There was a knock at the bedroom door.

'Will?' they called together.

'No. Sorry. Only Hilary.' Her voice was husky. Husky with grief, but also because that was Hilary's voice – big, rough, irresistible.

Gwen stood up and crossed noiselessly to the door, pulling her filmy white nightgown down around her knees.

'I was thinking you might have a sleeping pill,' came Hilary's apology as the door swung open.

'Poor Hil.' Gwen reached up with her dirty, thin-fingered hand to the height of Hilary's moon-white forehead, testing as if for a temperature. 'I don't know if we do, really. But let's –' She paused, feeling torn, stroked Hilary's wobbly, near-black screws of hair back against her scalp and her ears, then, as the hair sprang free again, said, 'C'mon. Lawrence has to get up early. Let's go downstairs and look in the kitchen. Maybe we have some hippie tea. Or maybe – what about whiskey?'

The story of Hilary's summer in London had rushed out chaotically at the big kitchen table in the basement when Hilary arrived from New York a few hours earlier. Now as Gwen turned on the lights at the bottom of the stairs and Hilary collapsed staring-eyed in a chair, it seemed to be still lying there in pieces which they could pick up and study. How did it all fit together? Did this piece interlock with that? Border or frame? Or endless, undifferentiated, disorienting sky?

The thing Hilary remembered most vividly from the last few months was eating lunch with Paul wherever they happened to be. It seemed as though they had eaten together every day that she had been in town. During the length of the mornings, working together, comparing this object with that one, discussing intrinsic qualities, history, whereabouts over the centuries and generations, the atmosphere between them would warm and thicken, a sense of anticipation would build up; they had to eat lunch, after all. It was unavoidable. He only suggested it once. After that, they repeated it by unspoken mutual agreement. They never made a reservation anywhere. Most of the cafés and sandwich shops they ate in were too simple for that, and making a reservation might have seemed to both of them to be too deliberate, like a date. It was as if, Hilary later reflected, they preferred to believe they ate together only because they had nothing better to do. And yet they seemed to go to lunch a little earlier each day, anxious to be sure there would be a table.

At the British Museum, for instance, they would desert the racks of antiquities and burst into the great, glass-ceilinged court-yard like travellers hurrying through a station for a train. Over their catalogues, over their notes, over their slides, they were reticent and businesslike; but in the bustle and clatter of that vast open space, they were relieved of self-consciousness and the excess of professional concentration that they practised in private. Among thick-shod tourists slung with umbrellas, cameras, guidebooks, parties of schoolchildren in windcheaters and knapsacks, squalling infants rolled along in their padded chair-worlds, they made a pair: experts from behind the scenes, carrying no luggage with them except what was inside their heads. The limestone facades, the wide, shallow stairs spiralling around the dome of Panizzi's reading room, the summer sky dimmed by luminous clouds and marked out by steel struts in hundreds of triangular pieces like a pale grey parterre, offered a monumental stadium for their quiet focus upon one another.

Hilary afterwards thought that this particular setting, with its combination of neoclassical beauty and ultra-modern engineering – the worship of the old enshrined in the temple of the new – epitomised the kind of magic that had bewitched her that summer. It seemed to sum up the whole effect on her of England: historical riches set off by soaring technical dazzle, a technical dazzle which she associated with America and which made her feel that she had been somehow misinformed. England – Europe – had gone on ahead into a future she didn't recognise, couldn't have predicted, and might not be able to keep up with. What rules were they playing by, she wondered, the members of this old culture, over which she had been taught, or had always assumed anyway, that the New World had some kind of natural, permanent, un-beatable advantage? How it all took her by surprise.

Hilary and Paul never spent much time studying a menu; it seemed to be of no interest to either what they ate. The first item listed would often be the one chosen by Paul, then Hilary might say, 'I'll have the same,' handing the menu back unopened. Or, if it was a cafeteria, each might grab the first plate on the shelf. But after every lunch, they would sit over coffee upon coffee – cappuccinos, double espressos, filters, cafetières, lattes – until they were shaking with it. Just to avoid leaving the table.

In the end it was all about being at the table, facing each other, with nothing in between them except what they might be about to eat or drink. In the Sotheby's café in New Bond Street, where they lunched on the occasional days when Hilary borrowed a desk to go through the old sale archives and to be in touch with New York, she liked the last seat on the slippery, well-padded brown leather banquette, in the corner, the back of her head against the mirror; they could both see what was coming, Paul by looking right past her into the mirror. This arrangement, too, was like part of a journey, two travellers in a compartment on board a train and the world flashing by. This was the table, private but not solitary, at which she had first begun to tell Paul about her engagement.

There seemed no reason not to. She was only in London temporarily; it was a moment out of time, out of her real life, and Paul seemed to be the most understanding, the least judgemental of people. He didn't know any of her New York friends. Who would he gossip to? It was a strangely exhilarating opportunity, something she couldn't have planned or foreseen – spontaneous, like their friendship. She had scarcely realised how small her circle of New York friends had become, nor how narrow her life was, how regimented by her work. But here in London, virtually alone, she felt free. His probings were delicate but surprisingly searching; she understood his curiosity as a form of commitment to their friendship. He seemed to concern himself more with her each time they lunched. She kept back almost nothing.

'Your fiancé was Edward Doro's lawyer?'

'He still is.'

'Was that because of you?'

'Because of me?' She felt on the spot, pink under Paul's gaze.

He dropped his eyes to his plate, cleared his throat, hesitated. 'Well, I mean – did you introduce them to each other?'

Paul was so correct, Hilary thought, so cautious. But this question was not really personal, this was easy.

'Oh, no,' she said with a hint of relief, 'the other way around. Mark, my fiancé, introduced me to Eddie. So I could help Eddie find the right person. It's just – the right person turned out to be me.' She laughed, tossed her head a little. Then she caught Paul's blue eyes straight on; their glow was intensified by the lenses of his thin-framed, round spectacles and yet insulated by them, as if by fireproof safety glass.

'So you – I mean, how did you – establish that?' He had to work at saying it.

Hilary thought that he was about to burst out laughing. 'Don't laugh,' she spurted.

'You're laughing,' he replied, with a lift of his coppery eyebrows, sitting back in his chair so that his dark pinstriped jacket fell open and his waistcoat showed, with its looped gold watch chain.

He was so young to dress like that, she thought, and so thin. Yet it suited him, the fussiness of his dress. The intention was polite, and the execution winningly rumpled, though never actually dirty. Even on the hottest summer days, he smelled of lime blossom, never of sweat, never of hurry or of being too long in his clothes. And when he put his thumb into his watch pocket to haul out the watch and study the time, he seemed to her like a character in a play, or like an impersonation of an English gentleman she'd watched in some long-ago black-and-white film, only he was more graceful and more slender than anything she could recall, his shoulders stooping around his hand as he studied the watch, his long back flexing in a deep, easy curve, the other hand half in, half out of his hip pocket, elbow lightly cocked. He had a certain formality, and yet a certain knowingness that skipped all the formalities.

'Forgive me,' he went on, 'it's just that it seems impossibly convenient – or impossibly clever of you. To be engaged to such a man. A man who could introduce you to one of the great collectors.'

'We weren't engaged then.' She said this as if it absolved her of guilt, though she didn't know for what.

'I see.' Paul crossed his arms and nodded. His look dared her to go on, as if he knew what she would say next, as if nothing could surprise him.

'He asked me to marry him the night before I left New York. Literally.'

Did this sound, Hilary wondered, like too short and too sudden an engagement to count? She rushed on with more details. 'We'd already been living together for ages. We rented places with his old college room-mates, and there was a room-mate of mine for a while, then Mark's law school people. Lately it's been just the two of us. It's sort of half his place, half mine. And I – actually, now it's not really mine. He took it over so I wouldn't have to pay rent while I was out of town and . . .' She petered out, unsure, seeing his eyes flicker away, scan the room.

'Very practical,' Paul said as the waiter approached.

And she thought to herself, Oh God, Hilary. Don't be so boring. Who cares about your domestic arrangements? For suddenly, her engagement didn't seem to be much more than that – arrangements, a matter of practicality and administration – as though Mark had asked not for her hand in marriage but for a guarantee, a security deposit, key money, and she had agreed only because her looming departure had somehow raised the stakes and just then she couldn't stand to lose one more thing.

'Another coffee?' Paul asked her, moving his fingers in the air like a trainer handling their waiter on an invisible leash.

She gulped a little, feeling reprieved. 'OK. Why not?'

'So the collection,' resumed Paul, leaning towards her again. 'Did you already know a lot about it before your fiancé introduced you to Mr Doro?'

'I – no. What would anyone know? I'd heard of Eddie. I guess I – knew about things he'd acquired from time to time. But he'd been at it for years, as we all now realise. Who could have imagined how much there was?'

'Why *you*? How did he – what made him choose *you*?'

'I think it was just – he trusted me. It's not that I didn't know anything. I knew a lot, enough to start on. And the fact that I was young meant I was – available. Plus – we got along incredibly well. He saw that I had a mind of my own, but he could tell that I wanted to find out what was in his mind; I was – well, I made myself – available in that way, too.'

'So,' Paul drained his cup, 'the perfect relationship.'

Hilary sighed. 'I guess – yes, in a lot of ways, it was perfect.' She felt odd assessing it; she didn't think about it as a relationship.

Paul was perching forward, quizzical, as if there was more to explain, so she said, 'The thing is, he decided the minute he met me that I was the one. He was like that. It was how he collected, too. Just with his eye – his instinct. He wanted what he thought was beautiful, what he loved. And that's why he wanted his pieces to stay together: because they represented a series of observations and decisions. A sort of work of art in its own right, you know? His contribution.'

'But,' Paul opened his eyes wide, lifted his thumbs, 'so much of it will be dispersed in this sale you're planning.'

'Yes. But Eddie's the one who's decided what to sell. And what to keep.' She looked at Paul with conviction, her round, pewter-coloured eyes steady, confident that she was hitting home.

'Of course.' Paul nodded, smiling. Then after a pause, he asked lightly, 'And how did you meet your fiancé?'

'Ages ago. College.' She struggled with it. 'Honestly? I guess it was Roman Law, which he thought, you know, that he should take. Not that he was interested in the Roman part – but the economics of it, the politics –'

What was it, Hilary wondered, that made these facts seem dull? Was it her voice? Her flat, inelegant American drawl? Paul, with his precise lips, his tongue knocking the backs of his teeth when he spoke, his almost sly poise and porcelain enunciation, seemed to supply every word he spoke with a special stylishness, an air of cultivation, broad knowledge, hauteur even, so that although they were speaking the same language, he seemed so much more in command of it than she felt she was. His way of speaking, Hilary thought, makes me feel that my life up until now has been entirely ordinary and that I hardly know what I'm talking about. Silently, she bolstered her nerve, dismissed such worries: Ridiculous. But even as she told herself this, she heard the very word, Ridiculous, metamorphosing inside her head as if it were being pronounced by a dandified English gentleman and with stinging disdain; it went on changing, so that she heard a shimmering stream of English alternatives for what she was trying to tell herself. After Ridiculous came Rubbish, Daft, Poppycock, Mad, Utterly Absurd. Words she herself would never say at all.

'You must be very comfortable with each other?' Paul smoothed his bumpy yellow curls around behind his ears. His cheeks were ruddy, unevenly blotched with schoolboy rose, and pricked towards the bottom with a gorse of brown-blond beard that from day to day came and went in no evident pattern at all, as if he just sometimes remembered that shaving was something he might do to his face of a morning.

Was comfort something to be desired? Sought after? Hilary wondered. Or was Paul making fun of such an unexciting arrangement? Was comfort missing from his own life? He never talked of it. This thought didn't wring any pity from her; she sensed a confidence in Paul, deep down, that he would get what he wanted in time. In fact, she sensed that he had some kind of plan, some long-term intention. Certainly he seemed to attribute far more long-term intention to her than she had ever consciously had, and far more ambition.

His view of her made Hilary begin to realise that everything which had happened to her in her life so far had happened by chance or through people she already knew. She had worked hard every single day for a decade since drifting away from graduate school, but she had never called any shots. She had simply accepted what life had offered in the way of work, in the way of friends. And she had been content. But now that Eddie Doro was dead, now that he had left her to sell off two-thirds of his collection of antiquities and build his museum, she was beginning to wonder if she needed to have something more like a vision, or at least an agenda. She had been relying on Eddie's. Would that be enough to complete the assignment? Such was Paul's effect on her – to make her feel as if he, Paul, could see her life much more clearly than she could see it herself, as if he could do the job she was intending to do better than she could do it.

'I am very comfortable with Mark,' she admitted, feeling a strange lowering inside, greyness, a lack of savour. 'And Eddie was comfortable with Mark, too. The plans have been perfectly clear for a long time. I mean – whether I actually go on to build and run the museum remains to be seen. Under the terms of the will, the appointment has to be confirmed by the trustees after the size of the project is finalised. But Mark chairs the trustees anyway. First the auction, is the thing. Maximise the cash. So – we better get back to the provenances, don't you think?'

She stood up, adjusting her limp, blue cotton skirt, studying the round scuffed toes of her flat, navy blue shoes. She didn't feel the least bit beautiful, and yet when Paul leaped from his chair and placed his hand for just an instant against the small of her back, gesturing gracefully with his free hand as if she needed to be shown the way and then propelling her gently through the doorway of the café and out into the main hall, she thought, He's incredibly attentive. He must like me. It's just that he's – so shy. It's this English thing, being nervous around girls. Boys sent away to boarding school too young, never seeing girls at all. I must ask him about that, she thought, as they walked to the stairs.

Despite her sense that each lunchtime with Paul was a kind of journey, he never actually agreed to travel with her around the other European museums and dealers. She was surprised, because this seemed to her one of the best things about the job she had hired him to do – trips abroad, nice hotels, introductions to other experts in the field. Paul always seemed to be committed to a bank holiday weekend in the countryside, amateur theatricals, an evening of singing, or visiting some aged former teacher. And he told her, in a confessional, apologetic tone, that his German was too embarrassing, even his vaunted Italian.

So Hilary flew off alone to Paris, Basel, Rome, Athens, lugging her notes and her photographs. While she was away, she worked like crazy, drilling through thick boxes of file cards, pinpointing every site of origin, every change of hands, dragging her eyes from object to object, her feet through gallery upon gallery, assessing, comparing, confirming; interviewing dozens of curators and dealers, picking their brains and at the same time building up their appetites for the auction. It renewed her confidence in herself: that she knew exactly what she was doing, solo. Still, wherever she went, she mentioned Paul by name, knowing as she did so that it made her feel important to say she had an assistant, and justifying such a weakness by telling herself that the connection might help him or her at some future unforeseen moment; in any case, she liked him and liked describing the two of them as a team.

On her return, she would spill her discoveries, her best anecdotes to Paul, and she would feel thicker than ever with him. If she withheld any details – out of shyness, half-conscious loyalty to Doro – she also flirtatiously hinted to Paul that he might make his own discoveries and his own connections if he perhaps came along on the next trip.

When the time came to go back to New York at the end of September, Hilary was beside herself. She spent her last morning rearranging papers that she might just as easily have thrown away or abandoned. She had already assembled by herself, without Paul's knowledge, a draft for the sale catalogue, checked every caption, checked and double-checked every estimate; she had provisionally numbered every lot; there was nothing more to describe. She had packed the night before, returned the keys to the service flat, and brought her suitcases to Sotheby's with her. There she sat at the borrowed desk in the warren of low-ceilinged back offices surrounded by computer screens, telephones, and glamorous-haired, multilingual women she still didn't know, waiting for lunch. Her concentration was ratty, her hands were trembly; she worried that she hadn't been thorough enough, but at the same time, she knew that she could have left yesterday, the day before; her mind flopped to and fro; words blurred on the page. She had meant to spend half a day around the corner at the Royal Academy before she left town, for her own pleasure, and she had meant to go shopping for Mark, a cashmere sweater or something, but she couldn't bring herself to leave the building and to venture down the street alone; she was afraid she would miss something, although she would have been reluctant to say what.

Paul arrived late. He breezed in at eleven thirty. She was in agony, pretending not to care, telling herself, Of course he's taking it easy, there's nothing left to do. She wondered if she should have invited him ahead of time to go along with her to the Royal Academy. But at their table in the café, Paul insisted on champagne. They both ordered lobster sandwiches despite the expense, and she allowed herself to be reassured that he shared her enthusiasm for this last precious lunch.

'A toast to our work,' he said buoyantly, lifting his glass.

'Our work,' she replied, lifting her glass to touch his.

'Shall we lay a bet on the outcome?' he asked, his glass still resting against hers.

She felt a little thrill of excitement, her throat parching with the sense that something was going to knock her off her feet. 'The outcome?'

'I'll lay you a round-trip ticket to New York that your sale breaks thirty million.'

The part of his wager that stood out for her was the round-trip ticket to New York; her heart leaped at it, a mixture of longing and fear. What was in Paul's mind – a trip to New York? Or even – if *she* won – a trip back to London for her? She struggled to say something rational. 'Dollars or pounds?' was what she came out with.

Paul laughed. 'Quite right to ask, you clever puss.'

She felt barriers collapsing, her chest expanding, the tiny room spinning away around them. She smiled and stared deep into his eyes, happy, letting herself go.

'I bag dollars,' she cried, the English idiom tripping off her tongue in a cascade of delight.

He pursed his lips, rueful, sulky. 'I haven't got a prayer of winning now, have I?'

'Poor baby,' she crooned at him, then snapped her glass to her lips and took a long triumphant draught of the silky bubbles.

They agreed they would stay in touch, and in the slosh of playful talk, exchanged addresses, schedules, plans. But there was a sense of an ending hanging over them which was explicit and somehow final. Hilary kept expecting something more to happen; the atmosphere of possibility seemed so rich, so ripe. They decided to extend to dessert before coffee; he recommended Eton Mess, which she had never heard of before, but which sounded like a sentimental journey they might yet take together into a charmed English world. It proved to be a familiar indulgence, grainy meringue smothered in sweet whipped cream, oozing with blood-red summer berries.

In the end, it was the usual thing, the waiter with the bill. Bewildered at the thought of Heathrow, the long, lonely taxi ride, Hilary insisted on paying.

'But I ordered the champagne,' Paul objected.

'You can pay next time –' she began.

'Next time?' He put one hand on her hand with her credit card in it, pushing her card away, and slipped his other hand inside his jacket, feeling for his wallet.

Hilary was liquid with warmth, 'Well, sometime . . . ?' She dropped the credit card on to the little tray just as the waiter snatched it from somewhere above them.

Paul helped her out to the pavement with her bags. 'It's been grand, hasn't it?' he said. 'I've adored getting to know you.'

'Yes.' Even the single syllable of American sounded yokelish, she thought. She wouldn't risk more. But her feelings were in spate, a running torrent. He might easily have carried her off if he had tried. He merely kissed her on one cheek, holding her arm just above the elbow as he leaned down to her, a whisper of flesh, soft and dry, halfway between her mouth and her ear.

Still, it heated her to nearly a sizzle and she added, 'I've adored −' stumbled, blushed '− you.'

Then she found herself in tears. 'I'm sorry − I can't help it. I'm going to miss you. I have to say it.'

'I shall − miss you, too −' Paul stood up straight, took a half-step backwards, sliding his hands into his trouser pockets. 'Naturally.'

She wiped her cheeks with the back of her hand. 'Oh God, I'm sorry.'

'Well, don't be. I mean − poor you. I had − no idea.'

'It's my fault. I should have said something. I wish we'd gone out, maybe, or −'

'How sweet you are,' Paul said. 'I'm terribly flattered.' With a glance up and down New Bond Street, he took his hands from his pockets and awkwardly wrapped his long arms around her, rattled her sportily in his embrace, then released her, stooped a little, peered into her face, stroked her unruly hair. 'But you've got to make that plane, haven't you? Come on, you can do it.' His voice was tender and encouraging. Now he pulled her against him with his left arm around her shoulders, raising his right in the air to hail a black cab.

Hilary let herself be held, melted against his willowy frame. It felt like heaven to her, this instant of contact, a brief crisis of bliss, as the taxi squealed to a stop, purred at them.

'Heathrow,' Paul barked at the driver, bullish, familiar. He lifted Hilary's two big black suitcases inside with his long right arm, letting go of her shoulders, taking her hand and holding it in his left as he reached through the yawning black door and she stood on the pavement beside him.

The driver poked at his computer, waiting. Hilary's mind went blank; time seemed suspended; she was in Paul's care; she felt she had admitted everything to him, everything that mattered.

'There,' Paul announced as he swung back towards her. 'You're all set. This chappie's been there a thousand times.'

And she nodded, accepting it. She felt entirely passive, a sleepwalker, partly because of the champagne.

Paul bundled her into the cab, one arm under her elbow, the other around her shoulder. 'Don't forget your seat belt; you have to, you know.'

She nodded, the tears welling as she slid back on the seat.

'You mustn't go all to pieces,' he clucked at her, leaning in one last time. 'There's so much traffic, is the thing. Better get going.' And he stretched his face towards her, creaking with effort, planted another, longer kiss on her cheek.

'Come to the airport with me?' Hilary was surprised at her own boldness. And she could tell that Paul was more than surprised. Shocked almost.

'I – I don't think I can. I mean – I don't think I should,' he sputtered. And then after a ponderous silence, a horn sounding behind them, he said with evident discomfort, 'After all, you're engaged to be married. I believe you must have mentioned it every day. So – hadn't we better leave it here? Mutual adoration and no bruises?'

It was a blow, but he said it so definitely that Hilary couldn't demur. And she felt she had no right to, since the impediment was on her side.

When she tried to speak, her lips shook; she was forced to wipe at her nose with a bare knuckle. Engaged to be married. She felt a surge of shame at her behaviour. So undignified, she reprimanded herself. What was she doing? Who was she, in fact?

She sat up very straight, dry-eyed, suddenly self-possessed. 'I'm so sorry,' she said solemnly. 'Please forgive me. Please.'

Paul was silent, opened his face to her. At least that was how Hilary thought of it afterwards, and that's what she was trying to explain now to Gwen.

CHAPTER 2

'There he was putting me into the cab, practically strapping me to the seat to stop me throwing myself at him, while I was blubbing my eyes out and trying to apologise, and the expression on his face was so – well, I don't know what it was. It was like he opened his face, made it – whatever I needed it to be. Made it an acceptance, or a forgiveness. A non-judgement. Without any sign that I could really make sense of.'

'You mean – blank?' Gwen asked. She had switched on the kettle, stood rummaging in the cupboards for mugs, tea bags.

'Maybe that's all it was. Just a blank. A make-of-me-what-you-will. And so I – I said goodbye, and the taxi pulled away and it seemed that anything was possible. That he had handed the situation over to me. That he would wait to see what I did next.'

'And what you did next was break off your engagement.'

Hilary pressed her lips together hard, looked feisty. 'God, you make it sound so cut and dried. Where the *hell* is that whiskey?' she demanded.

Gwen laughed and chucked the boxes of tea back into the cupboard just as the kettle began to spout steam into the air. She moved off towards the Welsh dresser by the floppy green sofa in the window alcove, bent to the screeching doors, the clinking bottles, and brandished a bottle aloft as she recrossed the room. She sloshed whiskey into the pair of mugs. Then she sat down at the kitchen table opposite Hilary.

The first sip made Hilary's voice deeper, huskier. 'Oh God, the lustre was off Mark completely. I *so* did not want to see him – like a kind of sudden revulsion. It blows my mind how fast everything came clear. I just wanted the plane to turn around and fly the other way. There were bubbles inside me, you know, this sensation of something fizzing, exhilarating – how I felt about Paul and that now he knew it. But I couldn't let the bubbles rise.

'It was weird when we landed. The wheels hit with that hard bounce, and it was like – the knock of reality. That smell you get of burning, the reek of the brakes in your nose. Utter destruction. All those years with Mark were some kind of lie I'd told to both of us. I was stale and sweaty and gross, but at least it proved I'd been working – an alibi. I was the sexless professional again, the same work jock I'd been when I left town. And I was thinking how free it felt. And how being alone was fine. Kind of thrilling, in fact.'

Gwen basked in it, Hilary alone.

'So – I was businesslike with Mark. Starting with, From three thousand miles away, I realised I didn't really want to be married . . . But I couldn't quite look him in the eye. Somehow you think the person's going to hit you or something. What is that? Some primitive thing. Your gut tells you that, basically, breaking up is a fight.'

'But you did say he was angry?'

'At first he didn't believe me. And then when he started to take it in, he thought it was just a re-entry thing. That I'd gone skittish or gotten self-conscious.'

'You mean because you didn't really kiss him when you first came in?'

Hilary went red. 'Oh, but Christ, I couldn't kiss him, Gwen!' Then she laughed.

'And the champagne?'

'That was terrible. A bottle of Dom Pérignon. The whole fiancé thing. And you know that he's not really like that, Gwen. He's much more beer and Chinese noodles. There were red roses, too, in this tippy glass vase on the coffee table. Like rolled-up bundles of velvet, on long, long stems. Completely ghastly. No scent; those waxy petals. The apartment was bare, as if he'd stuffed all the mess into closets or had cleaners come in. All so contrived. Then he opened the champagne while I was in the bathroom.'

Gwen grimaced. 'So you had to drink it.'

'Of course I had to. I was scared there was going to be a ring too. I kept looking for one of those little boxes, a bulge in a pocket. And I saw myself trapped there with only him for company, starved of something else I wanted. I knew I couldn't spend one night with him. And he was saying that I couldn't expect him to swear off me all of a sudden like that, after he'd been waiting all summer and looking forward to seeing me. Basically, he was begging for sex. I think he even had his hands like this.' She put her palms together as if she were praying. 'He never asked *anything* about my summer, about what had happened, or what I felt. So how could sex fit? Where could it come from, in a situation like that?'

Gwen tapped the whiskey bottle, raising her eyebrows at Hilary, but Hilary shook her head.

'We drank too much, Mark and I, last night. That was part of the problem – the crying and the screaming.'

'But, hey, you got through a lot of misery in one awful night.'

'I feel bad for him, Gwen. It was like I'd inflicted this terrible injury. That's how I keep picturing it – an open wound, bleeding and twitching.'

'Worse for Mark if you hadn't found out in time, hon.' Gwen was casual, like someone who'd seen it all before, lots of times. Then she stooped close across the table and spoke caressingly. 'It's bitter to betray someone – anyone – a lover, a friend. But don't you think when it comes to love and marriage – the lifelong deal, I mean – for that, don't you have to pay any price? You can't fake that. And if you want to have children? You did the right thing.'

Hilary was white-faced, dipping her finger in the dregs of her whiskey.

Gwen insisted. 'You have to leave this with ragged edges, Hil.

If he blames you or thinks you're a shit, then that's what he needs to do to survive. You have to let *him* deal with this – without you. Because if you're dumping Mark, you're dumping him. The thing is broken. That's life. It's painful.'

'Yeah. Painful.' Hilary's voice creaked. And then she seemed to shoulder it, like a burden. 'Listen. I know there were big things wrong with me and Mark. We were always part of some gang. Endless room-mates. Then with Eddie, a gang of three. Never a couple. Mark and I had been around each other for so long that it just seemed like time for something else to happen. The truth is, Paul saved me.'

She paused for a long time, leaned back in her chair. And then at last, she let it out: 'But man, I could never have pictured Mark's anger. His eyes turned red – flaming. In all our years together, I had never seen – this – creature in him who didn't get what he expected. Who couldn't make me do what he wanted. That was totally scary.'

'Stay away from him for a while, don't you think? Till he calms down?'

Hilary sat up. 'God, I'm stealing you from your bed, and Will'll be up early needing you.'

Gwen was easy with it. 'It's fine. Let's do the tea, huh?'

Hilary didn't fight her. 'Camomile or peppermint or something?'

Gwen switched the kettle back on, took clean mugs from the cupboard, talked with her back to Hilary, flipping labels loose from tea bags, extending their little strings. 'So what about all your stuff? How are you going to get it out of Mark's place?' She launched the soggy tea bags into the sink where they splatted.

'I don't have that much. I just need my books from Eddie's apartment. I miss those.'

Gwen rapped down the two smoking mugs, sat opposite again.

Hilary cupped her hands around one mug and shook her head. 'Mark didn't know about Paul, so he blamed Eddie, you know?

23

The stuff he said – aggressive, disgusting stuff. How weird I was to have a thing for an old man. Did I get off on Eddie's obsession, or was it the power I had over his money? Then shouting at me, "Where the fuck do you think you're going to go now? You can't get into his apartment if I don't give you the key. What are you going to do? Sleep in the warehouse so you can fondle his pots and his lamps and his statues? That's what you'd really like to do, isn't it? Sleep with him – with his fucking collection."' Hilary's lips curled back from her teeth, trembled ever so slightly.

'You think he felt jealous when Eddie was alive?'

'Maybe there was some power thing with them. Basically Mark never understood what all the excitement was about. He couldn't see what we saw – about the past. Turns out it made him mad. Made him into a kind of brute – a bully.'

Gwen lifted her mug to her lips, put it down again without drinking from it; there was something in Hilary's voice, disillusionment, a tone of fuck all. 'But you don't think he'd try to derail Eddie's plans?'

'He was kind of nuts with his threats, Gwen: "I can stop the whole fucking project. Doro's dead; he's buried in a hole in the ground. All that stuff in his apartment and all that stuff in the warehouse is dust and bones. It's dug up out of graves, stolen from tombs. It belonged to people who died thousands of years ago. What is this with you – dead people, the past? It's necrophilia, that's what it's called. You give me the creeps with your sarcophaguses and your burial monuments and your funeral urns."'

Gwen squeaked with outrage. 'But a *lawyer* – a trusts and estates lawyer – that's all about people dying, and about them trying to reach into the future with what they want – to exercise their will! I mean the word, "will" – it's all about enacting what you want from beyond the grave. That's Mark's job, it's what he *chose*. What's going on over there in America?'

'I know! And I said to him, "It's sarcophagi, by the way"; but,

God, I wish I hadn't! It just infuriated him.' At last she sipped her tea.

'Ginger and lemon,' murmured Gwen, watching her.

'I like it.' Hilary took another, longer sip. 'Up until I said that – "It's sarcophagi, by the way" – I think there was maybe a chance I could have persuaded Mark to give me back the key to Eddie's apartment. But somehow that one pedantic little remark changed everything. It seems trivial, but just as I was saying it, I realised that was the point: Mark and I weren't speaking the same language any more. I needed to be with someone who understood what I was doing – so I could remember who I was. All I really wanted was to go to Eddie's and sit there quietly and collect myself – Well, the thing is I couldn't even ask Mark, could I, because communing with Eddie – ?' Hilary stopped, raised her hands in mock horror.

'He would have thought you were trying to hold a seance –' Gwen said.

'It crossed my mind that I could get the doorman to let me in. There's one I'm friendly with. But there are all these procedures for access now because of the value of the stuff, and then Mark could accuse me of breaking the rules, and he'd have just what he needed to get me dumped for ever from the project. Imagine thinking that way, about a guy you were going to *marry*! And by then it was three or four in the morning and I wanted –'

The neglected undercurrent of Paul stirred between them. Gwen acknowledged it by lifting one corner of her mouth, not a smile, but sliding her lips around to the side of her face, making a squeegee sound inside her cheek. 'Right – you wanted to be with someone who understood why you cared so much about all those antiquities.'

'I got down into the street with my suitcases, and hailed a cab, and the whole thing just ran away with me. Arriving, departing. What was the name of any hotel, anyway? I felt all beaten up, and yet there was energy bubbling somewhere inside me. It was like I was right in the middle of a sentence with Paul, and I thought, Now I can talk straight to him because I'm free. So I told the cab driver to take me back to the airport.'

'I still can't believe you didn't phone him!'

'It was crazy. I thought – I *imagined* – that somehow he knew I was coming – or . . . I don't know. Paul and I never used the phone; we always just walked in and saw each other first thing every morning. It felt like such a sure thing. I had his address and I – I was so excited – so impatient – like I was running to his arms. I wanted to amaze him. I thought it would make up for torturing him all summer talking about Mark. I kept remembering that expression on his face, when he put me in the taxi – open to whatever I decided. And this would be my answer, my fabulous, dramatic answer. I thought I was in love, Gwen, that's the thing.' Hilary swallowed a sob. 'God, I'm sorry,' she said loudly, defying it. 'I'm so *fucking* tired.'

Gwen got up from her chair, slipped around the table, kneeled down beside Hilary, put her arms around her. 'It's fine. You have to give it time, Hil.'

'I pounded on his door for ever!' Hilary groaned. 'What was I *thinking*?!'

'You weren't thinking, you were feeling.'

'What was I feeling? None of it was real.'

'So maybe that's a problem people have about love. That they want it to feel passionate and impulsive. Maybe you did all this to make it feel like love when it wasn't. To throw yourself, to jump blind. Maybe you needed the end of the world as you knew it.'

'Christ, how does anyone ever *know*?' Hilary turned her chair with a raw scrape and laid her cheek on Gwen's hair; tears darkened the fine brown strands and swelled like beads on the flecks of green oil paint stuck to a few. 'Any normal person would have given up and gone away, realised he wasn't going to answer, assumed he wasn't home.'

'Shhh,' said Gwen, rocking her gently. 'It's just as well he was there so it's over already. One day you'll laugh about it.'

'When he finally opened the door, he was glowing. Hair tousled, no glasses, out of breath a little, giggling – and I still thought it was all for me. That he'd been waiting and hoping. He didn't have on a shirt, his trousers were only half done up. It's *so* embarrassing. I swear. I launched myself across the threshold, into the air, arms outstretched, before I even noticed the other man *right* behind him. This huge, hairy guy, half naked, twice Paul's age.'

Gwen shook with laughter. 'I'm sorry. I know how much it's hurting you, but you tell it so perfectly, and I see this – tableau.'

Hilary pushed Gwen's shoulders away, slapped at them, belligerent, half joking. 'Bitch.'

'Who talked first?'

'Paul. Handled it easily. As if he were in white tie and tails and presenting me to a duchess, but with this kind of blandness, like he was – under hypnosis.' She mimicked his English accent exaggeratedly: '"Ah – Hilary, what a surprise. Can I introduce you to my friend Orlando?" – or whatever the guy was called. But I didn't meet him; he must have been as surprised as I was; made tracks. And then Paul said, "We were just having a bit of a rest, actually."' In her broadest American accent Hilary added, 'Well, duh –'

'And how'd you make your getaway?'

'Badly. Really badly –' Hilary started to laugh, too. 'Some garbled junk about airplanes and how I had no idea what time it was and I was sorry and I'd call in the morning. To his credit, Paul did ask, "Is everything all right? *Quite* all right?"'

Hilary rolled her eyes. 'Perfect. It's all perfect. Can't you see? My life is completely perfect. What does *he* care?'

Lawrence lifted his head a little as Gwen slid under the covers.

'Sorry, darling,' she whispered.

'How is she now?' he muttered. 'OK?' He laid a hand on Gwen's thigh, squeezing it softly, then giving it a gentle shove, the cadence of goodnight.

'I've got to find her someone to marry.'

Lawrence snorted into his pillow. 'Wouldn't it be enough to find her a place to live? Or maybe a job?' He turned his head away, closing his eyes. 'Why does she need to marry anyone?'

'She still wants her old job. But we need to keep her away from Mark for a while. He's so angry, it's as if he's lost his mind. She definitely doesn't know how to pick men.'

His head came up again. 'Do you know?' Then dropped.

Gwen bent down and pressed her face into the nape of Lawrence's neck, rubbing against his bristling hair where it was cut close at the back, metallic with grey. 'OK,' she admitted, 'it was you who picked me. But by now, I can recognise the goods. Hilary *feels* so much, and she just throws herself at whatever – next it could be a passing car. I have to help her.'

Lawrence didn't answer; he was asleep.

Upstairs in the studio, on her thin spare pillow, Hilary was thinking about Lawrence and Gwen lying side by side in their wide bed with its massive, blackened oak headboard. So much presence, that bed. An institution in itself, she thought. The thick modern mattress supported by the Jacobean frame, five hundred years or more of ageing wood hewn by hand with an axe – an oak tree reshaped as beams, posts, creaking pegs neatly filling invisible holes in the tight corners, and the broad exposed planks boldly, impressively carved.

Generations were born and died in that bed, Hilary thought. She saw them in pairs, producing a life, producing a death. In her mind's eye, she only approximated the bodies, generic, strangely innocent, dressed in white like Gwen in her nightgown; what did Hilary know of their intimacy, in fact? She revered the idea of it. She pictured Lawrence and Gwen together throughout time, their hands folded on their breasts, not touching at all. Like figures carved in stone on a funeral monument. You could sleep for ever in that bed, she thought.

She had slept there herself during half of July and most of August when Gwen took Will to the cottage for the summer air and offered Hilary a vacation from the service flat. There had been a string of mornings so bright that Hilary had relished being called to them early by the birds. Relished dozing and dreaming in the half-light before dawn, under the pleasing shroud of Gwen's stiffly laundered cotton sheets, slightly abrasive with London lime on the naked skin. How lucky, how certain, how easy I felt in that bed. Before all this mess.

Hilary longed for sleep now, for oblivion. But her mind raced on. I could get to hate Gwen, she thought. Both of them. It might seem easy to tell myself I don't want what they have. But for whose benefit, that lie? The spinster's bitter defiance, life at arm's length. It's a marriage I admire, and it's *their* marriage. No way I can stay here more than a day or two. I have to tell her. Tomorrow – right away. Ask her to lend me money for one more ticket. Save what's left of the credit cards.

Trouble with goddamned *fucking* New York is everybody's apartments are so small. In London people have things like extra beds. She ran over in her mind the friends who might have room for her to stay, thinking how they were really Mark's friends more than hers, how they might have an opinion, either hate her guts or try to talk her around, and how she wouldn't be able to bear the interference. One or two from graduate school she could maybe impose on, her old PhD supervisor, for instance, who still treated her as though the world needed the thesis she had never finished writing. She pictured herself telling the whole sorry tale again on the phone to New York, and her stomach toiled with embarrassment.

Could Mark really kick her off the project? She'd been agonising over it, telling herself she was too tired to think straight.

Eddie wouldn't leave me so exposed. Eddie, whose last years had been haunted by the future, by planning, eventualities. And then with a shuddering ache, Get real, Hilary. Eddie was never planning with you in mind. He wouldn't leave his *collection* so exposed.

But it was hard to give up that fragile old-man voice in her ear, croaky, desiccated, the Bronx twang made fine by education and a certain natural delicacy: 'How can you be so sure you want to give your life to this when I'm gone? And the lockstep with Mark? Maybe I should set you free from that? There's always some other way, you know, with lawyers.'

How many times should Eddie have asked her? She had been so quick to reassure him, It's decided. I'm all yours. As if she herself were a piece he wanted for the collection. Because she knew his appetite, and it gave her so much pleasure to satisfy it. And because in his growing frailty, he was facing something so big, drawing closer all the time, and she could shield him a little with this indulgence; she could take his mind off his fear. 'The legal stuff's fine. Mark's good at that. Let him deal with it,' she used to say.

I left my*self* exposed, she thought. I had – a sense of expectation; she had to admit it.

After the funeral, Hilary had wondered how much she really cared for the treasures. All those years, had she been living off Eddie's enthusiasm? Until it all came to life again with Paul. Paul loved the collection with that unhesitating lightness of heart, that spontaneous certainty that she had come to feel she would never encounter again. The touch of boyish disregard that carried it off.

That was real, she thought, that part of my friendship with Paul. It was the same as with Eddie – we shared some things perfectly, others not at all.

At last she began to sink into sleep, feeling justified in something. She let go of trying to make sense; let the pieces of her puzzle fall apart into their jigsaw fragments. She drifted among bodies, among beds. Gwen, Lawrence. Eddie lying alone under his grand red canopy, lost in the magnificence of its height and hangings. Slipping away. Eddie in his wheelchair in the big living room. In the sunlight beside her desk. Safely dead at last; the silent move he made, out of reach.

I only slept with Mark's body, she thought without clarity. It felt like something she needed to explain. But not now, under the weight of the thin blanket, carrying her down. Don't try.

Then she had a sensation of hurt. A jolt, as if the pillow had dropped underneath her, the whole bed. There was a shuddering black edge around her thoughts as she was thrown back from sleep for an instant.

I knew Eddie was selfish. I made it easy for him. She tried to push past this discomfort, her sense of error and responsibility, still reaching for sleep. I have to go forward from where I am now. With what I know now. I can get back in touch with Paul, on a new footing. He'll help me.

And she was sure of Gwen. At least there's room for me here. With Lawrence and Gwen.

CHAPTER 3

It seemed obvious to Gwen whom Hilary should meet. Roland was tall enough, smart enough, steady enough, good enough. Did it matter whether he was handsome? Walking along King Street the next morning after dropping Will at school, she decided that handsome wasn't really the point. Up until now anyway, Gwen had never much judged people by how they looked. But he's got a great face, she reflected. Solid, intriguing. A lot of texture to his skin, a real beard and a head of thick, dark hair, a kind of masculinity and force. Maybe she had never before considered Roland on the question of looks. Did she know him too well? When had she first looked at him? When had she *ever* looked at him? Six or eight years ago?

He had been introduced by Lawrence as an Ancient History colleague; one of the few colleagues who seemed to Gwen to be actually alive. So many of those Oxford types, Gwen thought, as she made her way towards a cash machine through the sparse, early scurry, existed only as their academic selves – a constellation of starred alphas, named memorial prizes, Oxford University Press publications, sherry-stained gowns, high-table ripostes. But she had liked Roland right away. At one of those wistful gatherings in a barnlike room, everyone standing because the chairs were so far apart, so stiff-backed and so sunken-seated, a hot little drink in the fist. He had made jokes and asked her direct, friendly questions about herself, real questions, that sought out what was inside her, not the windy senior-common-room cross-examinations that aimed to position you on an imaginary list and then dismiss you as falling below some necessary level of academic accomplishment on that list. What are you working on? they felt free to ask once they had established that she didn't spend all her time looking after children, a house. Years ago, it had been her undergraduate degree in Greats. Then, when she gave up on that, she would answer, I paint. And it seemed to stump them. Hmm, they might reply, with a slight interrogative inflection, nodding vigorously, stretching the brows upward in a contortion of sympathy, optimism, goodwill. Some would venture on to a further question, What sort of things do you paint? Or even the informed probe, Figurative or abstract? But there the conversation would end. They couldn't taxonomise this particular activity, landscape painting. It was easier to look upon her as a dropout.

But not for Roland. He was good for my self-esteem, Gwen reflected, and he'll be good for Hilary's. She fed her debit card into the machine, her PIN number circling through her brain like a glimmering fish until she hooked it, stabbed the digits into the hard little keys. Roland has the energy to take a genuine interest in anything, and he has the nerve, too. He knows that there is plenty of vitality and conviction outside the locus of clever, singular answers, outside the high-walled, ancient quadrangles. Those dons go head to head with each other so hard and so long that they forget everything else – the rest of the world, for instance, what it's actually like. She bubbled with resentment, thinking about them. Their conversation, she thought, whatever the topic, is like a conversation about the weather, because they don't actually want to make contact. Real contact. They might have to follow that up with some expenditure of emotion. They can't afford to hear what you might have to say in case it doesn't fit into their train of thought, in case it might disturb some theory they are pushing towards. Some simplification of life. How she had hated those gatherings in college, attended with universal joylessness, another fixed commitment during which it was possible to kill a little time away from books and pens, rest their mighty brains, while eating.

33

The cash wheedled out crisply as if it were newly printed expressly for her. Then there was the thump behind the screen, the personal vault slamming shut.

But they're not all like that, she thought, folding the twenties into the pocket of her jeans, striding for home past the fountains playing over the smooth-paved piazza at her feet. Lawrence, Roland. Hilary will feel it right away. Roland's curiosity and his warmth. Gwen smiled, picturing it. Hilary's so tuned in. She'll find out how widely read and how thoughtful Roland is. Older and wiser than Mark or Paul. Will Hilary think he's too old? Lawrence's age? Nearly fifty? A baby, compared to Doro.

She climbed the black-painted front steps, grabbing up the milk and pinning the bottle under one arm as she let herself into the colourless, empty stairwell, struggled with the keys to the stiff little door of the flat. As to why such a cultivated, lovable man wasn't already involved with a worthwhile woman, Gwen glossed over it in her thoughts as she entered the ground-floor hallway, skipped down the basement steps to the kitchen. Or rather, she considered it rapidly as she flipped the fridge open and shut, and she decided, He hasn't met a good one yet, a good enough one. The right one. In the back of her mind was the flattering certainty that Roland had always been quite attentive to her. From this, she concluded that he liked American women and that he ought to meet more of them. She looked upon his chivalry towards herself as a promise, even a guarantee, that he would like Hilary, indeed, that Hilary was exactly whom he was waiting to meet.

She put Will's breakfast things in the dishwasher, walked around to the clammy back room, and started dragging towels and sheets out of the dryer, heaping them on the ironing board in crackling electric mounds so she could transfer the wet things in from the washing machine. She stopped to find Roland's number in the kitchen drawer, dialled it, and kept the phone clutched against her ear as she went back again to the laundry room.

'There's someone I want you to meet.' She felt unexpectedly shy – bent double, arse up, at the mouths of her machines, struggling one-handed to weed out little cotton items to dry on the rack, her knickers, a bra, falling on the dirty floor as they came untangled from the wet lump in the bouncing, perforated drum.

But Roland welcomed it. 'I'll drive down with Lawrence,' he said. 'Any day this week apart from tomorrow. It's only the freshers arriving now.'

'Lawrence thought he might be staying up for a couple of nights.'

'I'll give him a ring, shall I? And we'll fix it.'

That was it. She chucked more laundry into the washing machine and turned it on with the dryer, leaving the folding for later, everything churning.

Mentioning the arrangement to Hilary, Gwen was casual. 'There's a friend coming to supper. It's just the four of us.'

Hilary was horrified. She had woken up late and swayed down into the kitchen in her pale-blue-and-grey-striped men's pyjamas with a black V-neck sweater over them. Her dark tendrils of hair were pulled into a bright red scrunchie at the back of her head so that her whole face was revealed in the morning light, flushed, puffy around the eyes, but smooth with deep, long sleep.

She came on with a spoiling chill. 'I don't want to meet anyone, Gwen. I'm a wreck. I need to recover. I need time to – figure out what's going to happen.' In her alarm, she pulled her hair loose from the scrunchie, scowled as she plucked at its ends.

Gwen just looked at her for a few seconds, trying to tell from Hilary's half-veiled face why she seemed to be receiving the effort as an insult. But she couldn't see Hilary's eyes. An insult to grief? Gwen considered. Or to the seriousness of what's happened to her? How much time would Hilary need to mourn the end of her engagement? Gwen lifted her eyebrows and, at the same time, she blinked, indicating doubt, an attempt to be patient. She didn't speak.

'Don't get mad, Gwen.' Hilary dropped into the same chair where she had sat last night, reached for the box of Weetabix sitting on the table, studied the package.

'I'm not mad.' Gwen was trying to suppress her sense of investment in sorting Hilary out. She was thinking, It's a problem to be solved, let's get the ball rolling. Why dawdle and agonise? But she said, as casually as she could muster, 'Do you want me to postpone it?'

'I guess. I don't know.' Hilary looked a little dazed. 'Do you think I'll like this cereal? I never tried it all the time I was staying here. It looks so weird.' Hilary thought she was off the hook.

'It needs milk. Lawrence eats it,' Gwen said with sympathetic diffidence. Then adopting a perky, administrative tone, 'I can call him back and say next week instead of this? Is a week enough?'

Hilary put the cereal box down on the table and looked at Gwen. 'Is it really important? I mean, do we have to set a particular date *now*?'

'No. I mean – yes, it's important. It's harder for him to find the time once term starts.'

'So he can't come after I'm gone? I won't be here long.'

'He's wonderful. You should meet him.'

'Well, I don't want to waste that, do I? A wonderful man? But I'm really not in the mood to meet a man right now, Gwen. It's about the last thing I need. Don't you think?'

Where does mood come into it? Gwen wondered. Either he's the right man or he's not. And knowing she was grooming things ever so slightly, pushing her luck, she said, 'It's not a date or anything. He's an old friend of Lawrence's – of both of ours.'

'So you told him you want us to meet?' Despite her fanfared emotional helplessness and her sleepy look, Hilary was nobody's fool.

'He comes here to supper – all the time. You happen to be

staying with us.' Gwen lifted her hands, absolving herself of setting anything up. 'I haven't told him a lot about you.'

'What – that I'm roadkill? That someone needs to drag me to the shoulder before I get run over again and my guts squish out? Gwen, you said he's wonderful, and you said that it's important. So shouldn't I be – well, at least shouldn't I be looking my best? Maybe a few more days of real sleep, some exercise. I have to be ready to make an effort. Right now, I can't really think or talk about anything apart from – from everything that's happened to me since Eddie died.'

'Maybe you should try. You need to get your mind off what's happened. Just do something else. Distract yourself for a while, and let some time pass.'

'Can't I do that with you and Will and Lawrence? You guys are enough. And frankly, you're all I can cope with right now. Christ, you're bossy. And you must be at least two cups of coffee ahead of me.' Hilary gave Gwen a camp smile. She stood up and looked around the counters until she spotted the coffee machine that during the weeks she had stayed in the flat she had never used because she had hurried out each morning as if to meet her destiny. The clear glass jug was dark with coffee at the bottom and the little red light was on.

Without a word, Gwen opened a cupboard, handed Hilary a mug, went to the fridge for the milk, hangdog, slack-footed. She was suddenly remorseful. 'Hil. I'm sorry. Roland's not a lot more than just us. That's how well we know him. It's just one evening.'

'Do whatever you'd do if I weren't here,' Hilary said as she slurped. 'But I reserve the right to hide in my room – or leave before he shows up.'

Gwen saw she might get her way; she decided to drop it for a while. 'I got you some money,' she said. 'Don't know if you need it or not.' She pulled it from her pocket, held it out.

Hilary was surprised and embarrassed. Of course I need it, she thought. But despite herself she said, 'I can't take that, Gwen. God.' What she was thinking was, Why does it feel like she's forcing it on me? Is it just because she didn't give me time to ask before she offered? And how the hell will I ask for it now?

'Just in case you maybe don't have pounds?' Gwen put the money on the counter, and there it lay, her keen generosity, burning a hole in the slate. 'Do you want to go for a run with me now you're up?' Gwen asked. 'We could do a little circuit down across Hammersmith Bridge and along the south side of the river to Putney?'

Hilary's eyes focused hard at her; the glassy, washed-away blue brightened, sparked with enthusiasm. 'So forget cereal. Give me five minutes.'

Outside, the very first morning of October glowed at them; summer grown brittle, a little shabby, along the car-lined street. Gwen set off in front because the pavement was narrow and uneven, blistered by tree roots, and because she knew the way.

'These poor trees,' Hilary said, looking up and around. 'They made me sad all summer with their branches lopped off, trying to squeeze a leaf out of those knobs they have left. It looks even worse now that the green is turning.'

'It's what cities do, yeah? Cramping us all, making us into grotesques. The council prunes the trees like that because the roots are getting at everyone's foundations. Lifting them and breaking the walls.'

'All about insurance probably.' Hilary puffed out the words in even bursts. 'Just like the States.'

'How people think they can be insured against nature, against what grows, I don't know. There are just so many of us on the planet now. Everything, everyone, has to give way. In the country, you know, those trees would have room to achieve their true shape. It's why I can't paint here, except to finish things. I have to have the countryside. The city doesn't feel big enough. Or even – convincing. All hemmed in and restricted.'

Hilary called out to her as Gwen trotted ahead: 'I don't go fast any more, Gwen.'

'Neither do I. Don't worry.' Gwen tempered her pace ever so slightly, her feet making almost no sound as she loped along. 'Your legs are so much longer than mine, I thought you'd be tripping over me.'

'Why'd you move from the cottage, then? I thought you guys liked the city?'

'We like it. We need it anyway. Maybe people need a lot of things, not just one thing. It seemed like a question of survival for me – to grow. Some kind of abrasion. I was alone too much. And the company out there wasn't any you'd really choose on purpose. But now that we're here in town, I actually spend a lot of time trying to avoid people because there are just too many around. Especially if you have a child. All the school stuff. And if you really want to get any work done.' Gwen's voice grew expressionless with conserving breath.

For a little while, Hilary followed her in silence, feeling her brain sigh and expand with physical relief, feeling muscles let go that she hadn't realised were tense. Her back was stiff, her ankles were swollen, but these were local irritations, aeroplane-wear; underneath them, she felt strong, a flow of energy starting as her skin grew warm and damp.

At the Great West Road, by Hammersmith roundabout, they had to wait for the lights to get across the rush of traffic. They stamped around, hands on hips, elbows flapping, then crossed underneath the thumping flyover and the cool, stony shadow of the church, its great, gold-rimmed clock almost on noon. The wide world and the bright air opened all around them as they bounded on to the pale green arch of the bridge; the long slings of cable swooped up over their heads, the silver-brown river slid long and slow through the broad, exposed mudflats beneath, their shaking footsteps were lost in the size and glory of it all. Cars and buses roared by, and the acrid exhaust mingled in their noses with the salt stench of the ebb tide.

Down they plunged on the far bank, through the translucent, yellow foliage and the dank air hovering under the bridge, then settled their pace side by side on the pebbly path. Seagulls wheeled and called over the lonely, squint-making shine of the river, foraging the urban bend as if it were the ocean's edge. A pair of clean white swans nestled and waddled in the algae-streaked pools.

Hilary and Gwen grew easy with one another, slimy with sweat, breathing the layer of air that runners breathe, a chin length higher as the head tilts up and back ever so slightly. And in the depths of the mind, they were beginning to swim the channel of blue thought which grooves deeper, more vivid, with heartily coursing blood.

'I can't believe I never did this all summer,' Hilary said, happy. 'When was the last time we ran together?'

'Before Will?'

'But it reminds me of college. Along the Charles. When we used to train for crew.'

'And see – a boat appears before your very eyes as if you had summoned it.' Gwen stuck her jaw towards it. 'Maybe boys from St Paul's? There are boathouses back there, and more further along. Lots of crews working out here all the time.'

They were getting inside each other's heads now, inside the same flash of memory, locked in step as the boat slid towards them among the trees. They both heard the sucking slap as the pale blades cut the water, both delighted at the sudden, mighty thrust of speed as eight lean backs curled hard and round and the prow shot towards them, blades kicking free of the water again, flattening in the air with the deep, unison thunk against the oarlocks. Then again. And again. The boat wobbled a little between strokes, the boys' long, knobby bodies awkward, uncertain, as they came up their slides, arms and legs pretzeling crazily around their neat, clinging hands, the cox shouting, restless, his elbow flexed rigid up behind him in the stern.

'The cox is overruddering,' Gwen grunted. 'Throwing off their balance between strokes.'

She spun around and jogged backwards a few steps in the scatter of fallen leaves, looking on as the boat receded upriver, and she saw the fresh, devoted faces, tousle-haired, of the stroke, the seven, suffused with the blood of effort, eyes down, determined, bearing it. Then Hilary's face came between her and the boys as Hilary ran along towards her, so that she remembered how Hilary used to dive and pull, dive and pull, facing her in the stroke seat, her every movement perfectly matched to Gwen's commands. And behind Hilary, seven more gigantic, muscled Venuses, bulging, nearly cracking, with conviction as their thighs and stomachs doubled up then exploded, doubled up then exploded, lungs raging for air, nausea scorching chests and throats, arms and backs racked out to the edge of violence, and the hard pads of their calluses rubbed and eaten at by the slippery, fat, unquenchable wood of the blade handles.

Hilary used to be taciturn then, Gwen thought, pudgy and enslaveable. But that beastlike willingness, like the plunging salaams, had given way to something more sceptical, more self-regarding. And she was thinner now, Gwen noticed, lithe with maturity.

'You could still do it, couldn't you, Gwen? Cox that boat. You're light as a twig. Look at you, scuttling all around me like a spider. And your voice – big as ever.'

'I could cox a boat,' Gwen agreed, turning back to run alongside her.

It was exactly what Gwen had said the day they had met. 'I could cox a boat.' There had been no maybe, no hesitation.

'Remember when I came up to you in our Greek class, that first time?'

'On your quest for short people?'

'Was it just because you were short?'

Hilary had noticed her up in the front row and brought her along to practise the same afternoon, like a prize. Around this time of year, a few weeks earlier. Indian summer, humid, bright. The delirium of starting college still on them. Everything new. Everything desirable.

The others had treated them like a pair: here was Hilary's friend she was introducing. Which had made them intensely aware of each other.

In the shadowy quiet of the boathouse, a dozen or so big girls leaning up against the long, smooth-hulled shells overturned on their racks, a few more sitting on the concrete floor, bare legs crossed or negligently splayed, the coach droning on about trials. In their innocence. Most of them were there because it was offered. None of them had a clue. They were all nervous, eyes on the floor, faking cool, glancing up now and again to check the postures, the expressions, the chemistry of the group, furtively hunting for anything that could be pegged, judged.

We played along with it, Hilary thought, side by side through all the sizing up. And she could remember the anxiety, as the impatient seconds ticked by, filled with talking rather than the doing craved by every physique in the room. What did we know about each other? Only a hunch. And we both kept silent, poker-faced, made the same bet. That's how it started. Over the gruelling months that followed, unimaginable sweat and exhaustion, they privately crept towards the commitment they publicly seemed to have made already.

Every one of those girls knew how to do what she was told; Gwen quickly learned how to tell them. In no time at all, she vaulted upwards a level in the team hierarchy, practically a coach herself. But she did the same training as the others. She was knitted into the boat by it, felt the challenge. And Hilary, at stroke, remained her inward captain. Setting the beat, silently communicating to Gwen what was physically possible – how quick, how long, how many – and Hilary had to make it happen, bring the other seven with her, pull their oars in time with Gwen's commands. Gradually, Hilary and Gwen took complete possession of one another; it had to work between them or the whole boat failed. The adrenalin of the training, the races and victories, worked on them like a drug. They flew on it, face to face in the back of the boat.

'Don't you ever feel sorry about leaving early?' Hilary asked. 'Missing our last year?'

'Never.'

'I remember it as if you *had* been there, you know? That other girl who coxed after you, senior year. She was fine. But it wasn't the same. She never mattered.'

Gwen felt hit by this. But she fought it. 'Maybe I was there enough, if we both have such good memories. Maybe another year would have been less intense.'

'I just mean I can't picture her face, that girl. I can only picture yours, shouting abuse.' Hilary laughed. 'You were unbelievable, Gwen. If we could have harnessed your willpower –'

'If you could have harnessed my willpower, maybe I wouldn't have left!'

'You had us all completely under your control, Gwen. Your face was all I could ever see out on the river – my whole world was inside the boat. You could see all of us *and* the race, all the other boats alongside, out in front.'

'Other boats were never out in front for long, babe; you guys saw them all, too, once we passed them!' Gwen barked out, 'Pow-er *ten*,' and sprinted away in front of Hilary along the path, playful. But then she slowed down sheepishly and waited.

'It was a pretty big surprise,' Hilary said, catching up with her, 'you going off with Lawrence. Actually leaving the country. Like the boat, in a way – because to me, it felt as though I had my head down over work, over the school slog, and it turned out that you were looking around and seeing so much more. Seeing *all* the possibilities.'

'I wasn't looking for anything in particular, Hil. If you ask Lawrence, he'll tell you. I wasn't as sophisticated as you might think – trying to pick up some visiting professor.'

'You went to his office hours. I would never have had the nerve.'

Gwen laughed out loud, broke stride. 'Well, that's what they're for – office hours! I refuse to be embarrassed by that.' And she laughed again. 'You were no shrinking violet, Hil, shacked up with Mark by the end of freshman year as I recall. Maybe otherwise *you* would have had more nerve. Give me a break! I had questions for Lawrence. Who else was I going to ask? I hated what I was doing, and he guessed – I've told you that? Wrote it on one of my papers: "*You seem to hate Pliny. Why are you doing this?*"'

'Probably you could sue for that now,' Hilary chuckled.

'Yeah. And how could suing be better than falling in love, dropping out, running away together?'

'It seemed so womanly and grown-up – or no – old-fashioned. That's what surprised me. Because we were all such tomboys, you know? The romance between you and Lawrence was something someone would do who wore skirts to class, or who wasn't in college at all. Like something out of the 1950s, or even the nineteenth century.'

Gwen was a little stunned, irritated even. 'Why? Because he was English? I'm still a tomboy. Look what I'm wearing.' It was true; she had on men's track shorts made from heavy, dark blue cotton, probably ten years old, a once white T-shirt turned grey with washing, holes under the arms and along the edge of the neck band where the material had disintegrated with use and with sweat. It was all far too big for her. 'Not exactly a gym bunny's exercise outfit. Not a stitch of Lycra. I'm out here to sweat, not to vamp anyone.' She turned her head and looked Hilary up and down as they passed the Barn Elms boathouse.

Hilary was wearing a shirt she had borrowed from Mark and never returned; she looked at it now, smarting with dismay. And she had on skintight black stretch leggings, cropped at the knee, about which she self-consciously observed, 'I think the high-tech stuff is OK if you actually exercise in it. I know people go around in sports stuff as a fashion thing, at least in New York they do, and it looks like a state of undress. Running around town in pyjamas. But if you sweat in them and ache in them, you get to love them, like anything.' Next she said, 'Maybe I just never got the difference between a tomboy and an actual boy.'

'I found out the difference when I had Will – what a shock – *that* made me realise I was a girl. Man, I fought it – needing help. Needing anything at all. Maybe you'll be better prepared than I was. But sometimes I think our whole generation is confused about it. Did we think we *were* boys? I swear. Do you remember how, when all the schools in the States were going co-ed, it felt like we could go to college anywhere we wanted? And the real girls went to the women's colleges where they could be girls together, but the ones of us who went to the men's colleges – we went as boys. Hiding our femininity. Why did we do that?'

'Because the women's libbers were so goddamned embarrassing.' Hilary coughed up a laugh. 'So political, so filled with vengeance, so covered with hair. And because the only company they were ever going to have was each other's.'

'But if we wanted to pull men, why didn't we just become cheerleaders?'

'Didn't you have to be from the Deep South to do that? Surely it never crossed your mind? Anyway, pulling men – on *purpose*?'

'You're right. Never.'

'So you see what I mean about you and Lawrence . . . ? It looked like the real man-woman deal. Like something in a French movie. Adult. Or I guess it would have to be an English movie – one of the Michaels, Caine or York, or Charles Dance – with the wounded, pale-eyed glamour and the Shakespearean voice.'

45

'Lawrence has been telling me you have a thing for Englishmen.' Gwen smiled, thinking of Roland, dark as he was, his shambling brilliance.

'You and Lawrence started a whole mythology. We were awestruck. I was anyway.'

There was a little pause, their outbreaths whinnying, their shoes skiffing more lightly over the paved road as they passed the long row of boathouses at Putney: Vesta, Westminster Boys' School, Dulwich College. There were flags fluttering, powerboats and dinghies on wooden trailers outside open doors, boats moored along the waterfront, a jaunty, maritime air.

'But we *were* adults then, on the verge of it,' Gwen said at last.

And Hilary asked, 'Do you think we're getting too old to be tomboys?'

'Jeez. I haven't got any other self-image handy. Can't start primping now. I don't have time.' Gwen's tone was arch. After another pause, she said, 'Besides, Hil, the sort of guy we were interested in wasn't attracted to a woman already spit-shined and curled on a tray, fully cooked. Maybe we were embarrassed. Maybe we were being defiant. Or maybe we were saving the potent thing – like for a rainy day. For a man we really wanted. The gem in the rough – do you really want it cut, faceted? Cool was wearing the most disgusting clothes you could find because you knew you could dress up if you ever wanted to.'

'If you ever *met* a man you really wanted,' Hilary said sardonically. 'But, yeah. Maidenliness – it's girl macho, isn't it? Too easy if you use sex to get a guy. Any girl can use sex. Maybe even love is too easy. I got stuck there for ever with Mark – good friends who have sex on the side. The best I can say about it now is that it was completely reliable.'

This observation produced a brooding hiatus. They became a little separated as they threaded their way among the passers-by on the narrow pavement leading up on to Putney Bridge. The traffic swelled and crashed remorselessly; then they ran down on the other side among the faded roses at the edge of the grounds of Fulham Palace.

Gwen started in again with something bland and positive. 'You look better anyway than you looked then. I guess you know that. Your hair looks better, too.'

'We didn't have haircuts in those days, did we?'

Gwen laughed. 'I still don't have a haircut.' It was loose brown strands around her shoulders, some straight, some wavy, no obvious parting, fairly tangled, not even tied back to go running, wind-whipped, dark with sweat underneath.

'Mine doesn't cut anyway, even when the hairdresser uses scissors.'

'But among ourselves, we were comrades, hey, Hilary? That was a good thing about those days. How we were friends?'

'Not a lot of girls around, really. You had to be comrades.'

'And no rivalry.'

'Competition,' Hilary objected.

'It's not the same. Remember the girls who came from wher-ever on the weekends? They had haircuts. Hair*dos*, even. How they were desperate for dates – to get engaged before they graduated. And only the pretty ones had a prayer. That was rivalry. Completely poisonous.'

'It's funny, though, how when you left –' Hilary paused.

'When I left?' Gwen was waiting for a revelation, which she thought might be something funny; maybe Hilary and their class-mates had all begun to pay great attention to their hair or to their dress during senior year. But what she got was more of a spear thrust.

'It – felt like the ultimate move. That's all. Finished us off.'

Just then, under the long canopy made by the old London plane trees lining Bishop's Park and spreading without restraint over the paved embankment towards the river, they came up behind a woman walking with a baby in a pushchair. The baby was five or six months old, bright-eyed, alert, sitting up facing the woman with a little white blanket tucked up to its chest, its arms free and waving about sturdily with the joy of its ride and the excitement of the dappled golden light moving before its eyes. The pushchair bounced and lunged, its wheels catching against the blocks of the pavement, which were lifted at harsh angles here and there. The baby lurched forward then back, laughing and gurgling, as the woman strode steadily, wearily on along the green-railinged river.

'Hello,' said Hilary, stepping around the pushchair.

'Hey,' breathed Gwen.

But the woman said nothing as they turned and glanced at her. She stared ahead, into her baby's eyes, vague-faced under fair, bedraggled hair, blue circles under her own eyes, half smiling, bearing it.

When they were out of earshot, Gwen said, '*She* needs a good night's sleep. I can remember being exactly like that with Will.'

'What – a zombie? You have to tell me more about Will.'

'My ultimate move?' Gwen let the sarcasm sink in, but then she softened. 'It was just like that, you know. He was my cox. That woman back there, me, any mother – we're all galley slaves. You force the pushchair over the ruined paving, over whatever. Anything at all to keep the boat moving. The baby gives all the commands, shouts, shits, steers – whatever. Nothing else seems to matter. You can't hear the world, don't notice your husband. I guess from the baby's point of view it must be like trying to control a giant: the monster mother. Scary. Uncertain. Which is maybe why the baby is so ruthless in its demands. And you submit to it. Willingly. You throw yourself down, betray the man you love, whatever it takes – to please the child. It's a big deal. It's crazy.' She looked sideways at Hilary, half smiled with the slack corners of her heaving mouth. 'I'm ranting, aren't I?'

Hilary said, 'We've been out a while. It can happen – with the exercise.'

'Now. We have to go around this,' said Gwen, gesturing up to high white walls and fences marked Fulham Football Club.

On they ran into the silent neighbourhood, between the staring front windows of empty, midday houses, a deserted newsagent's, then weaved back once or twice to the north bank of the river, past outdoor lunches on pub terraces and gleaming café tables, laundry hanging out to dry, phlox spilling its clash of fuchsia over dark brick balconies above their heads, then at last back into the traffic, in rhythmic delirium, tired, surviving.

CHAPTER 4

The growing feeling of comfort between Hilary and Gwen made it seem easy, in the end, to sit down for dinner with Lawrence and Roland a few days later. Gwen didn't have to insist.

Will was still orbiting around his mother in the kitchen as she turned on the pair of gas burners underneath the shiny, submarine-shaped poaching pan, unwrapped the salmon, poked at the little potatoes rolling about in their cauldron. He managed to make himself the centre of everyone's attention for a good half-hour after Roland arrived with Lawrence, so that the jittery business of greeting, introducing, pouring drinks, was made even more chaotic than usual.

Will had a stacking top: five individual tops which could be made to spin as one if they were wound up and dropped in precisely the right way – accurately, quickly – before any of them stopped spinning. One by one, hosts and guests got down on the floor, giggling, absorbed. Nobody could get beyond three tops piled up and spinning at once – until they started helping each other out. Gwen was fastest at winding the tops, but Will had the surest touch for stacking them. The little group fell silent when mother and son got four of the tops going together. Then Will, his heavily lashed green eyes hooded and still, dropped the last tiny top on the whirling stack. The sharp point of the big, fat top at the bottom buzzed loudly like a little drill against the polished wood as the stack leaned ever so slightly and began to inscribe a slow hard arc across the floor, moving faster, becoming more and more unstable, alarmingly angled. At last it shot under the kitchen table, struck one of the legs and blew apart.

A deflationary 'Oh . . .' seeped from them all, the air going out of their game.

Then Hilary cried out, 'Look, they're still going!'

'Cool!' squeaked Will. Because three of the tops had landed upright and went on spinning separately, moving freely over the floor.

'Centripetal force,' Roland observed in his deep, imperturbable voice.

'Dead cool,' Gwen said, smiling, rising to her feet. 'We can do it all again tomorrow. Time for bed.'

She made no move to enforce this, but walked away to the stove, stuck a fork into the potatoes to see if they were cooked, then hefted them from the burner to the sink and poured the boiling water away.

Will grabbed up his tops, which were wobbling now as they spun themselves out, and took them to his father. 'Daddy, will you wind them up one more time? Pu-leeeze?'

And so Lawrence did, and the game began again, but with more tension now that bedtime was looming; everyone's hands were stiff and unsuccessful with it. The tops racketed crazily around the room, under the chairs, under the table, and Will fired the smaller ones carelessly at the bigger ones like bombs, laughing hilariously until he collapsed on the floor. His five-year-old stomach and its irresistible plughole of a belly button bulged unguarded where his striped pyjamas separated at the waist, and he was made the victim of a tough tickle from his father's big, relentless fingers, until he was overcome, and screamed, 'Stop, stop.' His legs kicked ferociously as he lay on his back; his arms flailed and swatted.

Lawrence stopped.

Then Will screamed, 'Do it again! Do it again!' tears showing along the corners of his grin.

Gwen slipped the fish into the simmering pan and replaced the long lid. 'C'mon, you guys. Bed.'

51

As Gwen moved with Will towards the door, Hilary said, 'I could read Will a story?'

'Do you want to?' Gwen turned, grateful.

'While you do the fish?'

'The fish is OK, actually,' said Gwen. 'It has to cook for a few minutes.'

Will said, 'I want Mummy to read me the story.' He took hold of Gwen's hand.

'It's going to be a short one, Will, since we're having dinner.'

'Two short ones?' he said engagingly.

'I can do the fish,' said Lawrence. 'And I'll send Hilary to you in ten minutes if you haven't reappeared. Don't worry, darling.'

'The spinach soufflé is in the oven. Keep an eye on it.' Gwen had a foot on the bottom step.

'G'night, Daddy,' said Will, tipping a half-cupped palm in the air, a stilted wave, suddenly shy.

'Night.'

The group in the kitchen, milling awkwardly around the table and the stove, turned back to the subject Roland had raised with Lawrence during their drive from Oxford to London – the question of whether Lawrence should be taking so much time from his big book on Greek and Roman slavery to be pursuing what Roland reckoned was a pretty tenuous connection between the *Satyricon* and *Les Misérables*.

Roland sidled up to Hilary, winking, conspiratorial. 'I've been warning Lawrence off trying to be popular. He's brewing up a scholarly piece on *Les Mis*. You must have seen *Les Mis*? Everyone has.'

'*Les Mis*?' she said, round-eyed. 'The musical? I – well – I read the novel, years ago. But I don't know any of the songs.'

'You needn't know the tunes,' Lawrence assured her, tearing brown paper off a round, crusty loaf of bread. 'Roland's faking. You haven't seen it, Roland. Own up.'

Roland's chin shot out; his face reddened.

In the burning silence that ensued, Lawrence opened his case, with a kind of polite indifference, to put Hilary at her ease. 'You remember the convict, Hilary? Jean Valjean? Tries to steal a loaf of bread — just like this,' and he whacked the bread down on a wooden cutting board by the sink. 'For this audacious, antisocial crime, he is sentenced to five years' hard labour.' Lawrence crumpled the paper showily with one hand and tossed it into the bin which stood lidless nearby. 'He begins his sentence in tears with an iron collar riveted on around his neck. Might as well be a slave, you see? Just my sort of thing.'

Hilary was silent, eyes on the floor, conscious that Roland was watching her, and that she hadn't responded to his opening gambit in the way he had evidently hoped she might. That she had failed even to recognise it as an opening gambit. She felt herself being caught up in somebody else's argument, and she didn't want to reveal sympathy for either side. Lawrence is only trying to be kind to me — that's what she would have liked to say to Roland — he wouldn't sideline his own friend on purpose.

Lawrence went on, gently but tenaciously, with his perform-ance. It was irresistible to him to try to capture whatever youthful, feminine attention was in a room. 'When he is eventually freed, the convict soon steals again.' He reached for a bread knife, unsheathing it from the wooden knife block with a dangerous flourish, high in the air, eyes aglow. 'But this time he steals from a bishop who has the power to free him physically *and spiritually* — by forgiving him. And as a sign of his forgiveness, the bishop gives the convict two silver candlesticks.'

Hilary looked up almost involuntarily and said, 'I remember that.'

Lawrence cut into the bread with energy, the toothed blade scoring loudly through the crust and sinking into the doughy middle, rasping and biting all the way down to the powdery surface of the well-hacked board. He cut another slice, then stopped and looked about the room as if he had forgotten something. He spotted a pair of pewter candlesticks on the Welsh dresser, walked across and collected them with a package of long white tapers from a shelf above, and set them at the centre of the table among the place settings. 'Perfect,' he said, spreading his palms in the air over it all and smiling with satisfaction. 'Maybe you'd put in the candles?' he asked, handing them to Hilary.

'You're an atheist, Lawrence; surely Hugo was not,' Roland grumbled. And he stalked off a few paces to sit down by himself on the sofa.

Lawrence ignored him, still smiling. He lifted the lid of the poaching pan ever so slightly with the corner of a spatula, looked at his watch. Then he began opening and shutting drawers, hunting. 'Jean Valjean keeps the bishop's candlesticks, despite the risk that they will eventually reveal his criminal past, just as Trimalchio – you know the *Satyricon* too, I suppose, Hilary? Being a classicist?'

Hilary looked guiltily towards Roland, then back towards Lawrence who was snatching and slamming at the drawers, rattling spoons, flaunting dish cloths, all the artillery of his domestic power. She fiddled with the package of candles, finding a way in through the cellophane, and nodded reluctantly, curious in spite of herself.

'Well, I'm sure you recall that Trimalchio keeps by him the candelabrum which once belonged to his master, despite the fact that it marks him as a former slave. Just like Valjean's candlesticks, you see?'

She approached the table, twisted the tapers into the sticks, straightened them.

'The candlesticks and the candelabrum are mementos,' he said, '– symbols, if you like – of the greatest moment in their lives: the moment of being freed.' There was an easy comedy in his voice, as if he wasn't insisting.

'But Petronius writes nothing about this!' Roland expostulated. Up he stood again. 'You are importing modern psychology into a text of which only fragments survive in any case. Where is the documentary evidence for what you say? Or any evidence at all? Are you forgetting that Trimalchio is not a real person?'

Lawrence turned away from the oven door where he was crouching to peer through the glass at the soufflé, his hands cosied in the two halves of an oven mitt. He smiled at Hilary as she stood tangled between himself and Roland. 'Petronius gives us extravagant detail! Trimalchio does nothing but celebrate his freedom. Hideous as he is, he becomes rich and he feasts – for ever, as it were – and in his own vulgar way. Feeding the appetites pent up in him as a slave.'

'We have one of the collars,' Hilary said. It burst out of her, as if it were proof of something. She lifted her eyebrows, surprised at herself. There was a little silence.

'Collars?' Roland bristled at her.

'A slave collar. Made of bronze. It's inscribed, so we know it's late antiquity. Early Christian period, fourth century. Found in Italy. I'll tell you what –' She paused, turned from one to the other of them and then raised her hands towards her neck, resting her fingertips on her collarbone, squinting a little in dismay. 'Sounds weird, but I put it on one time. It has a piece missing.' She held out her right thumb and forefinger, about two and a half inches apart to show the size of the gap, then rested her fingers back on her collarbone.

'I tried it with Eddie – Edward Doro.' Her hands moved ever so slightly as she recalled the stiffness, pulling the collar open wider, whether she would snap it, how the ragged edges scraped her skin when the two of them had nestled it into place. 'It's surprisingly delicate, actually – thin, like the leather strap you'd put around a dog's neck; it's not like you couldn't get it off if you were determined. It would have been more – well, also a symbol. Even with the tiny rivets soldered into place. Which just shows how completely the slave was resigned to the whole system, his place in it. A kind of settled, polished arrangement. It's almost unbearable to imagine –'

'Imagine. Exactly.' Roland pounced in triumph. 'Why would any slave resist a master who could torture him, have him crucified? Or have his head put on a spike along the road? Where was a slave to run to even if he didn't have a collar? The empire was monumental. You can't go around *imagining* history.'

But Lawrence pounced back. 'How the bloody else are we to understand it? It's not as if it's still here around us!'

Roland smiled, an artful, curling smile. He came towards the table, tut-tutting, reached for the white wine and poured himself another glass. 'Yes, yes. All right. But judicious use of same. In any case, these collars are a very late phenomenon. And by the fourth century, a freed slave didn't become a citizen of Rome, did he?'

'We have two or three branding irons, too,' said Hilary grimly.

'Touché,' said Lawrence. He was rinsing parsley at the sink, shaking water off it with a snap of his wrist. He reached across the counter and flung a few droplets on to the flame of the gas burner where they made a sizzling sound. 'As it were.'

They all laughed.

'Give it up, Roland,' said Lawrence in a congenial tone. 'We've scored a hit for the imagination. No history without it. No nothing, in fact.'

Hilary looked compassionately at Roland, and she said under her breath, uncertainly, 'What I meant was, imagine if you had to wear the collar yourself. It's degrading. And you feel that. Even though it is only a symbol of something else – real power, real servitude.'

Roland took a step towards her, holding his wine glass in front of his face, half obscuring it. 'You have to forgive us. We go on at each other like this all the time. It's part of our brief.' He looked down at his shoes, sipped the wine.

Lawrence set the basket of sliced bread on the table. 'Oh, yes, the brief. Nowadays we've got to fill out endless paperwork. What we plan to publish in the next five years – daunting to say the least. The whole department gets a grade. To ensure we're on to something worthwhile with our work, contributing to the gross national product. And they set our colleagues on us: Haven't we got something ready to go, something tucked away we could bring to print?'

'They are around *our* necks, speaking of collars, all these bureaucrats with their research assessment procedures,' Roland said contemptuously. 'What are we up to? they keep asking. Forgetting they have given us the nation's youth, and that some of us are devoted to teaching, which is, after all, very time-consuming. Otherwise it's, What do we need? What do we want? How can they make us happy? They should bloody well go away. People need to think life through for themselves or they don't learn to care about it. The state is mothering everyone to death.'

'I've taken on Roland as a mentor,' said Lawrence with amiable disdain, clueing Hilary in, 'and he defends me from the entire process of assessment.'

Roland giggled. He leaned towards Hilary and said, 'Or maybe we should say, Lawrence has taken me on as his mother – in this post-feminist era. We've all been turned into women, really. Oxford dons, the government, whatever. The men, the fathers – their time is gone.' He smiled and said to her with zest, 'You've won.'

Hilary was taken aback. 'Won what? I wasn't fighting for anything.' She felt strangely embarrassed by his pronouncement. She sat down at the table and Roland sat down opposite her.

'I had a mentor,' she said, as if admitting to a character flaw. 'Edward Doro. He died, and I've been at sea ever since.'

'That's bad news,' Roland said. 'I mean – forgive me. What happened exactly?'

Lawrence knew all about it from Gwen, but he was intrigued now to hear it straight from Hilary. He drew a little closer to the table.

But for a moment Hilary didn't say anything because she was wondering why it was that everyone she met in England assumed she was fighting for something, something of which she herself was unaware. Paul had seemed to think that she had an agenda of some kind. Were Americans more complacent than the English? Were they insufficiently political about day-to-day matters? Or is it me, she pondered, who has failed ever to become conscious of having any particular ambitions? Roland assumes I'm a feminist just because I'm a woman. Maybe I ought to be a feminist? But she and Gwen had agreed: it was out of the question for them, for a whole swathe of girls back in America, girls of their moment, of their type. Had she somehow misunderstood what it was, feminism? Had she received the benefits without signing up for the cause?

She looked up, sensing their expectation, wondering how to begin to answer Roland. 'Edward Doro collected antiquities and so that's what he taught me how to do.' She lifted her palms in the air, apologetic, self-deprecating. 'It was amazing — being with someone who always knew what he wanted. And who always *got* what he wanted — at least in the way of objects.'

She dropped her eyes, picked up a knife from the place setting in front of her, turned it end to end, idly, watching the gleam and flash of the blade, pacing herself. 'I got so that I could tell, actually, when he was going to go after something. Even from photos. And so when he was old and he couldn't really get out, he'd send me to look. And — it worked.' She put the knife down, lined it up straight along the side of the blue straw table mat. 'My eyes worked fine for him.' She sighed.

Suddenly she fixed them directly on Roland's, then away at Lawrence's, and announced with matter-of-fact energy, 'So, he left me to curate his collection, and I know exactly how to do it, but I've maybe wrecked my chance. Because I don't know anything about life. There you go.' Again she lifted her palms, the shrug of regret. 'What book could I have read to find out how not to screw up when I'd been handed everything on a plate? It was like an inheritance for me — or like the candelabrum you were telling us about, Lawrence, given to me after a long apprenticeship.' She wrapped a hand around the base of one of the pewter candle-sticks. 'How could I squander that?'

'Maybe you don't really want to look after the collection?' Lawrence suggested mildly.

'Oh, please, you're just like Gwen, telling me I didn't want to be engaged either.'

Roland flinched at this. 'You were engaged to him?'

Hilary laughed her boisterous laugh, and she looked at Roland with friendliness for the first time. 'God, no. That's an entirely different saga. Though not unrelated, I can assure you.'

Roland's heavy brows went up.

Before he could ask any more, Lawrence sat down with them, intervened. 'Seriously though. Perhaps you don't want to be a curator? It's not the same as collecting. Conservation, fund-raising, exhibiting. A public, institutionalised profession. It's about caring for something – as in the Latin – it's not about the hunt.'

Hilary relented. 'Sometimes the hunt came off Eddie like a smell –' she tapped her fingertips together under her nose as if there was something on them, savoury, dripping; narrowed her eyes, spoke intensely – 'this insistent – this urge to – *get* something. To possess it. The strange gratification. When he was like that, he couldn't think about anything except how he was going to do it. Any scheme, no matter how complex. Money was not a problem. It was persuading people to part with things. Oh –and the agony he went through when he wanted an object that had no provenance! He wouldn't let himself take a chance that something might be pulled out of the collection later if it turned out it had been stolen at some point or illegally exported.'

Roland and Lawrence were hanging on her every word. When she stopped talking there was a silence. To fill it, she said girlishly, with forced nonchalance, 'It's weird. Our whole partnership was about planning for death, but of course, you have no idea what that really means, dying, until the person's done it – moved on to wherever. I knew his mind so well – for me it still exists, in my head, and in his things.

'You've ruined the fish,' wailed Gwen, rushing in down the stairs and across to the stove.

'No, darling, I took it off. Don't worry. It's perfect.' Lawrence stood up, pointed at the big white china platter on to which he had delicately transferred the salmon. 'It's under that foil. It'll still be warm. I had to take the soufflé out; it was getting brown. But look – it hasn't fallen.'

Gwen gave him a look of sweet relief, nodded thanks without smiling.

He took pity on her. 'Poor you. I promised we'd rescue you after ten minutes. We got caught up in what Hilary was saying. But Hilary will say it again, won't you, Hilary?' He turned back to the other two at the table.

Gwen smiled, patted the air down with her palms, quietening him. 'OK, OK, the goddess is appeased.'

She didn't admit that she had lingered in Will's room just because she felt content there. Why should she resent it if her party was going well without her? That was the whole point, wasn't it? She hadn't been able to hear their voices from upstairs, but she knew they were hard at it, finding out all about each other. And they had probably only found out things she herself already knew.

'What about lighting the candles?' she asked.

Lawrence stood up. 'I couldn't find any matches.'

'The stove?' Gwen suggested.

So he lit one candle from the gas and then held it against the other wick until they flamed up together.

Gwen switched off the lights. 'Maybe everyone come serve yourselves?'

As they scraped back chairs, dished food, Lawrence announced in a non-committal tone, 'I think Roland taught this Paul fellow with whom you've been – working. Quite a young chap, is he?'

Nobody spoke. Gwen uncovered the potatoes and dropped the saucepan lid on the stove with a stupendous crash.

'You mean Paul Mercy?' Hilary said loudly, as if it should be obvious to them all. She put two potatoes beside her fish, and they rolled clumsily until they hit the soft mound of spinach. She levelled the plate in both hands, sat down. 'You're the one who taught him, Roland?'

'The one? To be sure, others will have taught him as well.' Roland cut off a large piece of salmon. 'Did you never teach him, Lawrence?'

'Never even met him,' Lawrence replied. 'Know nothing at all about him apart from what I ' he slowed '– hear.'

'Isn't he – I mean, Lawrence, was this to do with the post you were asking around about in the Easter vac, or maybe Trinity term. Last spring? And I suggested Paul, and I believe it was Clare Pryce, and I don't recall who else? Old students of mine, to be sure. All of them.'

The conversation was suspended, everyone waiting for someone to say something, to acknowledge some mysterious chain of connections by which they all were linked and of which they none were entirely aware.

'Gosh,' Lawrence muttered. 'I suppose I –'

There was another silence. Was anyone to blame? Were they all still on the same side?

'I gave you his name, didn't I?' Lawrence said contritely, looking sorrowfully at Hilary. 'I'm awfully sorry. I had no idea he would prove to be –'

'So irresistible?' Hilary demanded. 'Come on, it's not your fault. The guy knows his antiquities.' Her voice was raw, defensive and aggressive at once.

'Well, I'm glad to hear it,' Lawrence said sympathetically. 'But after all, a reference from friends. We ought to have been able to vouch for him personally, somehow. We ought to have –'

'I interviewed him,' said Hilary, bold, sarcastic. 'It was never a requirement that he subscribe to any particular code of conduct. That he be straight, marriageable, a match made in heaven –'

'Still, it's hardly professional –' Lawrence was grasping for some way to ease her pain, to let her off the hook.

'On the contrary. He behaved perfectly correctly. I was the one who lost my cool, wasn't I?' She seemed to be challenging him with her toughness and her hurry, insisting on keeping control of her own story, rather than be its pitiable victim.

'But the way you tell it, or Gwen tells it, he sounds rather – slimy. There's some level there of false ingratiation. And – something –'

He looked at Gwen, but Gwen was just as bewildered as he was. She only nodded. 'He doesn't sound like a nice guy,' she observed lamely. 'Not – forthright. I think – pretending to make friends – what is that? Leading you on. He knew. I'm sure he knew. After all, women are always getting blamed for that kind of behaviour – using their looks, their feminine wiles, to get what they want.'

Hilary nodded, suddenly speechless, self-conscious.

And Roland leaped in, in a schoolmasterish voice, summarising the merits and demerits of Paul. 'He's clever, of course. Very good company. But lazy, really – unless he's outgrown that. Quite a high opinion of himself – presumed he'd go far, I reckon. And he could do. Impressive grasp of detail, very strong sense of style. Gifted with languages. Even as an undergraduate, he had several ancient and modern ones.'

'Gifted with languages,' Hilary echoed, dry-mouthed.

Gwen knew just what Hilary was thinking – that Paul had lied about being lousy at Italian.

'Hardly a historian, and certainly not a philosopher,' Roland went on, unstoppable. 'Not that I ever taught him philosophy. Could have done anything he set his mind to, really, but he used to tell me that he hated talking about definitions and logic. Called them puzzles. Disdained Aristotle, Plato, metaphysics, ethics – plain old good and evil. What happens happens is what he would say.

Capable of memorising anything he read, but didn't want to think too hard. Not joined-up thinking. Text-based history suited him fine, but he wasn't much with analysing a problem. Useless with an economic model; he'd tell you what every pottery shard looked like, who made it, where it came from, based on certain visual qualities, but never get on to caring or understanding how the pottery trade might have worked in a pre-capitalist economy. Equally, the coins to him were lovely bright objects to collect and admire. He has the mind of a connoisseur really, an aesthete. And for ever stuck in the one-damn-thing-after-another school of thought. What, honestly, is the point of that? Life as a series of accidents? I take it, Hilary, that has somehow included you? Some – accident?'

'An accident,' Hilary breathed. She gave a tight chuckle, feeling that Roland was scolding her, taking her to task for having failed to see what she was dealing with in Paul. 'You seem to have the nub of it.'

Gwen thought, I've never seen Roland being so pompous, so cold, so unbelievably condescending.

Lawrence was diligently working his way through his plateful, head down, shovelling it in. 'Maybe he *was* quite happy to achieve some hold on Hilary,' he said with his mouth full, chewing. 'Maybe he did do it all deliberately. C'mon, Hilary, stick up for yourself. You mustn't let Roland be hard on you. Maybe Paul was after your – inheritance. Your candelabrum.'

Once again, Roland went red, realising he'd crossed some line. 'Do forgive me. I have no intention of being hard on anyone. And I don't think you should let Paul Mercy get the better of you. He shouldn't be allowed to – hurt your feelings. Or anyone's feelings for that matter.'

Gwen caught Lawrence's eye across the table as she poured sparkling water and he poured more wine. She was thinking that Roland, in some ghastly, awkward way, was trying to cheer Hilary up. She felt certain that Lawrence was thinking the same. She gazed at Lawrence, half smiling, considering that wine on top of fourteen years of marriage dissolved any barriers between their minds, that he knew even now what she was thinking as she thought it: that all this bluster was Roland's idea of gallantry, cutting Paul off at the knees, reducing him to a slip of an undergraduate figure, a schoolboy even, truant, with a lost homework assignment.

What is it with these dons? She wondered if Roland's efforts would succeed, looking at Hilary, looking at Roland. Surely Lawrence would never stoop so low, belittling a rival? Or were all men like that?

And now she heard Hilary starting in on how ridiculous she must have seemed, throwing herself at Paul.

'Here,' Hilary cried out, flushed with wine. 'Have my heart.' And she made a gesture, like throwing something down on the floor. 'Stomp on it for me.'

Oh, don't tell these stories against yourself, Gwen thought. She felt, suddenly, that the evening was destroying Hilary's morale. It's the tone of voice – abject, self-abasing. Come on, Hil, Gwen was thinking. You are not such a loser as all that. And why, *why*, tell Roland so much about the broken engagement. I mean not with such gusto. It's my fault, Gwen considered. She warned me, Not yet.

'Maybe Paul *was* somehow intrigued by you – authentically,' Lawrence proposed. 'Maybe he felt comfortable knowing nothing need happen between you. There are plenty of men like that, gay and straight.'

'And are there plenty of women like that?' asked Hilary, open-eyed.

'Plenty of women?' Lawrence echoed. 'For whom nothing need happen?' He felt strangely pinned down by her, targeted, and he found himself stuttering, 'No,' then, 'I don't know,' as it came over him that he had always presumed that women were not comfortable unless something did happen. Not a wise presumption, he advised himself. Yet he felt certain that it was true for this woman:

something would need to happen for Hilary to feel comfortable. Lawrence felt it distinctly.

Roland turned away just then from Hilary. Gwen felt his attention shift with a snap, like the mainsail of a boat going about in a stiff breeze. The weight of the evening fell towards her heavily, life jackets, picnic bags sliding down across the cockpit. He began to ask her about her upcoming exhibition.

'I've banned my dealer from my studio,' she announced. 'It's not until after Christmas, and he's already sold a piece. Had it shipped to Aspen to some movie producer. That was sort of – withering.' She hunched her shoulders up around her neck like a vulture, curled her fingers together in front of her face, miming avarice. 'He arrives from New York with this big black portfolio, peers at all the canvases, scavenges little scraps of drawings lying around. There's a lot of money on offer. The figures are going way up, which starts getting inside my head, right inside my imagination. Once I'm done with the paintings, OK, I'll want them all out – instantly –' She waved her hand imperiously. 'But I work back and forth from one to another and I need them all together until they're finished. You don't want someone buying your flat, really, if you're still living in it. Even though you might need the money. You want to find your new place first, where you're going to live next.'

'Same with books,' Roland murmured as if to himself, chewing, ruminating, so that Gwen had to sit up close to hear him. He swallowed, bent his head towards her, spoke more clearly, his lips near the curve of her cheek. 'I never tell a colleague, or even a student, something that I'm writing about; it's only natural for them to try to use it before I can publish it. Anything we say aloud – it's up for grabs, isn't it? Anything at all. But on the other hand, we writers don't really have to part with our books. Not like paintings. Everyone can have a copy of a book. More that the publisher worries nobody will want one.'

Gwen laughed at this. 'My dealer's pretty commercial,' she confided. 'American. You'd think I'd want big exhibitions and the high prices. But I feel a little pushed. A little packaged. Who are these clamouring millionaires? I need to paint without worrying about what sells; otherwise, I get on this roll that isn't my own. I hit one thing that someone really goes for, and I know I could do it again, and there's a lot of adrenalin there, and maybe even a temptation – a kind of challenge to please some supposed audience. But then, what would I really be doing? Are they hot for just whatever it is I'm producing? Or am I producing something they're hot for?'

She whirled her fork through the air. 'Sometimes I think I might have to run away from it, back to the country. So I don't become part of something dreamed up by other people. But right now, the work's OK. There's a lot happening fast. More coming. I can't stop. You'd have to pry my brushes out of my hands.' She gripped the fork hard, making a fist.

Now Roland laughed, a murmur in his chest, pleasure, interest, leaning down towards her. 'Part of art?' he asked, as if she knew what he meant. And when she looked bemused, he went on, 'To please the audience, to give them pleasure? Nowadays all parts of our culture are infected by a kind of marketing mentality. Even Lawrence. What do the people want? That question shapes everything – politics, education, health, transport. But can one ever be right in thinking one knows what the people want? And do the people want the right things in any case?'

Gwen poked at a nearly invisible fish bone on her plate, pushed it to the very edge, and without looking up said dreamily, almost as if she were thinking aloud, 'When I'm out in the landscape, looking, or even just being there, I don't think of any of that. It's something else – something that carries you right out of yourself, out of normal experience. Like some loophole you can get through in time, where it's slower or deeper – and actually *real* –'

'That's quite a palatable form of religion – nature worship. But quite primitive, eh? Pantheism, Wordsworth, the Druids. A sense of awe before the natural world? What about mankind, Gwen? What about civilisation? Or God, for that matter. Far more complex and intriguing.'

'What about *God*? What are you saying?' she demanded, sitting right up into the flow of his talk. 'I've copped out? Picked the easiest subject matter?'

'Not necessarily,' Roland said, smiling a smooth, almost syrupy smile, as if he were stroking her mind to quiet it. 'You're a painter after all.'

This was worse. 'So it's *painting* that's not good enough for you? What is wrong with this country, that painting isn't anything? And you've had so few great painters!'

He fell silent, looking confused. Then he said, 'Your paintings please me enormously. And I think art should please; it should be beautiful. Marketing, after all, is a lowbrow commercial name for something that has always been going on – and going on for perfectly good reasons. I like to see you think hard, that's all. You could do anything you wanted to. You might be more thoughtfu—' he corrected himself, 'more *analytical* – if you were pushed to it.'

'Watch your step, Henry Higgins!' Though she joked, Gwen was hurt. I reveal something personal, she thought, and he comes at me with that arrogance. Why does everything have to be an argument or a theory supported by evidence, a proof of something true or untrue? Who the fuck does he think he is?

Roland looked at her, down at his plate, at her again. Gwen sensed that he wanted in some way to apologise. She glanced at Hilary, wondering how the evening seemed to her, safely chatting with Lawrence.

'Of course I have my own favourites,' Hilary was saying, eyes on the hem of her napkin which she was folding and unfolding on the tabletop. Then she leaned a little towards Lawrence's reply.

'You won't ever be content if you let someone else get their hands on those. Will you?'

'I don't talk about it. It's not really appropriate to have my own opinion about the collection.' Hilary was demure and self-contained.

'But that's ridiculous!' Lawrence offered friendly outrage. 'You must have your own opinion! How can you ever have been a student of mine and not have an opinion? You must summon some nerve and tell me what it is! I'm longing to hear it!'

Hilary's cheeks darkened with his enthusiasm.

That's more like a conversation, Gwen thought. And it dawned on her that Roland was hardly coping with life away from Oxford. He was stuck after all in the tone of voice, in the useless style of put-downs and sparring. Roland only wants to please, she thought. Wants to be noticed and admired. But he doesn't know how to give ground. He doesn't believe as much as he pretends to believe in anyone else's vitality. He just knows how to question.

Tonight he had a chance – in theory, he had a chance for love. And he blew it. Before he even got into the room. He's the one who recommended the heartless Paul to be Hilary's assistant. So he's taking revenge on me as well as on Hilary. He won't even risk considering whether or not he likes Hilary, or how he ought to talk to her; he's just leaving her to Lawrence. He must have failed at this a hundred times, agonisingly, and he's trying to prove to us that he doesn't care – about women, about romance. Which shows that he's terrified. Gwen saw it all so suddenly and so clearly.

Oh, she thought with pain, he doesn't set out to hurt. He only needs someone to encourage him. To straighten his hair and spruce him up a little. Then he could shine. It occurred to her that, until tonight, she herself had been able to bring out what was gener-ous and alive in Roland because she wasn't a chance for love. She was already taken; with her, he was safe from failure, and so with her, he succeeded.

As she thought of this, she looked up at Roland with such warmth, such forgiveness, that he blushed brick red, almost purple, like a bruise, and the blush made a bond between them, a certain understanding. She could easily be the one if she cared to; he'd admitted it. It made the insides of her nostrils burn with surprise; she felt a flush of energy in her chest. She looked over at Hilary again, thinking, this should be you, Hil. And yet she felt a furtive pleasure that Hilary was still deep in conversation with Lawrence.

Gwen smiled a long easy smile at Roland. She felt gratified. She liked knowing she could be the one with him. She liked considering him as if she were single like Hilary. It was a long time since she had looked at a man with unmarried eyes.

When they talked about it, getting up the next morning, Gwen thought the party had been something of a success.

'Of course it was,' Lawrence announced. 'Everyone there was completely remarkable. What a privilege to be in the room with such people. And oh, the pudding!' He kissed his fingertips and tossed them in the air, then went back to scouring his teeth, toothpaste foaming from his jaws.

Gwen laughed, squeezing in at the sink. He had devoted himself to the store-bought chocolate cake.

Hyperbole often characterised Lawrence's most serious statements. It was like a superstition with him, making fun. He feared to value anything too much in case he lost it.

'But what do you mean by success? You want Roland to ask her out by himself?' He shook his head.

'You don't think he will?' Gwen whined a little, feeling mocked.

'With the wound of Paul that he and I inflicted on her? It's too much to expect him to make that up to her. Anyway, darling, you're the one he wants. He doesn't want her!'

She made an astonished face. 'Come off it, Lawrence. He wants a woman who will make sacrifices for him. You remember he told us that once? I don't make sacrifices for anyone!'

'You make sacrifices for Will every thirty seconds.' His voice trailed away as he went through the hall into the bedroom.

She scoffed at the mirror, spat into the sink. 'Not the same thing at all.'

Lawrence reappeared, buttoning his shirt, grinning devilishly. He watched her reflection over her shoulder and she watched, too – watched him, watched herself. Then she blushed, more from shyness than anxiety. They both knew he had a point, but it did them no harm at all, this tiny gratification she had enjoyed, Roland's attention. They laughed a little. It wasn't serious. It was like being caught eating ice cream straight out of the carton with the freezer door open; she felt slightly embarrassed. Why not sit down, have a bowlful? But a chair and a bowl would formally acknowledge the appetite; a chair and a bowl would make it impossible to pretend that the ice cream wasn't wanted, wasn't even really being eaten. As good as being caught; so who was kidding who? It was a delicate torture, to remind them both how intimately Lawrence knew her appetites and her sensibility.

As for Roland's admiration, Lawrence found it appropriate. It was further celebration of Gwen. Roland wasn't anything Gwen really wanted; Lawrence was sure of that. It enchanted Lawrence to surprise his wife as she tasted something she didn't really want; he loved the pathos of her inability to resist, and he felt a surge of strength in knowing she was his. 'Poor Roland' was what Lawrence really thought, but he didn't say it aloud.

He leaned down and around to Gwen's cheek, kissed her fondly. 'I'm not suggesting that you should sacrifice anything for Roland.'

'Hilary would make sacrifices, though,' Gwen burbled. 'That's what she's good at.'

But then she wondered uncomfortably, What kind of sacrifices? What kind of pleasure would Hilary have to forgo? Some deeply personal and necessary joy? Gwen remembered the sting Roland had administered with his comments about her private religion. What *about* mankind? she wondered. How could anyone drag their mind back from where it preferred to go? From its habitual satisfactions? In order to consider mankind? She felt angry at Roland, and she pushed the thought away.

'Maybe Roland *thinks* he wants a woman who would make sacrifices. But frankly, my dear, that's *so* last century.' Lawrence paused to savour the absurd trendiness of his witticism. Then he affected a more earnest voice, 'Don't you think he'd lose interest in someone like that? Walk all over her, use her up, throw her out? He ought to have a wife who could challenge him, amaze him. Do we know anyone that good? That tough?'

Gwen squirmed a little, knowing whom Lawrence had in mind. He reached for her chin, tugging at it in his cupped fingers, pulling her into his control. It was possessive, somehow tender, as if he wanted only to remind her of something.

'So, OK,' she conceded. 'Matchmaking's at least as hard as painting. For me, maybe harder, since I don't know yet how to do it.'

'I should think,' Lawrence agreed. He nodded, brooding, then added, 'It's a case of getting it exactly right once and once only. With painting, the more ways you can find, the more interest. And anyway, the paint *lets* you do it. But the people?'

CHAPTER 5

Gwen's studio was at the top of the house near the light. Already the autumn days seemed remorselessly short. Even if she didn't stop for lunch at all, the light didn't last as long as her appetite for work. She had ways of addressing this. She had systems, artifices, and she was always devising new ones.

Lately, she had one big, square canvas set on an easel directly underneath the vast skylight in the middle of the room, and another two wide, rectangular canvases facing the long window running across the back. Around the middle of the day, she usually worked on the square canvas underneath the skylight. Since it was October, the sun's zenith barely achieved the top of sky, and, even at noon, the light slanted in at an angle. But for a little over an hour, the quality of the light remained almost steady, so that the colours, as she worked them, held their value, ever so briefly, ever so precariously, and allowed her to see what she was making: a vista of dropping emerald meadow at midsummer in broad day.

Of course the light from her city skylight was nothing like the gradual passage of limpid sun at the cottage in June. But it didn't need to be. The meadow was a memory, a vision lodged in her mind long since. Gwen worked from what was in her mind. Catching what she could excited her for the hour or so that she tried. And she relished the time pressure because it reminded her of the transience of the scene at the moment that she had beheld it, of the urgency *then* of seeing it.

It wasn't a picture of a summer day anyway. It was an experience of moisture – clumps of grass that harassed her ankles or were dazzled by the wind as separated blades, trees caressed by mild English clouds along a tamed horizon, a festival of birdsong. In full summer, the English countryside always looked to Gwen pleasant, accommodating, long in use. Like a well-pillowed drawing room in nature, it was inviting, cultivated, but without any roof. She meant the picture to convey this, and yet while she painted, her mind dipped from time to time into something wilder and more crude that she half remembered from the brilliance and unbearable energies of her childhood in America. And when her mind dipped, deep, backwards, she would think, England is not like *that*, England is like *this*, making an implicit comparison; it was as if the scene she was painting held down some other scene and covered it.

On the pair of canvases by the back window, Gwen was doing something else, equally temperate, more mysterious: a pond in the woods, cloaked in mist, at dawn. And beside it, the same pond later in the day as the mist burned off so that the pond shone among the close-growing trees like phosphorescence. She liked to work on the first of these canvases very early in the morning, when the light from the window still reached long and low into its dank grey-green washes.

She would fetch the big wooden palette which she left tilted against the wall overnight to keep dust from clinging to the wet paint, and she would prod the little turds of colour with a small brush, with a knife, and with another, bigger, once white-haired brush, feeling how the colours had ever so slightly begun to seal themselves over in their sleep, like chrysalises around caterpillars. They would spread their wings, flatten out on to the palette as she waked them. She would snatch a brush into her mouth, clamp it there with wiry lips, tasting the white spirits she had cleaned it with, select another brush and another, until several bristled from her left fist as she narrowed her eyes again at where she had left off. She had hundreds of brushes in the studio, almost as many knives, stuffed upright into jars, flowerpots, pitchers, tin cans, all sizes, all shapes, each brush looking bleached and waterlogged as if it had rolled around the bottom of the sea, been abraded by sand, by surf, drifted ashore in harsh sun.

The sable hairs of her smallest brush would nip and sway at the soft mounds of Davy's grey, Payne's grey, burnt umber, terre verte, cadmium green, indigo, yellow ochre, probing the caches of colour. She would poke at the palette as if at a baby's meal, mix and blend the tiny portions in dabs, deliver them with the delicate fingertips and the anxious poise of a mother's hand towards an upturned mouth, then wait to see the effect before she offered more. On a clear day, the shafts of light reached closer and closer to the canvas as the morning wore on, and until Gwen herself moved on to the second canvas, where the mist was rising to reveal glimpses of brown and even purple reflected in the surface of the pond and ballasting the trees, bright yellow at their tops where the mist thinned to mere wisps, lifted in threads. The pond itself looked eerily on the move, as if through time, as if emerging from the past.

While she worked on these bucolic scenes, Gwen was mesmerised by their completeness, and she would think only from time to time of Will or of Lawrence – an instantaneous drift of face before her mind's eye, amounting to a serene recognition: They, too, exist, separately, safely. But lately, more and more continually, she thought of Hilary. Hilary didn't seem to be a discrete, settled fact; she not only existed but also suffered. Hilary was in turmoil, in trajectory, in a state of need. She was not constant; she was changing. Gwen saw Hilary clearly – wrinkles of fretfulness striking harsh verticals through the thick, pale flesh at the top of Hilary's long nose, between her forthright blue eyes.

One lunchtime not long after the dinner party, Gwen put down her brushes, flexed her shoulders, filled the kettle with water for coffee. The light was already hardening into the yellow-grey scowl of a smoggy London afternoon. She stared into the stained enamel sink, iridescent with wear like an old tooth, blue-black around the paint-clogged drain. She would fight it, she resolved, the premature onset of twilight. Will had piano after school and Hilary had offered to pick him up. Still time for the meadow. And what else?

She leaned back against the chipped edge of the Formica counter, the kettle roaring and spitting behind her. Around the sides of the room stood canvas upon canvas, a few with their pale wood stretchers and blank backs showing titles scrawled in black across them, others facing forward, one or two in trial frames, offering glimpses of a season, a time of day, a mood of nature. Her sketchbooks, warped and fattened with changes of atmosphere – raindrops, sun, the baking edge of the Aga at the cottage – lay here and there on the spattered workbench, the fridge, the disused cooker; one or two were propped open like tents so she could glance at them as they stood up with their wire bindings across the top. They served to remind her of what she had wanted to capture about a particular time in a particular place, like a diary of her intentions towards the paint.

A rickety panelled screen zigzagged halfway along the bed. On the floor one of Hilary's big black suitcases lay open, her linen skirt limp over one edge, her Lycra running leggings over another. Abandoned like that, the clothes seemed to Gwen poignant, vulnerable. They had pressed so near Hilary's skin that they might have been part of Hilary herself, her chosen outline, not her assigned one. But she isn't fully conscious of making an outline, Gwen thought. Not of how she looks or chooses to make herself look. And here they lay, her garments, with white flecks of Hilary's sloughed-off skin invisibly clinging to them, her odour and her sweat swelling each thread of the fabric ever so slightly, making it more airy, lighter than if the clothes had been newly laundered, dried, pressed. From all the way across the room, Gwen could see how intimately the fabric portrayed Hilary's person. Hilary who was always so unconcerned about such things. If her knickers, her bra, had lain on top of the pile of her clothes, even in a locker room, a public changing booth, she wouldn't have noticed, wouldn't have paused to fold them inside and conceal them, wouldn't even have turned them right side out if they were wrong side out. Was this really a woman? How like a boy, thought Gwen, a young boy. She noticed that among the pungent smells of the studio – white spirits, oil paint, linseed, sawdust – she couldn't, in fact, smell Hilary.

Next to the suitcase, Hilary's black nylon briefcase leaned against the bed, the pockets all unzipped, a laptop half in, half out. Plastic sleeves holding typed sheets and photographs spilled from one side. Doro's collection, Gwen thought, crossing the room, bending down to flip through the files, slithery in her hands.

Amphorae, kraters, statues, friezes, the likes of which she herself had once pored over with painful concentration. It gave her a start, their familiarity and their strangeness. How we both loved all this, she thought. Hilary still does; this is where she really lives, where she is at home. Is this something she should have to sacrifice? Slow-footed processionals and naked ceremonials, wars and games and crafts, kissing, killing, dancing, marrying, offering, giving thanks. There were human figures, animals, ritual fires, wreaths, gods, heroes, centaurs, satyrs, once known by name to Gwen, all poised in their long-ago occupations and obligations. Ideal bodies idealised – orderly, savage, in draperies, in helmets, in wings, in chariots, their white-ringed eyes sightless. The statues stood free and trance-like in their three dimensions, inky bronze, white marble, battered grey stone; the painted figures were silhouetted against red backgrounds, like the earth they came and went from, or, on the later vases, against black backgrounds, like the eternity of night into which, as they told, time carries everything.

Try something like this under electric light, thought Gwen. It can't change, so the light won't matter. It's not as if I ever experienced any of it as a natural world to begin with.

She decided on a tall, slender, two-handled black vase with

red-gold figures, and she laid the sleeve with its typed notes on the counter while she measured coffee grounds into her little cafetière, poured in the boiling water, stirred it. Then, leaving the coffee to draw on the ridged steel draining board next to the sink, she slipped the photograph from the sleeve to see the figures on the vase more closely: a wedding procession, mostly women, their hair bound with leaves, with linen, their golden earrings dangling, their gowns crisply pleated, their maidenly eyes downcast, their noses and their backs long and straight as they trod, following a man and leading a bullock, towards the longed-for state of marriage. How chaste a scene, Gwen thought, remote, inviolable.

One woman, the most maidenly, the most downcast, was carrying a vase exactly like this vase on which she was portrayed.

'Loutrophoros,' Gwen muttered to herself.

For there was the name of the vase shape typed across the top of Hilary's notes. Carrier of washing water. A vase as awkwardly tall and thin as a leggy girl – easy to sweep off its foot, narrow-necked, but with a wide, inviting mouth which was shaped almost flat like a plate to catch and funnel precious liquid so that none might be spilled. Did they mean it to seem like the way into a womb? Gwen wondered. This was the vase in which they kept the sacred water to purify you for marriage, or for your funeral if you died without marrying. Undamaged, like the virginal belly it suggested. Maybe it had been unearthed from a grave, buried with a maiden still unmarried at her death, and that's why we have it whole.

So what does that tell us about marriage for them? Gwen wondered. Right up there with death? They stayed at home with their children, they kept house, cooked and sewed. Submissive, hemmed in. Didn't get out much to chat to Alcibiades over a kylix of wine and water, or to throw javelins at the Olympic Games. What choices did they have? Gwen wondered. She simply couldn't imagine having no choices. They must have had ideas, sensations, plans. What did *they* sacrifice? They left nothing behind in words. On the other hand, neither did Socrates. We have only what the others recorded. And he was the Master of them all.

She put the photograph back into its sleeve, poured out coffee, thinking of Hilary, wondering whether this part of Doro's collection was to be kept or sold, wondering how much Hilary minded. I might catch something before it's dispersed, preserve it. Hilary might like that. She remembered eighteenth-century engravings by Piranesi. Earlier ones by Dürer, Goltzius. And hand-coloured things in books. The self-styled Baron d'Hancarville's illustrations of William Hamilton's collection of antiquities. Tischbein's. There was John Flaxman, the sculptor. Fascinated by Herculaneum, Pompeii, she thought. Lots of people were. Or much later, Beazley, the Balliol scholar, sketching vase after vase, making tracings, developing his method.

She merely fussed over the meadow, distracted by Hilary's face, by the vase, and by the little offering she had in mind to make from it. It wasn't long before she leaned her palette up against the wall, stuck her brushes in a jar of spirits in the sink, and began to sort through the bottom drawer of the mammoth brown chest that stood against the radiator.

She found a newish sketchbook; it was a good size, eleven by fourteen, with porous paper. She struggled with the drawer for a while, kneeling, lifting, pushing against its swollen groans. The weight was all on one side – clinking hammers, small saws, chisels, tacks. Needs rearranging, she thought, abandoned it gaping, and laid the sketch pad down flat on the workbench. Her hinged green tin box of watercolours was on top of the chest. She sharpened a pencil and stood over the photograph, calculating proportions. Then she sketched the geometry of the vase with swift strokes, thinking, To copy on to the shape of the vase a scene which contains the shape of the vase is called *mise en abyme*. First the potter, then the vase painter, now me. She felt the giddying pull of it, the palimpsest reaching right back through time, as if it were something she could dive into. I can lose myself in this, she thought.

She pulled up a tall stool and sat against the edge of it. As she outlined their forms and their faces, Gwen no longer wondered at all about the women on the vase. It didn't seem to her as if the women had ever been real. She could remember that when she had been a student, her professors liked to discuss what could be found out about life in, say, fifth century BC Athens, by looking at what was depicted on a vase. Social history on the side of a ceramic object. She didn't believe such a scene could be real. It came from inside someone's head. The very place where people part ways with so-called reality.

What she believed was that the clay was real and that whoever had made the clay into a vase was real and that whoever had painted the decoration on the vase was also real. Otherwise it was more like decoration on an Easter egg: it was what the maker had thought of on the day – a pattern, a momentary conclusion, at best a recollection. This might look nice, the painter had thought. Pleasing his eye, pleasing his patron, pleasing his master if he was a slave. But whenever Gwen had tried to discuss this with her professors they had always explained in a remedial tone, Ah, but the Greeks weren't like that. They weren't interested in self-expression. They were craftsmen. And she had always wanted to insist, No, that's not what I mean. I'm not talking about self-expression. It's just a practical fact about making something. It's how it happens, if you concentrate at all. You have to abandon what you *really* see and where you really are, to make a thing at all. But in those days, however rebellious she had felt, she had kept her eyes downcast, waiting for something. Because I was only a student, she mused. I wasn't sure of myself.

She was the painter now, making of the scene what she wanted to make. Something beautiful, she thought, evocative, balanced. Her brush stroked the figures, swept waves of Naples yellow, Venetian red, burnt sienna on to the rough, thirsty paper, which plumped with the moisture, its surface rising in welts. Her littlest finger, just touching the page, steadied her hand, delicately steered the image, gliding. Around them all, a black she mixed from ultramarine blue, raw umber and bright red. This chain of women, one man among them, the groom, and their expressions, their attitudes, belonged to her now; *she* was making them. And she was making them for Hilary because Hilary was still walking towards her partner.

Between Lawrence and Gwen's flat, which was on the ground and lower-ground floor of the house, and Gwen's studio which took up the whole top floor, there was another small flat, which was occupied by a young music student, Hugo Brackett. It was Hugo who gave Will piano lessons once a week.

The lessons had been initiated by a letter, cautiously slipped underneath Hugo's locked, expressionless front door.

Dear Mr Brackett, Gwen had written, with Lawrence standing over her advising what an Englishman expects. *In writing this, we are setting aside our considerable reluctance to invade your privacy, and we trust that you will not take it amiss. The hope that a truly gifted pianist might give our young son some encouragement seems worth the risk, especially as you are not only on our doorstep, but inside our house. Indeed, when you play, you are inside our very ears, and this gives us such great pleasure that we are moved to ask whether you do any teaching and whether, if you do, you might have room in your timetable for a five-year-old . . .*

To this well-calculated sycophancy, Mr Brackett had duly replied in writing, setting out his hourly terms, his expectations. He dropped his typed note through their mail slot during the night when they were asleep.

I do not, in fact, teach, and certainly not children. But I am prepared to give it a try provided you can see to it that he practises every day. There is very little point otherwise . . .

His tone was abrupt, beaky, an impersonation of a much older, much fussier musician, and reflected a certain ambivalence. As befitted a twenty-three-year-old student, Mr Brackett wished to avoid being appropriated by his older, richer, married, middle-class neighbours, or at least to ward off any expectation that a connection between himself and them could possibly bring about any significant result. It was as if he needed to be sure they recognised just what a serious thing he was engaged in – the preliminary stages of a career on the concert platform. But on the other hand, even though he seemed to be predicting that the proposed lessons would fail, he was clearly also saying, Yes, I will teach your son. It was later to become clear that he was not speaking in his true voice; but then, neither was Gwen. The lessons had begun solemnly and haltingly, with nervousness and long silences on both sides, at the grand piano crammed into Hugo's small sitting room.

Without even any bargaining, Lawrence and Gwen paid the twenty pounds per half-hour for Will's lessons, because Hugo obviously needed the money. But they reckoned the real reason Hugo had agreed to teach Will was that Hugo was grateful they had never so much as commented, until the phrase of appreciation in their letter, on the hours of practising which Hugo himself did in his flat. Hugo, they thought, must live in fear that they might object at any time. He hardly ever practised early or late. This could only have been the result of careful planning. Most likely, he took full advantage of pianos he had access to at the Royal College of Music. Nevertheless, sometimes without warning, Bartók or Prokofiev, Beethoven or Rachmaninov roared through their lives like a train – passionate, astonishing, and so powerful that it was impossible to continue unaffected in whatever frame of mind they might each have been in. If they were at home, Lawrence and Gwen were taken up by the music, shaken and rearranged. If it was Bach or Chopin or Liszt, the effect might be less shocking but it was no less complete: a mood lifted or lowered, clarified, or unimaginably expanded. And when the music ceased: a sudden melancholy, the ears left alone with silence, an aftertaste of longing.

In their big basement kitchen, in the window alcove where they sometimes watched television and in the laundry room and storage room at the back, Lawrence and Gwen and Will were far enough away not to feel the music, and only dimly to hear it – distant cascades muffled by two levels of floorboards, carpets, furniture, roomfuls of air. But upstairs in Will's little bedroom at the back of the house and in the tiny adjacent study, it was far more of an experience. And Lawrence and Gwen slept directly underneath the piano. Their whole room positively vibrated with the sound when it showered down around their bed.

In Gwen's studio on the top floor, the piano sounded intense and clear, but lighter, floating. Working there, she never felt disturbed by Hugo. On the contrary, the music seemed to move quietly just underneath her conscious thoughts, holding them up, sustaining them, so that when she noticed the music at all, she might have called it inspiring. There was no other word. It seemed to focus her concentration and to make her work progress more quickly. She felt that the notes rising up from below seemed to be heading to the sky, to heaven if there was one, or God.

Will himself practised on an electronic keyboard in his bedroom. Being an only child, he spent a lot of time at it, and before long he was making a success of the piano lessons, to everyone's delight. His ear was acute, and the keyboard sounded increasingly disappointing to him. It could make a lot of sounds that he liked, but none of the sounds was so like a piano as Hugo's piano. What's more, the keyboard lacked more than two octaves. The growling bottom notes and the piping top ones were immensely exciting to Will, who was developing a taste for drama. Almost every week he would put the same question to Hugo: Who uses those notes? And Hugo would usually play him a passage incorporating the lowest notes or the highest ones, understanding perfectly well that behind Will's question lay the real question, You use those notes, can I?

Hugo offered little studies that Will could move around to any octave on the piano, and then one day he suddenly invited Will to practise on his piano whenever Will liked, instead of on the keyboard. So, careful as they all had been to maintain the neighbourly *froideur* that is essential for privacy and the right to complaint, Will was altering the atmosphere in the house. Hugo was investing in him; Hugo wanted his midget protégé to prevail. Nowadays, when Hugo went out, he left his door unlocked, sometimes he even left it ajar, so that Will could play the piano on his own whenever he liked.

Today, when Hilary brought him home from school, Will would probably go down to the kitchen for a snack, then wander up the stairs to Hugo's whenever he was ready. He might play a few scales if Hugo wasn't back yet. Gwen knew she'd hear him starting any time now. Major scales, hands separately, C, G; major scales, hands together, more awkwardly. She could tell when a thumb went under, a three or a four went over. And so it began, just as she had expected, while she squinted at her loutrophoros: the Petzold minuets, the Bach minuet, the little tango, the samba.

But after a while Gwen suddenly stood up straight from where she was leaning over the workbench, her fine brush in mid-air. What had become of the music lesson? She heard nothing at all. She waited a few moments. They must be talking about something. She bent back to her picture, swirling the brush around in the brown water, tapping drops off against the jar, darting at the lid of her colour box, then at the paper, to fill in the last big areas of black.

Soon she'd go down. She pictured Will, seen from the back on the piano bench: small buttocks flattened across the hard seat, skinny arms and elbows emerging from his stiff, grey school-shirt sleeves, hands stirring steadily, almost imperceptibly, over the keys in front of him, his grey-trousered legs, his pilling socks, the thick rubber heels of his boat-sized black school shoes visible underneath the bench where his feet rested on the upside-down red plastic milk crate.

Hugo would be half perched on the wobbly three-legged piano stool beside Will, equally upright, skinny, engrossed, both long hands, long arms resting outstretched on his knees, occasionally reaching in front of Will to show him a fingering, a ritardando. Like this, try this, Hugo would say abruptly, then suddenly grabbing his hands back again, he'd work them into the tufts of his unkempt brown hair as if he needed to hold on to something in order to restrain himself from interfering too much, in order to leave the keys open for Will.

Gwen smiled inwardly at the charm of this picture. The life of her boy taking on this shape of its own, which she could never have predicted – friendship with an adult, growing skill as a musician. She felt almost sick with pleasure and with proprietorship. She couldn't help it. She was amazed by her son, overwhelmed with surprise almost every day.

All of a sudden from the silence below, she heard thundering chords, the start of a Brahms sonata, No. 3 in F minor.

Did I simply miss it? she wondered. The rest of the lesson? Was I not paying attention? Or had Will maybe asked Hugo to play for him?

She snatched up the water jar, the box of paints, took them to the sink where she threw the water hard at the drain, quickly rinsed the lid of the tin box, squeezed and fiddled the bristles of her brush under the running tap. Then she went back to the workbench, examining the vase, wanting to pin it up where Hilary would see it right away when she came in. She touched the gleams of wet, blew a little on a puddle of red, then wafted the paper through the air across the room and laid it flat on Hilary's pillow. Why rush and spoil it? she thought. Hilary will find it there. Let it dry. She hurried for the stairs, flying down and bursting into Hugo's flat, filled with the absurd, choking regret which she so often felt over missing some tiny, beautiful episode in the life of her son.

There on the piano bench were not Will's buttocks, but Hugo's; beside Hugo on the wobbly three-legged stool was Hilary, with her hands spread, just as Hugo's should have been, on her knees, a filmy gypsy skirt hanging long and low around her slippered feet. Across the room, in the relic of a yellow brocade easy chair, was Will, white-faced and still. It was not the scene that Gwen had imagined. Why was Will all the way across the room alone during his own piano lesson? Left out and forgotten? She felt herself quiver with rage.

The music was so loud that nobody heard her come in, and nobody heard her ask, 'What's going on?'

Will's eyes rolled slowly towards her as she fluttered in the doorway; a smile appeared on his face. He was happy to see her; he was tired. He went on listening to the music. Gwen stood still, confused. Then she drifted to Will's chair, sat on the arm of it, where the white cotton wadding was coming out in puffs, and he reached his hand up to her, laid the back of it on her thigh, until she picked the hand up and held it in her own.

When, eventually, the music ended, Hilary gave a slow loud clap; Will joined in. Hugo slumped, head down, as if he were bowing or as if the energy were now drained from him.

Gwen was flummoxed. At last she broke out, 'So – what happened? That was fabulous, Hugo. Sorry, I should have said – But Will's lesson? Wasn't it today?' She felt she was criticising and tried to hide her dissatisfaction.

Hugo turned towards her, and Hilary spun around on her stool. They were all smiling. All but Gwen, who felt the tension in herself striking absurdly at nothing, meeting no disagreement.

'Oh, yes, of course,' said Hugo. 'We just – well, Hilary – your friend – wanted – Oh, gosh, I am sorry, Gwen.' His hands went to his hair, troubled, restraining himself. 'We haven't kept to the timetable at all, and now I guess you'll need to go and have tea or something, won't you? Are there just a few minutes left for Will?'

Faced with this apology, this undisguised admission of organisational chaos, Gwen relented, and at last she, too, began to smile and to be drawn into the circle of their unconcern, their absorption in some other way of keeping time.

'The thing is, Gwen, I won this competition today. Will was chuffed, and so was I – we all were. I was telling them, I'll never play that piece again. I'm empty. I gave it everything. But then they started in on me; they wanted to hear it. And they teased me, and Will said that I had told him –' Hugo swelled his chest, dropped his chin, a child imitating the big voice and the pedagogic finger of his teacher – 'You're never really finished with a piece no matter how well you play it, no matter how far you think you've gone with it. You'll always come back to it and find more in it –'

Will giggled. Now Gwen felt thoroughly embarrassed about her anger, how quick and how misplaced it had been. They didn't hear what I said, she reassured herself, they can't have. But she felt uneasy all the same.

'Awesome playing, Hugo,' Will cried, jumping with sudden vitality from his chair. 'My turn.'

Hilary stood up. 'See you tonight,' she said quietly, touching Hugo on the shoulder, gathering her skirt to swing through the narrow space between his bench and her stool.

Gwen noticed how the skirt clung just below Hilary's waist, snug from the hip bones right to the tops of the thighs where it flared out, so that even with just the few small steps she made around Hugo, Hilary seemed to be dancing, a flashing, flowing thrust of pelvis.

'Eight?' Hugo asked almost inaudibly, tilting his small chin up towards Hilary, confidential.

'Eight.' Hilary spoke in the most ordinary voice, as if the pair of them had known each other for years.

Gwen was astonished. She sat paralysed on the arm of Will's vacated chair and stared at Hilary. Again, the hot quiver shook her chest. Why was Will being excluded? Or why – how dare Hilary – what was going on – between Hilary and Hugo? Had they somehow become friends during the summer, when she and Will had been with Lawrence at the cottage?

'Want a cup of tea, Gwen?' asked Hilary with a sleepy smile.

And Gwen felt shouldered away somehow, in her own house.

'No,' she said. She stood up sharp, hard-edged. 'No, I had coffee not long ago. But I can make you some tea if you want.'

Gwen led the way downstairs, and by the time they got to the kitchen, Hilary, tugged along in the wake of her rapid, turbulent passage, had already begun to sense what she must do.

'I can help Will with his homework, Gwen,' she offered, 'if you've got stuff to take care of. I didn't mean to delay his lesson and screw up the schedule. I was trying to give you a little more time to paint. Or I can fix supper if you want to be with Will?'

Gwen cracked a mug down on to the counter, snapped the tea bag from its packet, shrugged vaguely with her back to her friend. 'It'll be fine,' she announced.

'Come on, Gwen,' Hilary pleaded, standing very near her. 'Let me help.'

Gwen turned around on her suddenly, so that Hilary, without thinking why, backed away and took a seat, as if in response to a command, as if she had been told to sit down, to be quiet.

There was a silence. Hilary stared at the wooden tabletop; Gwen stared at Hilary.

And then Hilary, looking up at Gwen, blinking a little but not faltering, explained, 'I know I said I didn't want to meet anyone. But I ran into Hugo in the house, and I wish I'd gotten to know him better. Anyway, I definitely don't want to meet an imitation

Lawrence. I can see you're happy with him. But I want my own – an original. And I have to choose for myself.'

'He's twenty-three, Hil.'

'I wasn't exactly sure.' Hilary grinned, half embarrassed, half pleased. 'Still, the issue for you is that he's Will's piano teacher. Will's guru. Right?'

Gwen froze for a second, taking it in, then heaved a sigh of capitulation. Because Hilary knew exactly what she was saying. Will's guru. How can I be angry with a friend who sees that? Gwen asked herself. Who puts it so clearly, what I'm fighting for here? I love this woman.

Hilary went on. 'He's cute, Gwen, but it's not as if I'm thinking he's the one. Like you said, he's so young. Tonight's no big deal. We agreed to have a drink rather than talk over Will's head, that's all. We did realise, you know, that that was supposed to be Will's own time. Hugo said he wished he'd made plans to celebrate about this competition today. All his own friends are doing stuff, performing or studying or rehearsing. He's way too poor to take anyone out to dinner, and it's not like I'm rolling in it. It's just a drink.'

Gwen was telling herself that it was a matter of adjustment, getting used to this free, unpredictable energy in her house. 'Do you want to invite him here? To supper?' It made her feel better to offer; it made her feel more in control. 'There's plenty. We could wait and eat a little later, after Will's in bed. I'm not sure whether Lawrence will be back tonight. He didn't say. It'd be nice for me to have the company.'

Hilary seemed to consider it. She was silent, her eyes moving around the room, but there was something lurking in her, some tension or preoccupation; a stubbornness coalesced around her mouth. 'I don't know, Gwen. I don't think so. Let us go out. Just let us go.'

'I feel like a mother with a teenage daughter,' Gwen said.

'Yeah, well –' and Hilary rolled her eyes. 'I'm not a teenager.

Naive as I may seem. At thirty-four years old, I know what I'm doing, Gwen. I'm just making a new friend. That's all.'

'It took us for ever to make friends with Hugo.' Right away Gwen wished she hadn't said it.

'Well, you thought it would be better if you didn't make friends, hey? That's not what you were trying for. So why did you change your mind about that?'

'Because of Will.'

'Good reason. But because of me would not be a good reason. Don't let me start running your life. I'd feel bad if that happened.'

Gwen didn't respond to this. She was wondering, How does Hilary pick? What is it she wants? What does she think she sees in Hugo? Another young boy, like Paul, not gay this time, she thought, but not a partner, not a spouse. More of a playmate. A cub. Someone she might have been with in college, all over again, in her youth. Gwen was reaching towards some kind of judgement, a negative, dismissing one. But out of curiosity, she refrained. She felt herself wanting to know what it would be like – Hilary and Hugo. She wanted to go on thinking about it, letting her mind play on it.

Where would Hilary go with Hugo? she wondered. How close to each other would they sit? What would they talk about? Would they talk about her, about Will? But why should they?

She thought there might be rock music in the background, as the pair of them settled down into each other's faces, each other's snug smiles and bright eyes. And there might be young voices spilling around them, inquisitive, irrelevant, while other faces, other bodies checked one another out. Little shouts of laughter, the magic of the night, its dark proposals.

Hilary broke in on her reverie. 'I won't stay here with you for ever, Gwen. I'm not trying to turn your place into a commune. Don't worry. I'm picking myself up.'

'But I want you to stay. We all want you to stay as long as you possibly can.'

Hilary gazed up at her, a grateful glow spreading in her eyes, accepting it.

And Gwen unexpectedly said, 'The thing is, Hil, I was thinking maybe I'd paint you. If you've got time. A portrait. It might take a while.'

CHAPTER 6

They are so accustomed to showing their hip bones, Lawrence thought, that they mean nothing at all by it.

She reached up with her left hand to flop the long, stiff strands of her glossy young hair on to her bent neck. Her grey pullover was dragged even higher on the curve of her middle so that he saw, above the faded, flat, impossibly low waistband of her blue jeans, the rose-coloured, rick-rack edge of an undergarment which had worked its way clear as if to insist that the body itself would like to do the same, would like to slither free of the clothes. Above this ripe suggestion, her naked waist, fleshy and pale, matt with invisible hairs, stretched for several inches from where the jeans held tight all the slender way up to the prickling lace edge of some other soft, ribbed, off-white undergarment that hung down below her pullover from the fuller regions above. Her right hand clutched the trembly pages of her essay as she read on, restless, twitching between the arms of the little tapestry chair in which she sat.

Plate tectonics, Lawrence mused, deaf to her voice and thinking of the wrinkled surface that crawls and floats in pieces over the girth of the globe. Whose edges periodically knock against each other and rumple up in mortal tremors. The top layer of clothes is hardly significant, virtually unisex. Denim, big heavy boots. It's all about the underwear sliding about beneath the clothes, in and out of view, making us aware of layers, gaps, interstices, of the way the skin itself veils the bones, of the tender interior of the body protected by it all. It's a revelation of such intimacy and such completeness, because it is not complete. Calling attention to hidden places, to smells. Alerting us – he chuckled at this – to a molten core, a smouldering fire. And we can indeed smell it, at least subliminally, he thought.

The girl must feel something, dressed like that, showing the pelvis. She shifted again in her chair, uncrossing and recrossing her frayed bell-bottom calves, exposing the other hip, a pale wedge of bone shining yellow at him in the light, a riveting triangle underneath the new-moon edge of her belly. Nubile: this defines it, he thought. Because it's the pelvis, it's about the womb. Beautiful arms might be covered, beautiful legs, backs, shoulders, breasts might even be covered, but surely this whole generation of young women are offering themselves as mothers, crying out in their style of dress: Look where I will carry your child, in this smooth, unspoiled place.

And he thought, She will manage it, too, this young Fiona. Clever, warm-hearted, a little insecure. She still takes too much care about coming to her point, always a good point, but never before ten or twelve dutiful, wearying pages. So many of the girls are like that, thorough to a fault. They cover the material better than the boys, but they let the burden of it weigh them down. One day, when Fiona is pressed for time, Lawrence thought, when she has a child, a man she cares for, and also her work, she will become reckless; she will forge a straight, undoubting line with no detours through the what-ifs, with no homage to the many scholars who addressed the question before. And in that reckless adult moment, all that she is learning now will serve her; she will have it in her power. I'd like to be there for that, Lawrence thought; that's when what she has to say will be truly interesting. But for now, he could fully believe that Fiona would grow and change; he relished the uneven heat of her teenage grit, her potential.

She stopped reading, put her pages on her lap, sat very still. There was a little silence as she looked up, hoping. The light from the high, white-shuttered casement fell across her face so that she squinted at Lawrence, dazzled.

Her face is nothing as yet, Lawrence thought, plain, plump, without angles, because she is still growing. She is still taking in, like a sponge. But she is tenacious, like all of them, full of strength, which they show among themselves as cynicism. Not in front of me, though; they show me willingness and obedience, in earnest. Once or twice he had seen her in the cloister hand in hand with a bespectacled, ringleted boy. Kieran? Kevin? A chemist, Lawrence thought, grime on his jeans, grease in his yellow hair and on his raw, yellow-and-red blotched face. They are now another species to my own, Lawrence thought, the young. Part of them is hidden from me, even though they are more suspicious and more wary of one another than they are of me. He wished them well, Fiona and Kevin, finding a way into the open together, into what they deserved.

'Why don't you read out that last bit again, Fiona, just that last paragraph or last three sentences anyway, about how we understand Helen.' Lawrence got up and went to the window, unfolding the shutter to block the light so that she could see him. He was listening carefully now to what Fiona had to say.

'In the end, our view of The Trojan Women may indeed ride on how we understand Helen's repeated assertion that the gods, not she, are responsible for the fall of Troy. In his eponymous comedy about her, Euripides' device of the two Helens indeed absolves the real Helen from any blame in the sack of Troy, and the comedy suggests that the long war was not fought over the adultery of one Greek wife. War is made by warriors, not by women, and warriors will always find a reason to fight.'

'You've done a brilliant job, Fiona. I'm filled with awe. I don't know how you absorb so much nor write so much in a week. Clearly you are unafraid to lavish your grant money on printer paper. Once again, I can only urge you to take a step back. Now you've got to grips with all this, go have a bit of fun. Then perhaps take a long walk and mull things over away from the books. You have a fine mind; you needn't be so – respectful. Imagine you had been there, when The Trojan Women was performed; imagine you knew through gossip how the Melians had been scourged. *Were* these political acts, these plays?'

And she answered with nervous defiance, her voice strident. 'But it's not the same, Helen and the Melians, is it? With Helen of Troy, you have this intensely personal – thing – an abduction or a rape or an elopement – whatever it was.'

She ran her palms gracelessly along the thighs of her jeans as if her hands were sweaty, looking down at her feet, at the carpet. 'It's good, Euripides wanting the Athenians to think about what the state was doing – carrying on war after war – the barbarism it caused in their own people, the risk to political stability. When he has the Greeks throw the baby Astyanax from the battlements and they carry in the little body on Hector's shield – that must have really revolted some people in the audience. Even more than what happens to the Trojan women, enslaving them and sacrificing Polyxena.'

'But you're not especially impressed by *The Trojan Women*?'

Fiona rolled her eyes, took a quivery breath. 'I know it's put on a lot, Dr Phillips. And, OK, it's clever, how Euripides has Helen done down by Hecabe rather than by a man. You take that seriously. But the other play, *Helen*, is so far-fetched. Personally? I ended up hating Helen just as much as Hecabe hates her, for all the suffering she caused. I have trouble with the idea that she wasn't responsible for her own actions – even if she was chattel, or whatever. *The Bacchae* was better. And *Medea*. Those are the ones where you think about the play; with *The Trojan Women*, you think about all the historical context you need to know in order to read it right.' She gave a squawking laugh, a whinny of embarrassed excitement. 'I'm shockingly lazy, aren't I?'

Lawrence smiled, put his thumbs in the air. 'That's the spirit, Fiona. Lazy is one thing you are not. Of course, the historical context – we must find out all we can about that. Facts are awkward, intractable things. A vivid fiction may hold together far better than a raggedy hotchpotch of facts, even though the fiction may be altogether wrong. And it can be tough to clear a fiction out of one's head. You need to keep straight about facts, right from the start. Don't forget, either, that the Greeks may have believed far more in their gods than we can sympathise with in our secular age. Still, I'm glad to see you enter the fray and have a go at your elders. In the exam, you will have only a little time to demonstrate how much you know, and also how well you can think – how uniquely, how vigorously. You want to sparkle as we both know you can.'

She blushed crimson, struggling up from her chair with her legs pressed tightly together, the exposed flat of her chest mottled with pleasure and confusion. Her bosom heaved as she bent to gather her papers, held them out to him, lifted the long webbed strap of her green khaki military bag over her shoulder, grabbed up her flimsy, brass-buttoned, canvas jacket.

God, they are made of flesh, Lawrence thought, glancing at the pristine typescript. Only give them time to master themselves, to find their toughness. He thought of Hilary, claiming to have no opinion about the collection she hoped to curate, shyly asking to borrow books so she could understand what he was writing about.

Fiona was hardly out the door when the phone rang on his desk.

'Come out for lunch.'

'Clare –' was all he said.

'You've finished teaching?'

'Only just. Of course you know that, since I've picked up the phone.'

'I thought I'd catch you.'

'I was going to have something quickly in the senior common room. You could join me there?'

'Let's eat at Brown's.'

Lawrence glanced at his watch. Not because he didn't know what time it was, nor even because he was making a calculation of what time it would be when he returned from Brown's. But because he needed to pretend that he was somehow in control of what was going to happen now, of what was being decided. The next little bit of time was, in theory, his own. How would he himself like to spend it? Nearly two hours during which he could bolt down something light, something that wouldn't make him feel sleepy afterwards, and in which he could then try, however briefly, to focus his mind on his own work, on writing another paragraph, maybe even another whole page. How had it come about that he was reduced to such fine calculations? Where had the acres of life fled to?

'Don't be a bore,' Clare said archly.

He wanted to make a joke: was it boring that he wasn't answering for all these long seconds? Or boring that he didn't want to go out to lunch? Where did it come from, anyway, this current attitude that life should be one long continual party? One loud, eternal group conjugation? I like to be alone and work, thought Lawrence, because my work isn't boring. It's completely engrossing, when – if – I ever get down to it. What does Clare mean, a bore? She means, Don't do something that can't include Clare, don't be a clique of one, happy all by myself. Because that throws poor Clare back on herself, on the fact that just now perhaps *she* is a bore. A bore to herself, and in that case, almost certainly a bore to me.

It made him feel tired and reluctant, the thought of entertaining Clare. Could he summon the energy to walk all the way along the Broad, then dish out some kind of conversation while they sat over menus, waited among hungry, clattering tables to be served? Wasn't it raining outside? Wouldn't it be crowded? Lunch in college was already made, the big silver buffet dishes steaming with savoury beef stew, chicken curry, potatoes, noodles, rice. They could help themselves; it was free.

'I've got some things here I really ought to get to grips with,' he said apologetically. 'Shall we fix it for tomorrow?'

'Supper, tonight?'

'No more suppers, Clare. We've agreed on that.'

She steamrolled him. 'I'll stop by for you,' she announced. 'I can't manage it tomorrow, and I'm longing for a chat. We hardly see each other lately.'

'Right,' said Lawrence and hung up the phone. What was the point of even resenting it? He had first slid into Clare's hands through his own wayward inclination; he'd been trying and failing to get out ever since.

Restlessly, he scanned the page he'd written yesterday. There was a dense notation towards the bottom, hinting at where Lawrence had meant to go next; he had wanted to immerse himself in the insights slowly, to expand the notation in the many directions implied, to trace each delicate, elaborate connection in its fullness. Lawrence had wanted, in short, to think. But without enough time, now, he would have to hold tight to the kernel, the germ of it, and he had to hope the germ wouldn't wither and die before he could come back and nurture it.

Thought is a gossamer bridge, he mused, a tightrope. If we pass along it, we can surmount the greatest obstacles and solve the subtlest puzzles. We can cross an abyss, we can defy risk, because the possibility of a solution, a resolution, always lies before us. In thought, we can consider even what lies beyond death, toss our minds right to the other side. But interruption – falling off the thought, falling off the tightrope – well, it's a little death, isn't it? Every time.

It seemed to Lawrence that there were more interruptions nowadays than there had ever used to be. It seemed to him that it was harder than ever to have a thought. A complex, well-developed thought. Clare would burst in any second. What had yesterday's idea been? The candelabrum. Would he wear out the idea by going back to the beginning and starting fresh with it all over again tomorrow? Would the idea endlessly be there when he was free to pursue it? Would he follow the same process of thought? Or would he, perhaps unknowingly, follow a different one?

He studied his note, hunting out the germ. What had it been? Then he scanned the page again, running a finger along under the lines.

We feel surprised – yes, yes, he nodded to himself – *that Trimalchio shows no anxiety about displaying the candelabrum, despite the blemish it makes on his social status in linking him materially to his former position as a slave. The passage evokes a milieu accustomed to extreme social mobility. And it appeals to our modern notion of freedom, too, that Trimalchio shows himself to be free in another sense – free of shame about what he once was.*

Lawrence took his fingertip away, picked up a pen, his eye moving on.

Indeed, Trimalchio relished measuring himself against the candelabrum as he grew –

What word conveys that? Relish? Lawrence asked himself. Where in the text do I find that exact sense? He reached towards the back of the desk for his copy of the Latin, still looking at his own script.

The candelabrum thereby symbolises not necessarily, or not only, his lowly origin, but also the height he has since achieved.

Lawrence paused. Had Petronius intended to convey that meaning? Was he indirectly referring to Nero's own vulgarity? Does it matter what Petronius intended? Lawrence sat back in his chair, wondering about symbolism after all. What do we mean when we say, It symbolises . . . ?

He pressed his knuckles into the flesh of his cheek, the pen still loosely gripped in his hand. It was more than that, Lawrence thought, rolling the pen about between his fingers, then snapping upright in his chair again, tapping the tip of the pen against the page. There was Trimalchio's flesh being enslaved, the regular sexual use he endured by his master and his mistress. How he didn't much seem to mind this. How, on the contrary, it had built up in him something like an affinity, a familiarity – comfort – rather than the revulsion we might imagine. How his master made a pet of him, made Trimalchio his heir, secured his fortune. On the basis of this intimate physical relationship. Was this simply another aspect of Petronius' realism? Telling the reader, Here was a man, the sort of man, content to service others sexually when commanded. Dead to any finer concerns. Without personal delicacy.

This is not just some personal psychological hunch I am projecting on to the text, Lawrence thought with annoyance, as if Roland were perched somewhere inside the back of his head, disagreeing even as he tried to write. Yesterday I had that article about it. There was the real slave, the hunchback. Of no value to anyone. It's all in – Pliny. And anyone can go and read the hunchback's name today, in the wall along the Via Appia.

What if I'm right? Lawrence wondered. I might be right. He heard Roland saying, Are you forgetting that Trimalchio is not a real person? And he thought, But neither is Jean Valjean. Yet they come to life in the mind.

But now the words hardly made sense, his own handwriting, the scrunched note, were barely legible. Could he have lost it so quickly, in just a day? Leave it alone, he told himself. It's only because there isn't the time to review the facts and to develop it further that my mind is shutting down on me. He abandoned his paragraph because he thought it would be better not to be interrupted all over again in the middle of it.

E-mail, he thought, better check that quickly.

The computer screen perched on the pile of books at the back of his desk winked brightly and offered him another world altogether, a list of concerns so miscellaneous that it drove out all thought of his work and transformed him into a dozen other selves, all at once. A self who played chess with a man in Prague, a self who was pressing the College Librarian to expand the ancient reference section since the university and faculty libraries were now eliminating all duplications, a self who was assisting the Domestic Bursar in the search for a new chef, a self who permitted late undergraduate essays to be handed in as attachments, a self who had ordered a book so unpopular with other readers that it seemed it might never arrive at all from Amazon, a self who was arranging to go abroad skiing at Christmas, a self who had once dashed off countless flirtatious messages to Clare, a self who didn't really want to know the content of most of his e-mails, but who half consciously expected that one of them would bring extraordinarily good news, a vast quantity of money, a life-changing message.

E-mail has such a fragmenting effect on the mind, Lawrence thought. It introduces this, that – all possible, all real, all at once. Makes a kaleidoscope out of life – shifting, shattering, electrified, claiming to be urgent. He felt them tugging at him, all the little pleas and queries lighting up the screen, and he felt remorse.

That's how I forgot about Paul Mercy, he thought. I passed on Roland's recommendations without thinking. Pressed Send or Forward, like a corporate criminal. In e-mail life, we don't feel cause and effect, responsibility. The evolution of consciousness isn't up to that speed yet. Hers came as a request from a disembodied mind, not really Hilary, not the flesh-and-blood woman living at my house now. And it went back, through the e-ther, as if nothing real could come of it. He winced at the disservice he seemed to have done her, in a rush; he couldn't even remember when. Could it have been different if I had been paying closer attention? he wondered. Would I have known any more or conveyed any more about Paul Mercy in a phone call, a letter, in person?

Then, just as he clicked on the self who lately liked to swap thoughts on Petronius with a colleague in Providence, Rhode Island, there was a knock on his door, and the phone rang at the same time. It made his heart pump with a sensation of fear. But what was he afraid of?

'Come in!' he shouted brusquely, then picked up the phone. 'Hello?'

'Do you think that young woman would like me to try to cheer her up a bit about Paul Mercy?'

It was Roland. 'You mean Hilary Boyd?'

'Exactly.'

'How kind of you, Roland. I've no idea. Oughtn't you to ask her? Why not ring the flat? You do know she's staying with us? I'm not sure – I mean, what more would there be to say? I reckon she'd want to forget all about him. No?' He knew he was saying the wrong thing; Gwen would urge him to cultivate any excuse for further conversation between Roland and Hilary. How could he be so discouraging?

He dragged his eyes to the door, apologetic, gesturing with his free hand up and down in the air to indicate that he was helpless, in the grip of someone else's blah-blah-blah.

There stood Clare, tightly belted into a thin grey raincoat, arms crossed, the toe of one black pump tapping his worn wooden floor. She had her blonde head bowed, the dark parting splaying in spokes through it, and her eyes down to emphasise that she was not pressuring him with the fact of her arrival.

'The truth is, I've just had a long talk with Paul,' Roland said.

Roland's tone was rather stiff, Lawrence thought, as if he felt defensive about taking any interest in Hilary at all.

'And?' Lawrence felt the increasing strain of Clare not looking at him, not expressing her impatience.

'I like an excuse to keep in touch with him – and, to be honest, I've rather told him off. Playing on people's affections! I think he feels quite badly about the way things have gone for Gwen's friend, not to speak of the rather precarious future, now, of this obviously important collection. He wanted *all* the details.'

'Details?' Lawrence's heart pumped again. 'It's maybe a bit personal, don't you –'

But Roland cut him off, self-righteous. 'Naturally, I thought it best to be forthcoming. Once something's spoken of aloud, it's up for grabs – don't you agree?'

'Spoken of aloud?' Lawrence pushed back his chair and stood

up. 'I'd better ring you back, Roland. There's someone here and I –'

'I thought Gwen would like me to do something, you know,' Roland urged. 'I feel rather responsible. Will's godmother, such a good friend of hers –'

'Of course. We all feel responsible,' said Lawrence. And then, thinking of the outcome Gwen wanted, certain it would never happen, 'Why don't you arrange to have a chat with Hilary, and see what sort of help she really needs? You could ring her, talk on the phone and meet for a drink?'

There was a pause. Then Roland said, 'I had better chat to Gwen first, don't you think?'

Lawrence came over all smiles. This made sense to him. 'Of course you'd better. Gwen's far more likely to answer the phone at home anyhow, isn't she?' He felt entirely generous towards Roland. It was all rather charming, Roland's fascination with Gwen and his exaggerated awkwardness towards Hilary. Hilary was really far easier to talk to, and Roland had far more in common with Hilary, but that didn't seem to figure at all. He seemed hardly able to say Hilary's name out loud.

Lawrence hung up with a bloom in his cheeks. 'Sorry, Clare.'

Clare evidently thought that the bloom was for her. She crossed the room with a hip-dropping, high-heeled walk and stood right in front of him, very close, so that Lawrence had to lean back a little to see her face. He was determined not to move his feet, not to give ground. It was hard keeping his balance as he arched his shoulders backwards, peered at her thin, small nose, her blue-white forehead and cheeks, her big, misleadingly lazy-looking blue eyes, and as he wobbled there, she reached her arms out as if to steady him, which he rather appreciated as a companionable gesture. But then, while she had him in her hold, she reached up solemnly and planted a kiss on his mouth.

Lawrence accepted it, but he didn't respond. He felt he had to allow Clare to kiss him if she wanted to. Making a fuss would only increase her engagement. He was resigned. But he was not without a sense of comedy. 'I have to go to the loo,' he announced.

She reacted irritably. 'Couldn't you have done that before?'

He was ready for her. 'I was on the phone, you see. Awfully sorry.'

Clare looked at the phone, looked at the computer screen, took a step closer to the desk to read what was displayed there. But the screen went black, powersaving, and she looked up quickly at Lawrence, as if protesting lack of interest.

He reached into the tiny bedroom where his jacket lay across the dusty rows of books stacked spine up on the bare, narrow mattress, then reappeared, shouldering it on.

'I'll meet you at the porter's lodge?' he said. And he was gone.

Striding along the gravel by himself, Lawrence tried to recapture the sense of enthusiasm he had once felt for Clare. Down the basement steps into the darkness, fumbling for the light, he could remember it had once seemed inviting to be alone with her. More than inviting, a personal fleshly emergency. Her dense, womanly whiteness, unmuscled limbs forbiddingly garbed in tight skirts and stockings, rustling underwear, girdles, the complete costume of professional maturity.

It can't have been her, he thought, since now I know her I really don't like her much at all. It was something else I was attracted to. Something abstractly male/female making a mirage between us. With the right woman, he thought, the thing you want is part of her, inside her. But with all the others, it's something else you want, not the woman herself. Libido tricks us into imagining we might travel the whole trajectory of love through a new person and still arrive at the one we've already chosen, the one who is waiting at home minding the pram. With Clare, it was perhaps still Gwen I wanted. Gwen at some other, fresher moment, before I'd already had her. Or in some other format. But Clare is so unlike Gwen, so entirely unlike her.

As he peed, a rattling, urgent stream, he thought, If you fall for that, you get stuck with the wrong woman as well as the right one. A woman too many. I ought to have known better, Lawrence thought. Especially as I was perfectly happy. Perhaps in the trough of a wave, a bit ignored by my wife. She doesn't ignore me now, since Will started school. It was a phase she went through, child-bearing, loneliness, sorrow. Lately she has sprung back to life, vital, warm, continuously interesting. Continuously.

He had a sour sensation just behind his front teeth, where his tongue touched them, bathed in a light film of saliva; a tremor of repugnance lifted his upper lip. Because he suddenly remembered Clare's dry, deliberate way with sex. So much talking, so many clenched instructions, when he had expected liquid abandon. She had it somehow organised and planned. A strategic assault on joy. A list of things to cover. Conceived as bullet points, he ruefully imagined, maybe even a chart or a diagram. Certainly taken partly from books and nothing wrong with that; I've learned a great deal from books. But I've learned more by imagining or – just by impulse.

Did she have any impulses? Any longings? Proves I never cared for her, that I didn't take trouble to release her from her trap – to uncover her. Whatever, whoever she might really be under the clipboard. I was far too surprised, far too disappointed. Perhaps afraid there would be nothing there in any case, nothing to release. I used to be happy with most girls, any pretty one, any young one. Changed by Gwen. Didn't even realise it. Recalibrated somehow.

The thing about Clare is the sensation now of a dead end. He reached up and pulled the chain, made a last trembling spurt into the churning water, shook himself, zipped his flies. She didn't seem to feel it. She went on pursuing and trying to make something of nothing. It made her seem like a vampire. A harpie. Worse than that. It revealed in her some need that had been entirely hidden from him until it was too late. She had pretended to be someone in control of her own life, he reflected, a liberated woman, not interested in a dependent role, emotional or otherwise. It hadn't been like trying it on with a student, knowing how vulnerable a student is. Clare ought to have been able to handle it. Then she started to suck on me, on my life. Nothing ever grew between us. More than a year, two, since anything occurred which might be construed as passion? With Gwen, I've been making a family for a long time now – rich, tangled, thickening between us. I feel it even when I'm away from home. Something, Lawrence thought, that I couldn't always do in the past. At least, something that I didn't always bother to do.

He felt a twinge of guilt towards Gwen as he climbed up again from the basement and set out across the quad for the lodge. She must have known. And she must have known that it wasn't important, too. If she didn't know, it's because she didn't want to. He pictured her face, its brown, animal mobility, her hooded, unreadable eyes, remote, absorbed by work. He chided himself, You've forced this folly on her even if she doesn't know. It's the guilt that makes me Clare's slave for lunch, he thought. It's thinking that as long as I remain at least a little involved with Clare, Clare has reason to be discreet.

Oh God, what rubbish! He was angry with himself for having created such a rat's nest, and he stalked into the lodge with his hands shoved so hard into his jacket pockets that they were practically poking through to the outsides.

Clare was leaning on the counter, thin-lipped.

'Ready now?' she asked with a sweetness that felt sham to Lawrence, honey disguising desperation, rage, about how her whole life must feel to her, a narrow struggle towards some small, immediate, over-particularised goal, then another goal beyond that: him for lunch, and that over with, another lunch tomorrow with some other kind of prospect, a publication, a slot to speak at a conference, a free trip which she could tell about when she got back, a position on an editorial board, a pat on the back that she could wear home and warm herself with. In my case it was all disguised as a love affair; how did I ever feel that as love?

As she took his arm, Lawrence flinched a little, thinking he didn't want to walk through Oxford with a woman clinging to his elbow. Did she really feel so fond of him? Was she now intending to make a trophy of him, in public?

The thing is to tell Gwen myself, Lawrence realised. It's just so obvious. And maybe not so hard. That's the only way to get my freedom back. Our freedom, he resolved. He felt a kind of solidarity with Gwen — that he was bonded to her and liked it. Bring it into the open and make a formal end. Even if it makes Gwen unhappy for a time.

He unclamped Clare's arm gently from his, patted it a little and said by way of a practical explanation as he dropped it to her side, 'The pavements are so busy.'

Clare pouted a little, then lifting one eyebrow, turning her face up to his, asked, 'Who's Hilary Boyd?'

'Oh,' said Lawrence, suddenly thinking he understood Clare's possessiveness and, at the same time, seeing his way out. 'Will's godmother. An old friend of Gwen. She's staying with us in London. Gwen arranged for Roland to meet her, you see. But Hilary's not really Roland's type — if there is such a thing.'

Clare laughed at this. 'So what does she do?'

'She — well, she collects classical antiquities. Or she once did —'

'She needs help with that?' Clare wasn't easily satisfied.

'No. Or — Maybe. Actually, she has it in mind to be a curator. Perhaps. Nice woman. Not your — calibre. You'd eat her alive, my dear.'

'I'd prefer to try that with you,' said Clare.

Lawrence felt exasperated by this sally. 'Clare, honestly. We've agreed to lunch, on a plate, in a restaurant. Do we need all the sauce?'

'You needn't worry,' she said, deflated. 'I won't be vulgar.' She seemed embarrassed, a little hurt, and reached for his arm, putting her own arm through it all over again.

There was nobody near them; Lawrence didn't feel that he could pull his arm away another time. I am the one holding all the cards here, he told himself. This poor woman simply wants to go to lunch, simply wants to be friends.

He pictured Clare all alone, pathetically fighting her way, with no backing – no family, no supporters – along the Byzantine corridors of their institutional life, cut up as it was into hours and departments and colleges, with infighting and cold squalls of rain, wet feet, in between. A life that had no centre, no home, as it might once have done when the dons gathered around the same college dining table every evening.

Certainly there was no dining table in Clare's impressive suite of rooms, which were high-ceilinged, spacious, official. The shelves in her black metal library stacks were set in tall ranges so that every dust-jacketed book could stand bolt upright. There were no paperbacks. Matching black filing cabinets massed weightily behind her enormous leather-topped desk; the surface of the desk was clean. On the bare wooden floor sat a low, white suede sofa in the shape of a rectangular box, with firm, tightly fitting cushions. Pale, conical lampshades on chrome sticks threw brilliant modern light. The air smelled of citrus. And on the bedroom floor lay fluffy white rugs the size of sleeping sheep, clues – though Lawrence thought the clues were unintentional – to some superannuated farming background; the bed was covered in a black-and-white, smooth-haired skin. Pony? On his last visit, some time ago, the bedroom door had been closed.

Was it worth whatever sacrifices she had made? he wondered. Lawrence felt a rush of concern towards Clare, as if she were, for instance, a child alone, orphaned by her ambition, puny compared to the challenges she set herself. She is hateful simply because she tries too hard, he thought, is determined to boast, to swagger, that she needs no pastoral care, no feeding up or looking after. Was it the failure of intimacy between us that finally cinched Clare up so tight? Did I imply to her that I could save her? Suddenly, Lawrence felt that he was, after all, responsible for Clare, whether or not he wanted to be.

And so he let her lean against him all along the centre of the hurrying lunch-hour town, thinking that this little bit of warmth might make all the difference, might enable her to carry on by herself. He made no objection to settling opposite her at a tilt-legged table in the front window, lifted his elbows and his long, thin menu in silent unison with her so the table could be sponged clean of debris left by earlier diners.

'A glass of red?' he asked, instinctively undertaking to drown the boredom, the frustration, the assault on his time.

She gave a sly, familiar smile. 'And the duck salad.'

He chose the pork chop for himself. 'What about sharing an antipasti?'

'I'll share anything with you that you care to share with me,' she said in her barbed, unflagging way.

When the platter of cold meats arrived, she transferred one slice on to a bread dish, folded it into a neat package with her knife and fork, popped it between her lips and swallowed it almost without chewing, like a pill. Lawrence dangled slice after fatty slice on to his tongue with his fingers. They sipped their wine and she gossiped quietly to him about her life, the slow uncelebrated result that teaching brings, this and that prospect she had in mind for the future, how she might balance her commitments with new opportunities. And she solicited his ongoing support for her career as if this were somehow not guaranteed – with, Lawrence noted, a rather appealing humility.

'How do you give so much for so long when there is so little reward?' she asked admiringly. 'I used to imagine I could live continually in the ancient world, but in the end, you have to sell it to everyone else; you have to find a way to bring it all to life.'

'Easy to become discouraged,' Lawrence agreed. 'But the thing is to *believe* in change. It can't be stopped, whatever it is that seems to be pushing us to the side. We can only try to understand it. Maybe we can participate.' He began to cut into his pork chop, then paused and signalled for more wine. 'I'm struggling along with a little piece about *Les Misérables*. Roland keeps telling me it's a waste of time.'

'Aren't you glad I made you see that show?' Clare was glowing at him.

Lawrence sat up, opened his eyes wide and gave his head a little shake.

'Remember what a wonderful time we had, going down to London, the two of us? And you were such a snob about it – a musical.' She tilted her chin towards him, as if she were reaching for something in the neighbourhood of his chest, his heart.

He didn't like it at all – being reminded. The two of them brazenly out for the evening in public places, as if they belonged together. He scanned the restaurant uncomfortably as the episode welled up inside him. Only buried it from my own view, he thought. A trick I played on myself of complete forgetting. Other people saw us, might naturally remember just as Clare remembers. I've withdrawn my feelings, but the evening did in fact take place.

'I feel quite invested in your piece,' Clare went on. 'It's a new direction for you. When are you going to let me read it?'

'Well – I – when I've done more with it,' Lawrence said. He felt a taint on it now, as if it were founded on an error, something deeply uncomfortable. 'It was years ago, wasn't it? That we went?'

'Well, how old is your son?'

'My son?' What business is that of yours, he thought, feeling surprised she knew he had a son at all.

But the time came back to him, the trough of the wave. When he did as he liked, did as he felt he needed to do. When his family seemed to be two other people, himself merely orbiting. And he remembered what it had been like to sit beside Clare in the over-heated theatre, feeling as if they had a wind in their face, as if there were a light shining from the stage on to them. He had felt – inspired. Alert to details, nuances, which might ordinarily have escaped him. It was undeniable that she had played a part in it all. Constellated the energies somehow. Sexual energies.

She did make me relish it, breaking bounds into unfamiliar cir-cumstances. Entertainment aimed at the mob. She said it herself just now, vulgar; she has a natural vulgarity. With her I relished the brash tunes, the melodramatic storyline, the underdog, everyman hero with his cartoon-size gifts of goodness and physical strength. The constant fret and rustle of the crowd in the dark all around us, unwrapping sweets, sucking. Suddenly, he recalled the detail that had eluded him an hour ago looking over his notes. Trimalchio measured his height every day against the candelabrum in the hope that he might have grown tall enough to escape his master's sexual attentions. He rubbed oil from the lamp on his lips because he believed the oil would make his beard come in, make him a man, no longer the *puer delicatus*. The child-cheeked sexual toy. That's why he loved the candelabrum. Because he thought it might free him. For fourteen long years, he lived in hope.

Lawrence smacked at his pork chop, the fat shining on his lips and his chin; the acid of the green apple served with it stinging his teeth and his gums. He felt queasy. What have I done, he thought, that Clare is part of this thing I am trying to write?

As they strolled back through town, he hardly listened to her at all. He nodded, encouraged, promised, as his scattering thoughts drifted up side streets, spun in bicycle spokes, followed buses, as her words were caught by the wind, carried away. He had heard it all before. When she tugged him towards her entryway, he felt surprised; he had never intended to go up to her rooms. Never again. It seemed like a snare she had laid for him; was there any gallant way to say no?

'It's just not how I want to live, Clare, two lives. One is all I can handle. There's quite a lot going on at home.'

She seemed to be just as surprised as he was, as if he had somehow misled her on purpose. With the wine, they both lacked poise. Her face flushed with anger. She raised her voice. 'One life! It's all we get in fact! And you have never really cared whether I'm *happy* with mine!'

They parted abruptly. Lawrence walked on to his rooms, where he fell asleep on the sofa. He forgot about calling Roland.

But Clare remembered. Over the phone, Roland told her in detail the rather intriguing tale about the adorable, arrogant boy, Paul Mercy, whom she used to come across at his sherry parties.

'It's wonderful, Roland, how you keep up with us all. What would we do without you? You make us feel like family, all your old students. I must give Paul a ring myself one of these days.'

'You have his number?'

'Of course I do. Somewhere. But if you have it to hand, maybe I'll take it down?'

CHAPTER 7

At first, Hilary didn't know what to make of the watercolour Gwen had left on her pillow. She picked up the paper, which was stiffened and rippled, and which cracked a little as she handled it, then sat down on the bed with a sigh.

Did Gwen come up and paint this while Hugo and I were at the pub? Hilary wondered. The loutrophoros. Does she mean it to be an admonishment to chastity, or exactly the opposite – a kind of fertility dance, in case I hoped I would get laid tonight? What if that had been on the cards? What if I'd found this in a frenzied moment with Hugo? Pretty weird. My best friend's illustration of my proposed wedding procession. Would have scared any guy away. A reminder that Gwen wants to be the one to pick my husband? That I should purify myself, in readiness?

But it's gorgeous, Hilary thought, dropping the picture on the tufted white cotton bedspread beside her, twisting around to go on looking at it, her head hanging low, her springing hair lower still. She's got the long proportion of the vase exactly, and the figures. So detailed. Strange in watercolours. Light showing through as if it were transparent; the little pencil workings you can see underneath. Except in some places where the paint's on thicker. Romanticised. An aura. Almost like a phantom vase.

Hilary decided to be charmed by the picture. It's just a whimsy connected to me, she told herself. A beautiful object that Gwen knows I wish I didn't have to part with.

She took off her thin ballerina slippers, pushing them loose from the back of each heel with the big toe of her other foot, sighing again with a sense of exhaustion, then lay back among the spill of dusty, mismatched cushions with the picture beside her. I've got to get back to New York and sort out this mess, she thought. Sooner rather than later. I can't hide out here, sharing Gwen's fantasy that she's going to find me a husband. Or that I'll find one for myself. It would only make things worse anyway, since the collection is in New York and the museum will be there. Forget London. Hugo's completely right about that. And right about what it takes to get what you want in life. That deep voice of his, with the edge to it. Makes you know he's for real, like he's been out there, in the street, at work. She couldn't help comparing his voice to Paul's. Not so cultivated, she thought. Is that northern England, that accent Hugo has, of – was it resilience?

She heard him advising her, candid: 'It's just a physical thing, geography. You can't ignore it; you can't pretend you can live your life on some theoretical basis or among idealised possibilities. You have to move through time, through place, in a sequence – one actual thing, then another actual thing.'

You can see how a musician would have to be like that, she thought. But what about that strange energy of reticence and assertion? Telling me rather boldly, as if he *knew* at the tender age of twenty-three, 'You're hoping for too much. For some ultimate, universal solution. There is no choice that will bring you all the things you say you want.' Following that up with apologising: 'Sorry, but you know?'

Saintly guy, she thought, listening to my tale of self-destruction. And all those weeks this summer, passing each other now and again on the front steps or in the hall, a nod of ignoring, as if I owed it to Lawrence and Gwen in their absence to maintain a barrier, like remembering to lock their front door, to keep the perimeter intact. Was I so captivated by Paul that I thought I had more important things to do than meet the neighbours? And Hugo said he looked upon me as temporary. Therefore practically imaginary. Whereas now Gwen and Lawrence are home, it all feels real. I never heard him practising. Not even once. What if I had? Could it have been him instead of Paul?

His life is hanging from a slender thread like mine, she thought. The tiny bit of money from his fellowship, the sublet handed from student to student, the monumental conviction that he is a musician. Even with all that talent and all that commitment, it remains unclear how he will survive. Great that he has the slender thread, a few concerts on his agenda, the little extra time before he's officially done preparing. But it's something to negotiate, she thought. The time at which you leave the portals of education and somehow transform yourself into a full-fledged adult earning money to live on, maybe to have a family on. Amazing that more of us don't sink from view. How does anyone make it across the stream? All those stepping stones in your younger life and then suddenly no more stones, and a raging torrent all around.

I never did it, she thought. I never went out on my own like Hugo.

The next day, on Hilary's pillow, there was another watercolour, a statuette of a young man, a Greek warrior, broad-shouldered, narrow-hipped, full-thighed, and with a slight sway to his back – a long, diffident curve from nape to buttock. His arms hung lank, his big hands loose, long-fingered; his head was slightly bowed, in cold, impenetrable sea-green bronze.

Hilary recognised the little statue, but she raised an eyebrow at it, dived for her briefcase and her photographs. It was different, but how? She laughed out loud. Something like a Renaissance sensuality in the posture. Indolence cloaking the power. Was it there in the original? Or had Gwen introduced it?

Once you see it, Hilary thought, you will always see it. She was hypnotised by the pelvis, the ledges of muscles rising from the loins, framing the genitals. All of the youthful body, its visible ribs and armour of flesh, seemed to constellate around this flaccid

114

instrument, narrow at its dangling, uncircumcised tip like the melting end of a swirl of canned whipped cream. It's the way he's standing, she thought, so that everything curves protectively, self-consciously, around that unaroused display, which is thrust forward ever so slightly by the hips, but without self-assertion, just – permitted.

After looking at this, Hilary thought, it becomes almost scary to think how potent a man in the flesh might be. She considered Hugo. And she shuddered. The beauty gets more concentrated when you brood on it the way a statue makes you brood. Is beauty the right word? she wondered. For something so erotic? Then when you look back again at just – life – you start to notice things the artist might have noticed. Intimate things, she thought, on public exhibit, looked at by all the other people who ever looked at anything. She felt dazed by it, how the vigour of real life was heightened by looking at a picture of a statue, a picture which seemed to be showing her – *telling* her – how to look at the body of a young man – and she saw it now – a young man with hands and forearms like Hugo's.

In this case, the artist was Gwen. Hilary drew breath, startled at the thought of Gwen looking at Hugo in this way. Can a real person withstand all that looking, that focus of attention? she wondered. An ordinary person? Not that Hugo is necessarily ordinary, but even so. And who was Gwen when Gwen was looking at Hugo?

After the statue came more watercolour sketches, a new object illustrated every day, sometimes several. An Etruscan man and wife in a funerary embrace, smiling, uxorious, even in stone, in death; a marble figurine of a woman from the Cycladic period, Cubist in its simplicity, spaghetti arms akimbo, a long thin triangle for a nose, drumstick hips. Gwen painted the Cycladic figurine twice, the second time hotly coloured like a Pucci print, playing up its abstractness.

There was a charcoal brazier, Roman, made from iron, its three legs in the form of cloven-hoofed satyrs, each with up-hooking erection. The white marble head of a Greek goddess, vacant-eyed, separated from its body, from its locality, and worn away to a mere ideal by the damage of the centuries.

One day Gwen left a tiny picture of a coin, a head of Nero done not in watercolour but in charcoal, in rough, unoutlined areas of light and dark, like a rubbing from the coin itself. It seemed as though the actual coin must have been right here in the room, as if Gwen had laid the paper over it to trace the embossed profile. How did she do it? Hilary wondered. And there were many more vases, amphorae, kraters, kylixes, decorated with their tales of antique glory and antique pleasure, warriors, deities, maenads in their sensual distraction.

Hilary hardly remarked on the watercolours to Gwen, because she didn't know what to say. She felt simply amazed, almost as if she had been pressed back against the wall, a watcher, speechless. 'I like the one of the man and his wife,' she observed once; it reminded her of Gwen and Lawrence, an idea she had about them. But what more was there to tell? Gwen had taken possession of each object, one by one, in order to offer them to Hilary in her own version.

Gwen started hanging the sketches on the walls, and so the studio became a little museum. Sometimes at night, when Hilary lay down to sleep among the pictures, she wondered if something was now being fixed in her relationship to them.

All these sketches, gathering around me, pressing their claim. It's like being haunted. Am I still free to decide for myself whether or not I want to curate this collection? Or is Gwen deciding for me?

But Hilary couldn't see which way Gwen might be urging her. Does Gwen intend the watercolours to take the place of the objects I love? Or are they a reminder of what she thinks I ought to try to hold on to? Gradually Hilary became paralysed. It seemed more and more important, what Gwen was trying to tell her, and she couldn't understand what it was.

Nor could she ask. The watercolours stopped her mouth. And this was because there were a few facts about the collection which Hilary had never revealed to Gwen. Altogether Eddie had assembled four thousand pieces. He had chosen twelve hundred for his museum. Among the twenty-eight hundred pieces to be sold, there were sixty pieces which, over recent years, Hilary had tried and failed to persuade Eddie to keep. The more she had worked on the collection after his death, the more Hilary had wanted to keep each of the sixty pieces. The photographs and notes for them happened to be the ones she had packed in the side slot of her briefcase, because she liked to be able to get at them easily, to be able to look through them and to think about them. The rest of the files were in the big black suitcase which matched the suitcase in which she had packed her own clothes and which sat unopened on the floor of Gwen's studio.

From time to time, Hilary had considered that she might petition the board of trustees to allow her to hold back the sixty pieces from the sale and keep them in reserve against future cash needs. But she was uneasy about the plan; it was subversive, a betrayal somehow of Eddie's intentions, and so she had kept it secret. Now, simply because of the way she had packed her files, Gwen was painting and exhibiting all around them the very objects to which Hilary felt personally attached. It seemed like Gwen had somehow gotten inside her head, inside her way of seeing. Sometimes Hilary believed in Gwen as a party to her attachment; at other times she feared that Gwen was trying to expose her possessiveness. In any case, it was becoming disturbingly clear to Hilary that, in the recesses of her mind, she had been clinging to the little hoard as if it belonged to her.

After a few drifting weeks – shopping and cooking for Gwen to give her more time in the studio, rereading *Les Misérables* and the *Satyricon* with some photocopied articles Lawrence offered her, exercising, daydreaming – Hilary agreed to sit for her portrait. She thought it might dissipate Gwen's obsession with painting the little collection, and she felt she owed it to Gwen, to show her gratitude.

She sat in a dilapidated red moroccan leather wing chair from which Gwen swept a pile of hardened rags, paint-covered shirts, old newspapers on to the floor. The high sides, which Hilary leaned against, either one side or the other, made it easy for her to be comfortable, and they worked for two or three hours at a stretch.

Gwen tried bold, jagged outlines in various poses, on paper and then on old canvases painted out in white, painted out in crimson, discarding them from time to time. She pulled the easel a little closer to Hilary with each experiment, starting again. Until finally she said, 'You're disappearing into the chair. It's all a little too mysterious.'

Hilary flinched, strived to hold her pose. 'I feel you getting so close.'

'I want to see you,' Gwen said tenderly.

Cautiously, Hilary sat up a little straighter, her face coming into the light. 'What's happened to your landscapes?' she asked. 'I mean, what's making you want to paint Eddie's stuff? And now my portrait? Why do you want to do my portrait?'

'The challenge. The change,' Gwen said, eyes on the easel, her voice slight. Then her hand dropped, with the brush in it, and her voice sharpened. 'I'm not done with landscapes, but on the other hand, I wanted to move to London from the country. So what did that mean? Some new curiosity about – people? The problem with Eddie's stuff is it's just photographs, which are already flat, and so the contours, the way the light works – it's all prescribed. The objects are beautiful, but they don't change – whatever time, whatever day. In the end, anyone who looks at them can see what I see when I look at them. I can't show you something you don't already see for yourself.'

'What about your little Fauvist statuette? The Cycladic lady? And the Greek warrior? You've added suggestions – every sketch has some little new thing.'

Gwen threw her eyes around the walls where the sketches hung, half smiled. 'I want to do something alive. Get at the atmosphere around me, you know, the weather I'm living with. And I want three dimensions to work with – four. Time is the big one. Because all this visual stuff happens so fast. It can have such glamour, such impact, but then, poof. It's over, gone, before we understand it, maybe before we even see it, unless we work really fast. There are latent qualities that need bringing out if we're going to understand what we're responding to when we respond to – well – to life. And the reason it has to be *you* now is – you are a weathervane. You swing around with things, you change. I can feel it in you, or see it. Both. You are not always the same.'

'Nobody's always the same.'

Gwen looked puzzled. '*I'm* always the same. I mean – I get tired, hungry, go to sleep, wake up, but my personality is just what it is. A hard, bossy little knot.' She snorted out a laugh. 'I really can't change. Even when I've wanted to – towards other people, their chemistry or whatever. Their preferences, their levels of energy. I have to move away if things aren't right. Shift the scene around me until it clicks. You, on the other hand, pick up on the scene where you are – like a chameleon. You change colour in relation to who you're with. It's amazing. It shows how much you feel – the fact that you change so much so quickly. Like with that chair – you're hiding out in it and becoming this creature of red moroccan leather. Those long cracks in the leather and the stuffing coming out,' she waved her paintbrush at them vaguely, 'those make you look older and fragile, like a survivor of something – even kind of dried out, as if you need emollients and repairing. Your clothes don't fit with that – something you got in a depart- ment store – but I know you don't really care what you wear, so

119

I just ignore them. They don't have your masculinity, your clothes, and they don't have – your candour.'

'How do you know?' Hilary was irritated. 'There are tons of things to buy, and I have to decide just like anyone else. Maybe I bought this gypsy skirt last summer because I already knew I didn't have a home. And I think it's sort of sexy, the way it fits low on the hips, which is maybe how I felt. How I *wanted* to feel. Footloose. Ready. Maybe I was thinking like a girl when I bought it. A señorita.'

Gwen raised an eyebrow. 'Well, I can fake the clothes, can't I? Paint you how I see you. You don't always look the same from the outside. Maybe one portrait won't do, to capture you.'

'I'm going to wear this fucking skirt in *all* of them.'

Thus they were ensconced in the studio for several days, Hilary captive in the chair. During long stretches, they worked in silence, Gwen looking, stroking at the paint, looking, stroking again, focused so intently on this unfamiliar scenery, a human face, that she hardly thought about Hilary as the living creature in which she had professed such an interest.

Eventually, the intensity of concentration tired Hilary. Partway through one long morning, she mumbled like a ventriloquist, 'How much does it actually bother you when I move my mouth?'

There was no reply. So Hilary repeated her question, a little louder, parting her lips.

Gwen's hand stopped moving; she looked straight at Hilary, blank. Then she asked, 'Move your mouth?'

And Hilary eked out, 'Are you doing it now? My mouth? Can I talk?'

'If you need to. But – can you memorise the way you are now? To go back to the pose?' Gwen peered at Hilary, narrowed one eye, looked at her canvas, then barked, 'Wait. Just wait.'

She touched the mouth with her brush, rested the brush there for a moment, following the line of the lips with her eye, studying the colour, the way the flesh swelled and dimpled, the black line waving along the horizontal between upper and lower lip. 'OK,' she said. 'Are you getting sick of this? Are you tired?'

'What – of taking orders?' But after this burst of fight, Hilary was suddenly earnest. 'I feel like I'm supposed to be offering you something, but I don't know what it is. Can you see in my face that I'm trying to show a kind of willingness?'

Gwen just looked at her, and Hilary stumbled on. 'Because you didn't like it before when I started looking like part of the furniture –?'

There was a silence.

'The chair?' Hilary persisted. 'Remember I was turning into the chair?'

Gwen smiled and chuckled. 'It doesn't matter whether or not I liked it. It's just what I noticed. I couldn't see your face was the thing.'

'Is it pride?' Hilary asked. 'This wish I have to be recognised, even though I don't know for what? If how I look isn't impor- tant to me, it's pretty weird *you* taking such an interest.'

'Uh-huh,' Gwen said, a brush between her teeth, not seeming to listen. There was a long pause. 'You're doing a great job.'

'Is it a natural mood you're after? A characteristic one, that I have anyway? Because how I feel now is – that I'm having my portrait painted. And from my side of the canvas, nothing is hap- pening. I have this sense of expectation, this sense that you might apply the paint to my face or something. But I'm – just – waiting.'

'Yeah. That's just how I see you. Suspended. I mean as far as life goes, you haven't got anything to do now, have you? You're between things. Sort of – an empty vessel – or Sleeping Beauty?'

Gwen stopped painting and looked at Hilary, a little shocked at herself. She put down her brushes, spat the one from her mouth to speak more carefully. 'That doesn't sound good. Sorry. Let's turn on the radio. I listen to it a lot when I'm working – when there's no piano from Mr Delicious downstairs. Do you want classical? Rock and roll?'

Hilary paid no attention to the question; she spoke sternly. 'You know, at this point, you're really the one who's keeping me here, Gwen, with your solicitousness, and – your – painting! I'm *full* of thoughts; full of what I have to do. OK, I needed to rest and recuperate. You can't just go at it hammer and tongs the whole time without stopping to reflect –' But then losing the flight of her argument, she asked with a sudden smile, 'Mr Delicious?'

Now Gwen ignored the question. 'You are so damn brave. I really admire your fortitude.'

'My fortitude?'

'I wouldn't want to think so much about it, if I were reduced to – if I didn't have what I wanted.'

'Well, what else would I think about? And if I'm going to go back and fight for it?'

'I don't mean the ancient treasure.'

'What?' Hilary was astounded. 'A marriage that was clearly a mistake? Come on. And you can't possibly mean Paul?'

Gwen said reluctantly, 'I mean marriage in general. A happy marriage. A great passion. A child, even.' But it made her feel guilty, listing these things to Hilary, as if she was gloating over her own marriage, her own child; she didn't like to talk about it.

Uneasiness was building up between them. It was becoming more and more awkward to get a word out, an honest word, because each of them seemed to want to stick to saying things that would harmonise with the thoughts and needs of the other, and neither was confident what the thoughts and needs of the other might be. In fact, the life and lot of each seemed to comment on and to diminish the other, and so they were silenced by their wish to support one another – by an excess of love.

Suddenly, it cloyed with Hilary. She resented Gwen's carefulness, her tiptoeing tone of voice, and she said tartly, almost patronising, 'I relish my freedom, Gwen, hard as it is for me to be alone sometimes. I have to face the fact that maybe I don't make the right connections with other people because there's something I don't want to give up. You ought to face it, too, if you're really my friend. You ought to face what I'm really like.'

It was a slapping rebuke. There they were, with the easel between them: the likeness, the seeking after what Hilary was really like. It was somehow entirely compromising – what *was* Gwen doing?

'I suppose I would like to be married and to have a child,' Hilary said in a low voice. 'But maybe it's not something that's going to happen for me, Gwen. I still hope – I still assume – that it will. But it's not something I experience as a loss, you know. Because I've never had it. My relationship with Mark didn't develop that way, thank God. I guess somehow I didn't want to depend on him. We never really talked about it, in all that time. So I don't know what I'm missing – motherhood. Being around Will, yeah, I get thoughts I don't usually have. Maybe I don't allow myself much that way – warding off some element of longing. But that's natural, isn't it? Why would I want to wallow in something other people have, that I don't? Something you have? I don't want to live my life resenting and envying. I just want to take happiness as I find it. If I find it. I'm Will's godmother – I love that. I get the proprietary thrill. It's all a plus. It's not salt in a wound, in case that's what you're thinking. I don't need to be you and to have your life.'

'Well, how could I know that if you didn't tell me? I feel happy to hear it. And it makes me all the more admiring of you.'

'OK, you tell me – what's so great about your marriage? Is it something I really want, in fact? Tell me about having a baby.'

In the little silence that followed, there was an urgent knock on the door. Instinctively Gwen looked at her watch, forgetting that she always took it off to paint. The light told her that it should be hours still before Will came home. She felt strangely distressed. Was something wrong? Was Will sick? Had there been an accident at school?

But it was Hugo, flushed, perspiring, leaning around the door as he half opened it, reluctant to interrupt.

'Sorry sorry sorry! I've done something truly awful. It's all my fault. I was looking over a piece, and I completely forgot that I'd started to have a bath, and I let it overflow. It's a disaster! There's water everywhere, gallons of it. My flat looks like New Orleans. I ran downstairs because I'm horribly afraid it may have – burst through. But it's locked, down there. Do you think – could you possibly come down and let me in? And we could take a look?'

'Of course I can.' Hilary and Gwen both spoke at once. There was a strange pause, a sense of insult in the air, intense surprise.

Then Gwen backed down, smiling, abashed. 'Sorry, I thought you were asking me.'

'I *am* asking you!' Hugo cried. 'It's your flat underneath. There was no reply when I knocked, and I realised you'd be up here in the studio. Oh God, I'm sorry – it might be pouring through into your place. I'm thinking my bathroom is right above yours? At least that's what I'm hoping. I don't know your flat at all –'

He was all the way around the door inside the studio now, dancing with worry, his feet bare, the cuffs of his trousers dark with water. As they looked at him, he put his fingers to his open shirt placket, buttoning it over a long gash of tawny stomach, soft brown hair showing on its slimness. Gwen noticed that the flies on his trousers were zipped but not buttoned at the top.

'Maybe we should hurry?' he pleaded.

So they leaped up in unison, throwing down paintbrushes, poses.

'Will you come down with us, Hil?' Gwen asked, somehow not really wanting her to. She was patting her jean pockets, the work-table top, piles of rags and papers, hunting for her keys; suddenly she swept them down off the chest with a chatelaine's jingle and headed for the door.

She pushed past Hugo, avoiding looking at him, feeling rushed and self-conscious in his presence. She didn't look back as they thundered down the stairs, tried to bend all her attention on to the lock of her front door, which seemed to have become strangely unfamiliar since she had shut it only an hour or two before. It wouldn't accept the key; the key wouldn't turn; her hands were unsteady, her deft, artistic hands, as Hugo and then Hilary closed in around her in the hallway.

'Shall I help?' Hugo offered, extending his long, confident fingers in the air above her struggle. His untucked, half-buttoned shirt brushed her cheek.

Gwen felt the strength drain out of her shoulders and her upper arms. 'I can do it,' she bleated, floating against the door, clinging to the key. Her fingers somehow rotated the key without her, so that she fell inside, gasping, and fled from Hugo towards the bathroom, trying to remember why she had come.

But she could hear it, right away; they all could. The dripping. It was like the heavy, intermittent run-off of rain from the edge of a porch roof. And there was a smell of wet plaster and dirt. The carpet was soaked outside the bathroom door, the grey tile floor was slick with it. Incredibly, a lot of the water had landed inside the bathtub. It was spilling fast from the three tiny light fixtures in the ceiling directly above the tub, and more slowly from the line of four light fixtures running from the toilet towards the sink and the mirror.

They crowded in, staring, standing close together beside the tub.

'You could have your bath right here,' Gwen said, trying to make light of the catastrophe. 'But the water might be cold?'

Then she felt herself blush. She dropped her head and spun around as if to inspect the damage to the walls, the corners of the room, touching the white paint and the dampened towels on their rails. She saw her white cotton nightgown hanging on a hook on the back of the bathroom door, her cotton running shorts, knickers, dangling from the doorknob, hidden where the door was opened full back against the wall.

Hilary, sensing concern, reached for the door, snatched it away from the wall to see whether there was water leaking behind it, and the knickers fell on the wet floor.

'Sorry,' Hilary said.

'It doesn't matter,' Gwen mumbled, embarrassed, leaning past Hugo, past Hilary, bending down to grab them, whisking the shorts into the same hand as she stood up again. 'They're for the laundry anyway.'

'Should I call a plumber?' Hugo asked, staring all the while at the ceiling.

'What would a plumber do, though?' Hilary pointed out. 'Haven't you already turned the water off upstairs?'

'Yes. Oh, yes, it's off, now. I just thought − I realised it might be coming down here. But apart from that − I don't know a thing about a situation like this.'

'It'll be OK, Hugo.' Gwen was trying to regain her composure. 'It just depends how much water is inside the ceiling and whether it's finding a way out. If it's trapped, it'll gradually soak the plaster and then maybe the ceiling will collapse. We could make tiny holes, to let it through, but it seems as though the light fixtures are already doing that. Does it look like it's bulging anywhere?'

Hugo reached up to test the ceiling, and Gwen spoke sharply, 'You mustn't touch it!' Then more quietly, 'Sorry, but I think that can make it give way. Anyway − it looks completely flat to me. Don't you think? We should go turn off the light circuit, to be on the safe side. And just − get out of the room.' She disappeared to the fuse board with the ball of dirty laundry in her hand.

Hilary and Hugo eyed each other sheepishly, like scolded children.

'Can't you just picture it, if the ceiling comes down?' he said.

'Interconnecting flats?' But Hilary tried to reassure him. 'I don't think Gwen's worried about that.'

Gwen reappeared. 'I bet you don't have insurance, do you?'

126

Hugo looked blank. 'Insurance?'

She nodded, morose. 'Who would, at your age.'

'Actually, my piano is insured,' he said hopefully.

'That's good. Just in case it falls through the ceiling tonight. It's right over our bed, and it would probably kill us. I'll bet your insurance wouldn't cover that. You and Hilary would have to raise Will – OK?'

Hugo tried to smile, but mostly he just worked his eyebrows.

Gwen looked mournfully at the ceiling of the bathroom. 'I really just meant for the paint. Insurance might pay for redecorating. You see those little brown halos of dirty water spreading around the lights? Those will stain. I guess I could get up there and paint them out myself. On the other hand,' she put her hands on her hips, spread her shoulders, spoke with mock enthusiasm, 'maybe we'll all get to like them, lying back in the bath. You never know what you can get to be fond of.'

'I'll help you,' Hugo offered energetically.

'Get to like the stains? Or paint them out?' Gwen felt her heart hit one beat hard as she said it, like a bump, and she had to catch her breath.

'Umm – whichever you prefer.' He was bewildered, desperate to please. 'Both?'

'Let me think about it for a while.' Now her voice was sour. She was over some boundary with her playfulness.

She squeezed past him and opened the drain in the tub. 'I wonder why that plug was in?'

'Because I was going to take a bath after we went running,' said Hilary. 'But instead I went down and had a shower in the basement, right after you.'

The dirty water slurped down the drain, belched, was gone. They all smiled with relief at the sound.

'You do know how sorry I am, Gwen?'

'Yes. I think I do, Hugo. Let's leave it alone. Just let it dry. What state is your flat in? Have you got a mop? Towels?'

'We'll help you dry the floors,' Hilary offered.

Hugo stuck his hands in his pockets, looked at his bare feet. 'Yes please to the mop and maybe I need some old towels or something. But I'll deal with it. Go back to what you were doing. Please. I feel badly stealing your morning with this – with my – stupidity.'

Gwen was already snapping towels off the rails, loading them into Hugo's surprised arms.

'Use these dirty ones,' she commanded. 'I'll bring the mop.'

As they started back up the stairs, she left the door to the downstairs flat propped open. 'Air it out, don't you think?'

She stood the mop outside Hugo's doorway on the next landing and climbed straight on to the top without looking inside his flat to make any assessment, leaving him to get on with it.

When Hilary caught up with her, Gwen was looking out the window at the tiny paved garden three floors below, the awkward raised bed at the rear, the gasping, anonymous shrubs crowding around the tree which grew up towards the window, branching where it was allowed to, leafless and dingy. There was a hunched brick wall on the right, a sagging basketwork fence on the left, and the next-door gardens were equally grey, equally cramped, with their optimistic attempts at lawn, at box and gravel parterre, at Lilliputian water features, all overshadowed by the autumnal city, by the constant downdraught of traffic scum on to teak benches, on to children's abandoned fantasies – slides, Wendy houses, police motorbikes moulded in lurid plastic.

Hilary crossed to the window, looked out at what Gwen was looking out at, the sad, potted scene. Then she wandered among the easels, considering Gwen's landscapes.

Gwen turned from the window, walked to the easel she had abandoned when they went downstairs, and studied what she had done so far. She started to collect her brushes in one hand as she drew breath, considering what to do next.

From downstairs came the opening bars of Schubert's B flat

major Sonata. They looked at each other in surprise, then they both smiled slowly and completely.

'I love this,' said Hilary.

'He's trying to make it up to us.'

The ease of it, the measured beauty, longing and suffering made satisfying. It built through the studio, and they listened in absolute stillness.

Then Gwen said, 'We should do it as a nude, Hil. That would be the thing to try. Would it freak you out? It's just, you know, the clothes are all wrong. Or maybe they're in conflict with me – with my vision of you, how I want to see you.'

Wondering now for whom exactly she had worn the gypsy skirt, Hilary slipped it off. Then she began to unbutton her shirt.

'Let's try it,' she said. 'But the thing is, I'm so tired already. Can I lie down?' She laughed, partly because she was embarrassed and partly because of the precipitous slide which she knew Gwen would appreciate, from the sublime idea – a nude – to the ridiculous practicality.

'Good. Lie down. It's your own bed anyway. Mound up the cushions at the head, on your pillow. Push the screen all the way flat against the wall. I guess Hugo can't rush in and surprise us as long as we hear him playing? I'll turn up the heat.'

'What if I fall asleep?'

Gwen thought for a moment. 'Asleep?' Then she shrugged. 'Perfect. Sleeping Beauty, like I said. You'll wake up when the time comes.'

CHAPTER 8

When she arrived in Oxford about fifteen years before, Gwen had been animated by private emotions so intense that she relished the atmosphere of difficulty, of chill, of foreboding, which the stony city seemed to offer her. Wherever she turned, she had seen a cold wall rising, an ancient formidable gate, a narrow alley swollen and twisted with massed cobbles, slick with muddy water. The days were flinty, and they faded before they ever broadened to full light, as if the world was mired in a dark age, an age of ice or fog. The people she passed but to whom she did not speak in the streets, cloisters, courtyards, wore black or dark grey, as if coloured dyes had not yet been invented; they seemed to her to belong to a vast religious order, to be toiling towards some unspecified advancement in their woollen suits, woollen skirts, woollen tights, and, over the top, their black gowns, which fluttered at the armholes with streamers and ballooning sleeves that might carry the wearers, like wings, on an updraught of high thoughts, of hurrying, to heaven.

Only mailboxes, phone boxes and buses showed colour in Oxford – bright red. They seemed to Gwen to be the colour of lost Victorian optimism – and, like fire alarms, they seemed to be intended for use exclusively in an emergency: if you failed to cope with the local discipline, if you were weak enough to need to write a letter, make a phone call, escape altogether in a motorised vehicle to the outside world.

In those days, Gwen didn't need the outside world, nor much of the world she was in. Being shut out and cut off felt right to her, felt tonic and abrasive. She didn't want to enter anywhere, didn't want to join in, because she was party to a love affair so engrossing and so expansive that it made two a population for the whole planet. She had left her homeland, broken ranks with friends and family, abandoned her college degree, kicked over the traces. She would have done more. She would have crossed the ocean in a fifteenth-century sailing ship for Lawrence, dressed in rags, eaten rancid food, braved the plague. She had made a life-and-death commitment, and she wouldn't allow it to be ordinary. She wanted to nurture her sense of awe towards it. Modernity, electricity, running water – and her open road to middle-class comfort at home – they could all go; she was seeking, like something lost but well remembered, sensations more authentic, more complete, more profound.

As she squinted over her books, over page upon foxed page fingered by studious generations at hard, ill-lit, low desks – her nose stinging with mould in the never-adequate heat of this and that uncushioned, wood-lined, age-hallowed library – she felt that she was all the time engaged in a polar adventure, alone with Lawrence crossing the permanent twilight of the English winter, the mythical two of them, breasting the mystery, the blazing trail of their partnership. The fever of her conviction was enhanced immeasurably by its foil of darkness, dankness, discomfort, inconvenience.

Working on the nude, she tried to explain all this to Hilary, stopping, starting.

'I wasn't really in a normal state of consciousness, Hil. And I mean – it went on and on like that, the sense of elation, of being – can you get this? – transported. It was maybe a lot of things – who knows – all at one time. How can I unpick it now, and make you understand? Definitely it started before I left the States, the world falling away. Otherwise I wouldn't have left, would I?'

'No.' Hilary's voice was only a sigh, complying. 'You wouldn't have left.'

'And that's what it felt like, that's how I'd describe it – not so much falling in love, but the world falling away. Nothing else mattered. And once I got to Oxford, I was just so – excited. So awake to – the strangeness. As if nothing had ever happened to me before. So what was *that* then? Was that being in love? Or was it being in a new place? Because the difficulty of it, how shabby and old-fashioned it all seemed, that was something I reached for, ate up whole, as if it were – part of *him.*'

'See, Gwen. You *do* have moods; you've just described one. Being in love changed you completely.' Hilary was lying nearly flat on her back, her eyes roaming the yellowed ceiling and her lips gaping blindly at the air like a fish's.

'That's not what I mean by a mood – and it didn't change me, you know. It only made me more what I already am. Cleared the debris . . . from around me . . .'

Gwen fell silent as she studied the long pale thigh rising almost straight up towards her, narrowing into the bent, angular knee, with the bones of the joint pressing bloodless, dizzy yellow through the pink flesh. She was thinking, as she had been thinking since they began the nude, that she wanted to include every tiny contour of mortality and that she wanted at the same time to work her brush constantly around the whole canvas, capture Hilary's denseness, height, breadth all at once, the inscrutable curve of her doughy buttocks flattened against the bedspread, the ranginess of her limbs flinging themselves away from her torso as she lay there, her body at ease, her mind prowling over the great questions before them – love, life. She must keep the energy crackling, quick, over the whole form of her, move continually like the music rising from downstairs, which never stopped yet kept its theme always evident, continuing to become, as if naturally, something else which also belonged to or was a transformation of the same thing.

'But how did you know? In college?' Hilary eventually asked.

'There was just never anything I'd been more sure of,' Gwen said, the knee becoming itself under her brush, an aubergine shadow, green-edged, lengthening into the bony front of the shin, razor-sharp, vulnerable, and the blue looping flesh of the calf drooping down behind as it ran towards the square, strange foot, massive because it was so close, shamelessly strong and crude, yet showing helpless toes with their tender interstices curled sweetly side by side into the nest of the mattress. Beyond the leg, outstretched across the bedspread, Hilary's long, lazy arm scattered into fingers at its gnarled, snaking end. And as Gwen pushed up to it with her brush, she said, 'Because here was this man who – was – trying to set me free.'

'Free from what?' A note of more pressing interest sounded in Hilary's voice.

There was a pause, Gwen's eyes moved over Hilary, then pulled back into the painting, her brush went to her colours, hovered over them, sipped like a bee at a blossom, carried the pollen-coated bristles to the canvas.

'Just – free. I suppose if I had thought about it then, I would have said, free from convention, or free from whatever had been making me restless, making me feel constrained. Free from a way that I was being trained to think and didn't feel comfortable with. Or free from certain fears I maybe had. But I knew that it was real freedom. I felt no anxiety. To leap, launch, whatever. It was – an absolute.'

'Didn't he worry that he was ruining your life? That he shouldn't let you throw everything away for him?'

Hilary's breasts showed only as maroon tips of nipple above the cage of her ribs, the flesh of them spreading over her chest in two low swells. Gwen could see her pulse sucking fast at the small, deep cavity, taut-edged with tendons, at the base of her throat. And there was her heart, like a slow, slamming echo, rhythmically lifting her left side. It seemed like time, evident, passing; and it was proof of something so basic, so complex, the flutter and beat of life. Not that you could paint it. But you could paint everything animated by it.

'We had those talks,' Gwen murmured. 'Throwing everything

away. Or he made me consider it. But — what's everything? It didn't feel reckless. It felt like this was what everything — what all the other things were *for*. I don't think it felt reckless to him, either. Anyway, from a practical point of view, I could go study for a degree where he was, provided I could get in, but he had to go back to his job. He was done teaching in Boston. Maybe it's old-fashioned, but he was earning a salary. He was established, and he was in a position to help me in a way that I couldn't possibly have helped him.'

'I guess he had total sway over you. A professor? Plus — that whole English thing. The power is just — huge.'

'If you think about it like that. But how was he going to abuse it? We were both in love — not just me.'

'All the more reason he should have told you no. Should have told you to grow up first, then come find him.'

'This from the woman who has made her career to date out of getting inside the head of an octogenarian? Being his eyes, acquiring his taste, giving her body to house his ghost so that he can live on in a museum she will build for him?'

'You're not painting *that*, are you? A naked old man?'

They both laughed.

'People give themselves to what they give themselves to, Hil. I've grown up anyway — grown up more, grown up better. If it hadn't worked out, maybe Lawrence could be judged unprincipled; but it did work out. So he wins. And having the nerve to get what you want — didn't we talk about that? When it comes to the long term, something you're going to live with, you have to be ruthless. Anything else is sentimental.'

'But you liked that medieval deal in Oxford? It seems way more rigid and conventional than any place in the States. Weren't you lonely? You make it sound totally depressing. Like you were on some masochistic bender to prove how much you loved him.'

'The rigidity didn't really apply to me, though. It was all —

someone else's country. I was unofficial – beyond the law or something. The only thing I didn't like was Lawrence being out of the room. Out of any room that I was in, even for two minutes. I breathed to be with him, and nothing else figured.'

'So that's why you never finished your Oxford degree either? You never cared about it in the first place?' Hilary's voice was goading; she'd made a discovery, caught Gwen out.

And Gwen pleaded comically, half defensive. 'Wait. No. I did. I worked hard in the beginning. But you're right. And I was just blown away by – everything. Especially – something about the seasons here, something we don't have at home, and which took me by surprise.'

She scrubbed at her palette with the flat, square little brush she was using, dabbed and pulled at the crimson, the raw umber, muttering, 'Might need more of that.' Then she walked to the shelves above the sink, grabbed tubes of paint, stood there gripping them, talking intently.

'When spring came that first year, it was just so green and so heavy with leaf. You know how it's light here all night, in the summer? I never really slept at all, and the euphoria – it was almost like craziness, like mania. I guess there was some hibernating part of me that needed it and was waiting for it – for spring. It made me understand the idea of rebirth – really feel it – that's how alive I was. I had so much energy – too much. Can you have too much? It got scary because I loved that first winter, that primeval dark and cold, but when spring came, I realised that I was afraid to do it again – winter. I'm not kidding. Early in the spring, I thought, I can't go back to the dark – ever. I won't survive it a second time. And I started to dread autumn coming. It was still *months* away. I had never dreaded autumn before, but I was so in love with spring that the dark terrified me.'

She held the tubes of paint in the air, one in each hand, resolving it. 'We have to have a different kind of autumn, was what I thought.

Any change will do, so that we don't retread a path we know. It's not like you can cross the Arctic twice in one year. If you are going to dig that deep into yourself, you need to dig for something else, something new. So I persuaded Lawrence that we could get more of it – of spring, summer, of one another – if we moved out of Oxford. And I found the cottage. We just wallowed there, in the light and in the green. Hil, I had never even *seen* an English hedgerow. Have you seen one? In that countryside, they seemed to grow up over head height during the night! It was like *Jack and the Beanstalk*. It made me totally understand why the English have that story. That's exactly what summers are like here. And then I felt like I had to – do something about it – and – I started to paint.'

'It seems like you would have tried gardening.' Hilary played at humour because she felt a little overwhelmed by the drama of Gwen's story and by Gwen's certainty. Where did it come from, her strength? Her self-absorption? Clearly she had suffered a lot more for her impulsiveness than she ever let on – running off with Lawrence. And this whole heroic revelation, Hilary thought, this burst of spring and artistic inspiration was like some place Gwen had made for herself inside her head where everything would always be just how she needed it to be, intensely beautiful and satisfying.

'I always used to paint,' Gwen insisted. 'Before I knew you. All through school and high school. I took endless classes. I just had a lapse of conviction – that it wasn't something serious enough to do in college. Or maybe I mean responsible enough. I never wanted art school and to be with only artists. I wouldn't have met you or anyone like you. Whatever. At the cottage, I thought the painting would be just a dabble because at first I didn't realise the appetite behind it. There were times that felt a little – aimless – times I wanted to fill. When Lawrence wasn't back. Waiting was – always – heavy.'

Gwen paused, as if she had run out of energy for explaining, and Hilary thought, Unbearable; the waiting and the loneliness must have been unbearable.

Then Gwen lit off again, on a new breath. 'So there I was at the cottage, developing this obsession in his absence. Even in his presence sometimes. It became gigantic. I wanted to paint every-thing – *everything* – before it was too late, before autumn came. It was the long vacation, no lectures, no tutorials, no nothing, and gradually I abandoned my reading and my books and just painted all day long. Sometimes I painted all night.'

She bent over her palette, unscrewing a lid, squeezing watch-fully. 'I used a chestlamp for that, outside. Or sometimes I kept the studio door open, with the light on inside, so I could see what I was doing. Sitting out in the night, the cool of it – you know it brims with something, something whispering, moving – it's so fertile. Endless, edgeless. Can you see how it – seduced me? I couldn't leave the cottage. There was never time. There was so much to do, and the canvases got bigger and bigger and I kept on noticing more and more. Some days I thought, if I go outside again, I'll see something else and then I won't be able to leave to go buy food or even make a sandwich.'

'But, Gwen, no time to eat, let alone buy food? How on earth did you manage to get married? And you said you'd tell me about babies. That's really why I'm lying here for you. Because you said you would tell me about marriage and babies.'

'We were already married by then. We just went one day.'

'You so unconventional, severing every bond?'

'Well, I – felt it – needing the marriage – so did he. Not how you might think. It really was a way of getting free. What I said. Free from myself – from all the things that could hold me back, from desires that were too great. From sex.'

'Wait. What? Free from sex?'

'Oh God.' As she screwed the tiny lids back tight, Gwen stood up straight, rolling her eyes. 'Don't get me wrong – it's not some weird, English self-loathing thing. For ages, that was all we ever did.' She lodged the tubes back where she had taken them, grinning, shimmied her hips a little as she swanned back to the canvas.

'Sex *and* marriage: that's freedom. Because marriage – listen to me, Hilary –' Now she picked up her brush, lifted it in the air, looking down at her friend, admonishing, gesturing. 'Marriage brought an end to that whole trajectory of girlhood, all the wondering about what is my destiny, where is my man. Suddenly that was over. There I was; this was my man. And I *knew* it was my man, make no mistake. So what then? *Then* I was thinking from a position of complete, utter freedom. At last I felt I was an adult, not a girl. So – it was time to get on with my life. In my case, I knew I wanted to paint and that all the other stuff was beside the point – delaying tactics or fear or distraction – or dress rehearsal or preparation – or – I don't even know. Up until then I just had the problem that women have – I was waiting for someone to come along and sweep me off my feet, push me off my chosen path, interfere with my life, with my plans. So many women are waiting for that. In my case, someone came along and pushed me *on to* the path. So I painted. Non-stop. I couldn't get more than a step from that cottage – I had plans for further afield, but right outside the door, I had to stop and paint it all. I was a slave to it – for years.'

'So you're telling me I won't know what I want until I'm married?' Hilary lifted a hand in the air, protesting, let it drop hard back on to the bed in exasperation.

'Doesn't sound good at all, does it? I wouldn't like that to be true for women in general – because it's pathetic in a way. But – do you understand me? Maybe it's our age, you know, the generation we're in. That we still set store by pairing off. Or maybe a lot of women try to *pretend* it isn't so. But what I really think is that for you and for me, you have to get inside marriage to see out of it and to see – beyond the whole question of it.'

'You're making it sound like initiation into some cult,' Hilary said belligerently. 'I don't believe that at all. It's not a knowledge thing. It's companionship. A special kind of companionship.'

'Don't get pissed off at me. I'm not trying to lord it over you. I'm trying to tell you something I've found out. It *is* a mystery; it's esoteric; it's not evident; it's not transparent.' She paused, lowered her voice, tried to sound conciliatory. 'I'm sure you'll find out for yourself.'

But Hilary wouldn't be placated. 'I think I can see some things about it even from the outside, even without getting in. And fuck it, I think I can figure out my own destiny.'

Gwen drove her eyes, her brush into the darkness between Hilary's legs, thinking in frustration, in disappointment, that she didn't know how people learned anything, exchanged knowledge, were born or died. She could only see what she saw, and try to paint it. It was all there before her eyes, life as she cared about it, epitomised now in this figure of a woman. And she herself was a painter, nothing else. There was nothing more to her. No mutability, no alternative.

The balance was lost between them. Whatever Gwen was trying to give her could only enrage Hilary now. And yet Hilary was transfixed.

After a few ponderous moments, Hilary asked, 'So what about Will? Also a mystery?' It was only a little grudging. She couldn't help herself that she wanted to know.

Gwen barely tipped her head to one side, spoke unassertively. 'I think so.'

Hilary waited for more, then capitulated, pleading, 'You promised to tell me.'

It seemed to Hilary as though Gwen was being very careful now, thinking for a long time before she spoke, concentrating on some fine detail on the canvas. It made Hilary wonder if she would ever find out what it had been like for Gwen, giving birth to a child, and it made her wonder if she deserved to be punished like this for her jealousy and her rage, which were only natural. But she forgave them both, herself and Gwen, and she waited.

'Painting was nearly enough for me. I felt that. Especially when the technique came together. Which it does when you paint that much. Plus, I came up to London a few terms, went to classes again, for the practice. And to see what I was doing compared to something else, anything else. But I hated it. I hated the camaraderie. It was really distracting – everyone else, what they thought, what they had to say. There were people who liked my stuff, though. And the affirmation was good. It sent me back to work again. I only needed a little. Because Lawrence let me – He encouraged me to stay immersed. And it was glorious when we were both there, and no one else, in the depths of the country, in this – well – this vision. We used to work and go for walks, read by the fire, sleep out under the trees when the weather was warm. If the stream was high, it would roar so loudly that the rest of the world was completely blotted out – just that clean sound, that rushing white moisture when it was gorged with rain. We even used to swim in the pond, mucky as it was, freezing cold. We knew every tree, every stone, because we had time to notice it all. And he knew *exactly* what I was doing.'

She sighed, stepped back from the canvas, looked at Hilary, squinted to get the form, to simplify things. 'But he wasn't always there. Sometimes I *was* a little lonely, or just – overwhelmed by myself, because I didn't know how to stop – the craze, the hunger. I thought it was love, physical desire. Then I thought it was work. Nothing would feed it. Until one day it came to me, like the simplest idea: that I wanted a child. That I *lacked* a child. And I thought, I have to fill my belly. It was an itch that needed scratching. Worse than that. I mean – think of sex – desire – it was a whole new dimension. Frantic. Needing a result, the compulsion I felt about it. Sex had to *result* in something. How can a womb have hunger like that? The interior of you? How does the brain know? It was like an ache, a continual outcry. And it went on for a few years, or, I don't know, maybe longer, until finally it happened, and there was nature unfurling inside me – all that force that through the green fuse drives the flower or whatever it is that Dylan Thomas wrote – that can't be stopped, can't be controlled – the swelling, the miracle.'

'I haven't felt that,' said Hilary in a flat, matter-of-fact voice. 'Nothing so animal. I don't have that savage thing you're talking about. Not because I'm not married. I'm just not like you.' Bohemian, unhinged, she thought, feeling a little unnerved by Gwen, by her weirdness.

'Hmm,' Gwen murmured without conviction. 'I've seen you moved by things. To the point of earthquake. Look how freaked out you were the day you got here. And how you've chucked – basically your whole life – since Eddie Doro died. And I can remember you in the boat, too, in the old days. Savage is exactly the word I'd use – completely animal, how you'd give yourself to that pain in order to win what – a rowing race? How important is that?'

'I'm moved by different things, Gwen.'

'OK. And maybe moved by more than one thing at a time, more than one set of vibes? Trying to make things OK with everyone, all at once? That might dilute it – how it feels.'

Hilary objected to this, competing with Gwen now. 'Or make it more intense – eight people in a boat. Nine.'

'Yeah. So. If something comes along and takes you over – because it takes you over entirely, this new person trying to get into the world. It's not like you can resist.'

'So when Will came, was it a jungle birth? Did you raise him like a wolf cub?'

'You laugh, my dear.' Gwen's tone was arch. 'Lawrence wanted me to come back and live in Oxford, near the college. He was right, in a way, that we would need to be together more so he could help me. But I just couldn't do it. That wife of an Oxford don thing, adjunct to his institutional life, stuck in some generic role. And his is such a small college, a cul-de-sac for me. You just get pegged and reviled.' It was palpable, Gwen's disdain for the thing she had refused to be. 'I was determined to stay at the cottage. And wow. Talk about bondage – there is nothing to compare. I belonged to that boy.'

Hilary strained her head up for an instant and caught Gwen's eyes, the dull passion of them, inscrutable green misted with white. She remembered the woman and the baby they had seen beside the river that first morning and the outburst they had triggered in Gwen. And she dropped her head again, feeling unsettled, imagined smoke rising, as if from a sacrifice, from entrails. She wanted to make light of it. 'You let him drink your blood, huh?'

'I let him drink my blood,' Gwen repeated firmly. 'And I know I'll never be free again, not really. That's the bottom line. A child enslaves more completely than anything else. Takes you over, day and night. So – is that what you want, Hil, a child?'

Hilary was silent, feeling rebuked for something she hadn't done: *want* a child? It was too strong a word. She wasn't certain she would ever have the chance to want a child. It was the force of Gwen's voice, the impression she had that Gwen was gritting her teeth, even spitting, that made Hilary wonder: Is she angry at me? Or is she angry at Will? Angry at having had him? She felt shocked; this was a terrible revelation, like a warning against motherhood – that it was somehow just too hard.

But then Gwen said, 'It *is,* you know, Hil; it is what you want – a child.' Her insistence was aggressive, almost cruel. 'You won't be yourself until you have one. Go ahead and hate me for thinking that I know all about you even if you don't know yourself or won't admit it. But you're a woman after all. That's one of the things I've discovered about myself – that I'm a woman, hard as it is to be one. And I know it's true about you, too – that you're a woman.'

'It doesn't necessarily follow, Gwen, being a woman and wanting a child –' But Hilary stopped there, didn't make the obvious challenge, How can you know what I want? Because she recognised that Gwen was stuck. There was no going back on Will. Gwen only knew what she herself had done, and she seemed to want Hilary to do the same – to join her. As if this would resolve her ambivalence. I'm still free, Hilary thought, and maybe that's just about unbearable for Gwen. Hilary couldn't raise this aloud. She felt it would be like accusing Gwen of trying to trick her into throwing her life away, of saying, Marry, bear children, when Gwen seemed filled with rage that she herself had done exactly that. I'm not ready for that part of this conversation, thought Hilary.

Nevertheless, she wondered about having a child. Would I have the same experience of rage? Would I have regrets? But I'm *not* the same as Gwen, she thought. She was certain of that.

As she lay immobile on the bed, day after day, watching Gwen paint, Hilary felt a pungent, disabling fear spreading in her like something she had breathed in, something acrid and intoxicating. She thought about the hours Gwen spent here in this studio, about the chaos of it, the litter, which seemed so untrue to Gwen with her orderliness, her focus, her precise timekeeping. Hilary could see one thin, steady arm extended towards the canvas, so that Gwen seemed to be hanging from the activity which engaged her as if from a hook; Gwen's eyes were wide, staring, stupefied with effort. Her mouth worked and twitched or sometimes fell open, half agape, like the mouth of an old man, the flesh drooping from the jawbone that it must one day leave naked, the staring skull. Where was Gwen, in fact? She seemed literally to have left her body, to have abandoned it, to be operating it from wherever she had gone. Her subject and her canvas and the eyes that interlaced them were the only things that existed.

In the end what Hilary felt was that everything in the studio which was not part of the painting that Gwen was making at the present time had to be considered as part of a discard pile, as part of what was rejected from the frame. All around the room were rubbished sketches, on paper, on canvases. In the jar was the dense, brown sludge of white spirit into which Gwen dipped her brushes to remove the colour not applied to the canvas. There on her hip was the mushroom of paint made when she wiped on to her apron whatever she wanted off the brush. And there on the palette was the mess of paint, which had begun as a few simple, discrete splodges of colour, then grown more multicoloured and complex even as the painting took on particularity and the image became more clearly realised. At some indefinable turning point, Hilary noticed, the palette was lost to disorder, to chaos, and the image on the canvas emerged as defined, nearly complete. To Hilary, this became intensely meaningful; she brooded on it through the hours as she waited and longed to see the clear thing on the canvas, the one thing in the room hidden from her all day each day.

At one point, Gwen became fed up with her palette, scraped everything off it with a knife, poured white spirit over it, rubbed it with a rag, until only a deep mauve-brown shine of oily glaze lay over the grain of the wood. This, too, she wiped away with paper towel, and she threw the paper towel on the floor, in rich-smelling, soaked clumps, crumpled. Then she began briskly, care-fully, with fresh paint.

Could these discards be recycled, Hilary wondered, if the pile was turned over, shuffled, picked through again? Could they become part of a winning hand? The paintings which she had finished no longer seemed to interest Gwen at all; she never looked through the stacks leaning against the walls around the room. Evidently, it was the doing that drove her. She wanted a new thing to notice and to give an account of.

Among the things that frightened Hilary was her instinct that she herself would be discarded once her portrait was complete. Gwen would lose interest in her. And Hilary began to realise that she didn't want the portrait to succeed. Or at least she didn't want it to be completed.

I have to go to New York, she thought, and get hold of my own work again. I have to move on before Gwen does. It wouldn't be just losing her as a friend. It would be getting used up and discarded. I couldn't deal with that right now. Not on top of everything else, and everything Gwen's been saying.

She looked at Gwen, the absent, robotic stance, the arm still extended to the canvas, the ghastly mouth, sexless, speechless, the hunting, greedy eyes. It's as if she's exited her body through the eyes, and she's out there in the air somewhere, probing, seeking, getting at me, trying to snatch my soul.

Silly girl, Hilary told herself. But she felt terrified. Even Gwen's white apron seemed to be part of the costume of the anatomist, or the butcher, or the coroner. Ludicrous, Hilary scoffed, as she imagined the apron stained at the hip not by paint but by blood.

Just then, Gwen chucked her brush into the dirty jar, threw down her filthy rag. 'Enough. It's a good place to stop. I think maybe we're really getting somewhere now.'

CHAPTER 9

They worked for one more day before Hilary went to New York, leaving the house and the studio both full and empty of herself. The intensity which Gwen had felt about the nude portrait was ruptured. Once or twice, she tried to work on it, to push it along in Hilary's absence, but in the end she only sat looking at it, thinking about Hilary. There was so little in it of Hilary's face. It was the position they had chosen, reclining so far back on the cushions. Nose, eyes, even lips were visible at such an obtuse angle that they might as well have been tiny ragged hills, dark mysterious caves. There was no discernible expression, no likeness to recognise. She's all body, Gwen thought, a human landscape.

Across the back of her mind trembled the recollection, like a little jolt of self-consciousness, that she had been slow to get to grips with Hilary's eyes. There we sat, she thought, facing each other, trying to draw closer, and yet right from the beginning, I felt her disappearing – into the chair, into the distance. Did I ever really command her attention?

The light in the studio seemed to be dead now. Gwen felt that she was waiting for something to happen though she didn't know what. The landscapes she had been working on when Hilary first arrived seemed to her now to be finished; at least there was nothing more that she wished to add to them. She might have gone on with the watercolours of the antiquities, but Hilary had taken the photographs.

She's done me in, that girl, thought Gwen. How unexpected. I was so worried, that day she showed up, about the interruption to my work, but I entirely mistook what the interruption might be. Here I am, just like Mark, abandoned. Right in the middle of this intimate, important thing.

For the first time in a very long while, Gwen left off painting for a few days and devoted herself to housekeeping chores and to Will. She sorted through some canvases and left a telephone message for her dealer in New York, thinking she might encourage him to come around and take a look after all the next time he was in town. And she got ready to repaint the bathroom ceiling.

Lawrence knew that things weren't right.

'Can I see what you two have done?' he asked gently. 'Where you've got to, that you feel so marooned?'

'Maybe I pushed too hard,' Gwen confided, leading him up to the studio after Will had gone to bed. 'I need to catch up with myself. I've been thinking there might be some way that I need to grow by sitting still and by waiting. But it feels like torture.'

She opened the door, threw on the lights, held out one open palm towards the enormous canvas on the easel in the middle of the floor and then stood aside unhappily.

Lawrence was silent for a long time, staring at the flesh laid out point-blank, hotly coloured, right at the front of the canvas, groin on.

When he spoke, his voice was tight, breathless. 'You've never done anything like this before, Gwen. It's completely new.'

'I know.' She stood sunk in her thin, enwrapping arms, staring, then lifted one hand to her chin, covering her whole mouth with it as if she wanted to disappear inside herself. Her half-bowed head didn't reach as high as Lawrence's shoulder. 'But on the other hand it's the same.'

'Yes. It's the same, but it's completely different. A climate, an atmosphere. Entirely there, enveloping. A scene of nature . . . a conflagration.'

They fell silent again.

Finally Lawrence sighed out, in an exhausted voice, with no

play at exaggeration, 'It's very powerful. My goodness.' Then he turned towards her, smiling with pleasure.

She smiled back, excited, nervous. 'So what the hell do I do now?'

'On the cusp of this breakthrough, and your muse does a runner?'

Gwen nodded, still smiling, but embarrassed now, feeling it was somehow all her own fault and wondering how she had let herself get into a situation where her subject matter could have a mind of its own, could dislike the conversation, could get up and go. Because now she felt that no other subject matter would do.

Lawrence saw the trouble in her freckled, goblin face and in her quivering eyes, the risk she had taken with such confidence, the wound in herself opened and exposed. He knew that she couldn't go back to where she had been before, not Gwen. She would have to go on in the direction she was now headed.

'You get someone else to model for you.' It seemed to him obvious, inevitable.

Gwen only looked at him, raising her eyebrows sceptically, as if to say, Right; but who?

'I'll do it, sweetheart,' he said. 'Why don't I?'

Her eyes widened in surprise and then softened. 'It's a thought. I don't know. It's a thought.' She reached for his hand and kissed it gratefully, feeling charmed. Such a generous offer. 'How would you find the time, though?'

'How much time do you need?'

'All the time you have. Unlimited access if possible. From early in the mornings, when the light is good.' There was enthusiasm in her voice, but doubt as well, playful doubt. He couldn't be serious, she was thinking.

'I guess I'm not being realistic,' Lawrence admitted.

'Look, don't worry.' And to hide her disappointment, she told him, 'All my paintings are really about you anyway.'

Lawrence looked startled. 'Hmm,' he grunted. 'That's a revealing thing for you to say. But this painting of Hilary is not about me, Gwen. It's about something altogether different. Something – ferocious.'

'Ferocious?'

'Well, I don't know if that's what I mean. It's just – something I didn't foresee about you. Not altogether. Although, maybe I recognise it. Maybe I shouldn't feel surprised. It seems as if you've grown up in some way – or maybe grown down. It's deep. It hits the gut. Beautiful, the colours are beautiful – flesh and mud and jewel tones. Heavy, gorgeous. But if I hang around this picture long enough it's going to change my life. It doesn't leave one alone.'

With that he stepped away from the canvas, turned his back on it, as if to break its spell. He wandered around the room looking at everything else, trying to get abreast of Gwen, recollecting her excited reports of this and that progress, trying to feel his way into the sequence of her life lately and to understand her obsession with Hilary. 'I like all these watercolours.'

'It's our museum,' Gwen said. 'Hil's and mine.'

'I've never known you to take such an interest in civilisation,' Lawrence teased. 'Rather wonderful. All that we failed to teach you, we dons, flung back in our faces. Obviously we were appealing to you in entirely the wrong way. We should have signed you up for the Ashmolean. If Beazley hadn't figured out how to illustrate Greek pottery, you would have done. Hey?'

She gave him a poisonous look, comical.

'Not that I mean to diminish your other talents.' Then he said, 'Would you let me have a few of these? For my rooms in Oxford? I like them.'

'They're Hil's.'

'But she's left them. There are so many. How would she ever know?'

'She'd know. She knows every object in that collection. It's like her family, her children. Think about it, Lawrence. I can't take the stuff away from her all over again. The whole point was to make it up to her.'

'Ah, yes, because you failed to find her a suitable husband.'

'No! Because of her split with Mark, which might have lost her control over it all. And I'm not done with finding her a husband yet.' She said this flirtatiously, challenging him. 'She'll be back. Roland just left another message on the answering machine when we were painting the other day, and besides, I think there's a little something going on with Hugo.' She felt brazen mentioning Hugo, as if she was daring herself to get him out in the open. 'He's a little young, but what the hell. I can sort of see her point about him.'

Lawrence only half reacted. 'Who was the message for?' he asked.

'Me. But I still believe in it. I'll call Roland tomorrow. We need to catch up.'

Lawrence smiled and continued to poke around the room, looking. He bent down next to the bed and picked up something half under it. In her whirl of housekeeping, Gwen had stripped the linen and the bedspread off that morning to wash them.

'Trimalchio's candelabrum,' Lawrence murmured, looking at it, then held it out to Gwen. 'So what's this?'

Gwen had to rise on her tiptoes to see it. 'One of Hil's photos of the collection. It probably fell out of her briefcase, or out of one of those little plastic sleeves she keeps all her notes in. What did you call it?'

'Just a joke. Trimalchio – in Petronius, you know, in the *Satyricon*. He has a huge candelabrum like that in his house. It's what I've been writing about. I've told you.'

'Was I listening?'

'Do you ever listen when I talk about my work?' But he wasn't annoyed; he was quizzical. 'I'm not sure anyone ever listens. Maybe my students don't even listen. Although to be fair, I suppose I hardly listen to them half the time. Do any of us care, any more, about these ancient texts and ancient thoughts?'

150

'Of course we care!' She felt angry at the idea of Lawrence's work being neglected; then she caught herself on the irony, guilty. 'It's always more vivid for me if there's a picture. I mean – if your candelabrum, the one you're writing about, looked like this, then now I get it. So tell me again?'

He sat down on the blue ticking of the mattress, studied the photograph, tilting it backwards and forwards in his hands, feeling uneasy now that Gwen had asked. 'I've been trying to find a way to bring it all up to date. Squabbling about it with Roland – and with –' how to put it? '– other – colleagues. Any who care to hear what I'm doing.'

Gwen sat down beside him, very close, her thigh running along his, her hip nestled into him, and she bent her head again over the photograph. 'It's pretty fabulous, isn't it,' she said. 'Look how intricate the leaves are and yet how massive. And the fluting, too, so substantial. Too bad we don't have Hil's description. But maybe it's – what do you think? Bronze?'

'Almost certainly. The style of decoration is Corinthian. Acanthus leaves. It would have been expensive.'

'See that guy?'

There was a figure standing on one side in the background, a man in a dark suit, stooped; the candelabrum came to the rounded bulk of his shoulders, and one hand was reaching out to rest on top of it, but his head was out of the frame.

'That's what I mean – Trimalchio,' Lawrence chuckled. 'Measuring himself.'

'Or measuring the candelabrum. He must have stood next to it to give scale for the photograph? Don't you think? Maybe that's Eddie Doro. Or some dealer?'

'Was Doro hunched like that? He looks quite misshapen – at the shoulder.'

'I never met him. But maybe it's just age? He was way into his eighties by the time he died.'

'Uncanny,' said Lawrence, 'that he should have had a hunchback.

151

We must ask Hilary.' He held the photograph up in front of them both, then looked down at Gwen, considering. 'If he were of about average height that would make the candelabrum nearly as high as you. Hmm? The height of an adolescent boy.'

'So go on, tell me about Trimalchio. Was he a hunchback?'

He put his arm around her, encouraged by her warmth. 'No. Although he is probably a portrait of a real slave called Clesippus who was. According to Pliny, Clesippus was auctioned off as a boy along with an expensive candelabrum – a Corinthian one, mind you, exactly the style of Hilary's. Because of the hunchback, you see, he was considered worthless, and that's why he was thrown in, as part of the deal – a bonus – with the candelabrum. Which seems a bizarre coincidence, with Hilary's photograph. But only a coincidence, I remind myself –' Coincidence which can mislead us, trick us into making false connections, Lawrence thought. He drew a deep breath, as if he could draw discipline, clarity, from the air. 'Even though Clesippus was a hunchback, the woman who got him in the auction took him into her bed, and when she died, she left him her fortune. So eventually, he built himself a spectacular tomb – a "*sepulchrum nobile*", Pliny says, suitable for a nobleman. The tomb has long since collapsed, but the stones have been reused, as stones often are, and one can still go and read his name carved alongside his mistress's in this enormous piece of limestone, three metres across, in a modern wall just south of Rome. It survives to this very day.'

It was too much for Gwen, more than she wanted to know. But someone, she thought, must be interested. 'Have you told Hilary?' she asked, grasping faint-heartedly at it.

'I told her a bit, yes. The one night, over supper. It makes such an illuminating contrast to Jean Valjean, who has only an obscure grave in a remote corner of Père Lachaise and no epitaph at all. The point being that if his soul is really with God, he needs no epitaph. Valjean's life is all about compassion, about giving everything away –'

'Jean Valjean?'

'In *Les Misérables*. It's been so bloody popular, and people seem to know all about those candlesticks.'

'*Les Misérables*? Is that why Hilary's been reading it? How on earth did you ever think of that?'

Lawrence sat up. He let go of the photograph into Gwen's hand.

'It's just –' Gwen went on, 'I'm amazed anyone reads those big Victor Hugo novels any more.'

'But the musical,' he said, 'in the West End – it's been on for years.'

'Oh. Have you seen it? When was that?'

The time has come, he thought. He felt unexpectedly defensive, but he was quick to answer, as if it would affirm his intention to be forthright with her. 'Three or four years ago?'

She thought about it, inclining against him with her head bowed, and then she said quietly, accepting it, 'When Will was tiny.'

'Yes.' She must know already, he thought. She must have always known.

'You used to have to scrounge for entertainment, didn't you?' And after a pause, 'All the way down to London? I can't picture you at a musical!' She turned her face up towards him and kissed him on the neck. 'Poor you.'

'Well. I rather enjoyed it,' he said automatically. Then, feeling muddled, 'I mean – at the time.'

She studied his expression – as if he had swallowed something wrong – and she felt amused. 'And you kept it from me? Your slumming? What – you thought I'd sneer because it was commercial?'

'No. Not because it was commercial. I –' How much harder to begin to explain now, as she looked him straight in the eye, fond and familiar, so confident that she knew whom she was looking at, whom she was leaning against.

'I don't have any problem about popular stuff,' she laughed. 'I just don't like what's out there to control how I see things.'

'At the time – I didn't keep it from you on purpose. I meant to tell you. And then of course, I assumed you knew –' His voice staggered with effort.

'Whoa whoa whoa!' She still thought they were only playing, arguing some specious distinction between high and low culture. 'It really doesn't matter, Lawrence. I'm sure I wouldn't have wanted to know. I trust you on that.'

'But you mustn't trust me. You must listen. I think it's best if I tell you in full.'

She caught his tone. The edge of fear in it. It sobered her up. 'Let's not go back over those times, Lawrence. You know I hate the past. Hilary had me filling her in endlessly, hoping ours was some key to her own. It was kind of exhausting, and I'm sick of it. Honestly.' She turned her back into the curve of his arm, stroked his thigh. 'I'm sorry for – if I wasn't always what I might like to have been to you. But we made it through, yeah? Whatever desperate measures I drove you to. Can you bear to keep it to yourself?'

He was paralysed. It wrung his heart that Gwen should be the one to apologise. How could he force Clare on her if she was going to blame herself? It would be unjust, even if she only blamed herself a little. It's my own problem, he thought, as he had thought off and on for many months. We're in a good place now, the two of us. And Will. A safe place. But it sickened him a little, his sense of relief. It seemed like evidence of cowardice.

'Tell me what you're doing with it, what you're writing now,' she went on, insisting. 'That's more interesting, don't you think?'

He pulled away from her a little, then a little further, turning towards her, and he took her face in his hands. 'If that's what you really want to know,' he said. His thumbs glided ever so lightly down her cheeks. 'Forgive me,' he added.

For an instant, he wondered what Gwen herself would say

about holding back from anything that seemed so significant, whatever the cost. But I've decided now, he told himself, fighting a swoon under his lungs as the chance moved out of reach – the chance to be forgiven by her. He leaned down and kissed her on the forehead, sealing it. And then he felt it close around him, as if Clare were only now hardening into a lie, as if for the first time it was genuinely wrong, what had begun as a kind of personal allowance for necessary self-indulgence or experiment. Something which he and Gwen had merely not yet got around to addressing together. The rivets were in.

He struggled to his feet. 'Jean Valjean –' he began, squinting uncomfortably, snatching for a thread in his bundle of thoughts. 'Jean Valjean steals from the only man who is ever kind to him. And instead of sending Valjean back to prison, that man, the Bishop of Digne, gives Valjean his most valued possession, his pair of silver candlesticks. So, with the candlesticks, comes freedom – as in Petronius. But instead of the sexual intimacy between master and slave which you get in Petronius, Hugo describes a kind of spiritual intimacy whereby the bishop – the flame, let's say, in one candlestick – and Valjean the flame in the other candlestick – become "one" as a result of the bishop's forgiveness. There is a moment of spiritual ecstasy: the bishop floods Valjean's soul with radiance and takes him over for good.'

'Always a little on the weird side, don't you think?' Gwen teased. 'Religious and sexual parallels? Though acts of charity can be strange that way, the bonds they create. I remember you lit the candles like that when Roland came for dinner with Hilary. So what was that – a little magic ritual you were performing?'

Lawrence acknowledged Gwen's cynicism with a twisted, pre-occupied smile and began to roam the floor. For a moment, he pictured the two flames. Why is it, he wondered, that the exact sin must be confessed in order to gain forgiveness? Why isn't love in general enough to make the flames one? He rolled his shoulders backwards again and again as he walked, as if he were trying to roll something off his back, some wearying and unnatural burden. Then he stood up, opened his chest, shoved his hands into his trouser pockets. He wanted it to feel wonderful, telling Gwen about his work. 'So: Is Jean Valjean ever really free?' he asked loftily. 'Or is he now the bishop's convict – a slave of Christ? Valjean changes his ways, he rises in the world, but he never parts with the candlesticks despite the risk that they might reveal his criminal past.'

Lawrence halted his stride for an instant, pursed his lips disdainfully. 'Of course, to a Christian, spiritual servitude is perfectly acceptable. It makes for great drama – melodrama.' He swung towards her, chopping the air with both hands, then turning his hands flat, palms down, as if he were levelling something, shaping it. 'There are so many ways to travel with the discussion. In Christian ideology, the candle lit at the baptism stands for a man's life, for one soul. And we can trace that back to Roman culture. For instance, at the Saturnalia, the Romans gave one another candles, and the Latin Church inherited that use of candles in its Christmas rituals. The festival of the Saturnalia – just before the winter solstice – marked the turn in the year from growing darkness to growing light. Roughly, the 17th of December.'

'When the slaves were waited on by their masters.'

'Exactly. People are universally attracted to the energy let loose by turning everything upside down like that. And I've always thought how well that particular custom foretold the way in which Christianity and its slavish values – of humility, abjectness, mortification and so on – were to well up from the very bottom of classical culture, churning the Roman world over on itself, inverting its ideals and hierarchies. In modern times, social and ideological upheaval of that magnitude has generally been brought about only by bloody revolutions. The Romans seemed to think they could stave off such a thing by playing at it once a year, don't you see? Indulging the unruly impulse from below. *What*,

I ask you, made them so certain that the slaves would willingly return to being ruled the next day? They had nerve, the Romans.'

'Yes,' said Gwen. Her mind drifted to Hilary, the sudden departure, the unfinished portrait. An unruly impulse; a reversal of roles. I knew exactly what I was doing, she thought to herself. It's just that Hilary didn't know. And Gwen felt the unexpected loss all over again of the interest which had gripped her, which had been drawing her on with such intensity day after day. Why should Hilary ever want to return at all? she wondered. What was the benefit of it to her, being painted?

'I just need more time to work on it,' Lawrence was saying. 'I get interrupted all the time nowadays.'

She dragged herself back to him. 'Interruptions are almost unbearable,' she agreed.

She did feel sympathetic. She sat on the bed with the photograph in her hand, looking up at Lawrence like the pupil she had once been. In his face, she saw clearly the self-doubt which had been hampering him lately, his regal calm strained by effort, his pale skin creased with anxiety. How can one person know anything for certain about so vast a tract of time, so far-reaching and complex a set of changes? People do, thought Gwen. They believe they do. But Lawrence, who was so scrupulous about facts, so responsible towards any arguments countering his own? Here he was trying to be interesting when it was far more difficult to be correct, and correct was something she knew he could never stop trying for.

His excitement disturbed her. There was something about it that she didn't recognise. Something forced or lacking in authenticity. She pushed the feeling aside, trained her eyes on him and wished him to persevere.

'There's a chap in the States, you see, who takes the view that Trimalchio is trapped in a kind of underworld of ex-slaves, social climbers, vulgarians – a demi-monde.'

'So? Don't we think Petronius was a bit of an elitist?'

'Arbiter of taste to Nero? He looked down even on the Emperor!' Lawrence lifted his chin in mock grandiosity. 'This American has analysed the imagery. He's demonstrated that Trimalchio's world is really the world of the dead. His house is decorated like a Roman funerary monument.' Lawrence was muttering now, muttering at the chap in the States. 'Can anyone ever really be free? Maybe death *is* the only liberator. And that's why the funeral monument is so important – it's the final statement. Sums up the life. The free man wants to control that, doesn't he? His stature, his reputation after death. Any man does. Petronius, Hugo, all of us.'

'Edward Doro,' added Gwen.

Lawrence stopped pacing, looked completely stumped, then gave a slow nod. 'Yes,' he agreed at last, 'Edward Doro. Although one would like to think that his particular monument is not merely an attempt to glorify his name. I get the impression from Hilary that it's an extremely fine collection which we will all be lucky to see.'

'But he didn't leave it out of generosity.'

'Why should that matter? So long as it's justified by its quality.'

'But maybe Hilary thought so?'

He considered it. 'I see what you mean. Perhaps she's been disappointed in this mentor of hers, and that's why she feels so badly hurt. Wrongly idolised him. People often make such mistakes. Certainly one feels that she allowed him to rule her thoughts, which doesn't suit her. There's much more to Hilary than she lets on. Just as you've shown in the portrait.'

Beauty is not necessarily about generosity, Gwen thought. The collection will be a benefit in itself, if it's good enough. The same with the portrait.

She watched Lawrence as he lumbered past the long back window. The night sky was gathered just outside – lit above the rooftops by the neon, continual glow of London and marked out in the invisible brick wall on the far side of the garden by a few rectangles of light announcing comfort, huddled warmth, television. The studio seemed somehow too small for Lawrence, too low-ceilinged. But the night outside was far too big. She sensed in him the possibility of inward collapse, the threat of confusion. She wanted to ward it off.

Why must there be a lesson in everything? Why must Pliny provide us with a real slave to unpick Petronius's fiction? She hated Pliny. She wanted Lawrence to stop, to get out of her studio. Compassion doesn't interest me, Gwen decided. She couldn't bear to explain this to him. She felt so certain of what she wanted, and she was prepared to be ruthless about it, but just at the moment Lawrence seemed all astray in himself, weakened by equivocation, talking of mysticism, in wild generalities.

She sprang up from the bed with the photograph in her hands. 'I can paint the candelabrum for you, Lawrence. A watercolour. Hilary will like the connection, so she won't mind. You can take it to Oxford, and maybe it will inspire you in some way. In any case, it will give me something to do. Which we both know I need right now.'

CHAPTER 10

In fact, it was Hugo that Gwen decided to paint, because he had such a strong whiff of Hilary about him now. Some kind of heat had gradually transferred to him from the attention Hilary had paid him. Lying in the bath exactly as she had foreseen, staring at the small brown stains haloing the ceiling lights and planning to paint them out with the can of matt white she had bought, Gwen knew that she would never do it. She felt that it would be like painting out Hugo's eyes. It gave her a little twist of pain, bitter-sweet, like pity, or even self-pity, as though she would be hurting herself if she failed to appreciate Hugo in exactly the right way.

When she glided in now to the tail ends of Will's piano lessons and sat down in the old yellow armchair, she would quietly study Hugo's face. That's what I want to paint, she would think, not the bathroom ceiling.

It was such a clean, plain face. Hardly anything to it, a bright-ness around the brown eyes, eagerness, alertness, but calm and strangely boneless. She felt challenged by its youth, by its form-lessness, by its refusal to give anything away. What was he thinking? Had Hilary been able to tell?

When Hugo played the piano, the expression remained just as enigmatic, the face just as innocent of intention, and yet his leaping fingers filled the room with shifting moods, changing colours, a sequence of experiences. Gwen began to sense that he was like an actor, someone who could lend himself intimately to any musical role. Whatever style, whatever emotion was called for, he could articulate it with this complex, complete, evocative language. He offered details so subtle, so fresh, that she couldn't have foreseen them or described them, yet she felt familiar with them as soon as she heard them. Ah, yes, she kept thinking to herself as she recognised something new, Ah, yes, it's uncanny what he seems to *know*.

He didn't use many English words teaching Will; again and again Gwen would hear him say to Will, Like this. And there would follow a little demonstration. Will would show that he understood by copying – smaller, slower, the splayed, chubby fingers lisping Hugo's language of piano.

When Gwen listened from her bed or her studio to Hugo practising, she thought that the emotions seemed both profound and straightforward, and the more she considered it, the more she recognised that they were emotions which could not be expressed with thoroughness or sophistication in any other way than by playing the piano. He's a musician, she thought, because he has to be. Nothing else speaks for him. It's something that he has understood a composer was hearing in his mind's ear. That's why I can't tell who he is. He gives over to the idea. The idea is what he's certain of.

Could she show that? The face of this kind of an actor? One day, she arrived at the lesson with a sketch pad, thinking she might capture Hugo in the grip of something that drew him out. But although she opened the sketch pad and balanced it on her knees, she made no mark on it.

Afterwards, just as Will started out the door ahead of her, she asked Hugo whether she could sketch him sometime when Will wasn't there. 'Playing something – some piece?'

Hugo looked at the wire-bound sketch pad still pressed in her arms, opened back upon itself at the blank page. 'You painted Hilary, didn't you,' he said, as if it somehow explained why Gwen might want to sketch him.

But his way of getting comfortable with the idea made Gwen feel off balance.

'We didn't get to finish before she left,' Gwen started, thinking she needed to explain. She wondered what Hugo knew about the painting, what Hilary had told him. When had they talked about it? Where had they talked about it? In this flat? What room had they stood in? Or had they been standing up at all?

'I'd like to see the painting,' Hugo said in a friendly way.

She felt relieved to learn he hadn't already seen it, hadn't gone up to the studio with Hilary, some night maybe, when she herself wasn't there.

As she stood pondering what might lie between Hugo and Hilary, not saying anything and feeling drawn towards the open door and towards Will, Hugo offered her a bargain.

'Come in when you like and paint me or sketch me or whatever it is you have in mind. If it bothers me, I'll tell you, and – you'll just have to stop? Afterwards, you can show me your painting of Hilary. What do you reckon?'

'I guess Hilary wouldn't mind.' She hesitated, conscious of using Hilary as bait to get something she wanted from Hugo; it didn't feel right.

'I hadn't thought of her minding,' Hugo said. 'I suppose you ought to ask her permission? Is that how it's done?' Suddenly his voice was a drawl, pinched and dry; he straightened his knees and his back, drew himself up with rectitude.

Where had he been keeping that ultra-correct voice, Gwen wondered, that voice in which Englishmen discuss the rules of cricket? On impulse, she defied it. 'You can't possibly care how it's done. I mean – there *is* no way that it's "done". No etiquette. It's just – Hilary's a friend, and I – it's a nude –' She found that she was laughing, blushing.

'Mummy, are we having tea?' Will had reappeared in the doorway.

Gwen started, still red, then smiled at Will, a long, indulgent smile that soothed her, sorted her out. 'Yes, we are having tea. Right now.'

Then she looked Hugo in the eye and said in a confident tone,

'I can show you the painting whenever you like.' She felt reckless, taking full possession of the painting. But after all, it was hers, and she had other things to get on with. 'Tomorrow?'

Hugo looked at the floor. It had become an administrative question, an event to timetable. 'Tomorrow,' he said slowly, grabbing at his hair by the handful, tugging, thinking, then looking up again. 'Yes, I think tomorrow would be fine.'

'I'll come here first,' she announced, with a downward, finalising cadence. 'What time do you practise?'

'Oh – well – whenever.'

'I'll listen until I hear you.'

She stepped out the door, taking Will's expectant hand in her clammy one, as if his expectation could save her from something.

But the next morning, it was like trying to draw a picture of a windstorm. Schumann's *Fantasia*, the first movement. So much was going on, and yet none of the sounds showed on the paper. All her attempts seemed melodramatic – Hugo's face taken over by a generic expression of longing, somehow fake, almost ridiculous. She wanted colour, but she hadn't felt easy about bringing paints in with her. And she felt rattled, as if the air was thrashing at her.

I want just him, she thought darkly, not the music, not the yearning. I want the enigma. And I want him in my space, where I can really see him.

Finally, when he stopped playing, she simply asked him: 'Would you sit for me up in the studio, Hugo? I mean, if you have time. Maybe if – do you ever rest, between practices?'

He laughed. 'It's not something I need to rest from. Anyway, why do you want me? Seriously. I'm not trying to be coy. I can see in a mirror. I've got a pretty ordinary face.'

'I think that's really the whole point. I mean –' she rolled her eyes heavenward. 'Well, not ordinary, just –'

Now they both laughed, for a strange length of time. When they stopped laughing, Gwen opened her mouth to say something, but she thought that whatever she might say would seem irrelevant. The focus of their conversation had broken up. How could they negotiate the hole between them? They started laughing again.

'Go on, you can't hurt my feelings,' Hugo said. 'It's not about that, is it?'

'No. It's really not about that. It's about — There's a kind of vitality. Something that doesn't show itself on the surface. Not obviously, anyway.'

'Now that I've asked you, I suppose I already knew the answer.'

Gwen was a little frightened by this statement. She felt suddenly unprotected. She hadn't intended to explain to Hugo what she was interested in; she felt she couldn't explain it apart from painting the picture. That was how she meant to find out about him — by painting him. That was how she always did find out everything, how she mastered things. Hugo ought to understand that, she thought. He's — the same, in his own way.

She was sitting in the armchair, pulled up near to the piano keyboard, her sketchbook sullied with unique frustration on her knees. Hugo got up from the piano bench, unfolding his lean, endless frame towards the ceiling, reaching for his hair, burying his fingers in it. She jumped up, closing the book, so that he couldn't see what she had drawn.

'Whatever you want, Gwen. It's fine with me.'

She felt somehow stunned, looking up at him, and wondered how she had blinded herself to what was coming. I ought to have realised, she thought. It's partly about this. Of course. It has to be.

He took his hands from his hair and reached out towards her; she didn't move. So, with a step, he had her in his grasp, both arms pinned in his strong fingers, and he leaned down and kissed her on the mouth.

She felt she ought to be considering a lot of things just now:

whether kissing was a good idea, what effect it would have on everything else that seemed to be in play. It tugged at her, like Will tugging at her hand, what she ought to be considering. Hilary. Lawrence. But then consideration dropped away. The kiss seemed to be complete in itself. A world. An exciting, unfamiliar one in which she felt ready to lose herself.

There were piano legs, stools, piles of music books, which they knocked against, knocked down, hard edges, toppling thumps. They backed away from the discomfort, the anarchy, instinctively, without noticing, until they collapsed on Hugo's jittery bed, which was as long as Hugo, as narrow, as unwashed – the softest horizontal surface in the flat, smelling of his skin, nearly filling the bare, tiny room in which it stood.

Even on the bed, there were painful realities. Hugo seemed to Gwen to be all sweat and bones. Where among these knee joints, elbows, endless shins, was the pot of flesh that had enticed her? Who was she in bed with? Or what for that matter? A folding chair? Her mouth fixed easily to Hugo's with bliss-inducing suction, but all the other parts of their two bodies seemed misaligned. Whatever she reached for was further away, thinner, more muscled, or more unyielding than she expected. As they tussled and writhed, she began to laugh at the awkwardness of it, realising that they would have to resort to words.

For instance, 'Wait,' she said. 'Wait.'

She needed time to open her eyes and actually look at Hugo, how he was made. Who he was.

She had been brooding on him so intently that she had created some other Hugo, a Hugo of the imagination, a Hugo she already possessed.

He's not Lawrence, she thought. And he's not Hilary either. How can I feel surprised by that? For she knew she had been riding on them all – an inward wave of sexual energy. Dark, rolling sensations in which she wanted to bathe, as if they were liquid. The personages of her household, her intimates of whom she had no reason to be wary, moving around her, had drawn her animal spirits this way and that, loosening them from familiar, specific holds, enlivening them.

Still, it wasn't easy to immerse. Here was the fact of a strange man, a very young one as she had wished Hilary to recognise, bold, strong and unsure, like the boys she and Hilary had passed powering their wobbly shell along the Thames. A boy of whom she might need to take command.

I'm not used to that with sex, Gwen thought. Something in her drew back, read the pricks and kicks as a practical advisory. It won't work, she thought, making love with Hugo. It's not really what I wanted, his actual body. Is it? Not all anyway.

They were lying very still now, and Hugo kissed her again, sweetly and long, as if he felt a tenderness towards her that had little to do with sex. As if he was, indeed, prepared to wait.

We can get up now, Gwen thought. That's an acquittal. Kind, not angry. At peace with this thing about bodies.

He agreed to come to the studio, and he let her settle him in the red moroccan leather chair. They worked for a couple of hours starting the portrait. But sex built up between them like a thunderhead. Through her mind again and again ran the recollection of him reaching down to kiss her, gripping her arms. She felt startled by it repeatedly, trying to paint.

He wasn't a boy, after all; what did he want from her?

She considered that it was a particular challenge, now, to gather these energies back into the painting. Hilary and I just don't run to actual sex, she thought. It's sublimated between us pretty well completely. Two women. Friends. I never realised how secure it was, tilting straight at it. There was hardly any chance of undoing that taboo even if I thought I was testing something with her. But with a man and a woman – Well, she thought, how is it done? How do I keep him in the chair?

Hugo's eyes were jostling her, molten, bored with the deal they had struck. Gwen knew perfectly well what was in his mind, and she wanted to tell him that it was more electric in anticipation than it could be in reality. But the mere idea of such a conversation was a distraction. And eventually she began to think the other way around: that the thunderhead would go with a burst of rain. Until suddenly it seemed completely obvious, something she already knew about sex, which she had learned with Lawrence: that you could get free of its insistence if you went ahead and had enough of it. She and Hugo would have to try again, she decided, and maybe again, and it didn't matter whether it was any good between them; if it was bad, so much the better.

By lunchtime, they were in Hilary's bed. It seemed easy now for them to play. They became light-hearted, curious, talkative. Gwen began to feel that she knew exactly what she wanted from Hugo; nevertheless, she kept on being surprised by what she got. When he seemed most plastic to her desires, she was most aware of his. Who is the Pygmalion here? she wondered. Shouldn't it be me? And yet she felt herself come to life in Hugo's hands.

It was an ardent, unselfconscious adventure. Nobody was in charge. Nobody cared to be. Unless something intervened, now, right away, it was going to be a love affair. There were empty beds, empty rooms on nearly every floor of the house. How had they managed to avoid getting into one sooner?

What Lawrence noticed was that Hugo began practising the piano much later into the evenings.

'I never used to hear it much,' he observed to Gwen as they lay reading in bed a few nights later. 'I guess he always played when I was out.'

'It's my fault,' Gwen murmured without looking up from *The Princess Casamassima*. 'I'm painting a picture of him, so he's giving me the morning hours at the moment. Is it bothering you?'

'Of course it isn't bothering me,' said Lawrence. And then with characteristic grandeur, 'I love it. It's passionate – beyond words. Don't you think?'

He looked sideways over his glasses down towards her face, but she didn't look back. He laughed at her. 'By God, you are hard-hearted! How can you not be moved? I mean – the dear chap must be playing with both hands at the same time.'

At last she looked up, pink, protesting. 'I love it, too. But I hear it all day long. I filter it out. I have to.'

'I see.' Lawrence patted her hand, smiling. 'How I envy your concentration. Nothing interferes with you.'

She smiled at him now, grateful for his generosity and his enjoyment.

But she hadn't turned a page for a long time. She lay intoxi-cated under the notes fizzing around them – sparks from the fire-works exploding over their heads. She was drenched with sound, with excitement. And when they turned off the light, she lay swollen with joy beside her husband of fourteen years while her lover serenaded them both in the tumultuous dark.

Lawrence took her hand under the covers. 'Another nude?'

She didn't answer for a long time, then suddenly, as if starting from a trance, she said sharply, 'Oh, no. Not a nude. No. Just – a face.'

'Roland mightn't like a nude – of another man.'

Again she didn't answer for a long time, and then she said, 'Roland?'

'He's coming up tomorrow. For supper.'

'Oh God. His messages. I meant to phone him back.'

'I'm afraid we both rather let him down, allowing Hilary to slip away. I get the impression he assumed she'd be here indefin-itely.'

'Ah. He *did* want to see her again.' She said it as if she had accomplished something, a little win over Lawrence.

'He claims he was only ringing you to find out her plans –

about Doro's collection and whether she was keen to keep her position, because he is often asked about jobs.'

'So well defended, poor Roland. Hil's only called once.' Gwen didn't feel great about this. 'She's mostly spending her time in the library at Columbia. Working for an old teacher, to tide herself over. And thinking of approaching some of the trustees privately because Mark won't see her. You told Roland she went back?'

'Well, I have told him today, yes. It surprised me, really, that he was fussed about it. Hilary had only to leave town, eh, to make herself utterly desirable all round?' He squeezed Gwen's hand sympathetically, thinking about the abandoned portrait, then let the hand drop and turned on to his side. 'I thought we could make it up to him. He's been longing to see what you're painting. You promised to show him what's in your studio.'

'Did I?'

'I believe you did. Last time he was here?' Lawrence's voice was warm, cajoling, as he shifted about on his hip and his shoulder, burrowing into the mattress and the pillows.

'OK, so I will. It's not a nude.'

'I told him he ought to see the one you've done of Hilary, though.'

'That'll blow his mind altogether now that he's missed her.'

'It does rather make one think differently of her,' Lawrence observed.

Just then, with a great massing of chords – crescendo, ritardando, resolution – the piano fell silent. They heard the stool scrape backwards across the floor.

'Why don't you ask Hugo to join us for supper, too? Could you persuade him? That might offer a suitable distraction – meeting your new subject?'

Gwen was silent, stinging a little in the dark.

'Maybe if you gave him the morning off being painted, then he wouldn't have to practise all evening?'

*   *   *

In fact, Gwen couldn't get enough of Hugo, and it hadn't occurred to her that she had anything to hide. On the contrary, she felt as if she had something to show and to share, even if she wasn't intending to be explicit about it. There he was, a fleshly marvel, at the centre of their household, and they could all take pleasure in him. So she invited him. And he agreed to come.

After supper, the four of them went up to the studio together to see the painting of Hilary. It produced the same awed silence in the group that it had produced in Lawrence and in Hugo the first time each of them had seen it. It seemed to defy commentary.

The portrait of Hugo also produced a silence; there wasn't much to it yet, nothing to talk about. A green wash; the heart shape of an unstructured face; honeyed, unreal golden skin; holes where the eyes should have been; an empty space at the bottom of the canvas, so that the face seemed to float in the air, or on an updraught of wind.

Roland observed, glancing at Hugo, 'It's going to be tough as hell to get that, Gwen, so – lacking in obvious drama.'

'Ordinary, you mean?' asked Hugo mildly, both hands in his trouser pockets.

Roland winced. 'Sorry. That's my foot in it.'

'Not at all. It's what I've thought myself,' said Hugo. 'But Gwen says it's really not about that. She's after something else, some-thing not especially obvious, something she can sense emanating or animating –' and he turned to her, cocking an eyebrow, pulling one hand free from his pocket and reaching with it to his hair. 'After all, look what she saw in Hilary. What is that – force? That vigour?'

Gwen smiled beatifically at Hugo's embarrassment, at his sly teasing. Then she scolded, giggling at first, but growing more earnest, 'You all trump it up to such pompous heights. Just let me do it. There *is* something that the energy flows from, something you can see if you really look. I'll get it. Just let me. I'm going downstairs to clean up.'

The three men mooched around a little longer, until Hugo said, 'I could help her, couldn't I?'

'I should think she would love that,' said Lawrence. 'How kind.'

No sooner was Hugo out the door than Roland said, 'That young man is in love with your wife.'

Lawrence opened his eyes wide, stroked his curling, grey-blond hair smooth over his scalp with a few passes. 'You reckon?' Then he nodded. 'Well, everyone is. So it would make perfect sense. How can you tell?' He sounded only vaguely curious.

'He's just gone to help her do the washing-up.'

Lawrence laughed it off. 'That's not enough evidence.'

'He's letting her paint his portrait for Christ's sake.'

Now Lawrence took off his spectacles and put them on the draining board, then rubbed his face and his eyes for a long time. 'More like it,' he finally pronounced, turning his back to the sink and leaning against it casually.

Roland rushed on impatiently. 'Frankly, it seems quite obvious. The way he looks at her, as if he's prodding her with a special plea of some kind, as if he knows something and he's reminding her of it.'

'I suppose you'd be able to tell, Roland.' Lawrence continued to sound nonplussed. 'Has he tried to shut you out?'

'I've been shut out for years, so I wouldn't feel any difference. But I'm really thinking about you, not me. It's you I care for, Lawrence.' Roland's face bristled with indignation, with longing to be understood.

Lawrence lifted his eyebrows, taking it in. Then he looked solemn, honouring the statement. 'That's very kind, Roland. I'm grateful.'

There was a pause filled by shuffling of feet, crossing of arms.

Then Roland said with an air of thoughtful practicality, 'I can't tell how Gwen feels. The portrait of him reveals nothing. I mean, you have the female nude so unveiled that there is scarcely even any skin covering the anatomy, like something by Bacon, or – and

171

then there's this – this gold mask – in the wind. No body at all. Is that some classical idea? I've studied Gwen at some length, as you know, but women are quite simply opaque to me. Sometimes with Gwen, I sort of feel I'm getting the hang of them. But she – well, I don't know. She doesn't even return my phone calls. Yet she devotes herself to you and to Will, doesn't she? A very attractive quality.'

Lawrence felt touched by Roland's observations, though he found them slightly confusing and slightly out of harmony with his own sense of how things were in his household. 'Gwen's on the move just now,' he offered. 'There are great things happening with her work.'

Roland acknowledged this with a series of small nods, looking around at the canvases and at the watercolours pinned up everywhere.

So Lawrence felt surer and went on, confiding a little. 'I don't think she takes much notice of anything else. She had a wobble – a kind of crisis of confidence – to do with undergoing this big transition in subject matter. It was very painful for her, however brief. She can't handle that sort of thing, you know – a sinking mood, the loss of momentum. But she has her conviction back now. She's incredibly strong. It's all the better for her to have plenty of people in love with her. She thrives on it, don't you think?'

'Well, I wouldn't know. It's more a question of what *you* can cope with.'

'It makes no difference to me, Roland. So long as she's happy. So long as she's engaged with something she cares about.'

'Noble. Admirable.'

'Not noble. How else can anyone live? Gwen's not made for starving. Not that anyone is, but she needs food all the time. She needs difficulty or . . . you know . . . something to grapple with.'

*　*　*

In the kitchen, just then, she was grappling with Hugo, laughing, serious, pushing him away with her hips as she stood at the sink, elbow-deep in floating chicken fat, scalding soapsuds.

'We may as well be in the middle of Piccadilly Circus,' she complained. 'There's Will, maybe asleep, maybe awake, and Lawrence wouldn't like it, and Roland *really* wouldn't like it.'

Hugo wore dripping rubber gloves, bright yellow ones, and was trying to slide them inside the front of her shirt from behind her, dousing them both with water.

'We better get a little further on with that picture, my dear,' he crooned at her ear, pressing close against her. 'Or we'll be attracting attention to ourselves. It's hardly a mask for any-thing.'

'That's not what I meant by calling it a mask. You mustn't confuse the picture with other things.' And she shoved him away again with her flickering hips and one small foot.

He grew sober, marched around the room behind her, peeling off the gloves. 'You mustn't mind my mocking. I know you're for real. That's what I noticed about you right from the beginning. What I love.'

'I wanted to paint you, Hugo, and I still do, and I will. You want to play the piano, don't you?' She turned towards him a little, paddling with a wire brush in the roasting pan.

'I live to play the piano. And now, I live to play for you.' He made a leg like a courtier, his left hand on his breast, his right hand flourishing the gloves towards her through the air in little rising circles as he bowed, drops of water flying. 'College has become just this place to practise; home is where I want to perform. I want you to hear every note, to feel every note. To be stirred, to be ravished!' He broke out in a grin and extended his long arms engagingly. 'Ravished this very minute, in fact. How will I live until tomorrow morning? A lovelorn swain. Your troubadour.' He tossed the gloves on to the counter beside her.

'Play for us tonight.'

'For the two of you in your bed?' He was startled and displeased. 'I'm going to have to get in that bed and break that spell he has over you, that marriage spell. I think it will be tomorrow, the desecration.'

'Stop.' Gwen's voice was forbidding. 'He is nothing to do with you and me. You mustn't think of him that way. You mustn't think of him except as a friend. A wise, generous friend.'

'Sharing his wife with me? Penniless musician that I am, I'm afraid I lack any real bohemian spirit. I want to own you.'

'You can't own me, and I think you don't really want to anyway. It's just that this is – all very new, very thrilling. If you wanted to own someone, you'd choose an unmarried woman.'

'Like Hilary?'

The air seemed to judder between them. Then it filled with serious silence. Gwen felt stricken, failed to meet Hugo's eye.

'Hilary wasn't the one I wanted,' he said with measured force. 'Obviously.'

'What do you mean?' she managed.

'I just never thought of her that way. Not because she was too available. Not even because she was in such a mess. It would make more sense to say it was because she's too tall.'

Gwen felt a kind of amazement. Hugo hadn't gone after Hilary? Until now, she had assumed that she herself was the next thing after Hilary. Maybe even something sandwiched in between two rounds of Hilary.

She began to feel very differently about what was happening between her and Hugo – about its uniqueness and its importance. The air in the steamy kitchen throbbed with a risk she hadn't previously recognised. She was alone with Hugo; Hilary never really had been. And she had a strange deflated sense that she'd been struggling with some shadowy opponent who had never existed. I thought it was a triangle. Is that what engaged me? Not a pretty picture, she chided herself.

174

But then, she thought again, thought better. Or no, not a tri-angle. Just wanting to be able to do what Hilary could do. Because I liked Hilary's freedom to do it. That's what I was after. The fact that she *could* do it. I did it to be like her – to be *with* her. For the intimacy and – the companionship. Out of love.

But Hilary never even did it. I have no companion in this, no playmate – apart from Hugo.

Hugo shrugged, licked his lips, went on courting Gwen with flattering comparisons. 'Or because she's too steady and sympa-thetic. Too – easy. Nothing for me to unknot, delve into, find out. There's plenty of music I don't care to play either. Not that she isn't intelligent and sensitive – just – nothing crackled – I didn't fancy her is the common parlance –' Suddenly, he stopped and listened. 'They're starting down,' he said.

'God, I can't hear anything. You're incredible.' She felt trapped, cornered – the opposite of free. And she felt alone.

He seized her and kissed her feverishly, with the fever of last opportunity, and it reached her in her anxiety – the passion, and also the human kindness. She realised that she liked the fever for itself and liked Hugo for himself. His quickness, his self-confi-dence, his quixotic changeability. She liked the fact that he was a young man of no fixed habits and no fixed outlook apart from his mysterious and absolute devotion to his music. She liked the fact that for the moment he was also devoted to her.

By the time he released her and Lawrence and Roland came into the room, she was breathing hard, awash. Now what? she wondered. There was her husband, who made her life possible, whom she cherished and was accustomed to look up to. There was Hugo, towards whom some maverick energy kept pushing her. And she thought, Hold on to something until this passes, until it becomes possible to understand what is happening. She felt herself turning to liquid. What if it all washed away? Everything she could see? There was nothing to brace against.

She heard Lawrence say, 'What are you two doing? Drying them on your clothes? You're both soaking wet.' He laughed benevolently, collecting a dishcloth from the back of a kitchen chair where it hung, stepping up to the draining board, setting to. 'It would seem that you need professional help – of one sort or another.'

Gwen clutched at the countertop, knuckles whitening, then she stepped away from the sink, touched Lawrence's arm. 'I'll check on Will.'

'I'm sure he's fine, sweetheart.' But then he took in the confusion on her face. 'Go on, then. I'll deal with all this.'

That night, going to bed, Lawrence was reserved. He kept his eyes to himself, slipped noiselessly under the covers in clean, buttoned-up pyjamas and made himself comfortable, nesting at ease on his back, waiting. After a while, he turned on to his side, facing the empty place where Gwen would lie, as if to welcome her. He followed her around the room with his ears, with his heart, not speaking, as she folded clothes, matched shoes into pairs, slipped out once again to the bathroom. He believed he could wait for however long it might take.

He knew all too well what was happening to Gwen. It was entirely natural, hardly blameworthy. It would twist like a tornado, maybe leave a narrow, clean-edged track through the harvest, or maybe flatten the whole field of their marriage before it stopped. She will weather it if I do, he thought.

He couldn't help the fact that he wanted to see what she would make of it, what she would do. It seemed clear to him that she would chart it stupendously in her work. But it might cause her a great deal of pain. How much space to give her? he wondered. What was the right amount?

As he lay there, Gwen walked through the quiet flat, closing curtains, turning off lights, counting her blessings. Her finger on this or that switch, she looked it all over – the dishevelled furniture; the roasting pan left to dry upside down beside the sink; the corked half-bottle of red wine on the Welsh dresser; the bowl of fruit, grapes plucked from the nearest dozen stems; the litter of papers on the desk in the little study upstairs, recording sales, purchases, policies, achievements, obligations, plans of the members of the household; the sleeping child. Wind rattled at the windows behind her and smacked at the dim interior as she checked the front door.

She turned off the bedroom light and crossed the floor in the dark, thinking of Hugo's eyes blinking sleepily in the clear light of the studio. The fine, translucent skin as it slid down over the warm brown irises and the white surrounding globes, then slid up again in loose pockets below the brow bone when he opened them, reminded her of the veined and fragile pale brown skin of his scrotum and of the tender knobs within. She flinched a little, considering the holes in the mask.

CHAPTER 11

Towards the end of the morning, a few days later, Lawrence telephoned Clare from his rooms in college. He didn't intend to lean backwards on to their old relationship; he didn't think he needed to do anything like that. As he dialled her number, he was picturing the wide-spaced double hull of a catamaran and then training wheels on a child's bike. It's a question of balance, he was thinking. Ride straight through it, skim over it, without tilting, without bogging down. We'll have lunch, just to talk. About anything but Gwen.

He held the heavy, double-ended receiver away from himself out over his desk, on two fingers extended from his upturned palm, feeling the weight of it. The phone rang for a long time. Clare didn't answer.

It's just as well, he thought. It's an opportunity, at last, to engage properly with my work.

He closed his fingers around the receiver, flipped it over, dropped it back in its cradle. As he did so, he felt a vertiginous tilting, as if the whole planet was shifting ever so slightly on its axis. A shaft of light seemed to angle down sharply inside his head, and he imagined he heard marbles rolling away across the floor, barrelling over the brown-stained, time-warped, wooden boards beneath his feet.

It's not that I want to clutch at Gwen, he thought. Because I don't; I never have done. It's something else. Something broader. Everything between us is changing. She is approaching an apex. She is reaching her prime. I am not. I am past mine. I am on the wane.

For a long while, it has seemed as if we were going forward together through time, progressing along the same trajectory, a rolling road. Now it proves more like a solo escalator ride up, a solo escalator ride down. I'm already coming down. She is rising somewhere behind me, somewhere above; she is only setting out into the terminal, thinking about where she might like to travel, seeing for the first time the list of destinations on the big, clicking black board. She isn't following in any track I've laid, I'm no longer her teacher or even vaguely her mentor. She's on her own. I'm a kite tail, dangling, tugged about.

The shift had come about imperceptibly. How did it happen? When?

He pulled his papers towards him; Trimalchio, Jean Valjean, they need attending to. But then he stood up restlessly thinking, Man and his destiny, man and the world he has made, his tastes, his desires, his behaviour, his beliefs. It's of no use to me. There really *is* no proper conception of women, of what they had to do with it, in either of these books. Fortunata, Circe, the pair of crones, are only there to tempt, to fulfil, to punish the appetites of men. Fantine, Cosette, a far greater degree of verisimilitude, but the same. They reflect the aspirations of men. Had men so success-fully kept them down, kept them from becoming themselves? So it was said. Insistently, repeatedly. Surely it was only these particular authors who left the real women out? There are other kinds of men and other kinds of books. Flaubert, Tolstoy, Henry James. I've got copies somewhere about. And there must be earlier examples. Always there must have been the men who encouraged self-realisation.

What does Roland mean, that women are opaque to him? Doesn't he mean it's too painful to think about them? That it's easier to close down on them than to risk desiring them if they might not desire him at the same time in the same way?

'*Quis multa gracilis te puer in rosa,*' Lawrence murmured. Roland has consecrated his dripping garments to the god of the sea rather than suffer the pangs of inconstant love. A priest in the temple. Safe, but without understanding. Without even experience of life. But Pyrrha is so captivating, so infinitely preferable as an object of devotion. Even if she isn't real.

Lawrence walked to the high, white casement, put his forehead right against the glass, stared out at the college garden.

The leaves were half down already, layering over the mud-runnelled lawn. Not far away, a stocky, flannel-shirted man – wool-capped, moleskinned, wellingtoned, all in shades of green and russet as if he had fallen from a tree like a piece of autumn fruit – was raking up red-brown piles laced already with black rot, with leaf mould. Lawrence heard the rake scraping the soil under the bedraggled grass. And above, in the giant silvery limbs, more leaves – oak, ash – still dangled and turned in the light.

'Yellow leaves,' he murmured to himself, 'or none or few.' He waited to see a leaf fall, reflecting as he did so, how truly one understands one's own life – the difficulty of love, the passage of time – by external things; a leaf falling now would be for him a symbol and a confirmation. How rich life is with meaning, he thought, even when the meaning is bitter. Thus, he savoured his melancholy, his recognition this morning of what was irrefutably true about himself and about his circumstances. He took satisfaction in connecting it to Horace and to Shakespeare, certain that he understood with his heart as well as with his mind their various familiar lines. The process of making the connections liberated him from private anxiety, lifted him up and gave him, against all the odds, a feeling of delight.

There is probably nothing that intrigues me more than a woman coming fully into her own powers, Lawrence asserted inwardly and with a sense of injustice about it. Nothing I have ever given myself to more completely. Nurturing that. When women undergraduates showed up here in college for the first time twenty-five-odd years ago, it changed my life. Was that a weakness or a strength in me? he wondered. They wanted to know everything I knew and everything I thought. It was important to them, a matter of intense personal urgency. And I suppose there can be no question it derailed my career. Because I took such an interest in them. An inordinate interest. It's not about sexual awakening, some disguise for that, because there is all the other awakening, which is infinitely more difficult to achieve.

Nosing about in a low corner of the bookcase to the right of the fireplace, hunting for a little clutch of novels he felt he could once have laid hands on in a trice with his eyes closed, he flushed with the recollection of old enthusiasms, lost pleasures – innocent because they had not then been ruled otherwise, innocent because they had had no ill consequence of which he was aware – unless he counted the dissipation of his own scholarly energies, the day-dreaming. In those days one had felt ruled mostly by the clock. In an hour, another face would appear, equally entitled. Only a few had overflowed the boundary of time. Frank, playful appetites, tutorials rearranged for the end of the afternoon, the oak sported brazenly in the winter dusk, flesh gliding beneath tangling sheets. An Easter reading party, papers fluttering over swathes of bluebells in newly leaved woods, breasts bumpy and explicit in the chatter-making air, a hot, matted nest on a spread blanket. One ribald summer night in a punt, endlessly punctuated by lively, uncaptained criss-crossings with other people's drunkenness.

So many young women long to be kissed by their tutor, he thought. Praise isn't enough for them. They acquire a kind of transference. How close the air in this room used to get with it – expectation, longing. The windows would just about mist over. It starts somewhere underneath the intelligible conversation, underneath the articulate work of the brain. It starts in the glands, like woodwinds underneath the strings. There are hormones, olfactory sensations, a continual undertow in some other language, some other genre of human communication. Nature primes the male to respond to that. Is it predatory to supply what is wanted?

To wish to please? Nowadays we are advised to look upon them as children, as young of the species, not responsible for the messages they send us. And we are obliged to police ourselves. The alternative would be separating the men from the women, introducing the veil, that kind of thing.

But perhaps a kiss is the correct response? Say, a fatherly kiss and no more? What are these feelings *for*? Lawrence wondered, not for the first time. I have been made to feel guilty about them. Others have as well. Made to feel that I have behaved like a colonial adventurer, exploiting the young of whom I was in charge, over whom I was given such power. Abusing them. And yet so often a young woman walks away happily with her kiss; having won it, proved she could get it, she is generally satisfied. She feels esteemed, worthy, recognised. And in all likelihood, she then displays a new poise, maturity even, as if garnering the kiss were a rite of passage. She moves on, moves beyond the need, the transference. The kiss frees her – frees her from wanting it.

Ought such a kiss to have been socially institutionalised rather than outlawed? Lawrence wondered. He was on his knees behind a chair, squinting at spines stuffed in so tightly that they wouldn't budge even a little; he had to tilt his head over to read them, apart from the few on their sides across the top. He pictured a booth, a window in a curtained Punch and Judy show, in which a don might sit doling out kisses at the end of term. It's nothing like sex, in general; it doesn't call for a full bedding down. Frankly, the boys are in for something much more involved if they are in for anything at all. He chuckled. The hecklers, the crusaders, the feminist avengers; clearly they must be the ones we *failed* to kiss. All that longing turned to rage because we loved *too* discriminately. Of course, one acknowledges that there are some in positions of authority who are perverts, who are not interested in the students to begin with, but who are in need of a personal scratch for their pathetic, orphaned itch. They try to extract favours which are not on offer. Hard to imagine how. Can the moral rape indeed be worse than the physical? To say it's all the same is woefully obtuse. Crude thinking.

I wasn't much older than my students anyway in the early days. Now I've slipped away from them — Fiona, Kevin — slipped backwards from their time which continually bears down on ours and obliterates it, slipped out of range of the particular temptations they embody. Fifteen years older than my wife. And she would have no one but me. So who, in the end, was exploiting whom? How would the powers that be rule on us now, if they knew how we had begun? There is nothing I wouldn't do for her, give for her.

Somehow, although she seldom set foot in college, hadn't for years, Gwen had emptied the room behind him. Because she had made it seem irrelevant. The cottage, then London. And the way she wanted to create things rather than analyse them. Chucking her degree. Preferring experience to knowledge. It was as if she had moved on to something better, and though she had never said as much, she had left him with a half-conscious sense that his old habits were frivolous or maybe even juvenile. The sofa in its creased, near-blue covers and the dark wood coffee table marked with ink splodges, black-veined heat ripples, interlocking rings from glasses, its corners kicked and rubbed by sturdy, careless shoes, had once been the centre of a life. Students, colleagues, friends used to whirl in, slamming the door, breathless, cold-cheeked, throw themselves down, laughing, challenge him with ardent, shouted questions. How many slaves worked in the Athenian silver mines? How many manned the Roman aqueducts? Give three reasons why eunuchs, despite being barbarians and slaves, became powerful at court in the fourth- and fifth-century Roman Empire.

He would boil the kettle right there on the table between them, fish instant brown granules, powdered milk, into the pale green college cups with a dirty, sharp-edged tin spoon. It gave him a steadying influence over his guests, serving them. And it gave the guests something to hold in their hands to offset their excitement, their physical proximity to him, alone on his sofa with their bursting minds. Every conversation had been a high-wire act, a virtuoso display of esoteric knowledge cooked up and refined to impress and to engage the mind of the Oxford don.

And whenever he had worked in this room alone, often late into the night, there had been burning issues of his own. For instance, how did ancient slaves acquire money? It was easy to see how they grew rich from the demand for luxury goods in Rome and in Athens, since the aristocrats, with their strength in the land, had established slave-manned and slave-managed work-shops to make fine household goods, to build houses, temples, monuments, to trade goods, to run brothels. Slaves were artisans, artists, architects, merchants, whores. Expert ones. But what about slaves in the countryside – agricultural workers, personal servants? Lawrence had thought long and hard about this, studied and searched; there was simply no evidence. And yet it was clear that they had acquired money because so many of them had purchased their own freedom.

There were the tablets at Delphi which recorded how much they had paid their masters to release them. How the price rose during the two centuries leading up to the birth of Christ, so that they settled for buying only a promise of release, which was cheaper. They had to serve their master as long as he lived; they had to hand over their newly weaned toddler children into slavery. They could be chained up or beaten for disobedience. In what sense were they free? And yet they paid amounts that might have bought food for a whole family for two or three years. At Delphi, even this kind of manumission – freedom in hope – was nonethe-less marked by a solemn religious ceremony and written in stone. Apollo guaranteed it.

Lawrence could never help but be moved by so much longing for freedom and by such hapless trust in Apollo. His emotion was strangely intensified by the incompleteness of his knowledge, by the fact that the story itself was partly obliterated. He, too, longed for the illumination that might never come, the facts he might never unearth, the sudden, clear understanding of the facts he already possessed. And whoever used to arrive, unexpected, much anticipated, through his door, would be eager to know what was engaging his thought. Any paragraph he might be working on would be of interest and could be offered up for discussion. Any book that lay open on the table might be seized upon, read aloud, enthusiastically critiqued, even made fun of. Or they might gossip about someone else who had just been, who had just gone. What had made it all seem so vital and so important? For it had more than held his attention. It had held the attention of a devoted circle gathered around him as well. It had drawn a crowd to this very room.

Until his year in America, that boundless, shapeless, contour-less place. The one sharp-edged thing he had encountered there was Gwen, cutting all ways, like a creature trying to cut its way out of a sack, as if someone were trying to suffocate her, drown her, like a kitten. She was nearly free of it all when he met her – the institutionalised expectations that she couldn't quite see round, couldn't quite unburden herself of. And she bolted for the light when he opened the mouth of the sack.

He had seen at the time that by inviting Gwen into the life he already had and introducing her into his milieu, he had made evident to her that there could be any number of worlds. He never expected that she would settle for his. But he waited and she didn't move on. On the contrary, she had insisted that they marry. She liked to get in deep, Gwen did. She liked to do a thing completely once she decided.

I let her take me over, he thought, dragging the books out in clumps and reaching in behind them to feel for lost volumes in the hidden, dusty spaces. One book could have slipped through, he thought, but it's as if a whole shelf is missing. Where do things go? We collect them. They disperse. My thoughts, my books, on the loose. My former circle.

He replaced the little terracotta lamps that sat along the front edge of the shelf. Spoon-shaped boats of clay, made to hold oil, a wick; they were maybe ancient, maybe fake, picked up here and there around the Mediterranean years ago on student expeditions. White still with dust along some of their curves. My collection of antiquities, he thought, common as light bulbs; would we expect future generations to dig up and save our light bulbs? What could such a thing reveal about us? Undecorated, utilitarian. Without atmosphere or romance of any kind. He pictured a cartoon one, clicking on. Would light bulbs reveal that we had been absolutely chock-a-block with bright ideas?

What was I really trying for back then, around the time that I met Gwen? he wondered. I took it for granted that I would make my mark, that I had made a mark already. But a whole book can take a long time to write. So much praise can be heaped on an idea, on the promise shown in a doctoral thesis, on the spate of articles based on it. It comes to seem as if the book has been written already. The thesis and the articles seem to be a sufficient achievement. Everyone knows what the book would say. What news have you ever got for anyone at lunch, at dinner, on the blue sofa, if you just go on nailing down the one familiar idea? I wasn't prepared to be boring, was I? A different book, a newer book always seemed like a better one to write.

Oh, but how quickly that came to be two books he had not written. And in hindsight, he had always justified it: It mightn't have been a good book. It mightn't have been worth spending all the time on that. Better to try for something more important. After so long, they are expecting something big. Thus, having produced less and less on paper over the years, he found himself being mentored, being mothered, by Roland.

Where is that doctoral thesis? Lawrence wondered, abandoning his search for the novels. *Literature as Historical Text; Historical Text as Literature: The Problem of Slavery in Graeco-Roman Antiquity.* Is there a box under the bed? Perhaps I ought to read the thesis through again. Perhaps it might still make a book, another article or two. How good was I? I've got this idea now that Gwen is the real thing. Was I? Have I let her drag me from some path I was on?

Gwen has such pulling power, such centripetal force. It all revolves around her now.

He didn't go to look under the bed. He sat down on the sofa, staring around at his shelves, at all the books. Together they seemed to amount to something, an edifice, a set of convictions, or at least a set of questions – about how we have lived, and how we should live. Most of them he hadn't opened for a long time. After all, he had mastered the contents long ago; he had been drawing on the resources they contained for years, doling them out in countless spoonfuls, varied formats. If he were to take one down, to consult it, he would know where to open it, where to look for whatever detail he might want to check.

It's time I read all the books again, he thought. There will be things I've forgotten, pushed to the margins of thought, discounted. The books will die – what's in the books will die to the life of the mind; the shelves and the volumes will become mere objects loaded on planks, one beside another.

Nothing if not a good teacher, to the boys as well as the girls, he reminded himself. And as Roland assured him, it was a contribution. Year in, year out, there was the college's sturdy crop of seconds, the always startling crop of firsts, hardly ever a third, occasionally a congratulatory first. So hard to assess what was my share of their achievement, what they might have written in their exams if I hadn't taught them at all. Out they went into the world, writing, banking, teaching, advertising, raising children, staffing the museums, the Foreign Office, MI6. There had been so many; he'd rather lost count and mostly lost touch. With the undergraduates now, what did he really have to say? Was there anything new? Have I become boring to them? Or has it, in fact, gone cold on me? he wondered. Where is the glimmer that leads one on, the golden thread?

It all revolves around Gwen, he thought again. Gwen and Will.

Will's my real competition, Lawrence told himself. He had decided not to think about Hugo. It seemed possessive and vaguely pathetic, scrutinising the thing that was preoccupying his wife. Loving Gwen meant leaving her be and letting her find her own way, as he had always done. I wouldn't have liked her to scrutinise Clare.

Will has always been competition. Lawrence remembered how it had felt: as if Gwen took something back from me when that boy appeared. I suppose it's only natural. But how does any man stand for it? Giving up his wife's attentions to his newborn son, a thing he himself has brought into being – or so he believes. Not an uncomplicated adjustment. How likely to induce measureless rage and anguish in the male heart, the inconstancy of women. As a child, the very same man would have had to learn to accept that his mother had a duty to his father, that she might prefer his father. Betrayal on all sides. No wonder men tried to keep women down.

On the other hand, Lawrence suddenly considered, Will is my guarantee. He tests the relationship, proves it. He is a permanent bond to Gwen, and however much Will has divided us, Gwen will honour the bond.

He reckoned, as he often had done in the past, that his time with Will was yet to come, and that he could wait for it. She has never let me take the interest in Will that I have always taken in her. Will is her son still.

Lawrence looked at his watch and realised that he had better get something to eat in the senior common room before the college meeting started. And there was some other matter with the senior tutor about the tutorial board. A conversation he needed to have.

As he made his way across the quad, he thought, I must keep an eye on Will now in any case, if Gwen and Hugo are going to be – however they are going to be. He felt the cold through his corduroy jacket despite the full, high sun, and he was unexpectedly overwhelmed with the poignancy of Will's situation. It seemed hard to breathe, as if he were choking on the possibility that Hugo, even Gwen, might neglect Will – this pair whose attention to the child had been so exhilarating for Will and so reliable.

What if they now withdrew their attention to focus on one another? Could Will cope if he felt himself fallen from their grace? Hugo has brought him on at the piano in a way that Will is just about addicted to. Fed him on a kind of jet fuel of progress. Encouraged him to be obsessed. Gwen is like that anyway with Will. Ever since he was born – adoring. Her full passion for life aimed right at him.

Now that Lawrence considered it, Gwen had been irresponsible. She ought to have foreseen that Will would need to learn to be alone eventually. She ought to have been preparing him to do without adults. Lawrence wasn't aware of ever having had a dissenting thought about how Gwen was raising their son. But the prospect of Will's solitude made him afraid for the boy. How is a child to understand such a change, if I can hardly understand it myself?

Holding his half-filled white china plate in his hand – lamb stew, a cold potato – he suddenly turned from the sideboard, hurried over to the College Clerk, leaned down and whispered heatedly, 'Would you kindly make my apologies for this afternoon's meeting; I find I'm needed at home.'

The College Clerk – shingle-haired, efficient, Tutor in Law – had a forkful of steak-and-kidney pie hoisted halfway to her pearlised lips. She put the forkful down again on to her plate, twisted her bowed, bare neck towards Lawrence and pulled her face back a few inches in order to see his, which was very close. Then she turned slightly pink.

Lawrence pulled his own face back, too, thinking he had inadvertently violated her privacy, some personal space. He said, in a doubtful, half-apologetic tone, 'All right?'

But still she didn't reply. He couldn't think when he had missed a college meeting. He was a loyal presence, generally stayed up afterwards to dine in college, slept at the cottage. He knew perfectly well that others missed the meetings, a few with regularity. The Warden nearly always seemed to be away in America raising money. Was the College Clerk's mouth so full of food that she couldn't speak?

From across the wide, wooden table, the Senior Tutor, corpulent, whiskery, imposed himself jovially. 'Excuse me, Lawrence, you can't stay to deal with the business about Dr Pryce? We must at least agree how to cover her teaching in the short term, even if we don't get into any further discussion of her absence.'

'Dr Pryce's absence?' Lawrence recollected that Clare hadn't answered her telephone. 'But it's term time. Where on earth has she gone during term time?'

The Senior Tutor raised his eyebrows and nibbled at the buttered white roll in his pudgy fingers. 'She indicated — some sort of personal matter.'

'A personal matter?' Lawrence smacked his plate down on the table right next to the College Clerk's pale, unadorned left hand; the hand was snatched away. 'Is she all right?' he asked. 'I mean —' Then he stopped in mid-sentence, feeling he was being indiscreet.

The College Clerk, head down, spoke to her plate, under her breath, but with icy precision. 'I believe the phrase Dr Pryce employed in her letter was "importunate personal matter".'

Lawrence looked around the table, saw blank, expectant faces trained towards him, silent, masticating. Then he heard the Senior Tutor say, 'As the Tutorial Board won't meet until next week, I thought we might have a word later on today?'

'Yes, of course,' Lawrence said automatically. 'If you think it would be useful.' He reached down to pick up his plate again, feeling stung, uncomfortably singled out. The College Clerk leaned away stiffly.

What is being said in the college office and the senior common room? he wondered, still standing there. Some rubbish about Clare and me? It made him feel ill with irritation. And what is Clare up to? They seem to think I know. Then he spoke up quite loudly over their seated heads, with gruff authority, as if calling order among undergraduates so he could begin a lecture: 'Look, if there's college business for which I'm needed, I'll see to it that I remain for the afternoon. They can make other arrangements at home.'

That ought to shut them up, he thought brutishly, dolloping shredded carrots with raisins and lentils on to his plate. In case anybody thinks I was ducking anything on purpose. And he pulled up to the table sullenly in a corner chair, with no intention of chatting to anyone.

They have all adopted some view, he thought to himself, about me and Clare. They all think I know where she is and what's going on with her. She might have bloody told me. He chewed morosely, thinking of Will. He'll be at school now anyway. Struggling with that rumbustious monster who karate-chopped him yesterday, Maximilian. Or sitting on that long-haired red bath mat having stories. He's perfectly safe there. Those are exactly the struggles in which he needs to engage on his own.

But Lawrence found it difficult to be constructive about the business of the college that afternoon. He looked around at the rows of pale and ruddy faces – tweed jackets, corduroy, a few blazers and suits, cardigans, black leather, many sets of whiskers, one ponytail, the quota of shining and sleek feminine manes, countless knitted ties with arms firmly folded across them, eyes everywhere downcast – and he imagined he could smell eagerness, anticipation. A roomful of bored academics dying for a bit of scandal. Some dirt. About him. He didn't care. He defied them. His colleagues, many of whom he counted as friends.

The Domestic Bursar required to know whether there were any objections to hiring the College Steward's brother-in-law as the new chef. It was a set-up, a tactfully worded recommendation which would be accepted as a matter of course; Lawrence had already assisted in the decision by email. But he was overtaken by a subversive impulse to display some muscle.

'Why not, if he's qualified?' he demanded, staring at the Domestic Bursar's heavy-soled black brogues, one thicker to level his limping gait. 'Is he a good, experienced chef? Why should it count against him that he is the brother-in-law of the College Steward? Surely that would be how he found out about the job and thought of applying for it?'

'Highly qualified. Well recommended, as you know,' said the Domestic Bursar in his brusque Scots accent. 'We'd not have considered him at all otherwise, would we?' He was clearly taken aback, and, suddenly, the meeting sensed that there was something wrong about the appointment.

'But who else has applied for this post?' demanded the Tutor in French, sharp-voiced, petite Mademoiselle Hulot. She sat up very straight, snatched at her tightly tailored red blazer with her carmine-lacquered fingertips, tugged it downward over her middle. 'You cannot show this favouritism to the steward's brother-in-law! The others of our staff will no longer believe we have any just practices. We must of course look outside the friends and relations of our current employees when we make a new hiring. Absolutely.'

'That is an admirable view, Mademoiselle Hulot,' said Lawrence, rising patiently to a familiar role, advocate of real-life knowledge over high-minded theories of equal opportunity, and satisfied to have started a fight he could easily win. 'Funnily enough, it never seems to work that way. The college staff are perfectly savvy and a close-knit lot to boot. They can tell better than we can whether or not someone knows how to do a job properly. What's more, they feel well considered when the college takes their recommendations and their own family connections to heart. They are very loyal to us and to one another. If you think of it, there are several sets of siblings and spouses among them.'

'I am not aware of the personal relationships among the staff, and I do not consider this to be any of my business.' Mademoiselle Hulot grasped her lapels, lifted them away from her flesh as if to circulate air within, smoothed them down again. Then she shut her thin lips, also carmine, firmly.

The Domestic Bursar, clearly having no wish to offend, or even to be perceived as having a point of view, kept his eyes down, waiting. Now and again he shifted his gimpy leg about, maintaining all the while a bantam poise. After a decorous interval, he advised in an undertone, 'There has been only one other suitable applicant. I'm afraid that she herself happens to be the first cousin of the previous man in the post, and neither her skills nor her temperament come so highly recommended.'

'Well, the previous chef isn't going to be around to be upset by losing out, is he?' Lawrence expostulated grumpily. 'If you'll forgive me, Bursar, it seems you hardly need our opinion. It would appear you have no alternative.' And after his eccentric show of pugnacity, Lawrence just as eccentrically dropped the matter.

The Domestic Bursar gave a nod, looked around for further disagreement.

He got more than he expected from Mademoiselle Hulot, who asked, smiling graciously, 'What does this mean, her temperament is not recommended? Because she is a woman, one presumes?'

'I'm afraid I couldn't say why, ma'am. T'ould be a shame to spend time and money advertising when we have strong candidates to hand.'

Lawrence let out a sigh. He reckoned the Domestic Bursar might have preferred not to discuss such matters with Mademoiselle Hulot. She seldom dined in college. Lawrence had the impression that she found the food beneath her Continental contempt. And there was her personal life, generally presumed to be glamorous and time-consuming. And yet – had Mademoiselle Hulot had her share of kissing? Lawrence wondered. Maybe she had never been kissed by an Englishman. A don. Was that why she appeared so intensely to dislike them? Had she received kisses only from Frogs? Maybe the odd sexy Italian? The Domestic Bursar knew his job; he'd surely like to be allowed to get on with it.

Lawrence stopped listening. He was thinking that it was just as well he hadn't hurried home. Gwen and Hugo might be at work on the portrait or otherwise engaged with one another. They certainly wouldn't have been expecting him. I mustn't startle Gwen, create a panic, call anyone's bluff. I must behave as normally as possible.

All through the afternoon, the Governing Body swayed and ambled through its droning deliberations. Striving for correctness, for wisdom, for consensus. Inclining this way, then that. The Keeper of the College Pictures had agreed in principle to loan the Reynolds portrait of the college's celebrated eighteenth-century warden to the National Portrait Gallery. The Tutor in History was reluctant to see the portrait taken down, anxious that it was in need of restoration, shouldn't be packed, shipped, in its delicate state, the paint actually flaking in the lower, left corner, the image darkened, nearly obscured by discoloration to the ageing varnish, by cigar smoke from the late-night pleasures of the SCR.

None of it really seemed to matter to Lawrence, these household affairs of the college on which he had focused for years with authentic concern. His own life, which had felt so secure, so established around him only a day ago, was dissipating like a mist. Of what had it consisted? A wife, a son, a flat in Hammersmith. He was building up an unbearable impatience to get home and see if anything remained of what he loved. His impatience burned hotter as the afternoon wore on, until his anxiety became visible on his face as he sat silently, unlike his college self, in his chair.

I must be fair to my wife, he was thinking. I must be generous. Fear will not serve anyone. Take a long view. Give her time to get what she wants from this man so she can move on. Let her experience adultery, find out all she needs to know about it.

That, too, is a rite of passage. Indeed, in some cultures, adultery is quite successfully institutionalised.

But he had trouble thinking clearly of a good set of rules, an adequate code. What is the best way for adultery to work? he asked himself, thinking that he knew but had simply forgotten. It calls for discretion, self-control. Yet isn't it hallmarked by a lack of self-control? Isn't that how it comes about? Or at least, it's on a knife edge. We make the judgement that we can increase our happiness by a limited indulgence in something that we could not resist without a correspondingly greater increase in unhappiness. But then, like a little outcry from Lawrence's heart, came the question, What is each of the parties supposed to *feel*? And, with chagrin, he modified his question, What is the *third* party supposed to feel? He didn't like the term 'injured'; he didn't like the term 'betrayed'. Of no use, he considered. And he moved on to another point: that in some more traditional cultures, adultery is simply taboo.

At the conclusion of the meeting, Lawrence had to be summoned back from underneath a fixed grimace of dismay.

'Shall we sort something out preliminarily, about Dr Pryce?' the Senior Tutor was asking.

Lawrence became aware that he was receiving sympathetic looks from his colleagues as they made their way from the room. None of you has any idea, he thought to himself. It's nothing to do with Clare Pryce. He knew that they were simply misreading his face, misreading his pain. And he let them.

He allowed himself to be dragooned without demur into looking after her graduate students and her second- and third-year Greats students doing Plato and Aristotle, most of whom he taught anyway for history. He also agreed to contact Roland LeSeur to see if a few further hours' philosophy teaching could be found somewhere outside the college for the fourth years doing modern philosophers.

Dorian Summerbotham, who taught most of the literature for

Mods and for the Greats literature papers, agreed to help with Lawrence's own historians if Roland wasn't able to suggest anyone else. Summerbotham nobly restrained his exasperation so that the Senior Tutor could take note.

Lawrence looked at Summerbotham's blue-and-yellow-striped bow tie, his wan, weasel face, keen, darting eyes, and hated him for the first time in their long, productive, unfriendly association. How many times, thought Lawrence, have I given at your request a special tutorial in Homer, Theocritus, Sappho, Virgil, Horace, Catullus – this or that poet in the Mods syllabus whom you remind me is such a great favourite of mine and whom you always suggest it will be such a special treat for me to introduce to the first years myself? How you build it up for me, the informal opportunity for them to get to know me without anxiety, with nothing at stake, the chance for me to gauge the new talent, make my predictions, my plans for their finals papers. As if I haven't known all along that you ask me out of desperation, to try to ensure that your Mods candidates will get a decent result and you can hang on to your reputation as a good enough teacher. I always help you, because you haven't any other leg to stand on, hardly a publication to your name. A dull-witted schoolmaster at heart, without an original thought in your head, memorising everybody else's insights and passing them off to students as fresh meat.

But then, in mid-hate, it occurred to Lawrence that poor Summerbotham's feeble exasperation was just another sign of how desperate he was. Play-acting that you have something more important to do than teach second- and third-year history. How terrified you must be at the thought of tackling Herodotus, Thucydides, or, God forbid, Cicero, Suetonius, Tacitus – in front of clever, well-read, inventive undergraduates. And now *I* will fearlessly, foolishly, be swotting up on *philosophy* for them! Whose political arse did you lick to get this job to begin with? What theory did you pretend to believe in?

The Senior Tutor beamed at Summerbotham, rubbed his hands

together. 'Greatly appreciated, Dorian. Very gracious of you to be so uncomplaining in the circumstances.'

Then turning to Lawrence, the Senior Tutor admonished, 'If she doesn't come back, obviously we will have to make formal arrangements quite quickly. There are all of next year's candidates to weed through, the interviews in December, and so forth. Naturally we still hope she won't burn her bridges, but you might give some thought to your resources, Lawrence.'

'What do you mean, my resources?' Lawrence bristled. It was coming back to him that Clare had warned him, during their lunch at Brown's, that she was thinking of leaving her post. Moreover, that she had engaged his support and enjoined him to secrecy. He had paid so little attention. He really had not wanted to know. And they had parted in anger. Could she have moved this fast? But I never wrote any letter of reference for her, he thought, wincing a little. And I don't even know what job she had in mind to try for. A keeper in the Ashmolean? Had she said perhaps that she wanted real things in her life? That philosophy wasn't real? Wasn't satisfying? He remembered for certain how she hated the fact that there were no longer any books in the Ashmolean Museum and that the keepers had to walk around the outside of the building, rain or shine, to fetch their books from the new faculty library.

The Senior Tutor smiled and bowed like a round-breasted bird dipping into a bird bath. 'Only – what further time you may have to spare. For admissions during the Christmas vacation and the continuing teaching load. And of course, there are her lectures next term. We shall have to recommend someone to the faculty teaching committee. Perhaps you have some graduate students who would be up to it?'

Lawrence felt angry now, tricked and exploited. He wasn't having it – *all* Clare's abandoned responsibilities. It wasn't down to him. He threw Summerbotham a ferocious glance, and then he said with arrogant formality, 'You simply must enlighten me as to why you think Dr Pryce isn't coming back. And what's more, why you look to me in particular to take on such a large portion of her work?'

There was a silence. The Senior Tutor dipped towards the bird bath again, shook his head and shoulders as if shaking droplets from his plump, birdlike self.

'Well,' he said at last, with evident reluctance, 'it has begun to seem clear that she has for some time been considering employment elsewhere. She told me privately that she has been offered what she feels is a once-in-a-lifetime opportunity in the United States. New York City, I understand. On condition that she take it up right away, at least on a trial basis. If she makes a success of it, she will not return to fulfil her contract with the college.'

Lawrence was astonished, trying to take in the details, but he still fought his corner. 'What has that got to do with me? Everyone else in the college seems to know already.'

'Well. It has – Uh-uh –' the Senior Tutor cleared his throat. He looked at Summerbotham, his eyes popping with discomfort. Summerbotham made no move to leave them alone, folded his arms. The Senior Tutor dropped his eyes to the floor, lifted them again to Lawrence's, spoke apologetically: 'I've been given to understand that there are personal circumstances which made her position here untenable. Or so she came to feel. She sought professional counselling, and she made known to me and to the Warden and to one or two others that she left only under great psychological duress. We understood from her that she left with your blessing. Indeed with your wholehearted support. Ahhh – that you wished her to leave?'

Although he had thrown himself on his sword willingly, eagerly, Lawrence was surprised at the sensation of turbulence he now experienced in his gut. His eyes rolled back in his head. His mouth went dry.

There was another long silence.

At last, he said very quietly, 'That's what she said?'

'It's what she gave us to understand. What with one thing and another.'

'I see,' said Lawrence. Then, looking them each coolly in the eye, he said much more loudly, 'I have nothing to add apart from this: It's bollocks.'

And he turned and left the room, making his way directly to the bus station.

CHAPTER 12

That night at bedtime, Lawrence started telling Will the story of Jason and the Argonauts. It continued with great excitement for several nights, and then he offered the Labours of Hercules. Gwen felt herself less in demand, but she made no objection. She had laundry, cleaning, the letters and papers all over her desk, and plans to make for Christmas. It was right that Lawrence should spend more time with his son, she told herself. Lawrence was so seldom at home. Yet she worried that Lawrence seemed afraid to be alone, even for just a few minutes. Over the weekend, he proposed to look after Will so that Gwen could go for a run; he offered to help with homework, reading, even piano practice.

'He can stay here with me, if you like,' Lawrence kept on saying whenever there was an errand to do. 'Or if *he* likes.' He would look at Will in a friendly, non-committal way, without moving from where he stood or sat, as if to say, You don't have to stay with me, you know. I'm just here anyway. Will would shrug. He seemed attracted by the implicit offer of independence. And so Gwen left them to their own devices. She even got up to the studio for a few hours and did some painting.

Whenever Lawrence went up to Gwen's studio now, he took Will with him. He felt that it would be more natural if he happened upon Gwen there with Hugo. Even so, he took trouble to visit the studio when Gwen was out. He had never before asked her permission; why should he now? It would only draw their mutual attention to the change churning up the household. He didn't want to institutionalise it with the formality of any remark because he believed, or at least he hoped, that the change was still incomplete. With Will, his visits wore a certain lack of intention. Poking around, fiddling with this and that, was normal for a curious five-year-old boy, and the studio had always offered redress for boredom in dreary winter weather. Gwen often involved Will in little projects – drawing or painting, using her saws on bits of the leftover wood from which she sometimes made stretchers, fixing the wood into the vice on the table to cut it up, nailing the pieces together with her hammers. Will felt at home in the studio; there could be no harm for him in being there with his father.

But there was nothing casual about the way Lawrence studied Gwen's work once he was up there. He examined every canvas slowly and methodically, stared with ravenous, calculating eyes at paintings with which he had been familiar for months, even years, others that were newer, as if he were trying to memorise what he saw. For longer than Lawrence could remember, he had unequivocally delighted in the evidence of Gwen's gift. Every painting she made had seemed to affirm, to enhance, what he so comfortably knew and enjoyed about her. He had watched over the first outbreak of her talent, and she had blossomed extravagantly in the light of his absent-minded, unconditional approval, his benevolent pride. But suddenly, he felt that he needed to trace Gwen's development all over again from the very beginning. Perhaps there was something in the paintings that he had missed, or misunderstood, a crucial theme, a revealing motif.

'What do you think of this one, Will?' Lawrence was standing in front of the portrait of Hugo. 'It never seems to change much.'

'Maybe she finished it,' said Will.

Lawrence was stunned at the thought. 'Finished it?'

Will threw a glance up to the canvas and walked away to the sink. He stood on his tiptoes, leaned across the sink and, by making a little jump, managed to grab hold of a rusty wire scouring pad sitting on top of a piece of hard, yellowed soap along the back ledge. He stuck his arm up into the air, holding the scouring pad, so that the long sleeve of his grey-blue sweatshirt fell back from his hand, freeing his fingertips. Then he reached into the sink as far as he could and started scouring at the brownish ring around the drain where the enamel had worn away. With the rhythm of his scouring, the cuff of his sweatshirt slowly slid back down over his elfin wrist, and the material began to darken as it soaked up the few drops of water in the sink. The sleeve got heavier and dragged about after a while like a wet rag, but the brown ring remained the same, an indelible stain. With his left hand, Will snatched at the sleeve, pulled it up around his elbow, held it there, still scouring.

'Doesn't Hugo come up and sit for Mummy any more?' Lawrence asked cautiously, staying by the painting, watching Will.

'What do you mean, sit for Mummy?' asked Will. 'That sounds like a dog.' He lifted the scouring pad from the halo around the drain and started on some red paint marking the front corner of the sink, directly underneath his concentrating face. He hung over the sink with both arms inside as he worked. Some of the red came away with his effort.

'Sit still, in a chair or – on – the bed. So Mummy can paint his picture?'

'Mummy can paint fine without the person sitting there. She knows what Hugo looks like. She sees him at piano.'

'But she doesn't have her paints with her at piano, does she?'

Will stopped scrubbing and turned around towards his father. Lawrence felt uneasy – about what Will might say next, and about the way in which he himself was probing the boy.

'She did the ones of you when you weren't there. And those are her best ones. Definitely better than Hilary without her clothes on. Which came out like a man, all hot and purple and cross, with a red hole instead of his willie.'

Lawrence shut his eyes hard, then started to laugh at this outburst of clarity. But he couldn't stop himself from continuing to cross-examine Will. 'The ones of me?'

'Mummy didn't show them to you?' Will turned back to the sink.

I've got Will in over his head, Lawrence thought. He isn't sure what Gwen would want him to say. Lawrence considered that he ought to tell Will he hadn't seen the paintings. And he considered that he might add a loving guarantee that he wouldn't tell Gwen Will had mentioned them. What a bond that might have made between them, father and son.

But lately he had come to fear personally the peril of maternal desertion that seemed to hang over Will, and he pictured himself and his son as a pair – neglected boys, gamins, at the mercy of Gwen's passions, haplessly struggling to hold on to her domestic attention. So Lawrence told himself that Will's future depended just as much as his own upon whatever was going on in Gwen's studio and that it was right for Will to help work this out. He felt the malleability of Will's puerile cleverness like a ball of soft wax cupped in his palm, inside his fist. Lawrence was aching to get a grip again upon his wife. He knew perfectly well that he had been looking in Gwen's paintings for some reference to himself, some statement of her feeling for him or a comment on their destiny. She said they were *all* about me, he reminded himself, and I thought I knew exactly what she meant by that. Here's Will saying the best ones are *of* me. It made Lawrence optimistic, foolish with confidence that Will could show him what he wanted to see.

He wondered for a moment, Should I pretend I *have* seen the paintings and let Will off the hook? But he was reluctant to lie. Instead, he took a chance on another leading question: 'It's not a secret? Mummy didn't say it was a secret?' He meant this to comfort Will, to assure him that there was nothing wrong, but he recognised that it might also elicit further information.

Will trudged across the studio from the sink to the bed. Three feet high, lily-skinned, crowned by a nimbus of brown curls. The siren lights on his enormous white trainers flashed red then blue, warning of moral crisis with each step: Will was the unbesmirched, vital possibility, something we could not have foreseen, Lawrence considered. Where is he going? In Lawrence's mind, it was a general question and a specific one.

The boy kneeled on the floor in his stiff, clownlike jeans and reached under the bed, his bottom pointing into the air as he flattened his face and chest on the bedside rug. He dragged out some big, crackling sheets of paper, got to his feet, picked up the sheets and carried them to his father. The damp, baggy sleeves of Will's sweatshirt were now coated in dust, and even his face was smudged.

He was holding up a watercolour of Trimalchio's candelabrum, heavily wrought, dramatically lit, Gothic and grand, both in subject and in execution.

'Oh, yes,' Lawrence said, relieved. 'Mummy told me she would do this for me. It's for my rooms in Oxford.'

'Why are you wearing that suit?' asked Will. 'Is that your school uniform in Oxford?'

'No. I don't know,' Lawrence replied, studying the bent, headless man at the edge of the frame; it looked to him to be the unidentified man in the snapshot, illustrated exactly. 'Are you sure that's me?'

'It's you in the other ones. This one doesn't have room for your head, so you can't tell.'

Will dropped all the paintings on the floor, pulled a second sheet out from under the one they were looking at. Lawrence bent down, anxious about the dropping, the handling.

'See? This one is you. Like a gladiator or those Japanese fighters on television, those sumo guys.'

There was the candelabrum again, blue-brown, green-black, with its magnificent leaves, its fluted height, towering above a round-bellied little nude man leaning against the stem of it. Not me, but Trimalchio himself, Lawrence thought. Or Silenus. She's made a bawdy cartoon of it, to make me laugh. But he felt dismayed when he examined the face.

'See how his nose is kind of long and sharp around the holes? And he has bluish-greyish eyes, all curved in a slit like yours with the skin hanging down on them, and thick yellow hair that's grey?'

'No spectacles, though,' said Lawrence.

Will looked again; to him it was not the witticism his father had intended, but a practical issue. He said with decision, 'Spectacles are just part of your clothes. And he's not wearing those, too.'

There was a third picture. 'I like this one,' Will said, 'where you are a goat on the bottom half. With your willie standing way up. Mine does that sometimes when I wake up in the morning, but yours is dancing with you.' Will put his finger on it, his eyes glowing. 'Daddy, what's that tall stick thing you're leaning on? What's that for?'

'To measure yourself against,' Lawrence said. 'To see if you've grown.'

'Why does it need to have the little bowl?'

'You can put oil in that and make a light, a sort of torchlight. Or you can even fit a candle in it,' Lawrence explained.

'Why? So you can measure yourself at night? In the dark?'

Lawrence was finding it harder and harder to answer Will's questions. He thought he ought to start all over again about the candelabrum, but he only managed to say, 'I guess some people might measure themselves at night, in the dark, yes. Some people need to do it that way.'

He was far more distressed now than before he had begun trying to find out what was going on inside his wife. What could these watercolours mean? Himself as Trimalchio, puny in height rather than grown taller? Or was it supposed to be the tutor to Bacchus, fat and leering, his wisdom drowned in the lees? And the satyr? With his enormous phallus? Am I now hideous in my wife's eyes? Panting for her in some way she finds repulsive? Some way she wants to be free of? Does she see me as the scarecrow, Priapus, warning thieves away from her fruits? Why didn't she show the pictures to me? Did she show them to her lover? Had they laughed over them together? Hidden them under the bed before climbing into it? I need to know more, he thought perversely. I need to know much more.

Whether he was in Oxford or home in Hammersmith, Lawrence now found it uncomfortable to look at any aspect of his life straight on. One Sunday morning, waking long after it was already light as he could never do during the week, Gwen and Will out for a croissant, he saw a sliver of himself in his underwear in the full-length mirror on the back of the bathroom door. Did he have the nerve to look at that?

There were dressing gowns and abandoned clothes hanging on hooks and on the doorknob, covering most of the mirror. He took them down, tossed them on the floor behind him, and saw with a shock that his body was a no more familiar reflection of the man he thought himself to be than were his relationships with his wife and with his former mistress.

Is this what Gwen sees when she looks at me? Is this what she thought of when she was painting?

His height was as impressive as ever, but it was the only part of himself to which he could happily lay claim. From its majesty hung broad hairy mounds of breast and stomach, rounded and swollen; at his armpits and along his ribs and hips hung folds of soft, drooping flesh. The waistband of his pants rode high, with a grand circumference, so that the fabric stitched over it fell well away from his groin like a flimsy tennis skirt. From the leg holes protruded two massive, pale-haired thighs, outlined above the knees by semicircular rings of skin crowding down towards the lost kneecaps, the withered calves, chunky ankles, clog-like feet. His arms, like his calves, seemed miserably thin, knob-elbowed; his shoulders were sharp-boned along the top edges, down-curving, stooping, narrow.

'You look like a bloody dowager,' he remarked to his image. He took a step closer to the glass, turned his face to the right and to the left. His neck was joined to his head by a swinging wattle, a suspension bridge of empty skin. His jawline was smooth and plump, showing bristles of beard only around the mouth and near the temple, and his cheeks were rosy, strangely feminine, as if with the sweet renewed innocence of a woman past childbearing age.

He turned around, straining to see backwards over a shoulder. Down the sides of his torso fell the same cascades of rolling flesh. No matter how he twisted his neck and adjusted his posture to straighten his back, he couldn't smooth out the sagging effect which marred his vision of his back. Could it be that those wrinkles were always there, even when he wasn't trying to look at them? That swag of age looping between his shoulder blades?

Is it time that has done this? he wondered. Or complacency? Is it a reflection of inescapable reality? Or is it evidence of self-satisfaction? Have you been too arrogant even to bother being vain? Did it never occur to you that this condition would befall you, as it befalls all mortal creatures?

He thought of Will, and he thought grimly that he ought not to resign himself too easily to the ordinary fate – growing old. You are not fifty yet, Lawrence! Look at yourself. It's gluttony, oenophilia, laziness! You're not even up to lechery any more. You're too busy looking for your next morsel of food. When was the last time you missed a meal?

And then with petulance, self-hatred, resentment of his wife, he said sourly, aloud, 'Such a good cook, you've become, my friend. How happily you tie on the apron to look after them, tackle the washing-up. When you are not on the bloody bus to your other half-a-life with the colleagues from whom you have become so alienated that they are just as happy to jeer at you as to dine with you. You are a commuter – rootless, without purpose, without community. And your body has given way underneath the weight of your brain and your obsessively cerebral way of life.'

He kicked at the garments on the floor, kicked them towards the sink in anger and frustration. Gwen's running clothes, her old navy blue shorts, her smelly, rotting T-shirt. Then he picked them up and hung them tidily back on the doorknob and reached up to put the dressing gowns on the hook above the mirror. Keeping house for her, for his family.

Neither man nor woman, he was thinking. Neither husband nor wife. Lover nor teacher. Nothing. No one.

Such a fitnik she is, he thought, irritated, damning it. Then studying the shorts, the T-shirt: Those were all my own clothes once. He took them back off the doorknob, held them up, con-sidering the size. There were two enormous safety pins stuck through the elastic at the back of the shorts, halving the size of the waist. He undid the pins and put his hands inside the shorts, spreading his fingers, still considering. He put the shorts on. I need a jockstrap if I'm really going to do this, he thought. But the shorts were tight enough, especially with his pants crushed inside them. I'll just go a few blocks, he decided, excited, slightly frightened.

He whipped the T-shirt over his head. It stank of sweat, acrid and oddly strengthening. As he yanked it downward over the mass of his chest and belly, he felt the fabric give way somewhere behind, a soft, sighing rip along the collar. She won't mind, he assured himself, opening the bathroom door, going to the bedroom to look for trainers. I'll be back before they get home from the café.

He started out bemused along the uneven pavement, glad it was a Sunday morning, not many people about, and feeling exposed like a streaker protesting with his nudity, his unweathered yellow flesh lolloping in the December air. The hairs on his pasty legs rose with the chill, the wind played boisterously into his armpits. It was raw weather, drizzling, and he could feel the thin shirt clinging uselessly, like sodden loo roll, to his soft back; see his thighs and his forearms reddening with cold and with stinging blood. Tiny drops of water freckled his spectacles, and the lenses misted inside with the wet snorts of his breath. Step by step he built up a feeling of irascible, exhilarated defiance.

If I'm her, who the devil is she? he wondered. What does she feel like when she runs along this street? Strong enough to go just as far as she likes? Can I ever feel right again in my own clothes? Or has she got them away from me for good? Can they be shared? Will I need other clothes? Will she?

Then with a grimace, Maybe we are all too many people. Trying to live too many lives instead of settling on one and living it properly. Because it is hard to discover what the right life is, or to remain convinced of it. Rooted in it. Maybe we need pruning back, like these trees, so we don't grow too big down in our roots, where we are hidden underground, and so we don't knock down every wall in the city. Jean Valjean, he thought with interest, was a tree pruner. And the son of a tree pruner. It all began when his father fell from a high limb and died, making him an orphan. What can *that* mean? Why did Hugo choose that profession for him? Tree pruner? Is there some reference there to the tree of life? Should that have been the task of the father he never had? To forbid? To punish? Is that where I've gone wrong? Nurturing growth without ever thinking it might need to be disciplined in some way? In myself? In her? Is it my fault that Gwen feels entitled to do as she likes? It is a necessary part of cultivation – pruning.

And as he ran, stubbornly, beneath the burden of his body, fighting the heavy, unwieldy sensation in his legs, he thought that he needed to rediscover something, to unearth himself from the past, from the messiness of his life. Lost youth, he grunted, is a pathetic grail. Certainly I didn't know myself then any better than I know myself now. I didn't bother to think about who I was. I acted, moved towards things, never reflecting, never looking back. No. That is not actually what I'm after – not a return to youth. I'm after who I should now be, what or where I ought to have arrived at. Where was I going? What *was* I trying for?

He caught sight of the unruffled river, sliding like a mirror through the centre of the city, drawing the sky down between its bending banks, among trees, high cement buildings, the spume of traffic, and he felt a kind of poise in himself, a possibility of continuity. It's a case of going on, he thought, in a particular direction. That slow mass of water continually arrives, carves its way.

He was panting hard, and he ran ever so slowly, sweat pouring off him. He came to a handful of practical decisions, pounding them out with his feet: that, like it or not, he would have to spend more time in Oxford until the end of term, make his presence known and comfortable, and put paid to whatever rumours there were about himself and Clare. Get on with his work in a serious way, finish off the essay about Petronius and Victor Hugo so that in the new year his mind would be free to focus for real on the forever neglected book about ancient slavery. Quarry his thesis rather than let it lie shielded by imaginary glory. And he would take a run from the cottage at the start of each day that he couldn't be home in London.

During the holidays, just after Christmas, he would take Gwen and Will away skiing in the Alps as he had planned. There was plenty of money set aside for it. Gwen had been longing for Will to learn how to ski, and Lawrence had been looking forward to surprising them both with the trip. He had never attempted to surprise them before. Getting away from the house would be good for everyone. Everyone.

CHAPTER 13

Nick Hollander always looked sharp. He was broad across the shoulders, fleshy around the mouth and neck, substantial around the middle, but his clothes fitted him so well and his posture was at once so erect and so relaxed that he made it seem as though being any thinner would be somehow ungracious, even uncool. His bulk was one of the things that made him convincing; he was clearly entirely comfortable with any appetite, including his own. His manners were as heavy as he was, heavy with calm, as if nothing could surprise him, let alone distress him. And behind it all was a hint of swagger, perceptibly restrained, as though he wished to make clear that however certain he was of himself and of his judgements, it delighted him to give way to others out of civility and good humour. He chose to give pleasure rather than to offer any of the cynicism, the cupidity, the self-satisfaction, that might have seemed natural in someone who had so obviously seen it all.

On the morning that he dropped by to look at what Gwen had ready for her show, he was wearing a navy blue cashmere blazer thick enough to bandage a wound. He certainly required no overcoat even though it was early December. When Gwen opened the door to him, he stood at ease with the tips of his broad fingers slipped into his jacket pockets, his thumbs cocked in the air, elbows high. He gave her a big smile, extended one leg towards her in an elegant gesture that seemed to invite her to study his fine shoes or the vintage of his blue jeans or perhaps even to dance; then he drew his Gucci heels together and made a gallant little bow. 'Hey, baby,' was all he said. He could tell she was surprised and flustered; he made no move to cross her threshold.

'I called you,' Gwen announced, suddenly remembering that she had.

'You did.' He continued to smile. Then he held his arms wide, inviting a hug.

'And here you are.'

'Fresh from Manhattan.'

'Oh God, you're kidding.'

'Don't get jumpy. I was coming anyway. But you're top of my list.'

He fondled a gold button. 'Give me the hug now. Don't I deserve it?' And he spread his arms again.

Gwen held her hands out in front of her, turned them over once or twice checking. 'I don't want to get paint on you.'

'I love paint. Cover me in it.'

Finally she laughed and embraced him. 'Come on then. Come in.'

He ran his palms over his white mane. 'I'm not going to eat you, you know. I had breakfast on the plane. I just came to look. That's what you wanted, right?' His voice was booming, all-American, Ringling Brothers, Barnum and Bailey; he was a born showman.

'It's what I maybe wanted the day I called. Yeah.' She drew him inside, started for the stairs.

'Dames. You're all the same. Is that insulting, Gwen, for me to say that?'

'Not for you to say it. If anyone else said it, yeah. It'd be insulting.'

He laughed from his chest, puffing as they climbed. The stairs shook and echoed with the unembarrassed heaviness of his tread. By the time they got to the studio, he was out of breath, sweating a little. 'The romantic garret. Jesus Christ,' he said. 'I can get you a better place to work, you know. You don't have to keep on climbing all these goddam stairs.' He pulled a folded and pressed square of white linen from a pocket, patted his forehead with it.

'The stairs are fine, Nick. And the place. You don't have to run my whole life.'

'Just thought I'd offer. You always seem to know exactly what you're doing. But you should look after yourself. There are thousands of feet of wall space out there for you to fill, and your pictures are already living in much nicer places than you. Penthouses in the City, stinkpots in Seal Harbor, villas on the French Riviera. You think it would ruin you to have a little taste of all that?' He glanced around the studio.

'It just doesn't interest me is the thing.'

'Skanky is what you like, huh? You're all the same. Every last one of you brilliant kids. Down in the dirt where you can smell the shit that makes it grow. And I love you for it. You're the real deal, baby. We'll make damn sure you don't starve, yeah? So what have you got for me. Huh?' He began to promenade. 'What is all this stuff pinned up on the walls? A cabinet of curiosities? Where have you been?'

'Nowhere. I did those here, for a friend.'

'What friend?'

'This one.' She guided him to the portrait of Hilary.

He took it in fast, turned and looked at Gwen, eyebrows raised, and gave a gleaming smile bookended by thirsty-looking canines. Then he turned back to the portrait nodding. 'This is a big deal, baby. This is a helluva big deal. How many of these have you got?'

'That's the only one.' Then, after a pause, 'Except this, which I've just started.' And she pulled him towards the portrait of Hugo.

'You cunning thing. One hot, one cold. Wow. That's it? Just these two?'

Gwen looked at the floor, silent, her stomach knotting.

'Well, don't get all downcast. You need more time, that's all.'

He left her there by the portraits and stalked around the perimeter of the room taking in the abandoned canvases by the long rear window and under the skylight, studying each of the watercolours intently for a second or two. Then he said with confidence, 'We'll postpone the big exhibition here in London. I don't want to showcase these landscapes now; you're done with that and I can sell them all privately. I've got plenty of takers for your old stuff. Keep working on the nudes and the faces. See where you're going with them. And meanwhile, I'll show the watercolours; but maybe in New York instead of here. Let me think about it. Eleven by fourteen . . . I'll get you five or six thousand dollars for each one – say around four thousand pounds? There must be what, fifty or sixty of them?' He started counting under his breath, bouncing a finger at each of the watercolours. 'So that'll buy you a year easy – much longer the way you live.' He gave her a wink, as if it were applause. 'This way, we can bring in more first-time buyers and expand your market before the next show, which is going to be *big*. It's terrific, baby. Just terrific. You're full of surprises!'

'No shit, Nick.' Gwen was deadpan; she didn't let herself do the multiplication problem Nick was setting her. She refused to be moved by numbers. 'So you better listen to this: the watercolours aren't for sale.'

'Why the hell not?' He wasn't worried; his voice purred with the seasoned certainty that everything's for sale at the right price.

'I told you, I did them for her.' Gwen jerked a matter-of-fact thumb towards the picture of Hilary.

'Big fee, just to lie down for you. You must be painting way too slowly.' He laughed, testing her with this flash of facetiousness. Then, more sympathetically, he said, 'Is there something I'm not getting? Who the hell is she? A supermodel? You should let me negotiate this stuff for you. I can get them out of bed – into bed – for free for you.'

'Fuck off, Nick. She's my oldest friend. These are pictures of a collection of antiquities she planned to build a museum for. But her life's totally off the rails. She got into trouble with it and so – at the moment, these are it. All she has.'

For the first time since his arrival, Nick stood completely still for an instant. His face went straight and he said in a tone of acknowledgement, 'Those antiquities people are scary. It makes *my* hair stand on end. Half the stuff is hot, you know. And they'll shop their best friends to hold on to pieces for themselves. It's the good guys who get screwed in that business, I'll tell you. The ones who only break a few rules. The real criminals are cutting deals with the authorities. That whole market is unbelievably shaky.'

There was a little silence. Then he said, 'Hell. Where do I go to talk to this woman who owns all this work of yours? You're really not entitled to be giving it away out of the studio in this volume if you want to be with me.' He laughed again, a hoot of satisfaction, teasing her. 'If she's a friend, Gwen, she's got to be interested in your career. Let me at least meet her.'

Gwen looked at him, chewing her lip, impassive. Then she put her hands on her hips. 'It's a bad idea.' But it was like a drug to her, the possibility of something altogether new, and maybe a way forward for Hilary.

'Trust me, baby. Come on. I heard you when you said she's your best friend. And anyway, I can see from her picture that she's not to be trifled with.' He swept his cashmere arm towards the canvas, grinning. 'Whoa-no! I'm not planning a campaign of manipulation and intimidation. No campaign at all. I'm just intrigued. That's all.' He grew serious, soft-voiced. 'I tell you, I'm helpless with curiosity. That's the bottom line.'

'She'd be able to write an amazing catalogue,' Gwen said quietly. 'Or an essay, anyway, for a show.'

Nick cocked a beady ear. 'She need work?'

'I don't know. I mean – maybe she does. And – you know – money.'

'Well, if she needs money, she can let me sell her damn pictures for her, can't she?'

Just then, Hilary was stretched out in a sleeping bag between two massive old mahogany kneehole desks in a second-floor office near 125th Street on the Columbia University campus. She felt safer between the desks at night in case anybody managed to come in, and also there was a small rug there, which afforded some dusty padding under her hipbones, her knees and the bit of bruised shoulder she could fit on to the rug if she curled up small enough. But she wasn't asleep; she was deciding something.

At last, she unwadded herself from the sleeping bag and stumbled around the desks and the rolling, spinning, shin-barking office chairs to the door, which had a frosted-glass window in the upper half. She had to be wary of janitors; they were not on her side. But when she inched the door open and leaned out into the dark hallway, it was as still as a tomb.

She pressed the door shut again, trying not to let the glass rattle, and turned on the fluorescent overhead light which snapped and buzzed with nerve-racking loudness as it brightened. Then she dragged one of her big black suitcases on to the rug, laid it down, and unzipped it. Inside were dozens of plastic file boxes, lined up in tight rows. About a third of the file boxes were red, the other two-thirds were green. On top of them lay a little sheaf of papers, heavily written by hand, nearly all in her own writing, with a few notes added here and there by Eddie in black Rapidograph in his minuscule print. She took up the sheaf of papers savagely, as if to rip it in two, then stopped, looked around, and leaped to one of the desks, opening and shutting the drawers. The drawers were all empty; real professors didn't seem to have anything, or if they did, they kept it someplace else. She folded the sheets in half and put them into a bottom drawer, pushing them all the way to the back. Then she took all the file boxes out of the suitcase and stood them on the floor in their neat-edged, plastic simplicity. One by one, she opened them, emptying the bundles of individual clear sleeves, with their descriptions and their photographs, back into the suitcase.

She opened a red file box, then a green one, another green one, a red one, two more green ones. As she released the sleeves into the suitcase – slippery fish with snapshots for eyes and Times Roman print for scales, a few enlivened by the odd squiggle of calligraphy – she sorted through them, hunkering down until her knees cramped, checking for categorising features, certain notations, once in a while a tiny coloured sticker with a figure, a letter, a word written on it and which she removed. She stirred the growing heap inside the case, mixing the files up thoroughly before opening each new box. It took her more than an hour to empty them all. About halfway through, she got up and touched her toes, stretched her arms to the ceiling, strolled around the room.

Dumpsters were being juggled and slammed in the winter darkness outside by the time she was done. It was useless to lie down again. She sneaked along the broad granite landing to the Ladies room, brushed her teeth without making a sound, then, as she did every morning, fled back to the office in terror from the thunderous jolt the plumbing made when she flushed the toilet. She could hear traffic now on Amsterdam Avenue, intermittent whooshing, a shameless horn.

She rolled up the sleeping bag, slipped it back inside one of the two green metal trash cans, and put the trash can, upside down, into the bottom of the free-standing cupboard. Then she arranged the discarded file boxes on one of the bookcases, which were just as empty as the desk drawers, a row of red on top and a longer row of green underneath. She opened her other suitcase where it lay under the window, and changed methodically out of her sweatpants into a shapeless grey flannel skirt and jacket which she had bought on sale in the women's department at Brooks

Brothers. She put on a blue wool pullover under the jacket, even though it made the jacket uncomfortably tight, and she took out the gloves and wool scarf that she relied on to withstand cold walks around the Upper West Side and long waits at bus stops. Finally, she zipped up the big black suitcase, wheeled it out to the elevator, slamming the door locked behind her, and walked the suitcase across campus to Broadway where she could sit over coffee until it was time to catch the subway downtown.

Mark's office seemed to be full of people, which made Hilary feel hopeless and overexcited at the same time. She had half allowed herself to imagine a private interview for the handover, and an opportunity to ask some personal questions. Ranging from practical ones – about her clothes and her books – to more personal ones which she wasn't sure how to phrase. How have you been? Isn't there some way we can work this out – after all the years we spent together?

But clearly, there was no way they could work it out. A dozen telephone conversations during the course of the autumn had produced only more entrenched rage on both sides. Now she was looking at proof that Mark had no wish for a rapprochement of any kind, even on a footing of friendship: Paul Mercy and a blonde sat at their ease in the big tweed chairs flanking Mark's desk. Nobody stood up to greet her.

Bastards, she thought to herself as she dragged the suitcase through the door and flung it around in front of her on the little wheels which wouldn't roll on Mark's thick carpet. She was perspiring with effort and with anxiety.

The blonde was coolly turned out in a cream silk blouse with a drooping bow at the neck, a raw silk jacket in silvery charcoal and black flecks, a black pencil skirt hugging so tightly that it seemed to be sewn to her gossamer-weight black tights, and super-high black heels. On her raised, pinned-together knees, she had a little lilac-coloured laptop, which she now powered down and closed with a click, making a show of dragging her attention to the boring matter at hand.

'Just looking over the Met archive,' she said in a hyper-British accent, notifying nobody in particular of what preoccupied her. 'Their website's quite convincing. But we'll do more with ours once we settle on the designer.'

Hilary stopped in the middle of the floor, took off her jacket and hung it on the extending handle of the suitcase, yanked the pullover off, hung it where the jacket was and put the jacket back on, her hair a dark cloud of anarchy. 'Getting good use out of my winter coat, Mark?'

He sat up in his chair with a scowl and threw a glance at the blonde. 'I don't have your winter coat, Hilary. I don't have *anything* of yours. There are some garbage bags in the basement of my building which you might want to take a look at. Otherwise, it's about time I had the bags sent to the Goodwill.'

'You don't have *anything* of mine?' Hilary repeated.

Mark blinked and looked down, drumming all ten of his black-haired, manicured fingers on the trim stack of paper that lay in front of him. He opened his big desk drawer into his stomach, tilted his chair back on its wheels, and scrabbled around inside the drawer until he fished out a red rubber band – as if this might belong to Hilary: a rubber band. Then he fished out a paper clip. He stretched the rubber band over his thumbs, tested its give idly. Then he slipped the paper clip on to it, like a boy making a weapon in the classroom. He said nothing. It was insulting.

'You could have told me sooner,' Hilary said. 'It's been pretty damn cold for the past five weeks without my winter clothes.'

She hardly dared to look at Paul; when she let her glance fly sidelong over him, she thought he had his eyes on the floor. She noticed the well-worn and well-polished chestnut leather of his lace-up shoes, his thin socks with grey and navy fine vertical stripes, smooth-fitting on his slender ankles, the cuffed hem of his grey flannel trousers. Dandy, she couldn't help thinking, to the tips of his toes. Paul still didn't seem obvious to Hilary. Even now, she felt she could learn something she wanted to know just by looking at his socks. Why had he never answered his phone when she had tried to call him from Gwen's? Had he left town so quickly to make common cause with Mark? His perfect mismatch?

Aloud she said, imperiously, looking at Mark, 'What about my books?'

Still Mark said nothing. She could feel him bristling at her, his very beard bursting out through his bluish shaven skin, darkening his groomed face with something savage. His wiry brown-black hair, his heavy brows, might as well have been the fur of a wild animal, a caveman, right here on the thirty-second floor of this glass-and-steel skyscraper. When at last he looked up for an instant, his eyes were armour-plated, their muddy brown rolling in a field of burst corpuscles.

'Which were all at Eddie's?' The books were important to Hilary, and she was afraid there was a telltale creak beginning in her voice.

'Ah,' said Paul mellifluously, lightly, from his chair. 'Perhaps I can help there.' He seemed to speak from another world, where everybody was polite, sympathetic, unstriving. 'Could I trouble you to give me a list? I've noticed a few books about the place, and I'm sure it won't be at all difficult to find yours. Shall we agree that you send the list here, to Mr Bushette's office, and I can see to it that the books are posted to – to – well, naturally, to wherever you like?'

It's as if we had never even met, thought Hilary. How can he do it? The pose of courtesy, of serenity? He even seems – kind. 'Is that a promise?' she asked sharply.

Paul looked her in the eye, caught by surprise. The lenses of his spectacles flashed in the light. 'What do you mean?'

'Exactly what I asked. Is that a promise?' She had no problem now, holding her ground with him.

He appeared to think about it, grumpy, his slender figure in its natty clothes slipping down in the chair a little. 'Well, then –' He sighed slightly, as if to assert that he was an honourable man. 'I give you my word – if you feel it's necessary.'

Hilary had now secured from the situation the only thing she was absolutely certain she could. Anything more called for luck.

'The files are in this suitcase,' she said simply. 'I'll stop by your building this afternoon, Mark. Maybe you could tell the doorman I'm coming.' She turned to go.

'One moment.' The blonde woman stood up and spoke peremptorily. 'Wait outside while we examine them.'

'Have we met?' Hilary asked. In fact, Hilary knew more than she wanted to about Clare Pryce. Mark had boasted remorselessly about her on the phone – how highly recommended she was by 'your friend, Lawrence Phillips, and his colleagues'. She had tried not to listen, not to believe him. But asking around the department at Columbia, it had seemed to be true. And worse besides – rumours had circulated back to her that Clare Pryce was Lawrence's mistress, and that Lawrence or Lawrence's friends had wanted to get her out of Oxford where she was threatening to cause a scandal. This information had startled Hilary, and it had made her feel intensely disappointed. Now that she was face to face with Clare, Hilary also felt angry – at all of them, even Gwen. What did they amount to after all – Gwen and Lawrence? And how dare Lawrence or Roland or whoever unload this monstrous woman into the middle of her life?

The blonde woman bridled and looked down at Mark, practically spitting with annoyance.

Up bobbed Mark in his floppy, dark blue suit. 'Sorry, Clare. The formalities. Hilary Boyd – Clare Pryce. An Oxford colleague of Paul's? You *do* know Paul – right? Both of them are big experts.'

He nodded at Clare and turned hot pink, a blush of agony rather than enthusiasm.

Pathetic, Hilary thought. It never even dawned on me that you wanted someone to put a collar on you. She could feel it right away though, how helplessly, how happily, Mark was under Clare's heavy thumb. Was it like this between Clare and Lawrence? She found the idea bewildering and strangely hurtful. As if Lawrence had betrayed her just as much as he had betrayed his wife.

'I'm sorry,' Hilary said. 'I can't wait.' She dropped the suitcase flat, kneeled down and unzipped it, then stood up with the handle in her hand and flipped the suitcase upright again, hard, so that the contents spewed out on to the floor like a flow of lava. 'The files are all yours,' she said a little wildly. 'You know how to reach me if you have any questions.'

The three of them — Mark, Paul, Clare — rushed across the room squawking, flapping their arms. They grabbed at the files, tried to hold them back with their hands.

'How dare you do such a thing!' scolded Clare.

'How dare *you*?' said Hilary, folding her arms.

'Where's the disk?' demanded Mark. 'I thought you had it all on a disk?'

'I shouldn't worry,' Clare assured him, taking control. 'We can scan these in. It's just as well to have the original photos. These *are* the originals?'

Hilary didn't reply.

Paul was down on his hands and knees in the litter of plastic and paper. 'Four bloody thousand items,' he cackled. Then he swayed his face up towards Hilary, giggling, impressed. 'Absolutely no way we can be sure which are for the sale and which are for the museum! You were very canny about all that in the summer, weren't you?'

'Not especially on purpose,' Hilary said. 'But I must have had some instinct — as it turns out.'

Paul dropped his eyes, embarrassed. Then he stood up again and took Mark to one side, putting both his hands on Mark's forearm, whispering up to him very quietly, beseechingly. Mark became angry, shook off Paul's hands, turned away and shoved his own hands into the pockets of his big blue trousers. But Paul was unfazed. He pushed his delicate fist inside Mark's elbow, linking arms with him, and drew him companionably away to the window behind Mark's desk.

Hilary caught the phrase, 'My dear fellow'. After that, she could make out the conversation only from Mark's intermittent angry bursts.

'I don't care if we have to postpone the sale! . . . Not in any capacity whatsoever . . . That's exactly why we've agreed to hire Clare . . . you two'll figure it out . . . This stuff *always* appreciates. I won't go to the Board of Trustees with that . . . Look what she's just done! . . . Completely unreliable . . . a schemer and a double-crosser . . .'

Hilary sensed that it was a conversation the two of them had had before. It was distressing, and a little bizarre, to hear Paul, who had caused her so much pain, trying to persuade Mark to engage her help. Paul was ruthless in his way, practical, entirely unsentimental; but it was Mark who was against her. Mark who had been part of the furniture of her life. A big, heavy, unwieldy, immovable piece of furniture. Something she was so used to seeing that she never even looked at it. And she found herself hoping that Mark would continue to say no to Paul – how could she work with Mark or be involved with him in any way ever again? He'd have to go, Hilary realised, for me to be able to come back. And then she thought, Mark must have seen it all along – that we can't both be on this project any more.

Clare was counting the files into groups of twenty. She picked up the phone and asked for help. Hilary dropped into Paul's chair.

When Mark's PA scurried in and began to help counting the

files, Clare joined the whispered discussion at the window. Soon she approached Hilary's chair, the other two gathering behind her.

'Miss Boyd,' said Clare cuttingly, 'it is of little consequence whether or not you are prepared to clear up this mess you've made. Obviously, the most efficient way forward is to sell all the pieces Mr Doro left in the warehouse and to keep for his museum the ones in the apartment. I'm sure that will serve his memory perfectly adequately.'

Hilary was outraged. 'Mark!' She tried to look at him, to see his eyes. 'You know that's wrong! You know as well as I do that some of the stuff at Eddie's is there just because it's always been there — ever since he started collecting! And some of it is just really hard to move!'

Clare didn't let Mark reply. 'Fine, then,' she asserted. 'We'll do it the other way around. Sell what's in the apartment.'

'No! There's other stuff in the apartment that he only bought recently — he always had new pieces delivered at home first so he could get to know them. And also — and also —' she felt miserable getting it out — 'he had things there which he was having trouble making up his mind about — as to whether or not he wanted them sold. Near the end, he kept them close to him. He needed to look — every day — all the time —'

Hilary felt herself sinking into the sorrow that lay beneath her anger. She had carried some of those objects back and forth to Eddie more times than she could count, shared in his appraisal of them, each with its individual, ancient features. For some reason she thought of the black Persian helmet tipped with gold along the blade-like spine that formed its crown. '*Do you see, this must have been a bit of gold here, too?*' '*Oh, yes, how deluxe! How barbarous —*' She thought of the statuettes of Roman household gods — Lares, Penates, Mercury with his winged helmet and winged sandals. '*Don't you think we ought to have our own little god who can carry messages between the living and the dead?*' And then she thought of her favourite Etruscan couple, arms interlaced – as if it would do them any good.

'Mark!' she cried out. 'Don't you *remember*? Mark? You promised him –'

'We could make a terrific splash publicity-wise,' Clare breathed. She turned back to Mark and grabbed his hand, narrowed her eyes at him, inhaled slowly. 'Photographs of everything just as it is, in the apartment,' she said suggestively, 'with private views right there for the high rollers.' Her voice was gloating with greed – greed for a moment in the limelight. 'I wonder whether we could fit enough people to have the sale right there, in situ? And all the press in as well.'

Hilary was disgusted.

Paul was trying to interpose himself physically between Mark and Clare. 'Mark,' he urged, 'we ought to review this matter in private. Let's agree another meeting with Hilary in a few days' time, when we've been able to look over all these files and to reflect and perhaps to talk things through. We ought to consult one or two of the trustees on this as well. I feel I really must insist.'

Hilary let them talk on above her head. She began to think she could slide out of the chair and simply leave and they would never notice.

But then the alarm was raised over the missing files.

'Three thousand, nine hundred and forty,' whispered the assistant to Clare.

'Three thousand, nine hundred and forty?' hissed Clare.

'Three thousand, nine hundred and forty!' shouted Mark.

Paul looked at Hilary, his eyes lighting up with mischief. 'What have you done, you minx? You are never so sweet and simple as you seem. And so I always thought.'

But Mark was exploding. 'Sixty missing files!!' he shouted down at Hilary, his tongue protruding in a lather of saliva. 'What the hell are you trying to pull? Hand them over, or I will tie you up in court for the rest of your life and you will never have another job or a penny of cash or a moment of free time!'

'For Christ's sake, Mark. They're only *files*! I've been sleeping on floors, moving around. They're somewhere. And I'll find them.'

But Hilary was stricken. There were confidences she had exchanged with Mark along the way. About her ups and downs with Eddie. A while back, not so many later. Mark knew what she loved. At least, if he cared to think about it, he knew. And Paul could easily help him work it out. Once Mark had said to her, late at night, 'Why don't you ask Eddie to give you those pieces you always fight over? He's a selfish old bastard. You deserve something big for all this. So do I. Then we could sell them and get a great place to live outside the city. In case we ever —'

She had shut him up. 'I would never sell them, Mark!'

'Maybe I'll tell Eddie myself that he ought to give you something.'

She had earnestly begged Mark not to bring it up, and she had never allowed herself to think any further on what the suggestion revealed about Mark. Not until now.

She didn't like his knowing sixty files were missing. They were in her briefcase up at Columbia. She just couldn't bear to part with them. She had no other reason for keeping them.

Mark went on shouting. 'You know damn well they're somewhere. And I want to know where. Which sixty, Hilary? Those are not yours; Eddie never signed anything over to you. Not one goddammed item. Don't forget I was the one who introduced you to him. *I'm* Eddie's lawyer; *I'm* Eddie's executor. *I* was the architect of this trust. And I'm the one who'll build the museum!'

Finally, Hilary lost control. She shouted at Mark, at Paul, at Clare. 'You fuckers!! You better get straight about this collection. You better figure out exactly what you're doing, or I will write the biggest exposé you have ever seen. I can get this covered in the newspaper. I have friends. You're practically criminals, railroading a man's dying wishes to serve your own ambitions.'

She even tried a lie. 'I'll go to the police if I have to. I don't care if I implicate myself. I know which items in the collection can't be made public. Do you know? Do you know which ones can't be auctioned or exhibited? Which ones came through the Italian underground?'

She looked at Paul, daring him.

'Honestly, Hilary.' He was nonplussed as always.

'Do you?' She knew that Paul was as confident as she was that none of the items in Eddie's collection was stolen. But it was a hefty threat; even a rumour would drive away buyers. He held his tongue, and she felt somehow that he would continue to do so.

It was a day or two later when Hilary found Nick Hollander waiting for her up at Columbia. He had come straight from the airport in his jeans and his cashmere blazer, a camel-hair overcoat looped across his forearms. He was leaning against the wall outside the office where she had been sleeping, and he scared the hell out of her when he shrugged himself upright and approached her as she arrived a little out of breath at the top of the stairs.

'I'll bet you're Hilary,' he said buoyantly.

She glared at him and kept moving, one shoulder lowered towards him, as if to fend him off. She wanted to get to her laptop and her files, double-check again that she still had all the things she was relying on. Instinct drove her to get to them before this stranger could, to race him to her secret cache, and to beat him off if necessary.

'I'm a friend of Gwen's,' Nick persisted.

She slowed up, within reach of the door, about to knock on the glass in case anyone was inside.

'A friend of Gwen's?'

Nick beamed at her, expansive, reassuring.

'How do I know?' She wanted it to be true. She needed help;

228

she needed relief. Yesterday afternoon, crying into the mildewed mess of her personal belongings in Mark's basement, she had realised that it hardly mattered that nearly everything she owned was ruined. She had no place to keep it unless she was prepared to steal a shopping cart and wheel it around the city with her. She had pulled out her winter coat, three or four other pieces of work clothing, dropped them off optimistically at a dry-cleaner's, and abandoned the rest. It would be incredible if Gwen had sent a friend just now.

'Tough question,' Nick said. 'How does anyone know if someone's a friend?'

'Oh, come on,' Hilary said impatiently.

'Can I buy you a cup of coffee?'

'I'm really – in kind of a rush.'

'Looks like it,' said Nick, studying her pinched face, her weary posture. 'Gwen told me you could probably do with some TLC,' he went on. 'I was just with her in London. I couldn't get much out of her, except that I might find you here. And the kindly professor who was inside that office until just a few minutes ago told me it was OK to hang around for you.'

'So Gwen thought we should meet?' Hilary was sizing it up – Gwen's dauntless matchmaking, the look of the new prospect. It's like she has tried to send me a bouquet of flowers, Hilary thought, all the way from London. Even though – or because? – I've been out of touch. He's a little old. Or maybe he's a little young. And he's a little flash for what's left of my wardrobe. Does Gwen really think that at the eleventh hour some guy is going to walk into my life? Wouldn't it be something if she were right.

But then Hilary thought, Don't fall for that bullshit. You were never more vulnerable.

'*I* thought we should meet. It was my idea,' Nick announced. 'Gwen wasn't so sure.'

This made Hilary laugh. She looked at the clock by the elevator. 'OK. OK. We can get some coffee, and you can tell me all about Gwen. And about Will. Give me a second, would you?' She tapped on the office door as if she didn't quite trust that no one was there, unlocked it, slipped inside and closed it behind her.

She snatched her laptop from her black nylon briefcase in the cupboard, turned it on, and, while she waited for it, felt inside the briefcase to be sure of the sixty plastic sleeves of notes. Next, she rummaged for the handwritten list in the back of the desk drawer; there it was, where she'd stuffed it the other morning. Her software came to with its phoney flourish of strings, and she clicked through her files – all there. Why did it make her sweat so? What was she so afraid could have happened to her work? Sucked out of the computer into the air? Conveyed mysteriously into the hands of her enemies? Or simply evaporated? Gone for ever?

It was just as absurd how protective she felt about the sixty sets of notes with their photos. She had now been carrying them close to her for too long. As a substitute for everything else. She knew that they had become unreasonably important. A memento of the past and also some wish she had had for the future. To do with grieving, or with growing up. Exacerbated by Gwen when she had painted them, because Gwen had magnified her sense of conflict but had not helped her to resolve it. Hilary planned to take the notes downtown tonight and deliver them to Mark's office casually and anonymously after hours, as if she were a messenger boy. She was determined not to draw attention to them as something she wanted or had in any way singled out. She didn't want to show Mark any weaknesses, or give him or that Clare Pryce an idea of what to sell first, quickest, most cruelly.

She turned off the laptop, put it back on the shelf in the cupboard, and took the half-full briefcase with her.

'Did you go to school here?' Nick asked her as they walked down the wide shallow steps in front of Lowe Library.

'For a while, graduate school. I never finished.'

'So, what's the connection? What are you doing now?'

She clutched the briefcase tightly under one arm and squinted into the cold wind blowing up from the Hudson. People crawled past them up the massive steps, over the colossal grey granite paving stones.

'Not a lot. Some research. By the hour. For a friend who lets me use that office. The kindly professor as you called him. And actually, I'm thinking of finishing off my PhD, if I can get some teaching to pay for it.' She tried to laugh, feeling on the spot. 'What do *you* do? Why don't *you* talk?'

'I sell paintings. First I pick 'em out, then I sell 'em. Every now and then, I keep one I can't bear to part with. It's a great job. I love it.'

It made Hilary a little dizzy that a man like this, who appeared to be so in command of himself, might come across something he couldn't bear to part with. 'You're Gwen's dealer,' she managed to say.

'I didn't keep that from you long,' said Nick. 'So – cut to the chase. I've got a proposal for you.'

The dizziness hardened to a ringing in her ears. She knew he didn't mean Gwen's kind of proposal; she had completely missed the point about being set up with Nick. Something's coming at me, she thought. I can feel his managing way, his push. She strolled on beside him, trying to listen.

'Let me represent you.'

'Represent me?'

'Look after you, make you some dough.'

'How on earth – I don't have anything. I'm down to pretty much nothing at all.'

'So my timing's perfect, don't you think?'

'What do you mean?' She tried to picture Nick tangling with Mark. Clare he could do, she thought, oddly enough. Mincemeat in no time. She wasn't so sure about Paul. 'What *did* Gwen tell you?'

They were walking through the one-storey-high, black, wrought-iron gates letting out on to Broadway.

'Told me nothing –' He put his hand on her back, confidently, as the walk sign flashed green a few paces in front of them and he pressed her forward to catch the light and cross the street. But she stopped and turned towards him, eluding his touch, shifting the briefcase around on to her tummy, holding it with her arms linked around the outside, one in back, one in front. She was as tall as he was, but much thinner, shaking with cold.

Nick buttoned the top button of his coat, put his hands into the roomy pockets. 'Let's get you inside. Don't you think?'

'Here's good,' said Hilary. 'She told you nothing?'

'It's what she showed me, Hilary. Do you mind if I call you Hilary?'

'No, I don't mind.' She went a little red, teeth chattering, her face burning with a kind of curiosity about what she and Gwen between them had put on show. 'The portrait?'

'Totally amazing. You and Hugo, the music box downstairs.' He wiggled his eyebrows and said in an undertone like a parenthesis, '*There's* something you can maybe fill me in on later. I always thought Gwen was the constant wife. Or was she just fending me off?' Then returning to his main subject, 'But, no, Hilary – the Greek and Roman stuff. If you let me show that in my gallery here in town, I can sell the whole collection for you, and you'll have plenty to live on for a while. Or hire lawyers, or whatever it is you want to do. Grad school.'

She felt a rushing sensation. The wind seemed to whirl too briskly around her ears, numb as they were with cold; the traffic surged along Broadway as the light changed again, tyres whacking the manhole covers down into the tar, rubber and soot mixing in her nose. Then her stomach spinning. The briefcase seemed heavy, loaded with bricks, her arms weak, filled with air. 'You're just *all* fuckers!' she shouted at him.

His jaw dropped on to his camel-hair collar. Then he grinned. 'Excuse me?'

'Lay the hell off. You're like – some kind of sadist.'

'May I ask why?' His voice was tidy, deadpan, as near as Nick Hollander ever got to showing irritation.

'I don't know what you're trying to say about Gwen and Hugo. But you don't know what you're talking about. And the Greek and Roman stuff – you mean my watercolours? You had no business looking at those!'

'Whoa, whoa, whoa. Let's be reasonable here. True enough, I don't really know anything about Hugo. I was interested in a little friendly conjecture – called gossip – that's all. Of course I don't know what they get up to all alone in her studio. But it's not like she's trying to hide it. She's a friend, and I care about her. As a matter of fact, I care about her a *lot*. As for the watercolours, I'm her dealer, baby. Like you said. She *had* to show me those.'

Hilary felt double-crossed, deeply wronged. She knew that Nick was offering a way to get free of the trap she was in. She ached for it like the end of a boat race – release from the unbearable strain she was under, the pain of continuing to struggle. But she didn't want to be sprung; it didn't feel right to her. 'I don't want any fucking help from you – or from Gwen. Who the hell does she think she is?' Here was another asshole saying, We could sell them. Doesn't anybody get it? she wondered. I would never sell them! 'I told you I'm down to pretty much nothing. And now, I guess, one less friend!'

'Come on, you're not down a friend.' Nick was always bored by exaggeration. 'Gwen's on your side just as much as it's possible for someone to be. She told me not to mess with this. She told me to leave you alone.'

'I need to see those pictures.' Hilary turned away, suddenly thinking she might begin to cry, raging at Gwen for exposing her in this way, exposing the inside of her mind and the outside of her body. Man, Gwen she takes what she wants, Hilary thought.

Nick put a gentle hand on her arm. 'Look, Hilary. Do this. Jump on a flight to London. Go see her. And see your pictures. I'll pay. I've messed things up between you guys. It's my chit. And you know what? I'm sorry. I really am.'

CHAPTER 14

Hilary arrived back in London on the 17th of December, a cold morning under a muted sky, just after the end of Will's school term. Will led the way as she and Gwen dragged her suitcase and her briefcase upstairs and heaved them through the door into the studio.

As soon as Hilary saw the watercolours pinned to the walls, she cried out, 'God, you've still got them all up!' Then, with the three of them bunched together, hovering on the threshold uncomfortably close to one another, she said stridently, 'Everything you do makes it worse, Gwen. I had those assholes in the palm of my hand – without me, they have no idea what to sell and what to keep! And then your goddam friend Nick, your dealer or whatever, shows up with this idea of plastering your water-colours all over his art gallery for everyone in Manhattan to come and ogle! Which made me realise that I don't have a secret in the world or any control over what's happening in my life. And that maybe I don't even know who you are.'

Gwen took a few steps forward into the room, squeezing past Hilary, hands on Will's shoulders, shooing him along in front of her, head down as if she were expecting a blow. 'Forget about Nick. He thinks he can sell anything. He couldn't resist. He's always trying to solve all my problems, too, problems I don't even have. He's a mother hen. I told him to leave you alone.'

'But you told him where to find me,' Hilary said accusingly.

Gwen was silent, preoccupied by Will.

'I can see why you did it,' Hilary acknowledged, leaning against the door frame. For a moment, she was practical. 'I thought about the money a lot on the plane. But I wouldn't be able to control it; nobody would. If the exhibition was a success, it would just make the artefacts more valuable and that would actually help Mark. He'd be able to sell them faster and for more money, and I'd have nothing left apart from some cash. Not even your paintings.'

'So don't do it.' Gwen was definite. And then she asked, trying to puzzle it out in her head, 'But — so wait — the things I painted — they're in the auction? They're not going into the museum?' It was finally making an impression on Gwen, just how complicated it might be, sorting out the fate of four thousand objects.

'I thought you knew everything,' Hilary said caustically. But it wasn't really an answer. She started in another direction, her mood building. 'All the notes for the sale catalogue, the descriptions and most of the photos — it's all my own work. I spent nearly a decade on it, you know. Mark hasn't offered me a penny for anything. He stopped my salary right away when I left him. So upset! It must have been the first thing he did once I was out the door! My arrangement with Eddie lapsed when he died, and we were just going from month to month — no contract or anything. All this time, Mark's been yelling that he would sue me if I didn't hand over all my files. I don't have resources for a legal thing. Which Mark knows, and which he is *counting* on. He's a complete jerk. An arrogant *bastard*.' She hammered the door frame with the side of her fist, low down, by her hip. 'But I've turned the tables on him now. I just shuffled all the files together and dumped them on his floor! Absolutely nothing can go forward without what I know. He's paralysed.'

Hilary's voice and her diction were toxic. Gwen wanted to neutralise them any way that she could. She turned and smiled at Hilary, saying in a sugary voice, 'He'll hire you back in the end. He'll have to. After Christmas? He'll calm down by then, don't you think?'

But the poison kept coming. 'The goddam thing between me and Mark was too close; most of the board is basically relieved

I'm gone, and a crisp, clean professional relationship established with an outsider. On merit – whatever that is. So. He hired Paul to take my place. And the board approved it, thanks to Roland's enthusiastic support – all those goddam recommendations Lawrence sent them when *I* was hiring Paul.'

'Really?' Gwen glanced at Will. He climbed on to the freshly made bed and lay down on his stomach, watching them, elbows bent up on the mattress, chin in his hands, his feet waving around in the air over him. Gwen wanted Hilary to take note of Will's presence, so she sat down beside him and stroked his back a few times as she tried to fathom the force, the ugliness, of Hilary's anger.

'Paul's heading up the whole project now. And hiring in his friends. Mark is even more of a sucker than I am for the Oxford tradition, the British accent.' She said the last words with her teeth, scornfully mimicking. 'I feel like I was set up – start to finish. When I think back over the summer, how attentive and friendly Paul seemed, the sort of questions he asked me, which I so willingly – *eagerly* – answered, it's totally obvious he was just picking my brain.'

'Well, maybe he's an opportunist –' Gwen began, and then with a little gasp, half stifled, 'So – But Paul knows what's in, what's out? *He* could advise them about what to sell?'

Hilary shrugged. 'Maybe a few items he can identify for sure. But when he and I worked on the provenances, I had everything grouped by geography to make the travel easy. He was a fool not to go with me, because he'd know much more. Man, I put his name out there; everyone knows who he is. Still, there's a lot I never told him – fantasising I could hold his attention if I had a few secrets to tempt him with!' She said it harshly, all self-disdain, but then added, with a tremor that sounded like sorrow or nostalgia, 'Or maybe – I don't know – maybe there was a part of me that couldn't trust him with *everything* Eddie had taught me. Anyway,' her tone grew stubborn, 'I don't think he'll run an auction on hunches. There are risks, and he knows what they are. We need to command certain prices. I feel pretty sure of Paul, actually.'

'I'm glad you decided to come back,' Gwen said with warmth, trying again to change the atmosphere. 'We're all glad. Aren't we, Will?'

'Yeah.' Will nodded his head as much as he could with it resting in his hands.

Hilary finally took off her newly dry-cleaned overcoat and dumped it next to Will on the bed, then she walked around the room scowling at the watercolours, stretching and yawning. 'I hope you haven't been letting a lot of other people in here to see these pictures. I really love them. But there are a lot of clues here. Honestly, Gwen.'

She hesitated, still wondering what Gwen meant by the water-colours. 'You know – if you and Nick exhibited these pictures – It's almost like a list – of some of the most important items that have to be sold. You mustn't let anyone in here to see them. Especially not Lawrence and your so-called friend, Roland. They can't be trusted. You realise that, don't you? They could easily mention something, or even write out descriptions and send them to New York.'

'But who would they mention it to?'

Hilary gave her such an intense look that Gwen finally raised a warning finger in the air and pressed it to her lips, gesturing with her eyebrows towards Will. Then she said, 'Wait a second, Hil. I want to hear all this. I really do. Just wait.'

She turned to Will. 'Do you want to make something, Will? Maybe do some cutting over there at my workbench?'

He stopped waving his legs in the air, but he didn't look up at her. 'What is there to cut?' he asked non-committally. Then he slid off the bed, right over Hilary's coat, walked across the studio and climbed on to the stool, reaching towards the white china marmalade jar for the big pair of scissors that he had only recently been allowed to touch. They made a clink as he pulled them from the jar.

'I have some coloured paper,' Gwen said. She went to the

dresser and started rummaging through the drawers. 'We could make paper chains to decorate with. Hang them around the windows, or on the Christmas tree. We need to get a tree soon.'

She took the scissors from Will and began cutting a long straight strip of red paper, then another and another from the same sheet. 'Like this,' she said, rolling her lips around her teeth, squinting as she bent to the task. 'And you could do green with it.' She cut some strips from a dark green sheet. 'Which is Christmassy. You bend them through each other. See?' She made a ring with a red strip, pinching the ends together, then slid a green strip through it and pinched the green ends together to make two interlocking rings.

Will studied the rings in silence.

'Wait.' She put the scissors down, went back to the dresser for paste. 'You have to stick the ends together with this.' She unscrewed the jar and dug into its creamy contents with the little yellow plastic spatula, then smeared paste on the ends of the strips.

'I like that,' said Will.

As he squeezed the pasted places between the tips of his fingers, Gwen slid another red strip through the green ring, joined the ends, and said, 'When those are dry, you can paste this one.'

'OK.' He went on squeezing diligently. 'Is it enough yet?'

She smiled and nodded at him, and he put down his two links and picked up the third strip.

'Let's decorate the piano for Hugo, for the day he gets back,' Will said.

'That's not until after Christmas.'

'You choose the colours for his, Mummy. Hugo will like it better if you do.'

'Maybe.' She stayed by him, feeling edgy and protective. 'Shall we make one for Daddy, too?'

Will grunted.

'Cut lots of strips,' said Gwen, 'while I talk to Hilary. Then I'll help you paste them if you like.' She put her arm around Hilary and drew her away from Will towards the window.

'So why would Hugo like it better if you chose the colours for his Christmas chain?' asked Hilary in a confidential tone.

'Oh – I doubt he would,' replied Gwen, dismissing it. 'I guess it would really stink, to end up working with Paul?'

'I don't want to work with Paul. *For* Paul. And now there's also this unbelievably self-important woman called Clare who Mark has the hots for because she has the whole hairdo-and-suit thing down. Very professional, very aggressive. Tons of information at her fingertips, you know, just rolls off her tongue – about this and that collection someplace else, what objects they own, and how they manage them. Carries a laptop all the time. What the hell does *she* care about Eddie Doro? For her, it's a power trip. She wants her photograph in *Vogue* or whatever, at the big opening gala. It feels like she wants to wield a whip, too, behind closed doors. She and Paul have known each other for years. It's all totally incestuous.'

Hilary slapped at the window with the heel of her hand and cried out loudly in frustration, 'Oh why do I fucking *care*? I hate them hate them *hate* them. And I will get my revenge. I can do it. I know exactly how. I can easily trick them into selling all the wrong pieces, and they can never get them back once they've done it.'

'Hilary!' Gwen laid a hand over Hilary's, holding it still against the glass, amazed that the window hadn't broken, and frightened by the continuing vibration. She glanced back at Will, then pulled Hilary's hand towards her. 'You can't do that. Where would that leave Eddie? You can't betray his trust just to make yourself feel better. He relied on you. You'd just be sinking to some grotesque level – their level. That's not the kind of person you are or ever have been. Just to curate the stuff? To control it? What does it matter who owns it, who sells the tickets to see it, who pays for the electricity to light it? Let them. Just let them.' And she put the palm of Hilary's hand lovingly against her cheek, looked up into Hilary's eyes.

But Hilary yanked the hand away and narrowed her eyes at Gwen. 'And then when they open their museum,' she went on stonily, 'I'll have a great tale to tell – about Eddie Doro – about his vision. And how they destroyed it.'

'Hilary, stop.' Gwen's voice was brusque. 'It's disgusting what you're saying. It's – immoral. You don't mean it.'

Hilary came back at her menacingly, leaning against the window, towering over her. 'You know what, Gwen? I've been treated like shit, and I'm sick of it. Lawrence is the one who parked this whole God-awful mess on me, pretending to help. Don't you even realise that? Hasn't he filled you in on the details? These people are *both* his candidates – Paul Mercy and Clare Pryce – they were students of his and of Roland's. Or colleagues. And the board has complete confidence in their recommendations because I brought Lawrence and Roland to the board's attention as world experts who were in touch with the brightest scholars coming along at the moment and – whatever. How can I fight that?

'What kind of a man are you married to, Gwen? Who doesn't have the nerve to tell me that he thinks I'm no good at what I'm doing – or not good enough. Not as good as someone else he knows and wants to put forward in my place? English people are so polite, so gracious. Take you into their home as though you are a friend, as though they care about what happens to you. But it's not human kindness. It's just a way to get in on something – pick up information about the job market abroad. All this time, my English "friends" –' she raised both hands, curling her fingers derisively in the air to make the quotation marks – 'have been pushing some other, better friend, some inner-circle person. And you wanted me to go on a *date* with Roland! Did you all decide I could just marry him and move to Oxford? Was he supposed to be some kind of consolation prize?'

Gwen was aghast. 'I don't know what you're talking about, Hil. We never planned anything like that. You need to talk to Lawrence, that's all, and find out –'

'Yes, I need to talk to Lawrence! That's one reason I came back, Gwen!' Hilary was shouting now. 'Not to please you or to freeload off you or to get my portrait painted! Even Christmas and Will, frankly, are not much of a pull in the current circumstances.'

'Hi! Watch what you say! Come on.' It was an anguished plea.

Gwen was thinking that she needed to get Hilary out of the house away from Will, at least for a little while, until she herself could talk to Lawrence. But she was no longer on the most straightforward terms with him. She didn't want to have to explain that to Hilary. Not long ago, Gwen was realising, I could have counted on him; I would have known for certain that Lawrence would instantly drop everything for Hilary, for me, that he would come home and explain this, fix it. What have I done, that I can feel so uncomfortable about my husband? She didn't doubt that he would help her or help Hilary, but she doubted whether she could bring herself to ask him. She didn't feel entitled to his attention or to his concern. Could Hilary ask Lawrence herself? Could she call him? Go to Oxford?

Gwen fidgeted at the window, stared out restlessly without seeing anything but bland winter light. Then she turned back to the room, gazed over at Will still sitting quietly up at the workbench, painstakingly turning a piece of stiff paper in his hand, squeezing the flashing blades slowly together, ever so sharp, ever so close to the tips of his eager fingers. The blades rasped as they slid and bit. It moved her painfully, the commitment, the determination, of a small human being, any human being, unaware of whatever danger might lie about him, getting on with his work, with something he was devoted to. She had sharpened the blades herself a few days ago with her long round file and given him the scissors to use.

'Careful, Will,' she called to him. 'You'll be very careful with those scissors, won't you?'

He didn't look up. He kept on cutting. How Will deserved,

she thought, how anyone deserved, to get on with what they loved, with their work. Not to be disturbed.

Precarious, she thought; I've made everything so precarious.

'So, anyway, where is Lawrence?' Hilary asked in a gentler voice, still hanging over Gwen. 'Hasn't term ended yet?'

Gwen roused herself, defensive. 'He's staying at the cottage. He got stuck with a lot of additional duties. I mean – the interviewing that they have to do for next year's applicants. It's always at Christmas. He wasn't supposed to have to this year. It wasn't his turn, but someone skived off . . .' Her voice trailed away; she felt that she didn't really know what Lawrence was doing. Maybe he had been a little vague about it. It made her self-conscious – the condition of her marriage and what seemed to have happened to Hilary, while she, Gwen, was simply not paying attention. She perched uneasily against the window ledge, looking around the room. 'Do you want to go downstairs and get something to eat or drink? Or should we leave you to unpack?'

Hilary's eyes wandered after Gwen's, sensing her uncertainty. And then Hilary saw the portrait of Hugo, the edge of it, behind another newly stretched canvas. She sprang across the room and pulled it out.

'Oh, hey. Look what you've been up to. This is what Nick was talking about. How weird. Like –' She paused, staring at it. 'What *is* this? A Mycenaean burial mask? Beaten gold? Is he dead? Did you murder him in his bath like Agamemnon? Just for ruining your ceiling? Or – who did he betray?' She turned her eyes to Gwen.

Gwen flushed deeply, her scalp pricking with sweat. She couldn't help it. She was surprised at her own lack of self-possession. She stood up from the window ledge where she was still leaning and walked across to Will, cooing thickly at him, 'That's lovely, darling,' without really seeing what he had done.

When at last she looked up again at Hilary, she strained at brightness. 'Maybe Lawrence and Roland have sent this other person to try to help you out? What's she called? Clare whatever? Maybe they see her as some sort of ally for you, if she's a friend of theirs. What's she like? Shall I ring Roland and ask about her? Would that help?'

But Hilary wasn't buying it. She saw that she had been missing the point about a lot of things. She came right up to Gwen where Gwen hovered over Will, and she stared at her, breathing hard, putting it all together – what Nick Hollander had said to her in New York, Will's chatter, the new portrait. 'So where *is* Hugo? Why isn't he around during the convenient absence of your husband?'

Gwen ran her fingers through Will's hair, eyes down, then moved away from him again back to the window. Hilary pursued her, whispering angrily. 'You're telling me *I'm* immoral, Gwen. What's going on with you? None of you has any morals at all! You're all savages!'

And then, deciding Will couldn't hear her and that he wasn't listening anyway, Hilary said with considered brutality, 'Do you really think they sent Clare Pryce to help me out? Lawrence's *mistress*? What I heard in New York is that he wanted her out of Oxford before you found out about it. But you wouldn't care, would you, because you're so busy with your own betrayals! Evidently, she's been itching to bring him down in public because he won't leave you. Why the hell not, is what I'm wondering. Why the hell won't he leave you?'

The scissors made a slow, sharp snip. A chip of red paper fell from them, and then Will put the scissors down, attentive.

He looked across at Hilary with clean eyes. 'Hugo has performances now, Hilary. He gets paid for it and a lot of people come to listen because his friend has a very nice voice. Soprano. Which is the highest.'

This silenced her at last.

Gwen took a step back towards Will, as if in astonishment, and he looked up at her and asked casually, 'What is betray? Isn't that what Jason did to Medea after she helped him? Daddy said it was too frightening for children, but he doesn't really know that I *like* scary things.'

Gwen glared at Hilary, outraged, accusing her.

Hilary refused to be blamed. She held Gwen's eye and said evenly to Will: 'Betrayal is when you let someone down – trick them or break a promise. Your mother can explain it much better. She doesn't want me to betray my old friend, Mr Doro, the man I used to work for. But Mr Doro is dead now; he died when he was very old. And I was wondering whether it might be worse to betray someone who is still alive, since they could get their feelings hurt. What do you think, Will? If you promised to help someone and then actually made it harder for them instead of making it easier? Or if you promised to love someone and then went off and loved somebody else instead?'

'That would definitely hurt their feelings,' said Will. 'Hugo wouldn't do that. Nor Mummy.'

'Everyone has different ideas about what love is,' muttered Gwen, almost inaudibly, as if she didn't really want to be heard, as if her lips were numb. 'You don't love just one person.' I don't, she thought, and apparently Lawrence doesn't either. She knew it had to be true, that Lawrence had a mistress, and she thought she had brought it on herself.

Hilary had had enough. What was Will being protected from by this kind of talk? Rationalising. Vague. Didn't he need a clear and simple explanation? It seemed like Gwen was using his presence to shield herself from criticism. 'Maybe *you* have different ideas about what love is, Gwen. You make it what suits you on the day. You *and* Lawrence. You're so *greedy*. You lap it all up, everyone else's life, to satisfy yourselves. Try it all out. What about being true to something? Anything? To your own goddammed best intentions? Even when it doesn't taste so much like honey? I want these pictures off the walls. In fact, I want them back; they're mine, not yours.'

She swooped around the room, pulling the watercolours down, yanking them free without even taking out pins, without pulling off tape or Blu-tack, so that some of the pages tore. She bundled them in her hands, under her arm, page upon page, creasing them, spoiling them.

Gwen hung her head, overwhelmed by all the trespasses she was faced with. 'The pictures are yours, Hilary; you know I painted them for you. Take them − with all my heart. But I wish you wouldn't destroy them. I really wish you wouldn't destroy them.' It wasn't even begging; it wasn't hopeful enough. It was just a dribble of words, dying away. 'I'm sorry you feel so angry. I know it's my own fault about Nick and − about Hugo.'

But Will was set alight by his mother's uncharacteristic meekness and fought back for her. 'Stop, Hilary! Stop! You're ruining the pictures! You're tearing them!' He leaped from his stool, shouting, and ran at Hilary, pummelling her stomach and her back with his weightless fists. Then he dug his fingernails into her forearms and scratched her with all his might. 'Stop! You're making Mummy sad!'

'You little rat!' Hilary cried, as the blood sprang on her arms. She shoved him away hard with an elbow and the backs of her full, unwieldy hands.

Now Gwen couldn't contain herself. 'Don't you touch him!' she bellowed. 'What's *wrong* with you? He's a child! He's five years old! You can't stay here if you forget that!'

She darted at Will, wrapped herself around him and cocooned him on the floor between her crossed legs and her thin arms, laid her head on his, kissed his hair. 'Don't worry about the pictures, Will. I can make more. I can make plenty more. Just let Hilary have them. I made them for her. She can tear them to bits if she wants. It's probably better if she does. We'd all be better off without them. Let's you and I go downstairs and stay out of her way.'

But they made no move to leave.

Hilary threw the pictures she was holding on to the bed and went on taking the rest down from the walls. It was as if she was building a bonfire.

Will stayed in Gwen's lap in the middle of the floor crying a little and watching Hilary. After a while he whispered to his mother, 'You could put Daddy's pictures up instead?'

'Daddy's pictures?'

'I know there aren't as many. But it looks bad now without anything.'

He got up on his hands and knees and crawled to the bed, reached under, pulled out the watercolours of Trimalchio's candelabrum.

Gwen shut her eyes. She couldn't bear to look. 'I forgot about those. I might not put them up, Will. Those − were just for me really. They didn't come out so well. I meant to throw them away.'

'Daddy likes them,' offered Will reassuringly.

Gwen was silent for a moment, gathering her strength, and at last, with a sigh, she said, 'When did Daddy see them, hon? Do you know?'

Will's face was solemn. 'I'm sorry, Mummy.'

'Why?'

'If you didn't want me to show them to Daddy.'

Gwen felt a burning sadness. 'No, I didn't really want you to show them to Daddy.'

'But you didn't tell me not to.'

'But, Will, I didn't know you had seen the pictures. I didn't show them to you, did I?' Her voice was patient, apologetic, truth-baring.

'No.' He was crestfallen.

'You looked without asking me. In my things.'

He tried to explain. 'We always do, Daddy and me. We always come to look at your pictures. Everybody does. Daddy doesn't really like the Hugo one because it's always the same. So I showed him these.'

247

'I'll bet he doesn't like the Hugo one,' Hilary remarked sarcastically, turning to look at them from across the room, hands on hips, dipping her pelvis. 'He's lucky there's no death mask of him yet.'

Gwen felt it whirl around them, the chaos she had made, sucking her energy away, depleting her. There was only a little glow of anger in her gut – at Lawrence, at Hilary – because she blamed herself for what was happening.

Will looked at her anxiously across the pictures. 'I betrayed you.' He crawled back to her where she sat on the floor and she took him in her arms.

Hilary, loading the bed with her treasure, stopped to look at the pictures lying there on the floor. 'Those are mine, too,' she announced.

'For Christ's sake, Hil!' Gwen burst out.

'Well, it's Eddie's candelabrum. And see: that's Eddie standing at the edge. So we could tell how big it was. I took the photograph myself. He never liked his face to be in anything.' Then bending to the floor, studying the pictures more closely, leafing through them, she squeaked, 'You made him into Lawrence! And all this obscene stuff – my God, you're a strange woman, Gwen. How could you put Lawrence in Eddie's place! These are gross.'

She grabbed the pictures and threw them with the others on top of her pyre.

CHAPTER 15

It was late at night when Lawrence got home two days before Christmas; the house was dark. He crept into Will's room, studied the fuzz of hair damp with sweat at the ends, the drenched pillow, the petal mouth gaping around its delicate snores. He felt Will's forehead, his neck, pulled the top blanket away. Then he slipped out of his clothes in the bathroom and found his way to bed without switching on the lights.

Gwen rolled away from him with no sign of greeting. He fell back from his habitual expectation of homecoming, the half-conscious optimism.

'Gwen?'

'Hmm.' Sleep already preoccupied her; she was reluctant to be called back from it.

'Will seems feverish.'

'I think he's coming down with something. Or maybe it's – nerves, you know? Anxiety.' She sounded fed up.

'Christmas?'

'Or being used as a spy.'

'What's that supposed to mean?' He lay fast on his back, his hands flat on the covers, holding them down, holding himself down beneath them as the blood thumped through him.

'You and he – making trips together to my studio. Why didn't you just ask me to show you my work – or sneak in by yourself for Christ's sake? Are you afraid to go alone? Are my paintings that scary? Will feels torn apart. He can't handle it.' She saw the scissor blades flash in his hand.

Lawrence was silent, his heart grabbing in his chest. How he

249

wished this wasn't coming up now. How he wished it would never come up at all. 'Will's all right. I'll talk to him.'

He believed it; he believed children were resilient, especially Will, so well loved, so sure of himself. He felt Will striving, kicking, urgent with motion like a minnow, desperately alive, definite, in the flow of life, so certainly a boy, with gender but no sexuality marked on him, while the ocean around him teemed with ragged, snapping claws. Lawrence had never intended to be the one to deliver any blow from which Will might need to recover. He felt angry with himself, and he felt angry with Gwen. 'I didn't think I should surprise you in your studio; lately it seemed to me that you were needing – plenty of privacy.'

'So you brought along our young son to witness anything you might discover?'

'Gwen, stop it. That's not what I intended.'

'If you have reasons to be displeased with me, or if you have questions you want to ask me, then say so – ask. But don't use our child to try to make me feel guilty.'

Lawrence turned on his side, lifting his head, one hand up to support it. He spoke slowly, as if it could slow the pace of conflict building between them, but he was resigned to engaging with it. 'I thought this thing with you and Hugo would blow over. From the outset, I had no wish to talk about it or even to know about it. I propose to wait for it to go away.'

Her back curved towards him like a shell, her spine rounded, barbed with rage, all her maternity, affection, womanliness encased and concealed on the other side of her, the inside of her. She couldn't bear Lawrence mentioning Hugo. She ignored it, spoke hard and fast, uncompromising. 'And should I bring up your affair with Clare whatever she's called? Or have you gotten rid of her for good?'

Lawrence collapsed backwards again on to the pillow and lay silent for a long time. 'Did Roland tell you that?'

'Hilary.'

'Hilary?' He was genuinely surprised.

'She's furious with you.'

'She would be, wouldn't she? Your best friend.' He assumed Hilary's anger was on Gwen's behalf, and he didn't bother to ask how Hilary had found out about Clare. He breathed long and deep, dragging the moment out, exhausted. He felt that it wasn't worth explaining or asking questions. Everyone seemed to know everything anyway. What was the point of going into it all? A sorry episode. He deserved whatever might come of it. Gwen didn't, though. She didn't deserve to have to think about the trivial, loveless details. Beneath ordinary, beneath her.

'I thought you wouldn't want to know,' he said. 'It never mattered to me, Gwen, and for that reason, I allowed myself to imagine that it would never matter to anyone else. But of course, everyone else has only the facts to go on. And they take the facts as real. As somehow important.' He paused for a moment, and then he asked, 'Does it matter to you?'

She didn't reply. She realised that it was true – she didn't want to know. It enraged her all the more, how much Lawrence was right about. She decided not to provide him with any more information – not to tell him all the reasons why Hilary was furious with him. She felt him knowing too much already. She didn't want to go into the scene in the studio. It was a week old already, and she had reached a new equilibrium with Hilary; it had been either that or throw Hilary out of the house, wrong on top of wrong and utterly impractical. The pair of them had gambled once again on their old bond, exchanged something like renewed permission to get on with their lives, and they had barely referred to it aloud. It felt like a private matter. Hilary could take responsibility for her own relationship with Lawrence. Gwen wanted to get away from his knowing everything. She wanted to be free of his knowledge and free of his mistakes. She wanted to find things out for herself. To live for herself. To taste her pleasures as she liked, to rip into them.

At last she said, and it was an indirect answer, 'If you don't want to know about Hugo, why are you spying on me? Why are you trying to climb inside my head? Inside my imagination?' She would beat him off her, force him to let her go. 'Why are you in the studio looking for clues in my paintings? There aren't any there, Lawrence. Those are paintings, they are explorations of possible truths, expressions of insights. And they are about painting. They are not an account of my personal feelings or my affections. I make them. I make them up.'

As a philosophical point, this tempted him to argue. He couldn't stop himself. 'They evoke certain experiences, certain actualities.'

'Not in the way that you suppose. They don't show what I feel or think about a subject. They only show something it's *possible* to feel or think about a subject – what at one certain time it seems possible to feel or think – at the time the paint is committed to the canvas. Another time, something else would be possible. With the same subject or with a different subject. If you look too closely, ask too much of a painting, there will be nothing there at all. If you pin me down, that's what I'll be – pinned down. I won't be able to paint. I won't be anything. I'll just be caught, throttled.'

'I have no intention of pinning you down. That's precisely why I haven't mentioned any of this. I wanted to see where you were going – what you would do. What you *could* do.'

'I can't bear to be watched.'

'That's absurd. You're preparing to show the pictures off to the world – watching is what you want.'

'Not yet. The pictures aren't ready yet. And not by you.'

She got through to him with that, a great buffet of pain from inside his own bed. 'Goddammit, Gwen. I'm your husband. I don't care how you do it. I can give you all the space you need. But I can't disappear from the face of the earth. Nor from our household nor from Will's life.'

'I need privacy. You're the one who said it.'

'Fine, then. Have all the privacy you want. Haven't I been away enough this month?' Lawrence felt angry and bewildered. 'But you know, this love affair with Hugo? You should ask yourself, Gwen, what you really want from it, what you are getting. I've made this very mistake myself – out of idleness, really, boredom. And I suppose, to be honest, out of some strange, latent sense of rivalry with the young, with my students who are in the middle of it all – world-belittling love affairs. Are you sure that this whole thing hasn't blown up out of your rivalry with Hilary? Are you sure you care for Hugo? A boy of twenty-three? What can he offer you? What can you learn from him?' He drew breath.

And then he went on at her in the dark, admonishing, bearing down on her. 'Perhaps, Gwen, you just couldn't bear to think that Hilary would sleep with him and you wouldn't get the chance? You had your eye on her so closely – the way she was wasting the attentions of other men, attentions which you gave up long ago. What's completely obvious from looking at your paintings, Gwen, is that Hilary is the one you feel passionate about. Hugo is just a cipher. And something for you to play with and to mould. I'm sure you can make of him what you like. But for Christ's sake, Gwen, don't fuck up your whole life over a man you don't need, a man you never really wanted. It won't be worth it, not for any of us.'

She lay still, felt herself hovering in space, dry, a feather. Then she whispered, 'Sometimes you don't know what you'll find out from an experience. So you do it.'

Fear shimmered in her; she saw an opening, a space she was determined to get to and to occupy. She didn't know how big it was, nor what shape, but it had a quality of illumination. It drew her irresistibly. She couldn't turn back from it.

More loudly, she demanded, 'Why do I need to learn anything from Hugo? Why can't I teach *him*? Or just enjoy him? You're like some kind of stalker. A creep. I know you've been wearing my clothes. Did you go out jogging in them? To find out what it was like to be me?'

'But, Gwen, those are *my* clothes.'

'You gave them to me.'

'What difference does that make? I wanted to have a run. I don't have kit of my own here in London. I'll buy some if you like. Honestly, I didn't think you would mind.'

'Whatever you may think, I *am* in love with Hugo.' Her voice held the most transparent, the most girlish, note of challenge. 'It's nothing to do with Hilary. You *don't* know everything about me. You can't control me that way, by watching me.'

When she said it, Lawrence reckoned that he had forced her to. What was love, anyway? It was up to her to decide. He knew that he had only invited more pain upon them all. There was nothing he could do to stop it.

All minnows, he thought, not just Will. Blind, frantic, programmed by nature. What are we trying to prove?

Will woke before dawn with an earache, and Gwen took him to the doctor as soon as the surgery opened.

While they were gone, Hilary cornered Lawrence in the kitchen.

She had grown restless, aching to get out of town. Every day, she ran four or five miles along the river to exhaust her driving rage, to wear herself down into a semblance of a domesticated creature, and to pretend that she was doing something with her time. She also played endlessly with Will, regaining his trust. She didn't like to admit even to herself that she had no place else to go and nothing to do. And she was determined not to leave England without telling Lawrence what she thought of him and without forcing him to explain himself.

She bounded downstairs in her running clothes, steaming with warmth and sweat, a blue fleece vest over a new T-shirt Gwen had bought, pale bare forearms, ragged brown leather gloves, blood-flushed cheeks. She assumed that by now Gwen would have prepared Lawrence for what was coming, but he showed no sign of offering Hilary any opening, neither by defensiveness nor by apology. He was slumped in a chair at the kitchen table wallowing in his own misery.

Without looking up, he said morosely, 'I made arrangements to take Gwen and Will away skiing on Boxing Day, as a surprise. I expect Will is too poorly to go.'

Hilary sensed such a depth of disappointment in him, a sink-hole of melancholy, that she found herself trying to say something sympathetic. 'I'm really sorry, Lawrence.'

She bent down to untie her running shoes, doubling over from the waist with her legs straight to stretch the backs of them. Then as she slowly stood up again, she stepped out of her shoes, one at a time. The shoes squelched; her white socks were black with dirty water.

'I counted on it too much,' he observed, staring into a cup of tea, the tea bag floating in it, brown, sodden. 'Counted on it to make things right. As if there were a simple solution, like dosing Will with Calpol or putting a plaster on him to staunch tears. I've been working hard and been away so much. And Gwen –' He raised his eyes to Hilary's, wondering exactly how much Hilary knew about the situation between himself and Gwen; he saw a blaze there, barely restrained, which made him feel ashamed, so that he looked down after all.

Then he spoke again in an abject tone. 'I've made such a mess of things. To be frank, I don't see just now how it will come right. It's the darkest time of the year, isn't it? Only children look forward to this – that scraggly tree you and Gwen nobly dragged in, the magpie, tinselly bits.' He nodded towards it, in the window bay, with its forked, graceless trunk, its uneven veil of needles, its red papier mâché apples, gold bells, glass snowflakes, paper chains heavy with paste. 'Poor old Will, who's been counting the days – it'll all be over and we'll be out the other side and he'll have missed it.'

'If he's lucky.' Hilary's tone was acerbic.

Lawrence fought back instinctively. 'We can look after him,' he asserted stubbornly. And then he began to preach a little. 'We will – and you must help us, Hilary. You're his godmother, after all. It's circumstances like these for which one bothers to have godparents, eh? We must all protect Will a little. From our mistakes. Children need continuity and predictability. He needs that tree and some gifts and the turkey for Christmas lunch. It's something of a moral obligation for all of us – to hold steady.'

'What the hell do grown-ups need, then?' Hilary demanded. She took her gloves off and shoved them into the pockets of her fleece vest, making an angry-looking pouch along the bottom of her belly as she stood over him.

'Yes. Well. The thing is, grown-ups want freedom, don't they? And they must pay the price.'

He took it for granted that he was right; there was no effort of persuasion in his voice. He was just making an observation, quiet, nugatory.

It made Hilary furious. 'God, you and Gwen and your subtle thoughts! The crap you talk to justify doing whatever the hell you want and to persuade yourselves that it's a good idea. That it's exalted or it's artistic to risk everything for whatever it is that you believe – for the sake of experience or originality. That you're entitled, somehow, to have a mistress, as if you'd been forced into an unhappy marriage in consideration of property matters. How can you let your wife go to bed with another man right here in your own house? You think that's just a cost of doing as you like?'

Lawrence reeled a little in his heart, but he stood it, sat still, summoned the crisp voice of the common room, as if the question had nothing to do, personally, with him, pushed it away from himself, into generalised argument, and then back towards her. 'I don't particularly like it, Hilary, but it's up to Gwen. And – it's a venal matter, a matter of the flesh. Just the flesh. You Americans are quite puritanical about these things. Gwen's different, she's lived here so long. But you're quite – literal-minded – don't you think?'

'It's not because I'm an American. It's not just some cultural thing,' Hilary said irately. 'Behaving honourably.' She flounced away from him in her wet socks; her footprints showed, shining, slender, naked, across the wooden floor, then disappeared under his eye as they dried.

'Such matters generally are cultural, though,' Lawrence persisted, arguing for the sake of it, to arrive at a considered view, a cool view, a correct view, 'or perhaps we might say anthropological . . . even sociological.'

Hilary turned back towards him and repeated herself, more loudly, feeling she was hurling tiny darts at a rock face, feeling puny, condescended to, off on a tangent about sexual mores when what she really wanted to talk about was Lawrence's dishonourable behaviour towards *her*. 'It's not because I'm an American. It's because –' Then without really knowing whether she meant it, she suddenly said, 'It's because I'm a woman.'

Lawrence shrugged. 'Gwen's a woman.'

'That's what I mean. That's what you're not realising – how serious it is. You don't understand the risk you're taking – the risk *she's* taking. You don't understand what women are really like. Women place their trust in what's literal. They have to live in the flesh so much more than men. Submit to it. It's much easier for men to be cynical about the flesh, to detach themselves from it. Women take it literally because they might find they have no way out – there might be a child. Some response of the superego – for – for mental survival – makes them choose what's necessary. For women, every encounter of the flesh can be earth-shaking. Total. Every encounter. *Any* encounter.'

Lawrence was silent for a moment after she stopped speaking.

257

He thought of her footprints, their strange evanescent voluptuousness, the perfect mark of her flesh made on the floor through her filthy socks. Then he said, 'I suppose you're trying to warn me. And I feel grateful to you for that. But honestly, Hilary, Gwen is not like you, close as the pair of you are. She simply is not enough like you that this relationship with Hugo must necessarily change her life. Can't you think of plenty of examples of women who were, who are, just as cynical as men when it comes to sex? Maybe not you. You stayed with your fiancé a long time, but after all, perhaps you came to feel it was too long? Perhaps some physical aspect tricked you into setting too much store by it?'

Hilary recoiled visibly at the personal nature of this observation. He looked at her with regret, and she could sense his reluctance to press her further. But Lawrence couldn't resist the elucidation that might come from it, nor the possibility that it might somehow help her.

'Forgive me,' he went on gingerly, 'but had you considered – I mean, maybe you've been somewhat naive? And getting your feelings hurt by Paul Mercy? I imagine my saying so will make you feel angry. It's attractive, innocence – greatly valued by all cultures, one would think. But it's appropriate, in the end, to children. Like Christmas. The rest of us need to – wise up a little. The world spoils whatever is unspoiled – sooner or later.'

Hilary's face prickled with rage; she quivered with it, head to foot. Then she took a breath, and she bayed at him from across the room. 'What has happened to me is my own fault, is that what you're saying? How dare you! How can you delude yourself that it doesn't matter if you hurt other people? How can you be so self-absorbed? So blind?'

Why was she finding it impossible to blame him, outright, to his face, for ruining her life? Was it because he seemed to have ruined so much else, to be suffering so much already? She felt unexpectedly hampered by a lesson learned long ago, that blaming others for your failures was weak and self-pitying. And yet, there it was. Paul Mercy and Clare Pryce had ousted her from her job, got control over what she had once presumed was her future. And Lawrence had helped them. Would he be able to admit it, if she did manage to say it out loud?

He came at her now in a perfunctory tone, without evident emotion. He might have been giving her directions to the nearest tube station. He still thought that the issue between them was adultery. 'I don't delude myself that I'm not hurting other people. I see that I have. And of course it matters. I regret it enormously. But Gwen knows that I love her, and that I will do all I can to make things right with her. Our marriage is very important to me – to both of us. I'm quite worried about this thing with Hugo. However, it will pass. I feel confident of that. I'd like to get Gwen out of town, right away from him, for a bit. That's one reason I'd like to take her skiing. I thought that, in the mountains, we might feel free again.'

To Hilary his nonchalance seemed ludicrous. 'And after the holiday? Then what?'

'Clearly, we need to alter our domestic arrangements. It's hopeless with the lover sandwiched between her studio and our bedroom.'

Suddenly Lawrence laughed, embarrassed less by the intimacy than by the absurdity of their conversation.

'Won't you sit down? Can I get you a cup of tea?' He stood up, gesturing to the empty chairs around the table. 'You must be getting cold?'

But just as he began to introduce these social niceties, tried to settle himself and his house guest into a groove of safe and pleasant conversation, Hilary finally sprang.

'So is that why you shipped your own lover off to New York? Where she could sink her teeth into my fiancé and make sure I never got my own life back on course? Did you ship her off so that you could feel free again?'

He had gone to the counter and picked up the kettle to refill

259

it; now he dropped the kettle in the sink under the running tap, water hitting the shining side of it and spraying everywhere, wetting his shirt and his trousers, pooling on his shoes. 'I'm sorry?' He turned the tap off, snatched up a dishcloth, dabbed at the flood.

With his eyes on the flying cloth, he spoke sharply over his shoulder: 'Shipped my own lover where? I thought you had broken off your engagement?'

Hilary was heavy-voiced, imposing. 'Clare Pryce. Who you – *whom*,' she corrected herself grandly, 'you recommended to help Paul Mercy build my museum. After I poured my soul out to you here in this very room and told you how foolish I had been about him.'

Lawrence's hand moved in a vague circle over the counter, rubbing the water around and around underneath the soaked, useless cloth. 'Is that where she's bloody gone,' he said, under his breath, working it out for himself. 'It gets worse and worse.' Then he turned to Hilary, looked her full in the eyes. 'You've got to tell me how she did it, Hilary. I don't see how she did it.'

'How the hell would I know how she did it!' Hilary burst out, throwing her long arms wide. 'You recommended her for the job, didn't you?'

He leaned against the counter, feeling Hilary's exasperation, her astonishment, not two feet away from him. Feeling her height, her solidity, her sheer physical strength. Feeling her righteous anger. And feeling that he himself had no presence at all. He didn't know who he was or what he had done. He didn't know what he ought to do. It was as if there were no floor under him, as if he were trying to stand on a bit of wind, an updraught, to ride it somehow, to surf the air that moved when she moved.

'I – don't know. I don't know what job I recommended her for. Did I write a letter? Not lately, in any case. I don't recall writing a letter. I suppose I must have done in the past. There must be letters I have written about her. On file – somewhere.

Old letters. They can't be current. And one would think she'd want to show off some of her more recent achievements.'

How did Clare even think of applying for the job in New York? Lawrence wondered. Jumbled recollections came into his head, bits of conversations to which he had paid no attention because he had felt no interest in them. Conversations which he had sat through, survived, but in which he had never been engaged. He recalled how she had collected him for lunch that last time when he was speaking to Roland on the telephone. What had she overheard?

'Of course, I agreed in principle to support her if she decided to seek employment.' It was a stricken admission, followed by silence.

To himself, he finally muttered, 'If the old letter still works, why have a new one? Oh, crikey.'

Then he spoke up again, 'I suppose she's just used some old letter and they haven't bothered to renew the reference – to follow it up. Lazy of them, don't you think? I mean, if she's to run an entire museum, wouldn't they want to contact me by telephone?'

'Lazy?' Hilary rolled it around her tongue, appalled.

He dropped his eyes to his wet shoes. 'I've no right to say, of course. Since I can't even – Oh, Christ. It's all pretty shambolic, isn't it?'

There was a tense little pause in which he felt tempted to laugh again. It felt like comedy to him, or even farce, the number of misunderstandings and wrong assumptions that had piled up. He stole a look at Hilary; her face was marmoreal.

'It's serious to you, though, isn't it? If she's really got your job. Not at all funny.'

He was hustling, bustling, and he felt he would expire with it. 'We must get your job back, is the thing. She can't possibly do it as well as you, can she? She never even met this man, Doro, and I know Clare well enough to feel certain that she won't spend much time thinking about him. She'll be thinking about how to impress all the people who are not dead, who are still here to watch what she does and to applaud.'

'I can't believe this,' Hilary said. She fell into a chair, dumbfounded. 'I can't believe it turns out that it's all just — bumbling.' She was trying not to cry as it came over her. Nobody had even been paying enough attention to do her any harm on purpose; there had been no conspiracy. She had, in fact, done most of the damage to herself.

'These things happen,' said Lawrence soothingly. 'It will get sorted out. I'll get in touch with Roland. We've all been preoccupied with — personal concerns. Roland's bound to know what's happened. I'm surprised he hasn't told me all about Clare, but there's been the interviewing, and —' He stopped there, because it struck him that Roland had been a little odd with him that time, fishing about Hilary, about her job, how long she would remain in London; that, too, had washed right over him. He had registered that Roland was upset, but now he saw that it must have been because Roland had been feeling a bit furtive and cannibalistic. Lawrence couldn't bear to make things worse for Hilary by telling her. He looked at her with compassion. What have we all done, he wondered, to this striving, vital young woman? But he said brightly, 'Roland may have a thought as to how to manage.'

'It's all so much more complicated — so much more intractable — than you think. Paul is the one who really has my job, Lawrence. And then — and then there's Mark.'

'I see.' Lawrence dropped his chin in his hand, resting the elbow in the other hand which was crossed to his hip. His pale eyes settled on Hilary's. 'It's important not to overreact. We must first just — find out a bit more.'

Hilary looked doubtful. 'I've been so angry with you. Do you even realise that?'

'I'm sorry. I'm very much at fault. And I meant you nothing but well —' It was a valedictory observation.

'I figured you thought I wasn't good enough.'

'Good enough for what?'

'To run Eddie's museum. Because I don't have a PhD, and I didn't go to Oxford – and – whatever. It probably goes all the way back to college, when Gwen and I were in your class. You know, you never read my final essay? It was some graduate student.'

'I have no idea whether you are good enough.' There was more apology than surprise in his voice, as if he might indeed have judged her harshly. He was painfully aware how little he had noticed her all those years ago in his class. Were there things he had failed to teach Hilary? Things which he still owed her? He wondered crazily what had become of the essay, whether it was too late to read it now. But then he said without equivocation, as if there were a rule to the effect, a rule with which anyone would be familiar, 'But of course it's not for me to decide whether you're good enough. That was up to Doro.'

Hilary probed his judgement a little further, tentatively, like the old student hoping for praise. 'And also I thought you supposed I wasn't sure I wanted to do it anyway.'

'That seemed to be the case when last we spoke about it, at dinner here just after you arrived. But that was for *you* to decide – not me.'

His voice was gentle, fatherly. 'I'd do anything I could for you, Hilary, to help make things right.'

This assurance changed nothing, but she felt comforted by his tone of voice. It breached her solitude in a way that nothing had for a long time. As she continued to look up at him where he hung awkwardly against the counter, gripping the dishcloth and earnestly considering her predicament, she thought of Eddie, how sure of herself she had felt with him. Eddie had believed in her unreservedly – in her taste, in her potential. She had always felt certain that she could do whatever Eddie had in mind for her to do. More. It is only doubt, Hilary thought, which has been impeding me lately, weakening me. Doubt born of solitude. Why can't I do it alone, she wondered, if I used to be able to do it unassisted?

She pictured Lawrence in Eddie's suit, as Gwen had painted him. But then she couldn't stop herself from picturing him as the satyr. She tried to remember Eddie's voice, his tight, nasal, New York bark. His bony, hook-nosed face, his white baby skin hanging in powdery folds, innocent with age, his wasted body, hunching more and more at the top of the spine, confined at the end to a chair, to his bed. What the dead gave us, she thought, is alive in us. The dead are alive in us. She didn't want to let Eddie down. But how long should we go on measuring ourselves against the dead?

It occurred to her now that she would like to tell Lawrence about how she had shuffled all the files together. She guessed that he wouldn't judge her. That he might smile. If he smiled, she might go further. She might tell him, as he had encouraged her to at dinner that night back in October, that she did have her own ideas about Eddie's collection. Opinions that she hadn't mentioned to anyone else. What a relief it would be. Because she knew that Lawrence wouldn't be at all surprised to hear that there were things she and Eddie hadn't agreed on entirely, things they had argued about. Lawrence had assumed it all along. She wanted to hear Lawrence's thoughts about each of her favourite objects.

But she stopped herself from confiding in him; surely it was too soon to place herself in his hands all over again? It would be completely irrational.

How much better if there was a way to get Lawrence to place himself in *her* hands instead. And so she decided to offer Lawrence some help. He seemed badly in need of it. Why should she remain always on the receiving end, the begging end, of life?

'I'd like to do something for you, Lawrence.'

'For me?'

'For you and Gwen.'

'You hardly need to, just now. It ought to be the other way

round; it ought to be me who does something for you.' He was still fussing with the kettle, filling it with water, plugging it in, checking inside the dishwasher to find her a clean mug.

'I'll look after Will – here – if he'll let me. You go skiing with Gwen. We'll tell him you had planned the surprise for his mother all along. Why does he need to know that he's missing anything meant for him? I'd really like to do it, and to spend the time with him.'

Lawrence was taken aback. 'Gwen will never leave Will if he's unwell.'

'Maybe he'll be better – enough better.'

'It's such a kindness for you to offer, Hilary. A lovely gesture. But it seems pretty unlikely – don't you think?'

'Let's see when they get back from the doctor.'

Lawrence tipped his head to one side in vague acquiescence. The kettle had boiled at last and the steaming water, as he poured it from the spout, beat quick and deep on to the tea bag in the bottom of her mug, like cloth ripping.

CHAPTER 16

Will had a virus. The temperature was bound to go in a day or two, but one ear was a bit red. Because of the bank holiday, the doctor had prescribed an antibiotic, advising Gwen not to use it unless the ear got worse.

She set about organising treats and excitement for Will to try to enjoy lying down. Could Lawrence collect the prescription, could he get a bottle of children's ibuprofen to alternate with the Calpol, some honey lozenges, a candy cane if he saw one, ginger ale? Could he look for that Christmas movie at the video shop, *Elf*, which was supposed to be funny? Or would it be better to have something like *Mary Poppins* and try not to think about Christmas at all? Where were Will's magnets, the silver balls and the coloured bars that he liked to build with? Had anyone seen them?

Lawrence didn't have the heart to mention the skiing. Will was too floppy to care about anything at all. Gwen made a nest for him on the sofa in the kitchen alcove, and there he lay, glassy-eyed, hot-lipped, motionless, while she chopped onions and chestnuts for stuffing, cooked sausages. From time to time, she left the chores, perched beside him, held a glass of water to his mouth, urged him to take a sip. Every hour or so, she took his temperature, and as it rose and fell, she peeled his undershirt off him or pulled it back on, bathed his forehead to cool him or snugged a blanket around his chest.

Hilary disappeared to the studio. Later she came back down with books she had brought from America, and she read aloud to Will for a long time about a vampire rabbit, a cat and dog who lived with him. Will hardly seemed to notice, but when she stopped reading he asked for more.

The boy made a good project for the three of them. At supper time, they fed him buttered toast with strawberry jam. Afterwards they transferred him – limp, horizontal, trailing blankets – to his bed, along with his tray of medicines, the thermometer, his sweets, his tissues. They urged him not to worry about Santa Claus, that it would all be made up to him in due course; they told him that every year children fell ill on Christmas Eve.

And so they made it safely through to Christmas lunch, anchored to the house, occupied and preoccupied by kindness and necessity, and by the illness which they each suffered and which bound them together through the child. They managed to avoid directness. The world kept its seasonal distance. London was at peace around them.

At lunch, they got a little tipsy. Nobody was much interested in the turkey. Will cheered up a little, smiling, laughing, and at last opened a few small packages from his stocking – a balsa-wood aeroplane to assemble, chocolate racing cars, an off-round rubber ball that bounced to the ceiling then shot sideways across the room, a wooden whistle that sounded like a train's, a pair of snub-nosed, blue plastic children's scissors with metal strips lining the blades so they could really cut. But his ear hurt, and Gwen decreed that he would start the antibiotic.

'After that, you can watch the video Daddy got. Unless you want dessert?'

Will only blinked at her.

'It's *bûche de Noël*,' she said. 'Chocolate with creamy chocolate frosting inside.'

'Can I see it?' His voice was thin, a little strangled, and she could feel his glands as if they had swelled inside her own throat, the phlegm coating the roughness at the back of the tongue, gummy as he tried to swallow.

She went to the refrigerator for the box from the pastry shop, cut the curled pink ribbon with a knife, lifted the yule log out and put it on a dinner plate. Then she carried it to him, held the plate down low, bending over him. He studied the red-capped marzipan mushrooms, the green plastic holly leaves with gold glass berries, the dusting of cocoa powder on the ridged chocolate bark.

He put his germy finger on one of the mushrooms. 'Can you save this for me? For tomorrow?'

'Your ear will feel better after you start the medicine,' she promised him, trying not to feel sad at his lack of appetite and his unchildlike restraint.

She left the cake on the table, found the bottle of thick yellow amoxicillin in the fridge, the clear plastic five-mil spoon; came back to him, shaking the bottle, smiling; perched again on the edge of the sofa beside him. Then she leaned down to him intimately, catching his eyes, silently inquiring with her own. 'Hmmm?' she murmured, as if it were medicine in its own right, his mother wanting so badly to know just how he felt.

'Shall we open the champagne?' Lawrence called out from where he sat talking with Hilary at the table. 'The wine is finished.'

'If you want.' Gwen went gently on with her measuring and administering, tipped the spoon on to Will's pink reluctant tongue, handed him a tumblerful of ginger ale to wash it down.

'Gross?' she asked, gazing deep, her eyes locked on his.

He nodded, lifted his moist top lip so that it trembled a little and showed his seed-pearl teeth. 'Can I watch the movie now?'

'Good idea.'

She patted his outstretched legs as she stood up, looking around for the videotape. Once she had it running in the machine, she looked backwards and forwards a few times from the screen to Will's face, then collected her half-full wine glass from the table and disappeared up the stairs. Behind her, she heard the champagne cork pop; with a backward glance, she saw Lawrence holding a white cloth over the top of the bottle, three flutes on the laden table, and Hilary cutting the cake, both hands wielding the knife.

After a few minutes, Will began to gurgle with laughter. 'Where's Mummy?' he called out. 'This is so funny.'

Lawrence stood up, draining his glass, turned his eyes to the screen, smiled at the sight of a man in a bright green elf costume and a Santa Claus hat leaping on to a fully decorated Christmas tree and toppling it over.

'We need to replay this for her, Daddy. Can you pause the tape?'

'Of course we can. Where's she got to?'

And as Lawrence passed Hilary's chair, making for the laundry room, Hilary said under her breath, 'You should ask Gwen about the trip, when you find her. I think we'd be fine here. He's having a great time. Why don't you tell her about it now?'

'Right.' Lawrence turned from the laundry-room door, passed Hilary's chair again. 'She must have gone upstairs.'

He found Gwen in the studio. He could hear the radio at pretty well full volume from two flights below. '*When I look in the mirror to comb my hair / I see your face just a smiling there / Nowhere to run to, baby, nowhere to hide . . .*'

She was dancing. Her eyes were closed, her face serene – not so much smiling as deeply content. She shimmied around the room, her arms snaking in the air above her head, her hips sinking and turning. She might have been alone on the planet.

It made him feel happy, and he gurgled with laughter just as Will had done watching the film downstairs. He moved towards her, putting his arms out, swaying his hips in time with hers, to join the dance.

269

The radio blared and rocked them: '*I know you're no good for me / But free of you I'll never be / Nowhere to run to, baby, nowhere to hide . . .*'

She went on dancing, oblivious, but as she felt him try to take her in his arms, she scowled. He pressed against her, warm-hearted, but she resisted, shook him off, swivelled away, stepping her feet hard and flat, stamping, showing him only her back, her wish to be left alone.

She's a little drunk, Lawrence told himself. A little wild with Will being poorly, Christmas spoiled, everyone shut inside. But he felt taken aback. He doubted himself, and he wondered what was going on inside her, what she wanted. Was it Hugo? The music didn't tell him. Until now, Lawrence had managed to avoid being rebuffed outright; he didn't like it.

'Go ahead and dance,' she cried out above the music. 'I'm not stopping you.' It was harsh, crippling.

In his surprise, he fell back on a kind of false dignity, claimed a gentle civility, from which he could condescend to her savagery. 'I'm not that generation, Gwen, who dance alone. I prefer to have a partner, to share the pleasure. Maybe I'm not your generation at all.'

'Martha and the Vandellas, Lawrence. From before I was born. Get Hilary to dance with you. She's into old men and the past.' She tipped her head at him, a gesture of adolescent disdain, as if to say, Whatever. And she went on dancing.

Lawrence thought of his errand; clearly it was a risk to suggest anything at all to Gwen just now. But he steeled himself. 'I had a surprise for you and Will, which I have been wanting to tell you about. I rather suppose it's beside the point now.'

'Hmm.' She gyrated towards him.

'Skiing. I had made arrangements to take you both skiing tomorrow.'

'You don't know how to ski.' She laughed; it was ridiculous.

'Neither does Will. I thought we could learn – together.'

She laughed again, tinkling, brazen. 'You think you're not *my* generation. Wait till you try learning to ski with a five-year-old. He'll be bombing past you by the end of the first day.'

Where did it come from, this shattering hatred? Her evident disgust? He couldn't bear it. 'It's immaterial, isn't it?' His voice was imperious, scolding. 'Obviously he can't travel with this virus, and now the ear infection.'

Gwen made no comment.

'You and I ought to go anyway.' He seemed to offer it as a punishment. 'It's time we sorted ourselves out. We need a few days together – so we can find some kind of harmony with one another. Some kind of understanding –'

She stopped dancing, opened her eyes at him. 'Alone?'

He nodded.

'What about Will?'

'Hilary has very kindly offered to look after him.'

Gwen's face set hard. 'I'm not leaving Will with Hilary. Sorry.'

'It's such a waste, Gwen, not to take the chance. And a waste of money for the deposits –'

'I don't want to be alone with you, Lawrence. Not right now anyway. I'd rather be alone with myself. And I couldn't care less about the money. That's never a good reason to do anything. We'd only spend more money anyway, if we went.'

Her lack of concern for his feelings, for the trouble he had taken to please her and to please Will, made him so angry that he couldn't breathe. Cruel, insulting, outrageous – there was no word to describe it. He was beyond hurt. Who was this woman he was married to? He had to get out of the room, out of the house. Everything seemed to be screaming inside him, pummelling him, hard black rocks, the furies.

He turned from her complacent observation, stalked down the stairs and right out of the house along the road towards the river; then he began to run – in the clothes he had worn to lunch,

corduroy trousers, wool jacket, brown leather lace-up shoes –
because he thought it might quell his rage.

Hilary sipped at her champagne, cleared the table, started to wash
the dishes. Whenever she glanced at Will, his eyes were glimmering with the life of the television screen. Once he turned to
her, asking for his mother.

'Daddy's gone to find her,' was all Hilary said. That was enough
to settle Will.

Their basement world, rounded with comfort, plenty, glowed
steadily as it grew dark outside.

She scraped the Christmas leavings into the rubbish, pondering
the size of it, the waste. Even if we'd been hungry, she thought,
how could we have eaten half of it? We needed guests here –
Hugo, Roland. And she thought with humour and dismay,
Impossible. Gwen's matchmaking drove everyone away.

We never really sat down today, she thought. Gwen didn't. Just
a show of Christmas lunch. Poor Will. But Lawrence is probably
right, that you have to do it. Otherwise, pretty soon, you wouldn't
do anything at all.

She rifled the cupboards for little bowls, little plates, tinfoil,
cling film, storing the leftovers. Will and I can eat this again
tomorrow, she thought.

It alarmed her a little that she had offered to care for Will.
Food, even the virus and the ear, seemed easy compared to the
mystery of keeping him happy. It was clear to Hilary that his
mother was what Will wanted when he wanted anything at all.

Gwen seemed to be linked to him and to read him with a
kind of sonar that worked from anywhere in the room, as she
buzzed this way and that, then returned to her blossom, limbs and
lips sticky for him, with sweetness, with whatever it was she had
that he intermittently needed from her in order to thrive and to
be sure of himself. She knows just how long she can ignore him,

Hilary thought. Just how far away she can go. As an infant he would have cried for her, to be suckled, every few hours. It must be based on that. Does she hear an inward cry? Will she be able to hear him from the mountains? Will their bond break if she flies in an airplane? What if she never comes back?

It was a humbling promise, to care for another woman's child. But there were so many reasons just now why she wanted to.

Watching her hands in the soapy water, working the petroleum-coloured grease loose from the roasting pan, Hilary thought about Lawrence. How he had sat at the table, massive in his chair. The father. Most of all, she wanted to do it for him. That was why she had offered. She sensed with such certainty that he needed someone to do something for him; so she had to manage. She was resolved. Despite his intellect and his professional position, Lawrence seemed to have been sidelined from his own life, washed overboard from the raft. He was struggling. His head would soon slip under the water. The magnanimity of his nature, his enthusiasm for the progress of others, his natural, continuous habit of nurturing growth wherever he hoped that it might occur, seemed to have sapped his strength without his noticing. Hilary believed that she could boost him back up into his life, into Gwen's life, Will's life.

She considered the clarity of Lawrence's thought, the force of his powers of analysis, the fineness of his judgement, the generosity and self-deprecation of his instincts, the depth and breadth of his chest, the swoop and ease of his great round arms. And then with a lurch, a sickening shudder which plunged down through her gut and left her hands lying useless in the grey, filmy water, her elbows barely hooked inside the sink holding her up as she half collapsed on to her knees on the floor, she thought: Lawrence. It was as if everything in the world was falling away, leaving only him, isolated and vivid. Lawrence.

Exultation turned immediately to dismay. To horror. Lawrence is Gwen's husband.

I have to get out of this house, Hilary thought. Right away. I can't stay here. I can't fall for the husband of my best friend. The worst conceivable cliché. And at the same time, she felt mastered by it so completely that she was terrified. It's like death, she thought; it's that serious.

It rose over her, the sense of awe. It towered in the room, towered over the woman at the sink doing the washing-up, over the little boy on the sofa, watching a video and waiting for his mother. I had no idea, Hilary thought, no idea how serious, how immense it would feel. She understood in her flesh, in the savour of the breath entering and leaving her nose in snorts and gasps, why people killed for love. She could feel that their bodies were now mortally engaged – Gwen's, Lawrence's, her own, Will's. She could feel that they would never escape from one another.

I have to get out of this house, she thought again. She tried to stand up, to find a cloth and dry her hands, to call out.

And then she heard Lawrence coming heavily down the stairs, thumping, dragging, ungainly, towards her heart.

'Can you see if there's ice in the freezer? Sorry to put you to the trouble. I've turned over my ankle. Fool that I am. I think I've sprained it or pulled something. Stepped in a hole – that damned pavement which the tree roots heave. They need to be pruned much harder, those trees, if they're to be kept under control. It hurts like bloody hell –'

He stopped, seeing her twisted face. 'I'm so sorry, Hilary. Poor you, here all alone with our dishes, and Will. What an idiot I am. We none of us will stand another trip to the doctor just now and another invalid. It's too stupid.'

'Oh, my God!' she said, impassioned, hoarse, backing away from him.

'It's really not that bad.' He shook his head, easing into one of the straight-backed chairs at the table and raising the leg cautiously on to the seat of another. 'Honestly. You mustn't worry so.'

After a long pause in which Hilary stood frozen, apart from

her hands which were tumbling a damp white dish towel round and round themselves, he said, 'But if you wouldn't mind about the ice? I'd be so grateful.'

She looked across at Will; so Lawrence looked, too.

'He's all right,' said Lawrence, resting his eyes back on hers.

She swayed a little, turning pink.

Then she dived for the freezer, fingers trembling, nails scraping uselessly over slippery, frozen packages that wouldn't budge, that were hard and smooth as glass. Finally, she pried free a blue rubber tray filled with ice cubes, took it back and slammed it hard against the sink. Cubes and chips of ice flew everywhere, scooted across the floor, melted away in the dirty dishwater. She grabbed what she could, folded it inside the cloth she was still holding, smashed the bulging cloth a few more times against the sink, handed it to Lawrence.

He reached towards his foot, jerking forward like an inept rower, hopelessly. 'Trouble is, when I went down, I did something in my leg as well – or maybe it's my lower back. I've been running a bit lately, at the cottage, and the muscles have all got rather tight. Could I trouble you to take off my shoe? Not the nicest thing in the world, but if you could bear it?'

She drew close to his raised foot, at one side of him, and reached for his shoelace, then she suddenly pulled back her hands, as if from a fire. She had a kind of hunted sensation, a sensation that they were being watched, that they were being tested. She looked around the room, at the shadows gathering in the corners, at Will. She took a breath, grasped the laces in her fingers to untie them, pulled open the shoe around the tongue, loosening it. Then she eased one long hand around behind Lawrence's heel.

'I don't want to hurt you,' she murmured, and she looked up at him for an instant, checking his face for pain.

'No. I don't want you to do that either.' He smiled into her eyes, chuckled. 'Go on then,' he urged. And very quietly, 'You can't possibly hurt me as much as Gwen has done.'

Hilary looked back with so much understanding and so much sympathy that, for a moment, they both stopped breathing.

How does she know? Lawrence wondered. Clearly she does. Exactly how I feel just now – lamed as I am by my own rage and stupidity, my inability to deal with the fruits of my actions.

It smouldered between them, what they knew about each other. He felt the pressure of his sorrow and his anger slide off a little; felt a leap in his throat, a kick of life, unhobbled. Then gently, she wrapped her other hand around the back of his calf for leverage, and worked his foot free at the heel.

The shoe dropped with a thud.

Will cried out, 'What are you doing? Why are you taking off your shoes, Daddy?'

Will got up from the sofa, bare feet softly slapping the cold floor, and came to see.

Hilary was painstakingly peeling back Lawrence's thick green sock, exposing his puffy, big-boned, purplish ankle joint, his white-whale foot, damp toes, crooked yellow nails. Gently she nestled the bundle of ice cubes around the ankle, pressing them close, pressing them tight around the swollen flesh.

'Is that an ice pack, Daddy?' asked Will.

Lawrence leaned back in his chair and smiled with strange pleasure. 'It's an ice pack.'

'Have you had a bang on your foot?'

'Exactly.'

'Mummy always gives me an ice pack when I get a bang. You have to do it for twenty minutes, which is longer than you think.' He stood twirling the untied belt of his dressing gown around and around in the air.

'Yes. Well. We'll try to stick to Mummy's rules, shall we?' Lawrence said, raising his eyebrows at Hilary. 'Twenty minutes,' he repeated, thinking it would be far too short. 'Can you sit with me for that long, Hilary?'

At first she was afraid to reply. But Lawrence's eyes looked clear and unthreatening, only wishing to engage and amuse her. She told him the truth. 'I'll sit for as long as you want.'

There they sat looking at one another until Will grew bored. 'That's very kind what Hilary is doing,' he announced, and walked out from underneath the twined beams of their eyes back to his video.

'It certainly is,' Lawrence muttered. He turned away from Hilary to watch Will settle on the sofa and train his eyes back on the television screen. And as he watched Will, Lawrence said more loudly, 'It's the kindest thing anyone has done for me in a long time. I feel it's my Christmas present, being ministered to by Hilary.' Then, more quietly, 'And it deserves something in return.' Whereupon he reached forward with effort, taking hold of Hilary's elbow near his knee, tugging on it hard until she looked and then gave way towards him, startled. He pressed his lips against hers, letting them rest there without opening them, then nudged her roughly away, shoving his mouth at her mouth as if to deliver a silent challenge, What do you think of this? A kiss?

She thought she might burst into flame or dissolve in a puddle of tears.

She sat up straight, snatching herself back from him.

Lawrence saw a tremor around her mouth, a threat of earthquake, and he took refuge in reflecting upon the distinction which Seneca once drew between a *ministerium* and a *beneficium*. It had long intrigued him: Why would a slave voluntarily do for his master more than was required of him? Of course, in early Christian times, when so many values began to shift and to be turned upside down, many aspired to such acts. He wondered exactly how the terms had metamorphosed in ecclesiastical usage. Interesting to try to trace that, he thought. Everything was preparing for the transformation; for instance, among the Augustales, the freed slaves were keenest of all to worship the Emperor, because they already knew how to abase themselves, as if they had been Christians without even knowing it, well before Christ was born.

These were the kinds of puzzles, separate from their own, which Lawrence now felt he needed to rely on to carry him and to carry Hilary safely from the room.

CHAPTER 17

By the next morning, Hilary and Gwen had agreed to go away skiing together. Gwen had a hectic sense that she ought to get Hilary out of her house, away from her husband and her son. There was a penalty due to the airline, but it wasn't much, and Lawrence insisted on paying for everything as it was his Christmas present to Gwen and nobody would make such a trip alone.

But it was Will who persuaded his mother, cheerful, piping. 'It will be sad if nobody in our whole family goes. Since Daddy can't walk, the surprise will be ruined.'

He paused, head down, breathing noisily through his mouth. He was cutting up yesterday's wrapping paper with his new scissors. The metal-lined blades scraped against the paper with each creeping cut, then he laid the flimsy, brightly coloured strips side by side on the sofa, to make more paper chains. 'You can phone us when you get there and tell us. If it's really good? Maybe we'll be better by then and we'll come.'

They flew to Zurich and took a minibus to St Anton. Beside the spinning, traffic-riddled highway, the wet green farms seemed deserted, overhung with black-and-white winter light and dour clouds. At Lake Constance, the grey road rising and dropping as if from the sky, the slate-coloured water stretching wide towards alien, settled shores, Gwen felt a kind of exultation that they were away, alone, in an anonymous corner of the civilised world. She relished the bleakness, the unfamiliar, anodyne landscape, the damp scent in the air of frozen rain. When they crossed the border into

Austria and met the chill of officialdom – guards, dogs, wire fences – there seemed to be no turning back. Hilary smiled without opening her lips, dazed, struggling to pull free from her daydream of Lawrence.

They both babbled like children at the length and darkness of the mountain tunnels as they shot through them, cried out in delight as the white froth on the tree-lined ridges above and below them gradually thickened into snow.

It was late when they arrived. Lights twinkled in their hundreds under slanting eves, between quaintly painted shutters, through gauzy white curtains, on countless Christmas trees standing invisibly in the night. Along the melting roads, boots crunched and sloshed, tyre chains clinked and whispered. Woodsmoke rose sweetly in the snappy air, and the mountains silently hunkered in the inky, star-pricked sky. The charm of it was almost suffocating. And they were breathless with altitude. They fell asleep side by side under feather duvets in an overheated room lined with knotted yellow pine, gasping for morning and for the cold, bright illumination of the snow.

Over breakfast, they decided to hire a guide. But they had clothes and equipment to find, and the long, slippery main street bustled with lumbering crowds. By the time they finally approached a stern, red-jacketed officer of the *Skischule*, he only lifted his hands at the deserted slush around him, the cerulean sky, then, turning half away, lit a cigarette.

Hilary called out in German, 'Would you take our name? In case someone drops out?'

He snapped off his lighter and dropped it into his breast pocket, spewed smoke between his purple, leathery lips. 'You know the other school is bigger. Maybe they have someone free.' He waved at a distant facade.

They struggled along under their gear to find an argument

taking place between two big black-haired men in bright blue jackets splashed with yellow across the chests.

'What's this about?' Gwen asked under her breath.

'Being late to work,' Hilary whispered. 'The guy with the clipboard is saying that the clients waited plenty long enough and who could blame them for getting pissed off. Christmas week. Everyone is out skiing now. Why should they wait for a drunk?'

Hilary and Gwen exchanged a look, considering.

'Do we want to ski with a drunk?' Gwen asked, wrinkling her nose.

He flung a large, disgusted brown hand in the air, unzipped his jacket and shouted at his boss. 'I'm not drunk. I don't come to work drunk. You think I want to kill myself? Forty years' experience in these mountains?'

Then he rocked back on his heels and sat down low behind his bended knees with his backside cantilevered in mid-air, one fist and then the other punching upward towards the sky, as if he were working his way through big moguls. His jacket swivelled loosely around his hips. Without looking up, he added resentfully something it seemed he would have preferred to keep to himself, 'I was with someone. So.'

With a grunt of physical power, he stood up again, eyes flaming, and spat into the grey snow thinly covering the wet straw and the gravel on which they stood. Suddenly it became evident how much taller he was of the two.

'He says he's not drunk,' Hilary whispered, bending down to Gwen. 'And he's skied here for forty years.'

'Forty years? The one with the red ski boots?' Gwen studied the length of his slim, black Gore-tex-sheathed legs, the gash of light visible between them, the nonchalant zigzag of his stance at crotch and knee, the narrow flaps covering the endless zippers down the sides, and she considered the unconscious expertise with which he had frayed the fabric exactly where it was reinforced, around the scuffed wide mouths of his blood-coloured boots. 'He must have been born here. He looks pretty athletic?' She raised her eyes to Hilary's again, impressed, playful.

'Austria's John Wayne?' Hilary giggled.

'Or a tall Achilles,' Gwen suggested.

'How hard could it be to ditch him if it doesn't work out? We've got the little map. You think we have to pay in advance?'

'Ask. Might be better than trying to find good runs by ourselves.'

So Hilary clumped forward with her rented skis and poles balanced on her shoulder. 'Excuse me. We want a guide, and — if you've — missed your clients? Maybe you're available to ski with us?' She flipped the skis off her shoulder and let the tails fall heavily to the ground. They slapped together loudly at the bindings.

The two men started, squinted fiercely at her, then at Gwen. There was an uncomfortable feeling of exposure among them, but only for a moment. Then the men hurried to array themselves in an air of professionalism — squared their shoulders, flattened their fingers along their jaws as if checking they were clean-shaven, showed purring smiles.

'Helmut is free, yes,' announced his superior in stalwart, barking English. 'You are good skiers?'

'Pretty good,' said Hilary. 'Experienced anyway —' She hesitated and looked back at Gwen. 'We haven't skied for a few years.'

'And we haven't been here before,' added Gwen. 'We want someone to show us the fun places to go.'

Helmut's mouth slowly spread into a flashing grin. 'Fun places to go like the Krazy Kangaruh?' His shirt was open at the neck; he had a bright yellow kerchief knotted around his throat, the ends pulled wide, jaunty.

'Is that — a run?' asked Hilary.

Helmut laughed. 'We run there at the end of the day, the three of us, to fill the gas tank.' He extended a stiffly curving thumb towards his mouth and tipped his head back, guzzling, then he reached inside his jacket and produced a pair of black plastic sun-glasses, flicked them open, slipped them on; the mirror lenses lit up his tan like a neon sign.

His boss broke in on this show of gallantry with impatient pre-cision. 'Ladies, the bar is by your choice only. The session is four hours. You can pay cash to the instructor or go to the office after-wards. Have a nice ski.' And he walked off in his noiseless leather mountain boots.

Their first runs were a little stiff. Helmut was correct and dig-nified with them, looking back to see where they were, spreading his arms wide as if this would somehow remind them that they, too, had arms, bouncing with extravagant ceremony through his knees. Following his example, they inscribed S-curves down easy descents, rising and sinking. He stopped often to watch them turn, to comment on the flexibility of their knees, the edges of their uphill and downhill skis, the position of their centres of gravity, the rotation of their arms, their grip on their poles, but mostly he praised them. '*Sehr gut.*'

The thrill of it gradually coursed through them, wind pulling tears from their eyes, slashing at their hats, their hair. The un-familiar terrain delivered only small, pleasurable challenges.

Gradually, Helmut picked up the pace, telling them, 'Stay as close behind me as you can. This is safer when it's crowded.' So they took turns chasing him, following right on top of the flashing, black tails of his skis. They were like dancers, crook-kneed, strong-thighed, flex-hipped, held tight by Helmut's forceful lead, swinging and turning in a close chain along the spreading white way. Every arc Helmut made, they followed, now left, now right, down the crawling slopes, bonded in Helmut's swooping, writhing entourage.

When they finally stopped in the village, it was growing dark and a few flakes of snow drifted in the street lights. He waved them off abruptly. 'There's really not enough snow for you. It's too bad.'

'What about the Krazy Kangaruh?' Gwen called out.

He tossed his head, striding away already with his skis up on his high shoulder. 'Aren't you tired? I never met women like you before.'

'Tomorrow?' she suggested.

He turned around and called to them, walking backwards. 'You want to ski tomorrow?'

Hilary was bent low over her boots, hair tumbled around her face. 'Can we afford him?' she said quietly to Gwen.

'Sure,' said Gwen out loud, with gusto, answering them both at once.

'So. We take the bus to Zürs, ski over to Lech and back. Early. Around here is a waste of time now. It's getting colder; tonight this will freeze. Up there we can find maybe a little something more. Maybe even off-piste. They had already more snowfall there. Eight o'clock at the bus stop,' he said. 'I'll be waiting.'

Still Gwen teased him. 'We have to go to the bar by ourselves after all that talk, Helmut?'

He rewarded her with a leering, feline smile. 'Step into the bar; you won't be alone long. Later on, maybe I'll come and look for you, eh?'

But Hilary objected. 'I'm exhausted. I'm going to bed.'

When he was out of sight, Gwen said, 'You should have a drink with him, Hilary. Don't you think he's attractive?'

'He seems pretty jaded. And – I don't know – angry, in some weird way. Must be hard pandering to people who are on vacation, taking their money to show them a good time.'

She said this with a feeling that she was trying to warn Gwen of something or that she needed to restrain her. All around them, doors stood open to bars, discotheques, rented bedrooms; music spewed into the soft, snowy air. The sapping thrill of the sport, its cathartic demands on the physique, left her feeling defenceless against the lowlife invitation to go in from the isolating cold, to unwrap from heavy garments and eye-concealing lenses. Seduction seemed to suck at her and at Gwen. In her tiredness, Hilary had a vague, hallucinatory impression of the purity of the snow and the vast outdoors being encroached upon by dark energies, spots of disease like mould on bread.

She felt that she had Lawrence's wife in her care. It was an unfamiliar and an uncomfortable responsibility.

The next morning, Helmut kept them moving fast. It was snowing hard and the wind drove needles of snow into their reddened faces, lifting them backwards bodily as they schussed along the ridge above Zürs. From time to time Hilary wondered if Helmut remembered they were behind him; it was all they could do to keep him in their sight.

Finally, somewhere near the Zürsersee, they came upon a little mountainside hut, and he suddenly proposed that they stop to get warm. He took off his skis and went inside without waiting for them to reply.

Helmut drank glühwein; so did Gwen. Hilary had hot chocolate. Nobody else came in or went out of the dim room with its small windows and folksy curtains. After his second glühwein, he began to tell them stories, of ski races he had won, avalanches he had escaped, rich women he had loved and left. His face grew red; he leaned forward, smiling and gesturing with outspread arms. Even Gwen grew bored. She fell back against the pillows, perspiring a little with the hot wine.

Helmut leaned closer and confided, 'You know, if you pay enough, you can get a woman and kill her. Some of my clients tell me about this.' Then he stood up. 'Enough stories,' he announced. 'We go ski.'

Off they went into the storm, down the back of the Madloch. The world shrank down to a shroud of enveloping white, with Helmut, a phantom, slipping away in front of them into the silence, always at the very limit of their vision. They had no idea where they were, and the sinking slope was invisible, changing continually from sheer to rutted, hard to soft, powder to rocks, so that they had to let their skis ride blind, on and on, with leg-cramping anticipation. They both knew they were depending on Helmut entirely, Hilary with a kind of angry, clench-toothed resolve not to be defeated by his sadism, Gwen with a sense of terrified excitement, something closer to depravity. It was like a compulsion for Gwen, the faint fleeting figure of a man in the distance, bigger, stronger, a figure she couldn't quite keep up with, would never catch. The challenge was irresistible, to draw abreast of him, to make him turn to her, include her. She refused to be left behind, to be forgotten. The more she pursued him, the more she needed to. And she skied with abandon, without fear, as if she were tied to him by an invisible rope.

It was a long time before they caught sight of another building or any other skiers, and Helmut instinctively capitalised on their sense of relief by telling them loudly that they were Amazons, up to anything, tough as men.

'We ride up this chairlift, and then down in Oberlech we can have a fine meal. Toast our feet.'

So they had a long lunch in a warm, crowded hotel dining room, and he prevailed upon them both to drink wine. 'You need it,' he urged. 'I'm not kidding. If you don't want to ski these little baby trails to the bottom, we can ride down in the cable car. Then it's only the bus.'

They grew lazy and content in the steamy room. The windows misted over; the air smelled of wet wool. Nobody wanted to move.

And after a while, word bubbled through the pleasant fug that the pass was closed. Helmut pulled a waitress to him with a curled finger and spoke to her in German.

'What pass?' asked Hilary.

'The Flexenpass.' He leaned back against the banquette and smiled with seeming satisfaction. 'It's unusual so early in the year. So much snow at one time. And it fell, basically, on frozen slush. So.'

'So what?'

'I think they will open it soon. Perhaps during the night if they can blast.'

'What difference does it make?'

'Well, we have to find a place to sleep,' he grinned. 'The three of us. We can't get out, down to St Anton. Not tonight, that's for sure. I'll ask at the ski school.'

He chuckled at the consternation showing on their faces, looked from one to the other boldly. 'You can relax. We'll find something. Trust me. We may as well party.'

He poured out the last of their Gewürztraminer, splashing some on the tablecloth, and snapped his fingers for service so he could order more.

'Have you plenty of money?' he demanded. 'Lech is not cheap. Maybe we stay with a friend I have in town. I think he's here this season. We'll see. Only a floor, or maybe a sofa, but it's free.'

And that was how they found themselves, rank with sweat and wine, stunned with exhaustion, one arm of Helmut's around each of their shoulders, being introduced to a grizzled hippie called Axel in the open doorway of his apartment. His eyes, like the rest of him, were grey; they were enormous, liquid with sorrow, even as he smiled benevolently on their situation.

'It's my privilege for you to sleep here,' he said sadly, sweetly, throwing the door wide, stepping aside in his socks, his thin cotton shirt, his baggy corduroy trousers, so they could enter.

It was only one room, a sway-backed double bed covered in a brown-and-gold crocheted afghan, an electric burner, a tray of cutlery on top of a tiny fridge. In the single large window above the bed dangled a spider plant and a stained-glass medallion featuring an evil eye. A ski instructor's jacket, blue, black and yellow, hung on the back of one of the three chairs.

They stood around in silence, so Axel tentatively announced,

'Maybe Helmut finds another place for himself? And I go with him also? Of course, you have my bed, Hilary, Gwen.'

Helmut cried him down affably. 'This is fine for us all to share, Axel. Where else will anyone go? On such a night. You have heat, a toilet.'

Hilary and Gwen stammered out thanks, in English, in German, embarrassed and apologetic.

Axel invited them to shower. 'I have things you can wear, so you dry your clothes tonight.'

With an instinct not to become separated, they squeezed into the bathroom together, and when at length they opened the door again, they discovered two neat piles of well-worn, clean clothes on the floor. Helmut and Axel were both gone.

'So now what do we do for entertainment?' Gwen asked. She felt impatient at the sight of the empty room.

'We ought to call Lawrence and tell him what's happened,' Hilary said. 'What if Will got worse? Or missed you?'

'I don't see a phone, though. Maybe he doesn't have one?'

'We shouldn't use his.'

'Do we have the strength to walk out and find one?' Even as she asked, Gwen felt her blood lift at the thought of getting out into the town, into the night behind Helmut. 'I can go myself if you don't feel like it?' Her voice had a sudden push in it, like appetite.

It grated on Hilary, the impulse she sensed in Gwen to throw dirt on anything beautiful, anything sacred left in her marriage. What if Gwen just took herself to hell, Hilary thought, showed that she didn't love Lawrence, and that it wasn't worth his loving her? How easy that would be for me. Her heart whammed. She felt nausea rising and thrashing, a beast in her ribcage, self-disgust, black-breathed. I can't encourage her; I mustn't let her.

'I'll come,' Hilary sighed. Then, more definitely, 'I want to come.'

★ ★ ★

Nobody answered at the house in Hammersmith. It made Gwen and Hilary uneasy.

'What time is it there?'

Hilary looked at her watch. 'An hour earlier.'

'So where are they?' Gwen tried the number for the cottage, and Lawrence answered right away. 'Is everything OK?' she asked.

'Just about.'

'What are you doing up there? Isn't it freezing cold?'

'I've got the fire going.'

'And – I mean – how'd you get there? Is your ankle better already?'

'Roland collected us.'

'That was nice of him. But – so you don't have the car. What about food?'

'Don't worry about that, Gwen. We have plenty to eat. It's better for Will to be here at the moment. He needed a change of scene, that's all. He really didn't realise what it would be like with you gone overnight, how much he would miss you. Hugo's going to come for us in our car when he gets back to London. Otherwise Roland will drive us back again.'

'Wow. You've really mobilised the troops.'

'It seemed like a good idea.'

'What's going on, Lawrence? What's the matter?'

Lawrence was sitting in the clapped-out red armchair by the green-and-mauve-tiled fireplace. The buried cold of the chair, pressing on his buttocks and on the small of his back, smelled of mildew, stone walls, abandonment.

'Will went on a – kind of a – rampage. Up in the studio. I'm awfully sorry, Gwen. The trouble is that, with my ankle, I couldn't climb the stairs easily, and I let myself believe that he was perfectly content. He went up to play the piano. I ought to have noticed that I didn't hear any music. It never occurred to me. Of course, now I realise that, even in the basement, I ought probably to have been able to hear something. The doors were all open. But I was writing and –'

'What do you mean by a rampage? What did he do?'

There was a silence. Gwen spat out a summary to Hilary. 'They went to the cottage because Will got into the studio alone and made some sort of mess.' Then she said to Lawrence, 'It can't be those big scissors he loves or you'd be at the hospital.'

'Wait, Gwen. Wait just a second.' Lawrence struggled up from the depths of the chair, leaving the phone on its grimy arm, and limped across the flagged floor and the bright islands of thread-bare rug to Will's open door. He leaned inside, peered around to see the tumbled mess of hair, the half-circles of dark lash sweetly curling on the freckled cheeks. Then he shut the door quietly and went back to the phone.

'He's been making these paper chains, darling. That you showed him how to make for the tree? Manufacturing them in extraordinary quantities. And I guess he got the impression that some of your watercolours weren't wanted. In any case, he told me Hilary didn't like them, or didn't want me to see them? So he cut them up. He told me you wanted it done. It was those big scissors, as you say. He shredded – well – quite a lot of paper, really.'

'Quite a lot? But what exactly? Which ones did he shred?'

'All of them.'

'All of them? But that would have taken him hours!'

'Yes. That's why I've brought him here. I knew right away that he couldn't have done it all at once. He'd been up there several times, you see. Early in the morning before I woke up, and at it with real ferocity. It was a huge amount of work. It's astonishing really, the amount of work – or destruction. Depending how you – see it.'

Gwen felt a wave of awe rush downward inside her, her guts flushing. She thought she might faint with the sudden emptying.

'What? What is it?' Hilary demanded.

'He's cut up everything. All the watercolours. The ones I did for you.' Her voice was wan, almost inaudible.

'Everything?'

Gwen nodded.

'The whole collection?'

It was as if the objects themselves had been destroyed. They both staggered under it. Hilary grabbed the receiver out of Gwen's hand.

'Lawrence?'

'Maybe you two better come back. Is Gwen going to cope with this?'

'Did he cut them *all* up?'

'Well, I couldn't find anything else in the studio apart from the canvases. My movement's still rather restricted, but I crawled about on all fours for a long time trying to gather all the bits into a bin liner to preserve them in case – in case – well, I'm sure they can't be reassembled, so I don't know why – but anyway, I looked underneath all the furniture and so on. Then Roland came round to have a look and he advised I ring Gwen's dealer, but Nick's evidently gone to the Caribbean to have Christmas with his ex-wife and their children, which is maybe just as well. Who knows. I had to get Will away. It was rather like a murder scene or something. He was going on and on about betrayal, and I felt there was something really raging in him that I couldn't understand. He didn't like my discovering what he had done or searching round the room and looking at other things. And he went completely wild when I took Roland up, saying Roland mustn't see, either. That Hilary – that you – would be angry. That I'd have to leave. Once we got him away, he was much calmer, right away he was much calmer.'

There was a silence as the complexity of it fell on Lawrence and Hilary, and the sense of responsibility they shared for it. There wasn't much that Hilary felt she could say out loud; she thought Lawrence guessed this – that Gwen was still beside her, listening. She took a big breath. 'The thing is, Lawrence, we're snowed in.'

'What?'

'We came up to ski in another little town, because there wasn't much snow in St Anton, and now we're snowed in here. We literally can't get out. They're saying maybe tomorrow. But for the moment, we're trapped.'

Now it was Lawrence's turn to be surprised. 'Crikey.'

After a pause, his voice came down the line as a lamentation. 'This is just bloody awful. You've got to help Gwen with this. I know you can help her. A body blow, from one's own child. Maybe it's just as well that she has time there to get used to what's happened. Will needs her, but he needs her — as his mother. Not angry at all. He's in a pretty fragile state.'

Hilary tried to soothe Lawrence; she spoke coaxingly. 'Don't worry. You mustn't worry. It'll be all right.'

Her tone sent Gwen into a rage. Gwen pounded on Hilary's back, on her shoulders, screaming at her. 'Now you have what you wanted! Everything destroyed.'

Hilary ducked and held one arm up behind her to fend off the blows. 'Lawrence, I'll try to call you back. As soon as I can. Just look after Will. Don't worry.' And she slapped the receiver back into the cradle.

'Now there's no record of anything! I wanted to lift you up, to make you feel happy again. And you couldn't even receive that as — a gift! You're so obsessed with what's gone, with keeping everything secret so you can control it. That can't be what Doro wanted! And look what you've done to us — to my work. My little boy. My own sweet Will, look what you've made him do!' She was crying, hoarse with emotion.

'Stop it, Gwen! I'm not the one who's done this! You're upset. I understand.'

'Take my husband while you're at it. I know you want him. There aren't any others as good, are there? Any others that would ever really suit you. Practically in a wheelchair, which is just where you like them. And a classicist to boot. Maybe you can write his life work for him when he's dead and still hasn't finished it. Maybe you can inherit his notes, his hopes, instead of Doro's.'

Hilary went white at this. She took a step backwards in the soft snow.

Gwen went on berating her. 'Have my home. I invited you in, I offered. It's what I deserve. Obviously, I'm not good enough for Lawrence, with my indiscipline, my lasciviousness. While you, the figure on the vase, the gentle, grieving maiden, the still nubile girl, the hopeful, hardworking, undemanding, uncertain scholar, need only a little love, a little attention, a little advice and support, to make you blossom, to make you come into your own. You don't fool me for a minute. You just want to fuck up everyone else's life so you don't have to feel so bad about your own. I don't need anything that you can take from me, Hilary; I'm fine alone. I don't need some whole huge group to reassure me about who I am and what I want. Some gang of friends. I'm fine solo – no husband, no mentor, no lawyer, no assistant, no board of trustees, no collection of antiquities.'

'Gwen. Gwen. Stop. Please stop.' They were only whispers, floating away with Hilary's visible breath at the edge of the beam from the street light. Who was Gwen talking about? Had she really managed to ruin Gwen's life as well as her own? Gwen, who had seemed strong enough for both of them? 'You're not being fair – you're not –'

How happy Hilary had been to hear Lawrence's voice. She felt pulled to the telephone as if to a waiting meal, a banquet, but she didn't allow herself to go. She wouldn't call him back.

Gwen turned and walked away into the downpour of snow. Axel's clothes hung down below her ski jacket – his ochre sweatshirt, his thin, red fleece sweatpants, pilling and baggy, with the crotch falling nearly to her knees, the legs rolled up over enormous felt boots which shifted as she stumped along. She looked like an orphan, a waif.

Hilary stood and watched, her heart going along the road with Gwen in the spinning whiteness. She was thinking, That's the result of what I want. And I haven't even tried to get it.

CHAPTER 18

Hilary wiped tears from her stinging cheeks all the way back to Axel's apartment, arriving with an icicle of snot inside her nose, ready to climb in under his limp, lonely covers.

But she found him sitting at his table, silent and composed. He stood up and bowed slightly, heels together.

'Now I will do your chart,' he said with gentle conclusiveness, as if they had an appointment. 'According to the Mayan calendar.' He stood waiting, his big, sad eyes serene. Then he gestured to a chair beside his, and slightly bowed again. 'Please.'

Unsure what else to do, Hilary sat down and tried to focus on the folding plastic chart he placed before her and to answer his questions about her birthdate. She allowed herself to be summed up in a handful of coloured symbols: the red serpent, transformation; the eagle, vision.

She was more tired than ever, and she thought, What if it has nothing to do with me, any of what's happened? What if it's all because of this chart? Foreordained. Who I am, what I do.

Axel murmured on about the main sign, the minor sign, the third sign. A kernel of maize, potential. Death and rebirth.

'Mine, I also have the eagle,' Axel observed, 'and the green maize.' He went on telling her about his own chart and about Helmut's chart. 'Helmut has the serpent, but it's not so good with him because he does not have the eagle also with it. He has the monkey, you know, which is sex.'

There was a silence, and Hilary realised that Axel was making a joke about Helmut. She smiled, sniffed a small laugh. 'The monkey.'

Axel smiled back. 'Why not do Gwen's chart? You know her birthday? Because she is your close friend. And I can do it again for her, maybe later on.'

So Hilary summoned to mind the dates.

He raised his eyebrows. 'This one is not so often. She has the storm. It brings change. This sign can be very powerful, very destructive.' He paused, pressing his lips together in disapproval. Then, as if to comfort Hilary about possessing such a friend, he added, 'But she has also water, which is cleansing. So maybe after you get this turmoil, this energy, there is purity, a fresh start. And this one,' he put his grey-nailed finger on the sun, 'is very creative. So with this she has another mood, another energy.'

'Are you sure you don't have us mixed up, Axel?' Hilary asked. 'Could I be the storm? Maybe that one is mine?'

He sat back in his chair, gave a little sigh, seemed to be considering. 'Maybe this is true. Maybe if you spend a lot of time together with a friend, this happens. This kind of confusion, this kind of exchange with your energies.'

As she listened to him and watched his eyes, she thought how unspeakably wistful, how disappointed he seemed. All alone, evidently, in this little apartment. And she thought, It's hard to be alone. However straightforward it may seem, it's hard to be alone. Hard for me. And it would be hard for Gwen.

'So. The Mayan calendar finishes soon, in 2012,' Axel said matter-of-factly.

'That's as far as they wanted to think?' Hilary asked, trying to be polite, wondering whether, like a child bored by trying to count to infinity, the Mayans had decided that the rest was well enough implied.

He smiled, shrugged. 'After that, everything finishes.'

'You don't believe that, do you?'

'It's coming soon. We can see for ourselves.'

And Hilary thought, Fine for the Mayans; their whole civilisation collapsed long before they reached the end of time. She pictured the final implosion, the dust going up. Then, more accurately, high-stepped temples, jungle creeping in over the sacrificial altars, the gods carved as serpents and in feathers, the stone-walled ball courts. She had a sense about the Mayans that they hadn't tried to stop it. Was there some fatalistic attitude weakening the priests, the elite? Is that what it tells us about them – a calendar that *has* a last day? And yet there are Mayans around, scattered, at ground level, Mexicans now, intermingling with whatever else. It was only human nature to survive, to go on striving. There must have been intense, personal struggles. Somebody hoping there would be a future. Taking responsibility for it. Somebody who maybe hadn't had enough of everything yet. What difference would it ever make, otherwise, what any of us did? Hilary wondered. Why would we bother with paintings, museums, monuments?

'So after this calendar,' she asked, 'does a new one begin? Counting over again?'

'The end of the world,' said Axel. He smiled, opened his palms, lifted them towards her.

Gwen shuffled along through the snow, kicking at it, raging, with her hands shoved hard into her jacket pockets, her feet flinging about inside Axel's enormous boots.

She was burning up with frustration, with impotence, couldn't think, could hardly see, wanted to hit something, someone, to scream. All around her was the blanketing snow, settling thicker and thicker, white, cold and uniform in the darkness and in the pools of light she passed through. What did snow have to do with anything at all? What good is snow? And yet here she was.

I need to get home and fix what's broken; fix my marriage, be with my son. And I need to work. I need to start new pictures for my show. I need to paint like crazy. I need colour! Everywhere. She wanted the tubes of it, her palette, here in the white, undifferentiated blizzard, wanted to squeeze the pungent riches out on the snow all around her, colour it chrome yellow, rose madder, indigo, burnt sienna. Bring the whiteness to life according to her own invention, her own desire. She wanted the smell and the feel of her studio.

But it was impossible.

Water rushed alongside the road in the bright, open darkness. She was walking beside a river which cut its swathe between the mountains and through the middle of the town. It soothed her a little, the way the icy air freshened as the shallow current sluiced and gurgled over the rocks. The way the snow fell silently into it and swelled the river's strength and speed. On she pressed, nowhere in particular, along the road, up an incline.

And then she saw Helmut in front of her, a long way off. She recognised unmistakably the figure she had pursued all day through the white-out, and her instincts were roused at once. He offered distraction, something to experience in the blank, claustrophobic scene. She set her eye on him with the same heedless determination she had felt skiing behind him, and she began to walk a little faster, intending to catch him. He climbed some stairs beyond the bus stop and turned into a lit-up doorway on a big balcony above. A shout of music and laughter escaped as he went in. It was easy to find the stairs, and she climbed up and turned in through the same door, to have a drink, a night-time encounter, to sit close to him, talk to his eyes, drown in the loud music, the suggestion.

The restaurant was smoky, crowded with hot, heavy-footed bodies standing and sitting shoulder to shoulder, over beer steins, shots of schnapps, Poire William, half-globes of wine. She pressed through the jostling rooms on tiptoe, searching. He could see me, if he tried, she thought. And it hurt her feelings, ridiculously, that he hadn't already seen her, hadn't rescued her and taken her under his wing.

Then she spotted him, draped around a blonde, at the end of

the bar. The woman was turned out in white leather trousers and a fuzzy, white sweater with a plunging V-neck. Her skin was pallid with make-up, her plump lips scarlet. But Gwen could see right away that she was young. Too young. She could see that the vulgar, beautiful girl was too young because Helmut, so close beside her, looked grotesquely old. His skin in the fluorescent light from behind the bar showed pockmarks underneath the rose-brown ravages of the weather; his hair, combed back high from his forehead, was thin at the front, glistening with hairdressing cream. And Gwen noticed for the first time that its black colour had a reddish, translucent, shoe-polish quality. That his hair was, in fact, dyed.

She saw all this in a flash, as she moved towards them across the room, the girl within the circle of Helmut's powerful, long arm where she herself had intended to be. She froze in horror, revulsion. Why had she wanted to be that girl?

Or had she in fact wanted to be Helmut? Dissatisfied, flaccid maturity still praying for, preying upon, happiness, youth, love, fulfilment.

She thought of Hugo; she thought of Will. It was like a revelation. Like seeing herself from the outside, some action of her own mirrored in this tawdry scene. Accompanied by sudden illness, a sense of dread.

That was when Helmut looked up and noticed her. She felt his anger all the way across the room, read the snarl in his eyes, the hatred between his teeth. Why are you here? Are you following me around? Spying on me? Get lost. I am entitled to my privacy, to my pleasures. You haven't paid for twenty-four hours a day.

The girl looked up, a question on her face, innocent worry that she was failing to hold his attention. Helmut whispered in her ear. They both laughed, the girl tilting her head forward so that her forehead rested for a moment on Helmut's chin. Then she looked at Gwen, sized her up blatantly, defiantly, in an instant.

Gwen dropped her eyes and turned away. Her hand twitched with the inclination to wave at them, to wave it all away as a coincidence – that she had come here by chance, to have a drink on her own, happened to notice someone she knew. But she didn't wave. And as her eyes swept the floor, the trousered knees and dripping boots of the clientele, she caught sight of her own feet, her own thin legs, and felt strangely humiliated. She had forgotten how she was dressed. Snowed in during a blizzard, in a strange town, in a foreign country: how could it possibly matter what she was wearing? Yet she now noticed that everyone around her, drunk and rowdy as they seemed, was well groomed, prosperous-looking, in new clothes of expensive makes and materials. She was a cast-away, a refugee; it was absurd, really, but she left the restaurant as quickly as she could. She felt suddenly physically exhausted and overwhelmed; how would she walk another step outside in the cold?

All the miserable way back to Axel's apartment, she saw Helmut hanging over the girl, felt disgusted all over again, the gorge burning in her throat. The snow had stopped, the temperature was plummeting, the air closed in around her, gripping her face and her icy hands in her pockets.

When she finally crawled into bed beside Hilary, her anger was spent. Hilary turned a dry red face to her, hot with sleep, and Gwen whispered, 'Hil. I'm sorry.'

There was no reply.

She lay still and tense, thinking about Lawrence. About the paintings she had made of him and which Will had destroyed. Paintings of Lawrence as a party to her sexual foraging – applauding, crouching in the undergrowth, in the febrile shadows at the edge of her consciousness.

That's how we all are, she thought, and he has always known. Randy, cupidinous. I took it as some kind of encouragement. Because he held to no convention in physical love, satisfied my every desire, set no boundary. Not even requiring that I confine myself to his body, nor he to mine. It became destructive, all that libido.

It was during that long, uncomfortable night, her fingertips wrapped around the outside edge of Axel's thin, hammocky mattress, holding on so that she wouldn't roll down on top of Hilary's heavier, sleeping form, that Gwen began to wonder whether she would ever be able to go back to Lawrence in any real sense. Or he to her. She had taken things very far by herself, excluding him. She had begun to feel or anyway to act as though he were a threat to her pleasures. A threat to her work.

It isn't just Hugo, she thought. It's everything that obsesses me now. As if I'm just – done with that vision. Finished with some big, intense phase. What Nick said, that he won't show the landscapes now. They don't offer the old excitement. It's faces and figures I want; maybe I don't even know whose. But there will be others. And I feel guilty about it, but I can't change it.

Portraying Lawrence – I thought it was a joke. I might as well have eaten him alive. And I hid the pictures, so I must have known. I finally chose to see him in a particular way because that's what he's become to me. Something I used to believe in, swim and breathe in – merely antique now, objectified and diminished, like a fetish, a magic stone. Carved, specific. Powerful medicine in my own pocket that is now only my own power. A potency which I can use differently or throw away. Once, he was more like an aura. There was a gleam around him, like a caste of light over a vista, diffuse, ambient, something I could lose myself in endlessly. But I've used it all up.

By the time he began to follow me around and to spy on me, it was already too late. She couldn't recall that Lawrence had ever been jealous; he hadn't expressed it if he was. And why would he be, with someone else to interest him? It began, simply, with doubt. Eviscerating doubt.

Was it possible to take a thing too far? Freedom? The voluntary way that we thought we were adhering to? We're separated now by what we both equally know. Cast out by experience.

What is he to Hilary? Gwen wondered. How does Hilary see him? With a glory newly on him? The glamour spilling from his person like a halo? Shimmering where he walks. It's all possible with Lawrence, the field of light thing.

And she thought, It's my own fault.

When Gwen and Hilary woke up the next morning, the little apartment was flooded with sunlight. Axel had set bowls of muesli on the table, and when his guests stirred in his bed, he turned his back to them discreetly, making cocoa.

'Oh God, I can hardly move,' Hilary moaned, rubbing her eyes.

And Gwen said simply, 'Fuck,' pulling herself upright and unclenching her numb right hand from the edge of the mattress where it still clung.

'Maybe you skied a lot yesterday,' said Axel quietly. 'So now you are sore.'

They were eating quietly together when Helmut burst in upon them breathing steam. 'It's two feet of snow!' he shouted, spreading his arms in the air. 'The lifts are open. You should be ready! This is the day skiers wait for!'

'Well, cock-a-doodle-doo,' said Gwen. It hadn't even occurred to her – skiing.

Helmut put his hand on her back, oozed a grin over the three of them. 'Eh, you didn't find someone last night? Wearing Axel's clothes? Looking like a little child? I would have helped you, but, you know, I was very, very busy last night.'

He stood up tall, breathed in deeply, whipped a small black comb from his back trouser pocket and dragged it through his thin black hair, his free hand cupped around the front of the comb, following it, smoothing, patting. Then he put the comb back in his pocket, hitched up his ski pants under his jacket, and gazed at Axel, nodding his head, satisfied.

'Thank you for these comfortable boots, my friend. They have plenty of oomph in them!' He bent down and undid them, kicked them off, collected his own red ski boots and settled on the bed, slamming the ski boots about on the floor so that the buckles jingled and slapped.

'What about the pass?' Hilary asked.

'Not open yet.' Helmut grunted. The sour stench of his feet wafted across their breakfast. 'Maybe in a few hours. We have plenty of time.'

'Shouldn't we be around for that?' she persisted. 'Maybe down by the bus stop?'

Helmut was brusque. 'You'll get cold waiting there.'

Gwen felt just as anxious as Hilary to get out, strangely afraid. 'What if they open it and then close it again?'

'No. I have the responsibility not to leave you. And I say it's better we ski.' He smiled again.

Hilary and Gwen both turned to Axel, silently imploring him. They were tired; they wanted to go home.

Axel tilted his head to one side. 'If they open it, they keep it open. They don't do all that work and then close it again so soon.'

'What if there's more snow?' Gwen begged.

'If there's more snow –' Axel shrugged, conceded. 'But there isn't more snow. Look outside at the sky. There is no moisture in the air. It's too cold now for snow.'

So they went with Helmut up the mountain. Aching, reluctant, shivering with cold. It seemed better than fretting in Axel's tiny apartment.

Helmut teased them and urged them on. 'Not so tough, now, eh? Where are those crazy girls I skied with yesterday? Tired out before the real fun begins? So. I make it easy for you today.'

Once again, they were in his power. The azure brilliance of the sky, the dazzle of the snow, swept out their minds and bleached their hearts. The mountains seemed to open out for ever all around them, to the horizon, into the stratosphere; the still peaks, scattered with diamonds, bleak, windless, outlined with clear, black-edged light, held them up, cradled them under the astonishing heavens.

They crept their skis along in Helmut's deep, squeaky track, down a shallow incline, then a steeper one. Until, gathering confidence, gathering speed, they let them run on the virgin slope, hidden beneath the snow. It was like glittering clouds around their feet, bottomless and weightless. They began to turn in it, to dance, their legs dropping down and their arms rising up, up, up, without stopping. There was nothing to stop for. No limit, no boundary at all. On they danced, as if on air, growing hot, breathless, silly with adrenalin. Laughter bubbled in their throats at this magic distilled from the elements, and all three of them whooped out loud for joy — three grown adults, intoxicated, exhilarated, transformed.

They went further and further up, further and further afield, looking for broad, untracked expanses of fresh powder.

'So you like off-piste?' Helmut asked happily, his face shiny with perspiration, as they waited in line for a chairlift.

'I don't think so,' said Gwen. 'Maybe because we're American. You're not allowed to do it there.'

He looked perplexed. 'I thought you were enjoying it.'

'Yes. This is terrific. It's plenty,' said Gwen.

'But where we are skiing now, this is off the piste. Anyway, when the snow is like this, you cannot tell where is the piste.'

There was a little silence. Gwen looked at Hilary, and they smiled, embarrassed.

Hilary said, 'Well. It's great.'

'Whatever,' Gwen agreed, dropping her eyes. They both were utterly hooked now on being out of bounds.

As they approached the front of the line, Helmut gestured towards the signboard of trails and lifts, and the row of lights, red, green, yellow. 'Like I said. Now the pass is open. You see?'

Gwen and Hilary were startled. Then adjusting to the news, they were realistic.

'Let's go down,' said Gwen. 'I need to get home. I want to see Will.'

Hilary nodded.

'You like one more run?' Helmut asked.

They were nearly at the front of the line, hemmed in by sliding skis. It would be hard to duck out.

Gwen tossed her head, sobered and unsure.

'OK,' said Hilary with decision. 'One more. Then we're done.'

Helmut took off his glove with his teeth, pulled back his jacket sleeve to check his watch. 'It's a good time now for one great place. Still early enough. We try to find it. And then we get the bus.'

They made a long, sweaty trek back into the mountain from the top of the lift. Longer than Gwen liked; she felt more and more distracted by an underlying sense of distress, by her night thoughts. Helmut walked and skated in front, taking in the distance with easy, long glides, his poles flashing in the light. Hilary managed to stay close behind him, head down, arms slogging steadily as her legs scissored and closed, scissored and closed. It made Gwen feel her slight size, her lack of brawn. She struggled along, trying to stay in their track, but she couldn't get push from her arms because when she planted her poles, she met with no resistance at all; the unpacked snow seemed to go down for ever.

At last she drew near Helmut and Hilary beside a rising crest of snow. As she followed them down to the right of it, she could see that what was covered with snow at the back from where they had approached was a naked rock face in front – rough geometry of granite and ice – craggy brown, red, grey and yellow facets basking in the sun. The slope fell away below in a broad undulation, a long shallow bowl with a low ridge running down it sixty feet or so away on the right side. In the far distance, five hundred feet down through the crystal air, she could see tiny black shapes whizzing around the side of the mountain, a beltway, an easy road home.

Helmut dropped silently over the edge of the bowl, traversed to the right, up the incline of the ridge, made a sweeping turn back to the left, forming a deep, bluish S-gash on the side of the ridge, then another and another. Powder flew around his arms and his chest; behind him lay a serpent's path, a snaking chain through the pillowy white. Hilary hesitated, watching, amazed, summoning her nerve, and Gwen, panting, fed up with being last, shot past her down the centre.

Almost at once she was enveloped in snow up to her chest, the surprising weight of it pressing down on her, snatching her breath away, so that she fought to turn, felt her legs locked in, her skis lost to sight and even to touch as she clenched her tired muscles to no avail. She was in a kind of gully that had been hidden under drifted snow. She felt as if she were being sucked down into it, that she would be trapped, and she said to herself, Don't fall. You will never be able to get up again in this.

But she was moving a little, moving through the snow, moving with the snow, and she tried to recapture the lightness, the miracle, of only a few minutes ago, the sensation of turning in a cumulus cloud, a spray of joy, in nothing at all. If only I can *ski*, she thought, as she tried to feel it, to will herself forward, down towards the beltway she had seen, the black shapes whizzing by below.

She heard Helmut shouting, 'Go to the right! To the right!' And she thought she could see him waving his arm, a fleck of blue, intense against the blue sky on the margin of her vision. But she couldn't do anything by choice. She was in the grip of the snow.

She managed a sort of turn, leaning precariously backwards, her legs burning with it, and over her shoulder she noticed Hilary starting down above her. Still, the fall line drew her like a lead weight into the centre of the gully.

Little snowballs skittered all around her, then bigger ones, harder, hitting her in the back of the head. The snow was moving with her, faster and faster. Maybe Hilary shouldn't come down right behind me, she thought. There's so much.

And she felt the whole section of snow she was in, like a little continent, like a plate of the earth's surface, sliding as a unit with herself fixed in it, carried forward faster and faster.

Suddenly, with a far greater sense of urgency, a sickening realisation of what was upon her, she thought, I have to get to the ridge. I have to get out or this will bury me. Hilary will bury me.

Then she heard Hilary's voice, rich with command. 'Ski out, Gwen, over here. Ski to where I am! Gwen! You have to do it *now*!' And she realised Hilary had already managed to ski up on to the ridge. Hilary with her height, her muscles, was going to survive the avalanche.

'Goddammit,' Gwen grunted to herself. 'No *fucking* way she is going home without me.' She hunkered down, coiling like a spring, then uncoiled in a jealous thrust, up to the right; dropped down again into her knees, her belly and hips, thrust up to the right a second time. Her skis shot clear, rode up fast into the shallower snow on the higher ground. And she was out. She was free.

The avalanche raced down past them, its frosty wind hitting their faces, Gwen gasping for air.

'You are lucky,' said Helmut impassively. 'It's only a small one. It will stop there in the flat; there is a small valley so it can't reach the piste. This is crazy what you did, to ski in the gully. For God's sake, if you don't ski where I show you, you are going to get killed, you know?'

Then he turned and gestured down the slope with his pole. 'We stay up on this ridge. And we don't stop. You make your own track beside mine. Not too close, not too far. Like the pattern in a carpet.'

307

That was it. He set off again.

Hilary and Gwen exchanged a dark look, then followed like pall bearers shouldering a coffin, grim-faced, side by side, a corpse-width apart, locked together by the burden, matching their movements and their strengths, slowly, in deadly earnest.

CHAPTER 19

It wasn't until they were on the flight back to London that Gwen broke the silence between them.

'I want you to do something for me, Hil. Something important. Please?'

It was a long time before Hilary acknowledged it. Then, reluctantly, she only said, 'Hmm?'

'The watercolours are gone, so − everything is in your hands. I mean, there's no other record of your − of what Doro wanted kept or sold. Nothing to stop you from doing whatever you want to do about it. Make them sell the wrong pieces, whatever.' Gwen's voice was sullen, chafing against Hilary's mastery.

But then, abject, she gushed, 'Please, Hilary, don't do it to Lawrence. If you stitch up the people he's recommended − Paul Mercy and Clare Pryce − it might cause some kind of scandal. Either the poor judgement on his part, or − I don't know − the thing is, they might turn on him. Clearly, they're pretty ruthless, those two. Please don't hurt him, Hil. He doesn't actually deserve it.'

She gulped a little, then shivered miserably, turning away from Hilary towards the window and the measureless night hurtling past on the other side of it. 'He's going to be alone, is the thing. I'm going to split with him, Hil.'

Hilary pressed her head back into the unyielding aeroplane seat, closed her eyes, sat in silence. She felt a swirl of self-reproach sucking at her, like water down a drain. Urgent, very dark. She felt frightened of herself, of all the things she wanted, and of the possibility that she might be able to get them. But she felt more frightened of Gwen. Is Gwen placing Lawrence in my hands? she wondered. Is she trying to make me responsible for his happiness since she doesn't want to be responsible for it herself?

It's somehow like the watercolours, another strange boon of Gwen's. Announcing that her husband will be free, that I should take him on in some way, protect him from harm. Why does it have to be her giving all the time, rather than my taking? Her astride the inevitable as if it were a horse she could control? Does she think I can't get what I want for myself?

Hilary brooded for a long time. Tears slipped once in a while down her cheeks, and patiently she smoothed their salty trail. Give up the collection and protect Lawrence from whatever risk there might be of public humiliation, from the wrath of his colleagues if they now lose out.

It's not right, she thought, it's not just. To let so many wrongs and so much confusion collect around Eddie's intentions. Not right for me, either, to resort to trickery. Regardless of whether or not I want to protect Lawrence.

Lawrence and I would need to be clean, to be whole, to be in the right. It's all too shaky otherwise, she thought, built on a pretence that absolutely nothing has gone wrong. And anyway, what does Lawrence want? Why should it be up to Gwen to decide?

But then she thought, What if Gwen is only saying exactly what she means?

She considered the loss that Gwen had suffered at Will's hands, the destruction of the watercolours – the magnitude of it. Was this her response? To walk away from the rest of her life, too? From her marriage? It was awesome, really, Gwen's nerve. Clinging to nothing.

It wasn't until after nine o'clock, when they lay exhausted in the back of a taxi from Paddington Station, that she finally replied. 'You know what, Gwen, I'm sorry your watercolours are gone.

Sorry for both our sakes, and for the people who will never get to see them. They really were amazing – the most amazing thing that anyone has ever done for me. I want to tell you something about them that I guess you don't know.'

Gwen's face was still; her eyes, sad and serious, stared out along the Bayswater Road, rolling away backwards, then leaping forwards again, backwards, then forwards, in little jerks, as she watched the black-limbed trees flee past above the railings of Kensington Gardens. 'What?'

'The group of files you found, the ones you were painting from?'

'Yeah?'

'Those were my own picks.'

'What do you mean?'

'Those files give details of objects to be sold, but they were objects *I* didn't want to sell. They were my own favourites that I chose over the years – sixty of them, exactly. Eddie knew. I mean – Eddie and I agreed on practically everything, but those objects we fought about.'

Gwen turned her head, alert, concerned. 'And you couldn't persuade him?'

'I guess I never really tried that hard. He used to say I needed to have my own separate room in the museum. For my shadow collection. It was a joke we had. Sometimes I used to think – hope –' She bit her lip.

'Well, doesn't that just suck,' said Gwen with sympathy. She sat up, grabbing her seatbelt away from her throat, growing animated. 'I mean – it's even worse than I thought. So that big suitcase, that one you never opened, in the studio?'

'That had all the other files, yup. And I kept mine out because – well – when I was planning the auction, I liked to think that I could keep them aside somehow. Leave them out of the catalogue or else list them separately so that if the prices went high enough, then I might be able to hang on to them for the museum.

311

Anyway, that was when I had control over everything. Obviously, it was just a pipe dream.'

Gwen sat back again beside her, and Hilary talked quietly on as the taxi rattled through the yellow glow of the deserted west London streets, Notting Hill Gate, Shepherd's Bush.

'Eddie trusted me – he knew what I felt. He wasn't small-minded; it's just that he was so committed to each piece. He agonised. He used to lie awake at night trying to decide whether to part with this one or that one. He could only guess what sort of prices they would bring and whether he'd put enough really valuable ones into the auction. We talked about it every day. He'd wake up exhausted, knowing he had to resign himself. He was determined to do it on his own terms – letting go – and he couldn't bear to have somebody pick apart his plan, unpack his suitcase, just when he was ready to go out the door. Not even me.'

'I'm completely amazed,' Gwen said in a strange, wasted voice. 'Why didn't you ever tell me?'

'I think –' Hilary choked on this, and then said perfectly truthfully, 'Well, for one thing, I was embarrassed. Or felt guilty. *Greedy*. Collecting? What is it but greed? We cover it up with words like connoisseurship. How weird is that in me, though? To be fine helping Eddie – institutionalising *his* need to own stuff. That whole elaborate process – evaluating, locating, purchasing, archiving – it's just all part of some ritual that detaches acquisition from personal impulse so it doesn't look – as bad. You're an artist, and so you just make a thing, Gwen; that's when you're most engaged – when you're doing the painting. Collectors are – different. It didn't feel easy to me. It didn't feel exactly right.'

'But, hey, no collectors, no museums. What would we know about antiquity? About beauty? About anything at all? The public always gets in in the end.' Gwen laughed. 'Who'd buy *my* paintings? I like the hunter-gatherer types!'

'I know, I know. It's just . . . I lost that thread. Understanding another culture, understanding ourselves. The freedom you get through that, through knowledge.'

They sat beside a heaving red bus at Hammersmith round-about, waiting for the lights to change.

'And my little collection,' Hilary went on, 'what right did I have? It wasn't even my money; just my – opinion. It never seemed real to me. I mean, in my mind it was real, but it was very private, a fantasy I hoarded. It was all so intimate, between me and Eddie – we had our own language, our own code, that we worked in. We were the only two who really understood what we were doing. And when I fell out with Mark – well – think about it – I realised I had taken too much for granted and presumed on my role. I was never playing by the rules to begin with, which I was hardly acknowledging to myself, and then I screwed everything up –'

Gwen nodded dreamily, seeing it. 'And there I was making it better – or making it worse – painting those very objects and putting them up all around you on the walls. As if you could really keep them.'

'Or really let them go,' Hilary added with a shrug. Then, with energy, she said, 'The thing about it, Gwen – what you did affirmed something for me. I knew you saw what I saw – those objects – why I chose them. And you know Paul? He saw it, too. He spotted those files one day, went through them in his quicksilver way, and I swear to God, he said, "So what are these? The ones *you* don't think Doro should sell, eh?" When Paul said that – well, you can see why I thought we had something in common. He got exactly what I was all about, in one. Then he never even referred to it again. And I don't think he's mentioned it to Mark.'

'I'm glad you told me, Hil. I guess I thought you might not tell me anything ever again.'

'Maybe I won't, after this. Well – one more thing.'

'What?' The taxi was already stopping in front of the house. 'Wait!'

Through the bare branches of the pollarded trees, it was easy to see that there were lights on in most of the windows. They shoved their bags on to the pavement, fumbled for money in the dark, Hilary looking around behind her more than once, afraid the front door might open with greetings.

'You can't pair me off with Lawrence, Gwen,' she whispered fiercely. She stood very close to Gwen as Gwen reached into the taxi window to pay. 'If you leave him, you leave him. That's what you told me yourself when I broke up with Mark. You have to let him figure it out for himself. Don't you remember?'

Gwen picked up her bag to go inside. 'I remember.'

'It's a big deal, Gwen.'

'I know.'

'Much bigger than Mark and me.'

'I know.'

Hilary took Gwen's bag away from her and put it back down on the pavement, keeping her there as the taxi drove off. 'What about Will?' she demanded.

'I know.' Gwen looked away. She rubbed her open hands up and down her face and left them spread over her cheeks as if she were holding herself up from the jaw.

'How are you going to look after him?'

Gwen was silent. Her fingertips sank down along the flesh of her cheeks, pressing deep; she stared across the crooked pavement tossed up by the tree roots and across the lopsided kerb into the gutter; she could see the dirty yellow line painted along it. If the gutter was what she feared, then she ought to make herself lie down in it, she thought, and get comfortable with it. But not Will. What on earth was she getting ready to do, she wondered, with a child? How did it come about that she even had a child?

It was becoming clear to her that she had somehow considered Will to be part of herself, a satellite moving within the ambit of her own ego; whereas, in fact, he was autonomous, a person in his own right, who had his own destiny, who would make his own choices. At last she said, 'Can I leave my husband and take his child with me? Is that fair to either one of them?'

'For Christ's sake, Gwen! What do you mean? You have to fight for your son. He's only five; he depends on you utterly.'

'I don't want to hurt him.' Gwen lifted her eyes back to Hilary's face, as if she had found the answer, something noble, a sacrifice she could make for the sake of another.

'Why not? You're hurting everyone else!'

Gwen looked astonished. 'Aren't you cold? Let's go in.' It was too hard to face it.

But Hilary was going to make her. 'It'll destroy Will if you don't find some way to keep him with you. And you know it, Gwen. Especially now, after what he's done. You're the one he's hurt, not Lawrence. You're the one he's angry with.'

'What do you mean? I'm the one he's angry with?'

'That's why he cut up your pictures.'

'Lawrence said that he cut them up because you and I argued about them – to stop you being angry with me. To stop anyone else from being able to see them.'

'That may well be. But there's the more basic thing, Gwen. You left him to come skiing with me. Look at it from his point of view. Sure, we all heard him telling you to go, but when you did, it was more than he expected; he felt angry with you, so he took his revenge. He's only five, and he was pretty sick, and there's a lot of bad emotion washing around the house. It's a warning, Gwen. You *owe* that child. You really are not free to go – not by yourself.'

They looked at each other for a long time. Gwen looked towards the house, dropped her eyes to the pavement. She ran a finger along beneath one eye, wiping away a tear before it fell.

'It would destroy me, too,' she said at last. 'If I didn't have him with me.' She picked up her bag again. 'So we both fight. I don't know – let's hope we don't have to fight each other.'

Will was asleep on the sofa in the kitchen. Lawrence, with his injured foot up on a stool, was typing away on his laptop at the kitchen table. He must have heard them coming into the hall above, but even so he didn't stop typing when they arrived at the bottom of the stairs. It was as if he couldn't bear it, their return, as if he wanted to shield himself.

Gwen walked over to the sofa, bent and placed a silent kiss on Will's forehead, and crossed the room again back to Hilary. They stood side by side for a few bizarre moments, waiting, until at last Lawrence's eyes rolled to the top of the screen and he clicked on the save icon with a kind of flourish and looked up at them.

'Sorry,' he said sheepishly. 'Once he's asleep, I have to use every second. It's going quite well. The pressure does me good – and being away from my own desk. I've been all inside my own head for the first time in – I don't know – months, maybe even years. Absolutely no interruptions apart from Will. It's like a miracle. I can't get up and rush anywhere, so I don't even try. No internet set up properly at the cottage, nor here in the house. I just think. I know more than enough. In fact, I know far too much. I want to get as much written as possible before term starts again. Though maybe I'll go back with the bandage on –' He laughed tightly. 'Sorry,' he said again. 'How was it then, the mighty blizzard? The great outdoors? The Arlberg?'

There seemed to be no way to tell him. The homely scene in the basement contrasted almost absurdly with everything they had been through – strange, elemental – and Lawrence's hyperboles, his pat, grandiose tone, seemed calculated to deflate the world outside his reach, to tame it. His nervousness infected them all and divided them from one another.

In the bursting silence, with Hilary and Gwen leaning from one foot to another, each of the three of them began to realise what was wanted and what was necessary: separate conversations. Here it was then, among them, the fabled triangle. They were trapped by geometry; three was a public forum, a place, inevitably, of judgement. There was nothing they could talk about together. None of them had quite the nerve to acknowledge this in any way, nor quite the nerve to behave as though it were not the case.

At last Gwen drifted towards Will, bowing out. She perched beside him as if she had never left, felt his forehead tenderly with the flat of her palm.

'I'll take him,' she mumbled, not wanting Lawrence and Hilary to hear, not wanting to have to explain herself. She pulled his thin shoulders towards her own, folded his limp arms around her neck, gathered his bottom into her small, strong hands to lift him. He stirred and grappled with her, wrapping his monkey legs around her waist, squeezing his face in under her chin with his baby death grip; his sucking, suffocating love pressed on her throat, her Adam's apple, as she forced her wavering, exhausted legs to rise and to walk with him.

Without opening his eyes, Will murmured, 'Sorry, Mummy. Don't be cross.'

'It's all right,' she said as he struggled. 'You can sleep.'

He slumped at ease around her body, taking it for granted, as she bore him with great effort from the room.

'So —' said Lawrence.

Hilary pulled out a chair and sat down. She couldn't stand up any more. She dropped her face into her hands, and the coils of her hair spilled around her head, trembling a little in the light.

They sat like that for a long time in sorrow and anticipation until Lawrence said very softly, 'The work is a relief. I need to do it.'

'I'm glad,' she said.

This wasn't the heart of it, the conversation they wanted to have. They fell back from the effort, while the sense of crisis welled up between them. It pulsed in the veins of their hands as their hands lay without touching on the table. There was so little time; yet they drifted for an eternity. Building up to something, postponing it. They never looked at each other.

Eventually Hilary broached it. 'I love her so much. The flesh on her cheeks, her warped, insistent way. I feel all the time as if she's shouting me down, laughing, insisting *she's* more worthy of love.'

'We would need to be a million miles away from here,' Lawrence said. His voice was so deep, so low, that Hilary felt it as a vibration in herself, something she already knew.

There was a footstep on the stairs.

She looked up, white at what they were squandering – this singular moment, a chance. Lawrence could see a wild, untrammelled light in her eyes, and her nostrils flaring.

'I'm going back to New York for real,' she said, staccato, electric. 'I'll let you know what happens. I'll send an e-mail.'

It was Hugo coming down, smiling, lively, trailed by a silky, sweet-faced girl, pale hair splaying around her face and shoulders like a mantle, round spectacles glinting over shy, crinkled blue eyes.

'Good Christmas, everyone?' Hugo asked cheerfully. 'This is my friend, Svetlana. Sorry to come down so late, but we heard the taxi and all the lights were on. Is everything all right now?'

He looked suddenly alarmed, dampened, as Hilary stood up with an air of drama, dragged the backs of her hands across her cheeks. Svetlana stepped away again towards the stairs, lowering her eyes inside the curtain of her hair.

'Hilary has to leave soon,' said Lawrence. 'We were just – going over some – personal things – some –' His voice hung in the air, vague, as he struggled for a polite formulation that would make Hugo leave them alone again, make him take Svetlana away. How to imply that he and Hilary were entitled to privacy in this house, when he had never required that Hugo leave him in privacy with Gwen? As Lawrence pondered the ease with which he had ceded such rights and never minded, never even noticed, as he pondered the fact that he now wanted them back, he felt angry with Hugo for the first time since he had known him. Why didn't it bother me, with Gwen? he wondered. Walked in upon, interrupted, cuckolded. It was all fine. My whole life was just a result of everyone else's actions and choices. I want you out now, Hugo. I need this time. I am trying to talk to someone.

But already it was too late. Here was Gwen with her neck stretched forward, periscoping her eyes down the stairs to see what lay below as she tentatively descended. She gave a thin, sceptical smile. Lawrence knew she was thinking it, too: What now? What more?

Hugo bounded towards her, uncharacteristically puppylike, kissed her on both cheeks, beamed at her. 'I've got the most fantastic tour coming up!' he crowed. 'Australia, New Zealand and Japan! Can you believe it? I'm accompanying this gorgeous singer I've been working with all the holidays. Six recitals, and then three solo recitals of my own that she's been able to arrange. Maybe one more in Japan. And there's a Wigmore date fixed for me when I get home. It's all starting to happen!'

'Congratulations,' said Gwen, smiling with the outermost layer of her lips, frozen inside. 'You deserve it. Lucky them, down under, to hear you play. Lucky them.'

Her voice faded away, and she looked around self-consciously at Lawrence and at Hilary. Then, affecting a brassy nonchalance, she spoke with sudden ungauged loudness. 'Is this your singer for us to meet?' She rushed at Svetlana, pumping her surprised arm.

'Oh, no,' Svetlana said in her thick Russian accent. 'I am not singer. I am pianist. For Vill?' And she smiled charmingly, hopefully.

Hugo put his arm between Gwen and Svetlana, rested his hand on Gwen's shoulder, pushed her gently backwards, looked her carefully in the eye. 'I wouldn't leave without finding a teacher for Will.' He was very calm, very focused.

He looked up for a moment, towards Lawrence and towards Hilary. 'I never meant to be a children's teacher, you know.' It was an apology. 'But he's a very special boy. And he's – he's a good little pianist. So I –'

319

Then he looked at Gwen again and spoke gently. 'I'm sorry, Gwen. You of all people can understand. Svetlana is going to take over the flat, you see, and have my piano. We've worked it out as part of our arrangement. She'll teach Will. It's all fixed. I've told her everything about him.'

Gwen looked at him, waiting for something more. But this was all Hugo had in mind to say. It was a terrible blow, so hurtful and humiliating in front of her husband, in front of Hilary, her rival, both privy unexpectedly to the denouement of her love affair, to this painful moment of becoming the discarded mistress of a much younger man.

What a strange initiation, she thought eccentrically, what a strange rite of passage – the woman given back from adultery. Has anybody ever painted that? And it was a haven for her, the idea that she herself might be a subject for a painting. Because she was determined not to cry, not to crack. She would not linger on this or any loss, on any personal hurt. Not when she had invited it upon herself and wanted it. What was there to learn by looking backwards? She relished what was yet to come, what she had yet to discover.

She tried to smile at Svetlana, wondering, Are you my rival, too? Or is it the singer? Both? I can find out, Gwen thought; it won't take long to get traction, to engage.

She shook herself down, spoke mellifluously to Svetlana, with a girlish directness. 'We must become friends. I mean – depending on your time – how much you have and when you're around and so on. You'll tell me when I should send Will up? He's free any time in these holidays, obviously. But once school term starts, it has to be afternoons, really.'

'Yis, I know this.' Svetlana nodded. 'Vill be fine, afternoons. He can come vinever he likes. I have small brothers in Moscow and I am used to play with them and also vork. I am missing them. So for me is nice. Hugo is choosing very carefully for Vill. Also for me.'

She dimpled at Hugo, blushed borscht-coloured, nodded. 'I look forvard to meet him soon. So, goodnight. I vish you good-night.' She turned and flew up the stairs by herself, two at a time, the huge bell-bottoms of her jeans swishing against one another.

Gwen strode straight on at her penance. 'So where are the watercolours, Lawrence? I want to see what's happened to them.'

'Wouldn't you wait until tomorrow, Gwen? You must be tired. It's – a lot to face.'

'I really want to see them now. I won't sleep anyway.' She wasn't just paying for a few days out of town; she was paying for every-thing. 'I need to get past this and get back to work. I have a lot of painting to do if I'm going to have any kind of show in the new year. The landscapes aren't finished. There are only two por-traits.' Even as she said it, she was thinking about new ones. Maybe the self-portrait, in fact; and she had other ideas. 'I've got to try to get hold of Nick tomorrow afternoon and talk it all through with him. I need to be ready.'

'Everything's in the studio,' Lawrence said. 'Roland helped me collect it all – long, thin shreds, ribbons – into bin liners – you'll see. But wait. Wait for me, Gwen. The stairs take me a long time. You mustn't do this alone.'

Gwen didn't miss a beat. It was still her house. Her voice came lilting, absolute, 'Come with me, Hil? We can drag your suitcase up while we're at it.' She would still dispose the sleepers to their beds.

As they started climbing, Lawrence heard her saying to Hilary, pulling her in, 'Maybe Svetlana will sit for me. She has a kind of winsome simplicity. Something Spartan underneath. Like early winter. Like dawn. Don't you think?'

CHAPTER 20

When Hilary telephoned from the airport, Paul suggested meeting in a Starbucks near Eddie's apartment on the Upper East Side.

'Awfully sorry Mark and Clare couldn't join us,' he said, grasping her hand without really shaking it. 'They won't be back until after the New Year. Seems a shame not to chat in the meantime.'

'What are you having?' asked Hilary.

'Ah,' Paul scoffed, 'just tea for me, thanks.' He swept the room with his bespectacled blue eyes, letting her handle it, the food, the drink.

As they jostled towards the cash register, tense, uncommunicative, Paul kept his back towards the glass case of pastries and sandwiches and one shoulder towards Hilary while she ordered, handed over her money. Then he lounged silently against the high counter on the other side of the coffee machines, cleaning his fingernails between his teeth, until he eventually accepted his mug of tea from her hands as if summoned from a dream in which he had altogether forgotten about it.

'Oh, yes, yes of course,' he said. 'Thanks ever so.' He bowed over the tea and trailed her to a table in a far corner.

'Lovely to see you,' he pattered across at her, putting his hands into his jacket pockets, smiling. 'Had a good holiday?'

'Not really,' said Hilary. 'Not so great.'

He looked contrite, fell silent for a moment, then started in again. 'The thing is, Hilary, I really ought to apologise – I – I imagine it's not entirely ideal, having me fill your old spot – and, and – But I – I know what I'm about. I will do it properly, and if only you can help me out for a time about the sale, it really would be a great gesture towards the collection, and –'

'A gesture?'

'A contribution – a – a – Oh, call it what you like. We may as well be frank. Obviously, I can't hold the auction without your confirming for me what Doro intended to sell. Clare's just aching for her and me to split the collection up according to our own judgements. Is that what you want?'

'Of course not. I wouldn't have come if I wanted that. It's not about what I want anyway, Paul; it's what Eddie wanted.' She scowled. 'You really are a complete shit, you know?'

Paul sat back and laughed. 'I imagine it might seem that way.' Then he blushed, swept the room again with his eyes, leaned closer. 'You've got all the wrong idea about me, you know. It was never a plan on my part. How could you think I was that organ-ised? That calculating? After you worked with me all summer? All the advantage I *failed* to take of you?'

She felt a little taken aback. 'What do you mean? How do you know what I think?'

'My dear, honestly. I am great friends with Roland LeSeur. I thought you realised that. *Great* friends.'

She rolled her eyes at him, curled one side of her upper lip. 'Is there some coded revelation in what you are saying? What does that rubric allow for, "*Great* friends"?'

He waited for her, watched in feigned innocence as she struggled. He didn't interrupt and didn't help her.

'I mean –' Hilary forged on, 'I thought Roland was –'

Paul only nodded, smiling blandly, expectant. At last he said, 'Roland reckoned that you simply hadn't made the connection at all.'

And then she did: It had been Roland in Paul's apartment that awful day, the last day of September. How could she not have realised it until now?

'Are you lovers?' she blurted out.

'That would be a bit of an exaggeration,' he laughed. 'Poor Roland. He's a dear chap. Always been fond of me. But you know, he's not one for – getting terribly involved with other people. And I – well, nowadays he and I often speak on the telephone. I wouldn't like you to think we had gossiped about you behind your back, but –'

'But you did,' she interjected sharply.

He took her up quickly. 'We're all chained quite close together in this, Hilary. Roland is old chums with Lawrence Phillips. You're friendly with Phillips's wife – and so on. You mustn't feel annoyed about it. Naturally, Roland told me all about your situation; he genuinely thought you wouldn't come back to New York – that you would never want to work with a man whom you had once intended to marry.'

'Why didn't you ask *me* what I wanted? Why didn't you answer my calls?'

Paul had the grace to drop his gaze. 'Roland felt you didn't really know yourself what you wanted. And there wasn't much time –'

'Time? While I was still at a loss?' She was halfway across the table at him, eyes on fire.

He aimed his voice at the floor, a little off to one side. 'Roland's ended up feeling rather remorseful that he messed you about, though doubtless he'll never admit it. I'm not happy myself, to tell you the truth, and I made no bones about telling him. Imagine me – arriving in New York to embark upon what I presumed would be, as they say, a new life. A truly exciting job. And then he persuades me I ought to take on Clare Pryce. Now there's no getting away from her!'

'So. You've decided to make amends with me because you can't stand her?'

'If that's how you care to see it,' he admitted. 'You do put a fine point on things. Oof! But seriously, Hilary, I'd like us to be sorted – to be friends again.'

'Were we ever friends, Paul?'

He seemed to consider for a moment, and then he said, 'I rather thought we were friends, yes. Frankly you make a much better friend than Clare. And perhaps you can give me some advice about Mark, whom you had the good sense to leave. The two of them have got some rather surprising ambitions for the collection. For instance, just now, on this – holiday they've taken, they're looking at a factory space in Ohio, where they intend to produce a line of house wares and furnishings called Classic. Based on objects in the collection, you see.'

'What?' Hilary sat up, wide-eyed.

'They've hired two designers and a marketing team.'

'That's *completely* bizarre. What are they using for money? You haven't even held the auction yet!'

'They've got a backer. They tell me the auction will bring much more money if they launch this – product – first and – you know – give it a higher profile, or however one puts it. It's not my world, and I have to say I am really not interested. I'll have charge of the collection, but of course, it feels to me as though that will soon be a secondary consideration for the foundation. Who knows if we'll ever get round to building the museum at all. Although, they say that's what they want the additional money for.' He gave her an artful, dubious look. 'The pair of them together – Mark and Clare – give a whole new meaning to the phrase, thick as thieves.'

'It's – appalling.'

'Quite.' He was terse, practical. 'You see how badly I need your help. There's far more at stake here than who gets to curate Doro's collection. It's a question of what it means to be a curator at all. Preserve, make accessible, make inviting even. But Mark and Clare are out to bury the past under newly manufactured objects.' He raised his eyebrows at her, looked glum and somehow a little older. 'Let's face it – the passage of time obliterates the past anyway. It needs no assistance. In fact, the opposite – we must work to restore it. But if everyone buys an object and takes it home, will they bother to come and see the originals? Is this an appetite we want to feed? The appetite for a poor imitation, cheaply made, easily possessed, but which has no aura, no essential beauty?'

His hands were in the air, expostulating, fervid, and he knocked his mug over with his elbow, spilling the tea. 'Oh, Christ!' he said. 'How idiotic of me.'

Hilary dropped a wad of paper napkins on the milky pool of grey-brown, left them soaking it up. She looked at Paul, impassive. Spilled tea is about what I'd expect from you, her expression seemed to say.

Paul fluttered on. 'So perhaps – if you could accept my apology? And if you could bear to work with us? With me?'

It didn't take her a moment to reply. She had made up her mind on the journey back from Austria; it was time to let go. Gwen had persuaded her. In fact, Gwen had inspired her. Clinging to nothing. 'No, Paul. I couldn't bear to work with you. Not with any of you. Sorry. Especially after what you've just told me. The collection is – only *things*. Things I love – but it's just time for me personally to find out what else there could be.'

There was a little silence. He put his fingertips on the wet napkins, pushed them around, streaking tea sloppily. 'That's a great disappointment to me,' he said soberly. 'I had hoped since you came all this way that you might have in mind some kind of arrangement. I've never told them, you know, what nonsense you fed them that day at Bushette's – that some of the things might be stolen! I considered it rather a bond between us – to rein them in together, with that quite reasonable fear. And I never told them –'

Hilary's eyes flared at him; she didn't want to know. 'OK then. I'll sell you what I know for a percentage of the proceeds from the auction. I want three per cent of the sales. The gross sales. For that, I'll tell you everything; I'll see you through in whatever capacity you want, and afterwards I'll go away.'

Paul put two fingers over his rounded lips, as if to stop himself letting out a whistle. With a sage little nod he said, 'A lot more than the round-trip ticket to New York for which we once laid a bet.'

She shrugged. She wasn't going to be pulled in by nostalgia for their old camaraderie; she didn't believe in it.

'I don't think it's going to happen, Hilary,' said Paul at last. 'I think you're asking too much.'

'To give up my life's work? The percentage seems fair to me. I used to think about it during the autumn. Actually I need the money.'

'I'll have to speak with the others. Mark and the board. Maybe if the payments were spread out over a period of years. It's not something you and I can agree to privately, here and now.'

She shrugged again, pulled a little handwritten card from her bag and snapped it down on the table between them. 'You can reach me at this number.' She stood up to go.

'Right,' said Paul, jumping up, leaping around to her side of the table and touching the back of her chair with an implication of gallantry, a hint that he was pulling the chair out for her. Standing close, with his arm alongside her, so that she couldn't easily move off, he spoke into her ear, nearly touching it with his lips. 'I have the key with me, for Doro's place. I thought – I mean, forgive me, but I know how you care for these objects, and you've been denied any sight of them for so long. Wouldn't you – I mean, we could step round there and have a little look? It might prove to be the proverbial last chance. The guard knows me, and the doorman, of course, so there'd be no problem.'

She looked around at him, right into his eyes, stony-faced, furious. 'The doorman knows *you*?'

But she saw in his eyes a kind of melting invitation, a sweet sympathy. 'If you'll allow me,' he said, 'by way of – well, it's something I can do, isn't it?'

The temptation was too great for her.

327

He ushered her out, his hand hovering near the small of her back, never touching her.

They walked briskly along the cold, teeming streets, and Paul looked warily to the right, to the left, grim-mouthed, light-footed. The lank cuffs of his grey flannel trousers flapped from side to side over the shining brown leather toes of his shoes.

Hilary felt that she was walking backwards in time. The store-fronts and the awnings were intensely familiar, bathed in a vivid light that seemed to penetrate her chest as well as her eyes, stirring in her a sensation of possessing and of lacking, an indescribable longing. For many years, this had always seemed to be her own street, and she felt that she had hardly realised it until now. She scanned the faces they passed, wondering, Do you recognise me? Do I recognise you?

As they approached Doro's long green awning, the row of planters filled with bay trees and ivy, the brass handles on the gleaming glass doors with their little windowpanes framed in dark green, Paul remarked with a disarming sensitivity, a neutralising wit, 'Maybe it's a new doorman?'

But it was the same doorman. Portly, assertive Robert O'Reilly, with his merry, rolling, Irish voice. He touched his black-visored green cap, smiled. 'Miss Boyd. Nice to see you back at last. Happy New Year for tomorrow.'

'Happy New Year, Robert,' she answered automatically, feeling she was arriving home, bubbling inside with joy that she was trying to restrain.

Eddie won't be there, she told herself in the elevator. And then she thought, But I'm used to that. She remembered the hot, melancholy spring days which she had spent alone in the apartment after the funeral. Taking stock, making plans.

The guard, young, black, jowly, was half asleep in a hard wooden chair in the elevator lobby upstairs; he jumped up when the elevator doors opened, then immediately sat down again, his holstered pistol knocking against the arm of the chair, gouging his ribs.

'You going to sign in this young lady, sir?' A clipboard lay beside him on the floor.

Paul only nodded at him, clicked briskly across the floor, unlocked the apartment door, switched off the burglar alarm.

'Nothing's been moved,' he said confidentially to Hilary, addressing with his uncanny telepathy an anxiety which, until that very moment, she scarcely realised she had. 'It seemed essential to keep everything exactly as it was since we didn't have the documentation. I think Mark will be arguing with the board for quite some time as to whether the apartment will be sold or used as a residence for – the – ahh – foundation staff. Since the museum's going to be outside the city, I haven't a prayer of living here anyway. Evidently, he thinks he does.'

She had stopped listening. In she stepped, on to the black-and-white marble floor of the two-storey oval entranceway. It was lined with high mirrors, deep, treasure-laden glass shelves, and a half-oval of six ebony pillars topped by white marble busts. She breathed in the smell of clay and thick dust. Then she began to pace ever so slowly around the shelves, sighing with pleasure, with the momentary dream of repossession. Serenely she smiled upon it all – vases and bowls of countless different shapes and sizes; drinking vessels of gold, silver, electrum, cunningly embossed; figures of ivory, clay and bronze; helmets, swords and shields burnished with the drama of mortality; braziers, tripods, cauldrons, ladles; fragments of relief work and of friezes showing intricately patterned actions, of pairs, of groups, in sandstone, limestone, marble.

How we both loved all this, she thought. The silent, strange, familiar evidence of a lost world. Gods, heroes, men, women and beasts. Illustrated, sculpted, implied by what they used and cared about. By what they made and left behind.

After she'd walked twice around the dim entrance hall, she went on through the colonnaded double doors into the living room and opened the curtains at each of the three tall windows. Silently she strolled, light flooding in over the sprawling clutter of antiquity hauled in piece by precious piece, meticulously and precariously set out on every level surface. Tiny glass bottles; coins and seals swarming on tables and trays; the gaming board made of wood, ivory, lapis lazuli and crystal; spills of jewellery. In front of the glittering wall mosaic that nearly covered the inner length of the room, she began to weep, and she stood pretending to study its orchard trees – lemon, pomegranate, pear, fig, plum – and its songbirds opening their downy throats among the ripe fruits and the jade-hard leaves – oleander, myrtle, laurel – with red roses meandering upward from the rich, imaginary ground.

Paul leaned quietly in the doorway, looking at her from time to time, then stepping along to examine an inlaid Persian dagger, a stone triton, a gold cloak pin from Roman Spain. After a few minutes, he coughed and said, 'I thought you needed to see it all. It's just so outstanding. And especially here, in this setting. Private. Such perfection. I could take you to the warehouse as well, if you like. Tomorrow? Are you free?'

She didn't answer, continued to wander, dashing at her cheeks with the backs of her hands. Here at last were her books, a pile of them on the high stone bench she had used as a desk under the window; she had never made the list for Paul. Here was the bronze Corinthian candelabrum that Gwen had painted as Trimalchio's.

After another few minutes, Paul said, 'I've often wondered how the two of you never thought simply to put little stickers on everything. Just for your own sakes, red dots, for instance, for the objects he intended kept. Such an easy device, really, as a fail-safe.'

'Oh, we did think of it,' said Hilary, a little choked. 'I did. I tried to convince him. But he would never allow it. He said he didn't want anything stuck to anything while he was alive. He wanted to go on enjoying it as it was.'

'But why not on the other things, out at the warehouse? Surely that wouldn't have affected his enjoyment? And there are so many more pieces there.'

'I never understood it then,' Hilary said meditatively. 'But now, I think I do.'

There was a silence.

'And?' urged Paul.

'It was to protect me from exactly what's happened. It was to guarantee that I had total control. That no one else could know what I knew or figure it out. He placed everything in my hands –' her voice trembled – 'in my trust.'

'So you haven't gone round removing any little stickers?' Paul ducked his face down towards her, trying to catch her red-rimmed eyes across the room.

'How dare you? How dare you say such a thing!' She turned to him angrily, then away again, her hair swinging around her shoulders.

'Well, I have to be careful, don't I? Actually, it was something Clare brought up. She found sticky spots on some of the objects, or fuzzy, you know where a little label might have been put on and then removed.'

'Honestly!' said Hilary. 'You two make me sick.'

'Feel this, for instance,' said Paul. 'On this vase.' He tipped the vase to one side where it sat on a low chest, and rubbed his finger underneath the base, then gestured for Hilary to do the same.

'Oh, yes,' said Hilary, drawing near. 'I love that one. It's exceptional.' It was the first one that Gwen had painted, the black loutrophoros, tall, thin, narrow-necked, wide-mouthed. She reached underneath and touched it where Paul had. 'I sort of see what you mean. Maybe that's from before Eddie's time? Some earlier sale? I never noticed it before.'

Paul set the vase upright and moved away.

She bent again and stroked the length of it, looking at the red figures – the women, the man, the bullock, the maiden in the wedding procession carrying a vase like this one on which they all appeared. As her hand reached the lip, she peered inside, thinking of water, of how hard it would be to fill the vase, how hard to spill the contents. And she caught a glimpse of something white. She lifted the vase a little with both hands and shook it once, ever so slightly. It rattled, a hollow papery sound.

'What's in it?' she asked. 'What have you put inside?'

'I haven't put anything inside. Why would I?' Paul watched her from the window where he now stood.

She lifted the vase higher and with effort turned it upside down, shaking it again, a little harder. A rolled paper fell out on to the carpet, heavily typed. There were more papers inside; she could feel them and hear them moving, but they had unrolled inside the vase and didn't slide out.

She put the vase back on the chest, snatched up the paper from the floor and began to read it silently as Paul advanced towards her again across the room.

It was a letter, addressed to Mr Mark Bushette.

Dear Mark,

As we have discussed, it is my intention that if for any reason whatsoever Hilary Boyd chooses not to undertake the task of curating the Doro Collection after my death, then she is to receive sixty items from the collection which are specified on the attached list or sixty of comparable value of her own choosing from the entire collection before any sale or auction takes place. With them, she is to inherit my apartment and any contents of furniture and household goods deemed not part of the collection of antiquities regardless of any clauses to the contrary contained in any earlier wills that I might have made . . .

Hilary sank on to the carpet, next to the vase. 'What does this mean? Is this real?'

'Let's see,' said Paul.

But she kept it from him. 'Go look in the kitchen drawer,' she ordered. 'Find the tongs. The big top drawer left of the stove. There are more papers inside the vase.'

There was Eddie's trembly signature across the bottom of the letter. And Robert O'Reilly, the doorman, had signed as a witness.

She couldn't breathe. You bastard, she was thinking. You fucking bastard. Tears streamed down her face. She shouted for the guard. 'We need help in here! Guard, please come and help us!' She wanted another witness – a witness to her discovery, and to whatever might happen next.

The guard put his head around the door, then came in on tiptoes, looking from side to side, his eyes wide in amazement, just as Paul reappeared from the kitchen with the tongs and several skewers.

'Give them to me,' Hilary insisted, grabbing the tongs.

'You'll need me to tip the vase upside down again,' said Paul. 'Those won't be long enough otherwise.'

The guard stood over them with his clipboard in his hand and watched anxiously as Hilary and Paul extracted the other papers from inside the vase.

'So what's up, Hilary? Come on.' Paul set the vase down again and craned over her shoulder reading and breathing rather fast. 'My God,' he drawled. 'No wonder you don't want to work for me.'

'But I had no idea about this!' cried Hilary.

And yet there was some part of her that had known. The other papers were a long list of objects, numbered one to sixty. It was her own sixty; Hilary was certain before she even read it.

Paul knew, too. 'It's your little collection that you always kept by you – your clutch of favourites. Surely you did know?'

There was a long silence, blurred by the quiver of her hands, the cracking noise of the pages.

Then Hilary looked straight at Paul; they were both pale. 'How has this not come to light until now? Why has nobody told me about this letter?' Even her voice shook, with accusation and with distress.

Paul lifted both arms in the air, protesting his innocence. 'It's something Mark will have to explain. Something he has – must have – overlooked. Perhaps Mr Doro changed his mind after he signed the letter? I imagine Mark would have wanted to avoid hurting your feelings and –'

'But look at the date – the week before Eddie died!' Hilary snapped at him. 'Call Robert. How on earth did the papers get into the vase, for Christ's sake? Did Eddie think he had to hide them? Or was it Mark who hid them? You've got to call Robert and get him up here. He signed as the witness. He'll know.'

The guard drew closer. 'I'm thinking this is not a good location to engage in any kind of arguing,' he said. 'And maybe we need to have Mr Bushette present if there's any kind of a problem?'

'There's no problem,' Paul assured him. 'Mr Bushette's out of town. Can you get the doorman to come up?'

'Nobody comes in here who's not on the approved list, as you know, sir. Which this young lady is not. And who would be on the front door, in that case?'

'I don't suppose you could do that? For ten minutes?'

'No, sir. Not and leave you all in here like this.'

'Well, can't Robert just – lock up for five minutes? What does he do if he has to use the toilet, for goodness' sake? It's really rather important.'

'Of course he can,' pronounced Hilary. 'He used to help Eddie up and down with the wheelchair. All the tenants have keys to the front door.' And she ran to the kitchen and called Robert through the intercom.

'It's perfectly clear in my mind,' Robert said, smiling as he came in the door, removing his cap and self-consciously fingering his pink scalp through his clipped white hair. 'And Mr Bushette knows all about it because I delivered the other set to his office myself; Mr Doro asked me that favour, like, after work one day. He was tired of waiting, is what he said, on paperwork and lawyers. How do you think I knew you were to live here, hey, Miss Boyd? I was only witnessing that Mr Doro signed, but he told me to read it through first because he said nobody should be comfortable signing a paper which might have anything at all written above, you see. There's no mystery about it, apart from he did ask me to keep it from you – it was something to find out after he was gone.'

'So why were the papers in the vase?' Hilary pressed.

'He signed both sets. Well, people do, don't they? A copy to keep for himself. You know he couldn't reach much from his chair. But he pushed the papers inside there himself – the tall vase, eh? With the young girl on it. Getting married.' Robert paused and gave Hilary a soft, twinkly look.

'He showed me all about the figures, you see, and was telling me how you'd appreciate it when you came across the papers inside. A little joke, like. How a young girl who didn't marry might take such a vase to her grave. Gloomy, but it was those thoughts he had; we used to curse it together, hauling the chair up. We used to curse old age. But why else does anyone make a will? And he thought he might go at any time. So I couldn't say no to him.'

The group fell silent, and Robert, as if to reinforce his story, waved his cap at the loutrophoros and walked over to it. 'This one here,' he said. He put his cap down on the chest and tipped the vase to one side, feeling underneath just as Paul and Hilary had done. 'It'll be marked on the bottom.'

He looked up at them, still feeling the base of the vase, his skin flushed, his blue eyes puzzled. 'For certain it was this one.' He began to walk around the room, checking other objects, the Cycladic figurine, a single coin, the bronze Corinthian candelabrum. The tails of his stiff green overcoat swept worryingly near the crowded tables and shelves as he trod heavily here and there.

'They can't all have fallen off,' he exclaimed. 'We used a packet of the little red dots, like, which he said you kept giving him, Miss Boyd. Took a few minutes, if you don't mind my saying so.

Sixty of them. Though if you have the list there, it's no matter, eh?'

'Unless someone took them all off on purpose,' Hilary said bitterly.

'Gee. Do you think so?' Robert was surprised. 'Well, there's been more and more of you coming in lately. It used to be only you and Mr Bushette. So. I better get downstairs now, unless there's anything else I can help you with?'

Hilary took one of Robert's hands in both of hers and held it for a moment, looking him steadily in the eye. 'Thank you, Robert. You've changed everything for me. I can't tell you how grateful I am.'

He shuffled his feet, his bulk swaying awkwardly. 'For sure you were kinder to him than either of my daughters is to me!' He chuckled, red in the face, and waddled out the door.

'The faithful retainer,' said Paul in a mocking tone. 'Will there now be a goatherd to tell us he raised you in simple circumstances after a tragic misunderstanding between Doro and your mother, and that you are in fact Doro's own long-lost daughter?'

'We can leave,' Hilary said curtly. Then to the guard, 'We want you to lock up and come with us, please, to copy these papers and FedEx them to various people who – who need to see them.' She had in mind to send out several copies, to Gwen, to Lawrence, to her professor friend at Columbia.

The guard looked dubious. 'Nothing is supposed to leave this apartment. That's what I've been told. So that includes any papers.'

Hilary drew herself up. 'I'm not leaving unless we can take these papers and make copies for safekeeping.'

Nobody spoke; nobody moved.

And then she flashed out, righteous, imperious, 'Paul! You with your eye for beauty. Don't you see how beautiful this is? In this vase, of all vases, like a dowry. Mine whether I married Mark or not. Mine if I chose not to curate the collection. And that's what I've finally chosen. Eddie foresaw all of this. It's such a generous act, to set me free to follow my own inclination. To make it possible. Mark was clearly dragging his feet about altering the will or drafting the letter or whatever. I can't leave this to chance now, and I certainly can't leave it to Mark.'

'Surely Mark would have told you sooner or later. He would have had to –' Paul ventured.

'When? After our wedding? When he had control of everything Eddie left? When the hell did he peel the red stickers off the pieces Eddie and Robert marked for me? He's even lied to you about that – Clare doesn't seem to know.' She was shouting now. 'Did he plan to say I didn't *choose* not to curate the collection? That he fired me, and so the letter isn't valid?'

The guard put his hand to his holster. He looked at Paul.

Paul spoke with gravity, 'She's entitled to do this. Fully entitled. We really mustn't stand in her way. In fact, we must help her now as much as we possibly can.'

As they left the room, Hilary's eye fell on the candelabrum that Gwen had painted for Lawrence. Trimalchio's candelabrum, standing beside her old desk, her books.

'Wait, Paul.'

She walked over to it, held her arm out straight: the palm of her hand rested on the top. Then she stepped in close beside it, between two of the curved legs, and measured herself alongside. It reached Eddie's shoulder in the photo, she thought, and it reaches mine.

I'm going to give this to Lawrence, she decided giddily, stepping free again. She couldn't wait to share her good fortune, to give it away. I'm going to give the loutrophoros to Gwen. She can put it up in the studio; maybe she'll paint it again – from life. Anyway, it can remind her of what she's lost.

'Are you free to come to New York before term begins? I want to show it all to you, and maybe get your advice. I can offer you a bed.'

How incredible, Lawrence thought as he came to the end of Hilary's long e-mail. How completely incredible – and wonderful.

He was in an internet café in King Street. Will was waiting for him at home, getting ready to leave for the cottage so Gwen could start on a portrait of Nick Hollander. When she tracked Nick down in Barbados, he had offered her the time before she even finished telling him what Will had done. 'Hell, I'm lying still here for the sun, and it's not like *that* colour's going to last. It's not good for me anyway. Let's do me in oils. I can give you five days.'

Hilary's news made Lawrence feel that his own life was a quagmire of commitment, obligation, scheduling, administration. Gwen had moved up to the studio as soon as Hilary was out the door. It had fallen into place without much conversation, and he knew that somehow, without realising it, he and Gwen must have been preparing for the split for a long time. But she wanted to be back downstairs with Will as soon as possible, so they had agreed that Lawrence would move permanently to the cottage as soon as Will started again at school. There was bound to be endless toing and froing over Will.

Hilary might as well be a million miles away, Lawrence thought, remembering the words they had exchanged that last night at the kitchen table. I won't ask her to come to me.

He tried to picture her as he had first seen her in his class fifteen years ago, in the back row, silent, waiting her turn, the one girl he had somehow managed to overlook. Then, feeling the pressure of time on him, the obligation to get home and take his share of responsibility for his son, he typed, 'I can get free. Once Will is back at school. For a little while.'

As he clicked Send, he felt a rush of laughter. The icon lit up and changed colour, throwing out its coy, bright blush. Then as the cursor pierced the glow, the icon changed into something else altogether; it seemed to swell or explode, and then it disappeared. Sent.

It's like the sperm and the egg, he thought, the arrow making for the icon, penetrating it, and the impulse already multiplying. He felt himself as the minnow, the message, striving through the ether, a journey of which he could hardly be conscious. And which might bear unimagined fruits.

ACKNOWLEDGEMENTS

My heartfelt thanks to John Bodel, Stephanie Cabot, Jackie Edgar, Melanie Essex, Isabel Fonseca, John Fuller, Grey Gowrie, Matthew Greenburgh, Bettina von Hase, Linda Heathcoat-Amory, Lucy Maguire, Robert and Polly Maguire, Robert McCrum, Blake Morrison, Roger Pasquier, Erik Tarloff, Susan Watt.

ALSO BY KATHERINE BUCKNELL

Canarino

What price perfection?

Elizabeth is a woman of peerless beauty and refinement; David, her husband, is an American investment banker working in London. They have two children and their marriage seems perfect. Why then does she want him to retire and move home to America? One summer evening David, alone in their empty mansion, receives a phone call from a long-lost friend. So begins a transatlantic tale of friendship, marriage and betrayal, filled with unexpected reversals.

In Katherine Bucknell's first novel, beauty and passion are stalked by desolation. Beneath the novel's polished surface lie psychological depths both uncanny and haunting. *Canarino* is a remarkable debut: a novel that lingers in the mind.

'An artistic triumph'   *Sunday Telegraph*

Leninsky Prospekt

October 1962. Nina Davenport is struggling to come
to terms with her new life. The lonely wife of a preoccupied American diplomat, she has returned to the
USSR at the height of an international crisis – there are
nuclear missiles in Cuba; the world holds its breath.

Raised in Moscow, once a student at the Bolshoi, Nina
escaped to the West – and her return is reckless at best.
Now she must confront the demons of her girlhood.
Hemmed in by official restraints, followed everywhere,
longing to make contact with old friends, she becomes a
tool for some in the American Embassy who have a hidden
– and dangerous – agenda. An agenda of which her
husband knows nothing . . .

'A pleasure . . . powerful, moving, intense and intelligent
fiction'   *Observer*